WHISKEY

JACK

By the same author:

WHISKEY JACK

Greenwing & Dart
Book Three

VICTORIA GODDARD

Underhill
Books

Grandview, PEI

2018

Copyright © 2018 by Victoria Goddard

Book design copyright © 2018 Victoria Goddard

ISBN: 978-1-988908-11-3

First published by Underhill Books in 2018.

Underhill Books

4183 Murray Harbour Road

Grandview, PEI C0A 1A0

www.underhillbooks.com

Chapter One
An Under-appreciated Genre

I WROTE MY final paper at Morrowlea on the masterwork of Ariadne nev Lingarel, one of the last of the classical poets and, in my opinion, a much under-appreciated writer. Her poem, *On Being Incarcerated in Orio Prison*, is commonly reckoned one of the finest extant examples of a Third Vertical Calligraphic long-form ode, but since that particular genre was promoted only by a small group of closely-connected poets writing what could be deeply solipsistic allusions, that's not saying much.

In a fit of insight that for various reasons I did not actually end up defending before my tutor and the assembled faculty, I argued that Ariadne nev Lingarel was not only playing 'the game of two sticks and a stone', as this particular group of poets called their art, but also was a puzzle providing a key to the architecture of the prison in which she found herself. She had been condemned to life in Orio Prison after an exceedingly unpopular stint as Governor of the then-very-new Imperial Province of Northwestern Oriole, and had devoted the rest of her life to her masterwork.

I examined my own cell carefully. It did not inspire me to poetry.

Mind you, Yellton Gaol was built in a sturdy vernacular style with no pretensions to architectural merit or grandeur, and I had not been in there long. And unlike the fair Ariadne (I took leave to imagine her as beautiful; the one picture I had been able to find of her in Morrowlea's library was an etching of her death-mask at the age of eighty-two, at which point she looked remarkably magisterial for someone who had been incarcerated for thirty-nine years), I had no clear idea why I was in gaol nor how long I could expect to remain there.

My cell was roughly wedge-shaped, with the door at the narrow end. The long walls were eleven paces long; the wide end eight and a half; and try as I might, I could conceive of no system even remotely pertinent to the barony of Yellem in South Fiellan whereby those numbers were significant.

I paced them out several times until I had the numbers secure in my mind.

The walls were made of the rough yellow sandstone common to Yellem—nothing like the shelly limestone or gold-glittering-granite of the fair Ariadne's cell—and various previous incumbents had scratched rude graffiti on them. A sump drain in the corner away from the door provided a dank air and an unhygienic chamber-pot; a small window above the drain was thickly barred, looked out onto the main square, and was moreover far too small for me to get more than my fist through.

A few stray lines of *On Being Incarcerated* emerged out of the loud chaos of thoughts in my mind, to do with the colours of the flowers Ariadne could see on the sea-cliffs and the sight of distant storm clouds out over the ocean.

I glanced at my cell again, to see if anything had changed. Nothing had. I sighed and used my foot to nudge at the only furnishing, a mildewy straw pallet. I did not want to sit on it. My friend Hal, who was teaching me the rudiments of magic, had so far taught me a handful of theories and incantations, of which keeping insects at bay was one. I had not tried it on anything more numerous than three houseflies; I feared the pallet's fauna would outmatch my skill.

I prodded the pallet again, for want of anything better to do. My foot hit something hard. I crouched down to investigate, wishing for a stick with which to poke the straw, but I had not accoutred myself for anything beyond a long-distance run that morning and therefore had nothing so useful as a swordstick. I had not brought a hat, or gloves, or even a wallet of money, which the gaol-warden had appeared most disappointed by.

I'm not much of a gentleman sometimes, I'm afraid.

Finally, with a faint thrill—for if not taboo, magic was certainly desperately unfashionable—I murmured the words of the insect-away spell. *Eako ekaino ekalo.* The Old Shaian meaning echoed in my mind, snagging on a line of *On Being Incarcerated*, where the poet played on all the various meanings of 'ward'.

I was disappointed to find only a rock.

***

After a while, which felt like hours but was very likely much shorter, I fell to studying the door.

I had, of course, investigated it when I first arrived in the cell. I had duly noticed its heavy oaken planks, its great iron bands, the massive unyielding grandeur of its hinge assembly, the hinge-pins as wide as my thumb. I fiddled with my ring, which was a habit I was trying to stop, and turned the energy to playing with the rock instead. It was a granite cobble or sett, about two pounds in weight, and of a pleasant light grey flecked with dark grey and little shiny bits of mica.

That about exhausted my knowledge of stones. The cobble was a bit too heavy to hold pleasantly in one hand, but its curved edges made it rock pleasantly on the floor. I rocked it back and forth with my foot and stared at the door and wondered which of my life's choices had ended up with me here, and had just about decided on blaming Mr. Dart's ducks when the door opened and two other men were thrust in.

I was glad I was standing. I would have felt at an even greater disadvantage had I dared sit on the noisome pallet.

My two fellow prisoners appeared experienced at the ways of gaol. Unlike myself, they made no protests; they made no futile gestures of defiance or anger; they did not even appear to need distraction from their plight by excessive analysis of antique Shaian poetry. They simply walked in, ignored the door clanging shut behind them, exchanged one sharp glance with each other, and focused in on me.

"Er, how do you do," I said, bowing with what elaboration I could manage given the space and the absence of my hat.

They stared at me some more.

The one to my right was barely taller than me, and looked like some wicked version of Hal's distant future: *wizened, wiry*, and *canny* were the adjectives that came to mind, along with a certain inevitable curiosity as to which high-ranking family he was black sheep or backside relation of, for apart from situation, clothing, and scar tissue he was clearly of noble Shaian family. He was also somewhere north of seventy, possibly eighty, so there was no telling where in all the old Empire he originated.

I had the worrisome sensation, as he grinned at me, that he had probably killed more people than I knew personally.

"G'day to you," he replied, still grinning, with an accent I could not even begin to place. He scratched his side through a ragged tunic of equally indeterminate origin and age. It was a strange greyish-orange colour that almost worked against his dark skin. He put his shoulders against the wall, which impressed me even more by his total disdain for anything so missish as squeamishness.

I turned to the other man. He was younger than his partner in (I presumed) crime, though easily old enough to be my father; I guessed maybe in his fifties, but his rough beard and almost theatrically villainous eyepatch made it hard to tell. He was a bit taller than I, rather stockier, and appeared—from what I could see of his figure through the layers of tattered garments he wore—to be made entirely of sinew and bone.

Unlike the older man, he did not give the impression of a naturally lean and wiry figure. He looked as if a very long and hard road had carved away every inessential from his being. It was a fanciful thought but once I had it I could not keep from thinking it. I could not but think that more than his eye was missing.

When he spoke his voice was unexpectedly deep and hoarse. His accent was roughly local—like his dark brown hair and mid-pale skin, it could have been from any of the four duchies and most of the rest of Northwest Oriole.

"Jack," he said, jabbing a thumb at himself. "He's Ben."

I covered my hesitation by bowing again. Then: "Jim."

It was the first time I could remember ever deliberately misleading someone about my given name. It was faintly thrilling, much like my small act of magic. Unlike with that, I also felt a small pang of disappointment in myself.

I could name five Jacks and seven Bens in Ragnor Bella alone. My given name, on the other hand, was so unusual that I knew of only one other person named it. Anyone asking for a young man named Jemis would immediately be directed to me—all the more so because of some small notoriety I had earned my first month home from university.

Not that it was my fault the local magistrate's wife and sister-in-law were deep in the thrall of a criminal organization growing pernicious drugs on his estate.

Nor that someone had started a cult to the Dark Kings and was sacrificing cows at the Ellery Stone.

Nor even that a dragon had demolished the cake competition at the Dartington Harvest Fair.

I sighed. I was Jemis Greenwing, Mad Jack Greenwing's son, the Viscount St-Noire (a long story), Fiellanese scholar at Morrowlea, and current incarcerated felon. Two questions would be sufficient for anyone to find me.

Jack and Ben nodded and performed much the same inspection of the cell as I had earlier. It did not appear to move either of them to poetry, either. After Jack had lifted himself up to look through the window (with a casual display of strength I admired silently from my corner next to the drain), they exchanged another glance, then each squatted down against the wall in silent reflection.

I wondered how long they had known each other to develop such intense skills at non-verbal communication and what exactly they did to require it. I sat down gingerly on the pallet to ponder, though to be honest I was almost immediately of the opinion that they were highwayman on their way to or from the Arguty Forest.

***

The only other gaol I had ever been inside was the tiny one in Ragnor Bella. My father had taken me there, the summer I was nine, with what I could only assume was the intention of dissuading me from taking up either crime or law enforcement.

At the time I had been resolute in my desire to follow my father to glory in the Astandalan Army. It would have been difficult to follow on his heels, recipient as he was of the Heart of Glory from the hands of the Emperor himself. Only the Fall of Astandalas dissuaded me from this plan, and I still sometimes felt vaguely cheated that I could not buy my colours (or even enlist as a regular) and see what I could make of myself.

Inveragory for law, my current plan, was not all that appealing. Nonetheless, I could not expect to work for Mrs. Etaris at Elderflower Books forever. One day I might want a family—and rather sooner than that I wanted to do my duty for the Woods Noirell—and most urgently of all I wanted to clear my father's name and reclaim his—now my—inheritance.

The granite cobble was a hard lump just a little too far under my thigh to ignore. I shifted position awkwardly, aware of how both Jack and Ben—though the latter was feigning sleep—were immediately alert at my motion. I glanced aimlessly and, I hoped, unthreateningly around, and discovered the deeper significance of something I had seen but not comprehended earlier, which was that the hinges of the cell door were on the *inside*.

Chapter Two
Gaolbreak

IT TOOK ALL three of us a considerable amount of effort to lift the door off its hinges. The granite cobble served its purposes—first to loosen the hinge-pins, and secondly to act as brace and pivot once we had lifted the door.

"Could do with some oil," I said breathlessly as we manoeuvred it against the wall.

The two men had entered just before dark, which was half past four this time of the year, and thanks to the short November days it was not yet six by the time we made our escape. Based entirely on my limited knowledge of the habits Mr. Etaris (the Chief Constable of Ragnor Bella and the husband of my employer), I surmised that the Yellton gaol-warden would be dining at the bourgeois countryman's hour, which was a good hour earlier than that favoured by the gentry. I also reasoned, with more certainty, that six of the clock made unexpected noises and people alike less alarming than they would be later in the evening.

All that was sound as far as it went.

Unfortunately this was only as far as the back door of the gaol, where we—all right, I—tripped right over the constable on guard and sent his dinner flying.

We split immediately. Ben and Jack forked right while I launched into an all-out sprint down the main street of Yellton.

This was not perhaps the wisest action I could have taken.

I am, however, a fine runner, odd though it might be to describe myself that way. After a few weeks of being embarrassed to be caught running for pleasure and exercise, I had entered my name in the three-mile race at the Dartington Harvest Fair, to the wonder and wagering of the barony. Due to an unexpected encounter with highwaymen hired to delay (or possibly to kill) me, I had come second, but the main benefit of the whole affair was that I had openly proclaimed myself a partaker of the sport, and added another layer to the reputation for eccentricity I was fast developing.

My friend Mr. Dart said that I was already sufficiently eccentric for a man three times my age. He also pointed out that it seemed hard to have to wait until one was sixty to have fun. I myself did not actually *endeavour* to be eccentric. Running was the only way I could make sense of my life. I had started having strange dreams and occasional nightmares since the dragon-slaying and curse-breaking and so forth, and running the barony in the morning was a major help in anchoring me to the present day and situation.

After a fortnight I had traversed almost all the roads of Ragnor barony and also developed a few favourite routes. I supposed I should have borne in mind that if my running was no longer a secret, well, neither was my route, and incredible as it seemed, there were several people who seemed dead-set on being my enemies.

One of them had, presumably, arranged for today's excursion.

There were a lot of people out on Yellton's main street. They did not appear to know what to make of me or of the cries being raised behind me, but it was surely only a matter of time before someone put two and two together and came up with 'gaolbreak'.

Sudden turns were not a large enough proportion of my training, I discovered as I grabbed a defunct lamp-post, swung around it, and endeavoured to launch down the alley behind it without pitching over onto my face.

In these post-Astandalan days, with magic erratic and out of fashion, only the houses of wealth or pleasure had torches illuminating their forecourts. Most towns still had the lamp-posts up, perhaps in the hopes that magic would return to both fashion and use, but they were now symbols mostly of the fall of Empire and the collapse of rational civilization et cetera. Contemporary poets probably made great use of them, or would if any of them were interested in the complex interactions of sign and significance and sense that had once been all the rage.

The alley was dark as a close November night. Initially this seemed a good point; the downsides I discovered when my foot landed on something soft and moist and I went flying.

"This way, lad," came a rough voice out of the shadows. Rough hands grabbed my arm to haul me upright. I gasped, winded from the fall, and could not help but follow Jack as he led me into a shadowed recess that led, it appeared, into an inner court.

Ben was sitting on a stack of wood. He shook his head at me. "You've something to learn about the fine art of escape, lad."

"Lack of practice," I replied, annoyed that my voice was shaky.

"A spectacular fall," said Jack. "Now hush."

I hushed.

Feet and incoherent voices went by on the other side of the gate. After no longer than a held breath they tromped back again, the voices and even the steps sounding this time frustrated. I sat on the wood next to Ben, cold and smelling ruefully of dog shit, and wondered again just how I had gone from out on a run in the middle of Ragnor barony to being incarcerated in Yellton gaol.

Try as I might, I could not bridge the time between reaching the White Cross and entering the cell.

Since Jack and Ben made no move to leave, I let myself focus on trying to remember.

It was the custom in South Fiellan that at some point during the last of the spur weeks, once in the week before the Furlough of the Spring, and again in the fortnight before the Winterturn Assizes began, you went to visit the graves of your family and leave a gift-offering. The spring offering (which usually coincided with my birthday on the come-and-go 29th of February) was of the first flowers, hope for a new life; the November offering was the last fruits of the year, hope of a legacy well remembered.

I had gone with my stepfather's second wife and my half-sisters and step-sisters to lay our offerings on the four-month-old grave of my stepfather. I had taken my two half-sisters to our mother's grave, though even Lauren, the older, was really too young to remember her. Both of those graves were in the village cemetery on the high ground north and west of the Rag.

I had delayed going to my father's grave, not sure what the rules were for someone who had been buried ignominiously as a suicide and a traitor and a potential wakeful revenant under a cross-roads at midnight. I was quite sure one was not supposed to leave offerings to the criminal dead.

But my father had not been a traitor, and I was increasingly un-certain whether he had been a suicide or a victim of murder—and he was my father, whom I loved.

I had taken my gifts of wheat and starflowers and apples with me on that run. I'd gone very early, one very misty morning when sounds echoed and ebbed strangely.

In the pre-dawn twilight, the last week before winter began, a few days off the anniversary of his death, I had run down the highway to reach the waystone at the White Cross, and—

"Cheer up, lad," said Ben. "You're not in such dire straits as all that."

I started, recalled where I was, smiled lopsidedly at how much I had forgotten my current predicament. "No? I must admit this is a new situation for me. Do you by chance have any advice?"

"Assuming we do have the experience?"

I smiled more genuinely at the old man. It was hard to imagine anyone looking more like a rogue than him, unless it was his piratical companion. "Forgive me the presumption. It could, of course, equally have been your first time."

"With the Yellem constabulary, yes, but we've seen our share of cells before, eh Jack?"

Jack grunted. "Time to move out. You coming with?"

There wasn't much point in hesitating. Besides, I'd never find out the truth if I didn't go with them.

***

Escaping from a mid-sized town's worth of alarmed citizenry and annoyed constabulary required my attention. I put aside all questions of *how* along with those with *why* (for both were equally baffling: why would someone kidnap me from the White Cross? And why would I not remember them doing so?), and followed

Ben and Jack where they led.

I could not help wondering, as we passed through gardens and yards and someone's unattended haberdashery shop, just what my father would have thought to see me.

"No, lad, head *down*," rumbled Jack. "Don't you know *anything* about poaching?"

"Just the card game," I muttered, obeying. The snide question reminded me of Mr. Dart's recurrent invitations to go 'picking mushrooms', which I equally recurrently declined. An unwary acceptance my first weekend home had started what I considered the melodrama of the past month and Mr. Dart insisted on calling *adventures*.

"Now on your belly, under there."

I followed Ben under a fence, over an outdoor privy still odorously in use, through someone's raspberry patch, and wished Mr. Dart were here, since he would certainly be having a great deal more fun.

I scratched a finger on something I didn't enquire too closely into and nursed it, taking comfort from the cool comfort of the magic ring I had won in my last game of Poacher.

There were far too many oddities in my life of late. It *was* a melodrama. Some days I felt like writing to Jack Lindsary, celebrated author of that hit play of the summer, *Three Years Gone: The Tragicomedy of the Traitor of Loe*, and offering him the opportunity to write a sequel about what happened when said so-called traitor's son came home from university.

Past the raspberries the escape was a blur of occasional torches, a seeping damp cold, the lingering aroma of dog shit, dark gardens, and light edging around heavy winter curtains in warm snug well-fed homes. After a while it started to snow.

Ben and Jack exchanged another glance. Perhaps they were communicating mind-to-mind, as Voonran wizard-mystics of Astandalan days had been reputed to do?

Jack said, "Thin first, thick later. Blizzard if the wind picks up."

This showed an impressive knowledge of South Fiellanese weather patterns. Perhaps he was a local? I squinted, but could make out nothing except for a pale blur between eyepatch and beard. Not that there was any reason to suppose I would be more likely to recognize him than I had in the cell.

South Fiellan had never been populous—Yellton, with somewhere between seven and ten thousand inhabitants, was the largest town of the three southernmost baronies—but after the Fall, the hard times of the Interim had cut the population considerably. Ragnor Bella and the barony around it had not been as horribly affected by the out-of-control magic as some, but we'd had our share of pestilence, famine, and maddened animals—and men—before order began to be restored.

There was a large stretch of farmland between Ragnor Bella and Woods Noirell that lay abandoned. Not all those people had perished. Some had given up fled to what they hoped were better lives. Many of those had ended up in the larger cities, Yrchester, Kingsford, even Orio City—and many had ended up in the wastelands and no-man's-lands and the Arguty Forest.

Jack peered out of our current hiding spot, a lean-to woodshed, and came back to nod decisively at us. "Wind's picking up. In five minutes no one will be able to see us or our trace."

"How will we keep our way?" I asked, which seemed a logical question to me but which caused both men to appear startled.

"Rope is traditional," Ben said.

"Have you any? I don't wish to be obstructive, but I'd rather not be sacrificed for your escape, either."

Jack snorted. "We're not so far gone as you imagine, lad. We'll not abandon you until you prove an enemy to us."

I supposed I had to accept that. If I had no idea how much I could, or should, trust them, they had no idea about my character, either. There were certainly young men of (nearly) one-and-twenty who were hardened criminals.

Women, too, of course. My ex-lover Lark was a fine example of the type. She had drugged, beguiled, bespelled, and finally betrayed me, and quite conceivably was behind today's activities.

I felt proud of myself for being able to refer to her in my thoughts as an ex-lover. I used to write embarrassingly bad poetry to her apostrophizing her as 'my goddess'.

I did rather better at deciphering poetry than I did creating it. Violet had always laughed at my efforts. We had ended up writing coded messages to each other in Old Shaian to practice our ideographs.

Violet was Lark's best friend, confidante, and very likely second-in-command. I had found out too late, alas, that Lark was actually one of the Indrillines, those criminal kings of Orio City, and Violet one of their agents.

Once the drug and the enchantment wore off I could be angry at Lark. Every rational impulse of my soul suggested that Violet was not a good person to fall in love with.

The rational impulses of my soul do not, alas, always have much weight.

I tugged my thoughts back to the present. I didn't reckon much on my chances alone, all told, what with the blizzard and the darkness and the unknown country and the angry populace, so I said: "Very well then. I have some fishing line, if that will suit?"

For although I might prefer the card game to the dead-of-night crime, I was coming to learn that fishing was *always* a good excuse.

***

Linked together by fine cord invisible in a night become white as a nightmare, I travelled between Ben and Jack in a peculiar state. All my senses were alert and straining, but there was only ever the snow and the wind and the faint tug of the line on my wrist to sense. My feet, in their light half-boots, were long since numb, and the snow was the heavy wet type that stuck to my face and slid off in lumps.

It was not truly cold, but I was sincerely concerned about hypothermia. Once we stopped moving we would be in grave danger.

I fretted over that for a while but thoughts of bright fires and hot wine and delicious food and warm, dry, *warm* clothing intruded. I fell into a reverie of the Winterturn feasts at Arguty Manor with my elder uncle Sir Rinald, when my father was alive.

I had loved Arguty Manor, dark as some found it with all the oak panelling everywhere. It was a house full of strange details; I had spent many happy hours searching the wainscoting for the seven carved mice my uncle swore were there and for the entrance to the secret passages Mr. Dart was sure had to exist. We never found them, but the hunt for treasure and mystery and adventure had never palled.

A tug on my wrist recalled me to the present. I turned along the motion, drawn as a fish to the fisherman to the still dark shape

in the swirling darkness. Jack, waiting for us to gather round, aston-
ishingly certain of his whereabouts and route.

"In here," he said, and pushed my shoulders down.

***

Down was a jarring drop of a few feet into what felt like a
face-full of roots. I started sneezing, a matter complicated by the
fishing lines, the darkness, Ben's precipitous arrival behind me, and
whatever-it-was that had set me off.

Jack disentangled himself from the line. Ben pushed past me
with a muttered observation I thought it best not to hear, and I
indulged myself in a good long sneeze.

Feeling slightly dizzy, I recovered myself to find that I was in a
dark tunnel. It was not quite so dark as it might have been, for both
light and blessed warmth flowed from the direction my unlikely
companions had gone.

I collected myself as much as possible, knowing that dignity
was far too much to ask for, and proceeded along the tunnel into
a hurtful brightness.

After a few minutes this resolved itself into a cave with a fire
in the middle. Ben was doing something with a pot; Jack glanced
at me. "There's another blanket in the corner there and some dry
clothes."

"Thank you," I replied gravely, too grateful for the change of
garments to worry about where they might have come from. An
unwary peasant fallen on hard times, I suspected. They were dry
and warm and its was far better than hypothermia—and if I had
fallen in with highwaymen, at least they were gentlemanlike ones.

Sadly, none of us were dressed well enough for the part of nobleman-in-disguise from a ballad or a play.

Ben passed me a tin cup full of something warm that turned out to be broth. I supped it even more gratefully, reflected that *I* was technically a nobleman in disguise, reflected briefly on what Jack Lindsary might do with that tidbit in a new melodrama, and presently began to be decidedly puzzled.

I looked around the cave. It was definitely a cave: thready roots hung down from its ceiling, and thick roots, the size of my arm, snaked down one side wall. There was the tunnel by which we'd entered, another dark opening from which blew a steady but gentle draught, and a sandy floor.

Besides the three of us and the fire it held a collection of useful-looking items: bed rolls, blankets, two bags like larger versions of the rucksacks Hal and Marcan and I had borne on our walking tour in the summer; a few dishes, some comestibles, and in two piles, one near to Jack, the other to Ben, their weapons.

These were old and well-used, the familiar pair of Astandalan-army regulation shortsword and daggers. Even as I watched Ben turned to pick one of his daggers up. Despite his knobbly arthritic joints his motions were sure and skillful.

"Well?" said Jack, who had been narrowly watching me. "Your assessment?"

"Ex-army," I replied promptly. "Probably one of the calvary regiments. Also, you must be a local."

"Not I?" asked Ben, chuckling. He cut a slab of cheese with his knife, another of bread, and handed the result to Jack before cutting another for me.

"No, sir," I said seriously. "None of the local families are anywhere of your colouring."

It was a simple statement of fact, for the three baronies of South Fiellan had only one imperial title among them (mine … or rather my grandmother's), and otherwise it had never been much of a magnet for Shaian settlers. There were a few people of Shaian ethnicity scattered around, mostly in the village of St-Noire south of Ragnor Bella, once the last village of Alinor before the Border crossing on the way to Astandalas the Golden. Most of the diversity of Fiellan was to the north and east—and south and west on the other side of the mountains, to be honest, for Ragnor, Yellem, and Temby baronies were all always somewhat backwards. We had the Imperial Highway going through, but the old joke went that no one ever left it before they got to Yrchester. Ben's skin tone was numerous shades darker than any of the locals, almost as dark as Hal's—and Hal was an imperial duke.

"Mmph," said Ben, which was a splendid noise perhaps aided by his own mouthful of bread and cheese. "Well, yes, then, we're old soldiers. Jack and I mustered up in the Seventh Army, long ago now."

"Didn't stay calvary long," Jack muttered.

I ignored this tempting diversion. "Which division?"

"Sixth, why?"

I was caught by my own eagerness. I wanted very much to explain, to crow my exultation at the vindication of my father's name—but at the same time I knew that the mistaken connection with treason was still all too current.

I temporized. "I'm from Ragnor Bella. Everyone knows about Mad Jack Greenwing of the Sixth."

Which was, alas, only true.

Jack swallowed half his bread in one bite. "Load of stuff and nonsense, I expect."

"Oh, yes, sir," I agreed—for that was also only too true, and it cost me nothing to be polite. I didn't feel up to an extended game of dissembling, so took advantage of a sneezing fit to change the subject. I couldn't think of a delicate way of asking the most pressing question, so just came right out and said: "May I ask what you were in for?"

"Loitering," Ben replied immediately. Jack made a rumbling noise I realized after a moment was his laugh. "We're honest vagabonds. Don't laugh like that, Jack, you'll affright the lad. We were taking a rest along the wayside when some officious constables came by and scooped us up. We didn't wish to be press-ganged in the morning, so when you made notice of the door—welladay and here we are. And yourself?"

"Oh, murder," I said inattentively, focusing on the new item in what Ben had said. "What do you mean, press-ganged?"

"What do *you* mean, murder?"

His voice was so hard I was for the first time truly concerned for my own safety.

I smiled deprecatingly. "I haven't murdered anyone. I was thrown into Yellton Gaol on the charge of murdering Fitzroy Angursell in the form of a dragon."

Chapter Three
The Troglodyte Kingdom

"AREN'T YOU WORRIED about the snow?" I asked as Ben and Jack collected their various belongings together into remarkably compact bundles.

Jack spoke through a mouthful of the strap he was tightening. "Aren't you from round here? Early wet snow like that doesn't last past mid-morning."

"We don't usually get any snow in Ragnor barony until the start of the Winterturn Assizes, and they're not for another week."

I trailed off on that thought. The Winterturn Assizes were in a week, or just about. I had to sort out whatever was going on with the Yellem constabulary before then, because I was fairly certain that even if it were lawful for someone going through an active trial on count of murder to attend probate hearings, it surely wasn't a good idea for someone on the lam for said charges (allegations? I wasn't totally clear where things had ended up) to attend.

My non-attendance at the Assizes, as it happened, was altogether unacceptable.

The law in Fiellan was that before a will could finish its journey through probate, all parties named in it had to be assembled together before the chief magistrate of the deceased's home barony during either the Midsomer or Winterturn Assizes to hear it being read. Due to the fact that I had been wandering around Ghilousette in a slough of despond (as I believe is the technical phrase) in the summer, I had not been able to be informed of my stepfather's death in time to make even the tail end of the Midsomer Assizes. Although I was not anticipating more than a very small competence, I was nonetheless a named party and therefore required to be there. As a result of my absence the settling of his estate—including all of his Rondelan business dealings—had to wait.

I could not miss the Winterturn Assizes.

Though everything in me revolted at the thought, I might have to let myself begin a murder trial for a crime I did not commit. How sensational a trial it would be! The son of Mad Jack Greenwing—hero, reputed traitor, subject of the staggeringly successful new play *Three Years Gone: The Tragicomedy of the Traitor of Loe*—tried for the murder of Fitzroy Angursell (of all people!) in the form of a dragon (of all things!). Whoever had set this up, I mused gloomily, had certainly wanted it to be disseminated far and wide.

Jack and Ben gave me a blanket and some strapping with which to tie together my still-damp clothes from yesterday. I formed a bundle less elegant than theirs but portable. Ben dowsed the fire and Jack inspected the cave for what traces we had left.

"Good enough," he said eventually, his raspy voice again surprising me. I didn't know why I was so surprised by his voice, which certainly wasn't at odds with his appearance—quite the contrary, given eyepatch, bristling beard, rough queue of grey-streaked dark hair.

I watched him take a werelight from Ben, as easily as if magic had not gone awry in the Fall and become decidedly unfashionable in the years since.

I made an involuntary noise, mostly of amazement. Ben said sharply, "Hush, lad. Jack needs quiet to find his way. He hasn't been here for nigh on twenty years."

"Not quite that long," Jack rumbled without turning his head. "I've spent my time in the Forest, that indeed I have."

He set off down the tunnel at that. I wondered why he had hesitated, given that there were only the two tunnels to choose from—the one by which we had come in, the other one, which we took now. Perhaps there was magic in the tunnels- –or magic beyond the werelight. I spun my ring. I had the faint prickle of a sneeze in my passages between nose and throat, but that could as easily have been from the soil around us as anything else. I had not progressed far enough in my studies to reliably sense magic at work.

I walked along behind Jack, the dim werelight casting strangely multiple shadows. We ducked roots, skirted damp patches, startled the odd spider in its quiet corner. My question about the snow seemed retrospectively foolish.

***

The Arguty Forest had for generations been the haunt of outlaws and misfits of one sort or another.

The Forest was large, wild, ran up into the uninhabited mountains, and not many people cared about Ragnor barony to its south. On the other hand, the Forest also had rich pickings of game—and of travellers, for the Imperial Highway to Astandalas ran through the western edge of the Forest. This had always been something of a problem.

Usually such things were the province of local authorities, but the Marquisate of Noirell to the south had enough to do with managing the actual Border crossing and the magic-haunted Woods Noirell, and for some reason my friend Mr. Dart would probably know, but which I didn't, neither the baronet of Arguty nor the barons of Ragnor or Yellem had the imperial title or duty. Instead of their wardenship, a division of the Army had been garrisoned in Yellton and given the job of ensuring the highway's safety.

That, of course, had ended with the Fall of the Empire, and no doubt what soldiers had been present at the time had either married into local communities, gone seeking family or fortunes elsewhere, or ended up on the other side of the law in the Forest themselves.

Probably Jack had been posted to the Arguty garrison at some point. Two or three divisions of the Seventh Army had been, though never my father's. It was standard practice that local officers never served within three prefectures of their home. The Seventh Army was a blend of Alinorel and Zuni divisions, with, I vaguely recalled, a few Voonran regiments as well. A blend of the peoples of the five worlds of the Empire, back when travel between the worlds was made possible by the magic of Astandalan wizardry.

Jack and Ben were old enough to have travelled far. Ben's odd accent could as easily be Zuni or Ystharian as from some distant corner of Alinor.

I would almost certainly never see anywhere but Alinor, probably nowhere farther than Northwest Oriole—once only one province among many, now most of the civilized world.

I was old enough to remember the Empire—I had been ten

when it Fell—but soon enough the tales of its riches and wonders would be just that, tales.

I stumbled on a rock and brought my attention back to the present with a jerk. What was *wrong* with me? I was never so prone to woolgathering before—

I sighed. Before I spent three years unwittingly drugged on wireweed, besotted with an unscrupulous wizard who used the drug to steal my then-unknown gift at magic and ensure my abject devotion.

It was infuriating in so many ways. Not just that Lark had been doing this under the noses of the entire university, but that as a result I didn't know which of my behaviours were truly my own, and which were residues of drug and enchantment.

Was I naturally prone to wandering thoughts? Possibly. Probably, even. The only counter I could think of was my single-minded focus when I studied for the Entrance Examinations. But the Entrance Examinations were the gate through which the future could open for anyone, and that was the year after my mother had died and my stepfather had remarried. I had only had one thought in my mind, and that was to leave without relying on him.

I had done so: I had come second in the duchy, coincidentally also second in the kingdom, and won a seat and a full scholarship to Morrowlea, the most radical of the Circle Schools. I could have gone anywhere but Tara, and chose the one where all exterior trappings of rank, including surname, were left behind the doors.

I was the son of a man reputed the most infamous and reviled traitor of the Emperor Artorin's reign.

My roommate Hal had turned out to be the Imperial Duke of Fillering Pool.

Much to the consternation of the local gentry, Hal was staying with me in my lodgings above the bookstore. He would be a little concerned about my whereabouts by now. I had been gone for—

I frowned. I had been gone for … at least a full day. It had been early morning when I went for my run, and it was early morning again now. But … But I had the niggling suspicion that something else had happened between reaching the White Cross to make my spur week offering at my father's burial site (one could not, really, call it a grave) and being pushed through the door of the cell in Yellton Gaol.

Well, obviously plenty had happened. I had somehow traversed the Arguty Forest—indeed, traversed the entire distance between the White Cross and Yellton, which was fourteen miles. I had not intended to run that; I hadn't wanted to go into the Forest. I had … I frowned again, turning it over in my mind. I had intended to run … where?

"Walk a little faster, lad," Ben said from behind me. "We've a long ways to go."

***

We walked underground for a long time.

I had no way of measuring time. I was the owner of a most up-to-date pocket watch, gift of my stepfather on my sixteenth birthday, but I had not taken it with me running. After a month I had a good sense of the lengths of roads in the barony, and I had a very steady pace on a practice run of exactly six and a quarter miles an hour.

Walking through a twisting tunnel at the pace Jack set, I had no temporal markers at all. My—companions? comrades in escape?

captors?—whatever Ben and Jack intended, they showed no inclination to talk. I fell to pondering again.

My thoughts wandered to the perfidious Lark and, naturally, from there to the dashing and dangerous Violet, whom I was more than half in love with despite every rational thought in my head and her own stern warnings. It was cold comfort to think that as an Indrilline spy she could not really quibble at my being on the lam.

On the lam. Yes, I did like the phrase. The reality, not so much.

As a matter of principle I did not approve of trying to evade justice and the law. Yet I had not even hesitated, had immediately sought escape.

I amused myself for a few more minutes querying whether the Faculty of Laws at Inveragory would be more or less inclined to take someone with a criminal history as spectacular as mine was shortly going to become. Jack Lindsary, the author of *Three Years Gone*, could pour all the clichés and melodramatic literary tropes his soul could hold into a sequel play, and they would probably fall short of reality.

Possible titles for said sequel amused me a bit longer.

Were we *never* going to come out of these tunnels?

I had a blank between leaving the White Cross and crossing the gaol threshold. I would not even recognize the gaoler by sight. Perhaps by hand, as he'd held it out for graft or whatever he'd wanted.

Did the Ragnor constabulary take bribes? I considered Mr. Etaris, the Chief Constable; decided that he must, but nothing so crass as a handful of coin. His corruption lay in subtler form, in whom he looked at and how and when and what treatment was meted out. The Honourable Rag, the baron's son, was indulged in all his vices of gambling and poaching and riding roughshod over

crops on the cusp of harvest; Jemis Greenwing, ill-loved nephew of
the new chief magistrate, was scrutinized and accused by the court
of public opinion of every sensational act in the barony.

I made a tally of said sensational acts attributed to me. All right,
I had rescued a mermaid from a burning building, and I had slain
a dragon, and the two of my university friends who had so far
shown up had been a beautiful cross-dressing Indrilline spy and an
Imperial Duke, and I had broken a curse on the bees of the Woods
Noirell, and I had been involved in the strange matter of the disastrous Late Bastard Decadent dinner party given by Dame Talgarth,
but that was incognito, as was the small matter of the cult to the
Dark Kings sacrificing cows at the Ellery Stone, which Mr. Dart
and I had witnessed.

The *rest* of the rumours were totally wrong. I had had nothing
at all to do with the summer's flooding, the wireweed at the Talgarths', the existence of said cult, the rumours of a twa-tailed vixen
running around and not doing any of the things said magical creatures were reputed to do in the Legendarium, any of the multiple
groups of highwaymen in the Arguty Forest, or the government's
deliberations over whether to change the inheritance laws of the
kingdom and institute a barrel tax on whiskey.

And we were *still* in the tunnels.

I sighed and started reciting poetry to myself.

I was deep into the sequence of odes from the Gainsgooding
conspirators when Jack stopped suddenly, cursed once under his
breath, and shoved me back several awkward yards to a cross-path I
had entirely missed on my way up. Ben gazed at him intently; Jack
said, "*Tufa*. In there and silent, lad."

'In there' was inside the branch tunnel, which was not really a proper tunnel, not like the one we'd been following. A musty, heavy scent saturated the air. I pinched my nose against the certainty of sneezing.

It was a badger sett, I realized. Ben caught my arm and pulled me to sit on the cold ground beside him. Jack glanced at us, then pulled—actually *pulled*—the roots above us until bushels of dirt and sand showered down. I buried my head in my knees to muffle my reaction.

When at last I recovered sufficiently to lift my head everything was dark and I could hear the knocking.

I pulled a handkerchief out of my pocket. Even running—even after a month as bemused owner of a magic-induced sneeze-suppressing magical ring (my acquisition of it was a long story; the background to the ring, or indeed the sneezes, remained an item on the long list of things about my life I did not fully understand)—I had a goodly store of handkerchiefs. Nearly three years under wireweed had ingrained the habit.

I repaired myself to the best of my ability. The knocking faded off into the distance. It reminded me inevitably of my adventuresome first weekend back in Ragnor Bella, when Mr. Dart and I had stumbled headfirst in the competing—or possibly colluding—activities of the cult to the Dark Kings, the reprehensible business affairs of the Indrillines, and the even more reprehensible activities of their main rivals, the Knockermen of the Isles.

It did not stretch the imagination unduly to suppose that the Knockermen might be involved in mysterious tunnels in the southern portion of Yellem barony. It could even have been the Knockermen of the Legendarium, for they were traditionally associated with mines.

I weighed the merits of encountering the human criminals versus the bloody fey.

I was enough a child of the Empire to believe in the power of reason and law, and enough a man of the new order to have a deep-seated distrust of unschooled magic.

I breathed slowly through my mouth, thinking of things other than my tickling nose. If I had to meet one, I'd prefer the criminals. I was an enemy of the Indrillines, and might conceivably be able to bargain my way to safety with the Knockermen, though every gentleman's instinct in me revolted at the thought of selling out my former lover. Even if she had drugged me, deceived me, stolen my magic, and finally betrayed my deepest confidence. And somehow had power over Violet …

What was Violet doing this evening? Safely ensconced in the counsels of the Indrillines, presumably, dashingly dressed and surrounded by dashing criminals—

O, Lady, I was a total idiot.

At last Jack said, "They've reached further than I'd heard. Must be a good harvest this year."

"Is this about the wireweed?" I asked quietly, hoping tone hid any nervousness my voice might have belied.

"Wireweed?" Ben said incredulously. "Has the blight reached so far?"

I blinked, uselessly in the darkness. "I beg your pardon?"

"There's an epidemic of addiction—and worse, death and, well, I don't know how much you know about wireweed."

His voice was suspicious and cold. I felt cheered by this small and possibly mendacious indication that whatever they were up to, it wasn't anything to do with the Indrillines, the wireweed, or the cult.

"More than I'd prefer," I replied dryly, but decided not to expand on my up-close-and-personal acquaintance with the drug. "I travelled in Ghilousette earlier this summer."

I felt them relax. Something made me add, "About a month ago the chief magistrate of Ragnor Bella's sister-in-law was found to have been growing wireweed on the premises."

"Not old Justice Talgarth?" Jack said incredulously.

"Yes. To be fair, he was away for the summer."

"Surely to the Lady he's not still the magistrate after that going on at his estate?"

"No." I sighed involuntarily and realized I'd dropped my hand-kerchief. I started to fish around for it in the dark, hand closing on the damp earth below me and then someone else's fingers. "Oh, sorry, Jack, I'm trying to find my handkerchief. The acting chief magistrate for the Winterturn Assizes is Sir Vorel Greening."

There was a pause. I felt sure that had there been any illumination whatsoever I would have seen Jack and Ben exchanging one of their meaningful glances. Whatever they were up to, the identity of the chief magistrate mattered. Well, it probably would, to highwaymen.

Finally Jack said carefully, "*Sir* Vorel Greenwing?"

"Yes, he's a baronet." I was quite pleased at how neutral my voice was.

"He any relation to Mad Jack?"

I smiled wryly into the darkness. "Younger brother."

Ben said thoughtfully, "I seem to recall Jack boasting endlessly about his son. He's not the baronet?"

The question hung there for a moment while I digested the idea that my father had boasted of his son—of *me*—to such an extent that his comrades would remember it ten—twelve—who knew how many years on.

I gripped a handful of earth tightly, swallowing against my always-too-ready propensity for tears. When I could speak tolerably unemotionally, I said, "Mad Jack was found hanging in the Forest some weeks after his sudden reappearance. His death was ruled a suicide and proof that the accusations of treason were correct. As a traitor forfeits his patrimony, his son was therefore attainted and his brother received the title and estate instead."

The silence was very nearly absolute. I could clearly hear my heart beating.

I was glad withal for the darkness.

Ben said, "The knocking's stopped. Shall we go on?"

"You've the light," Jack replied in a low rumble. When Ben lit the were light and passed it over, Jack picked up the white square of cotton that had fallen between us. He smiled crookedly at the Old Shaian character monogrammed in the corner. "'Racer'?"

"Thank you. Yes, I like to run. A friend embroidered it as a joke."

I didn't add the second layer of the joke, that I'd been named for my grandfather's favourite racehorse. "That's what I was doing, running, when I was taken up."

"Not running from?"

"Just running. The poor man's steeplechase, my father used to call it."

"A man after my own heart," Ben said jovially, not clarifying whether he meant me or my father. "Lead on, Jack, you know the route."

"I know our destination and that these tunnels used to lead there."

He set off walking again down the taller and less musty main tunnel. "Who built them?" I asked diffidently.

"These? They're part of the smugglers' network along the Magarran. The Tufa are looking for tippermongeramy. Not too much trouble usually, but better not to have to deal with them, especially not this time of year. Surely you've heard of them?"

"The smugglers, yes."

I could hear the amusement in his voice. "And spent plenty of time looking for them?"

"We didn't come this far in."

Mr. Dart had read about the caves in one or other of his beloved histories (being the sort of boy who'd read histories as soon as he could read), and had been most insistent we go looking for them. This was when we were ten or so, in the summer after my father's departure for Loe but before the first report of his death. It was the last of the gilded summers before the Fall of the Empire.

In retrospect we'd not gone anywhere deep enough to reach the limestone country and find the caves. We'd been sternly warned against the dangers of the Magarran valley, which were full of sudden sinkholes and treacherous waters. Then again, we hadn't really thought there was treasure to be found. As the rest of Jack's explanation was gibberish to me, I said, "What do you mean by the tufa? What is tippermongeramy?"

"Well said," Ben muttered. "Took me three tries to get it the first time."

Jack rumbled again. "Tippermongeramy? The natural caves are full of stalactites and stalagmites, which condense a kind of magic-enriched water. The tippermongeramy is algae that grows at a certain level of magic and nutrients. The Tufa—well, that's the name for a kind of rock, but in this case it's also the name for people who come harvesting the tippermongeramy. The Tufa are a very old community, as old as anything in the kingdom. They do something with the tippermongeramy and sell it for use in cosmetics. It used to be illegal for anyone below the rank of provincial governor to use it. The taxes made the Governor of Northwest Oriole rich."

I blinked. Several times.

Ben laughed. "I wish you could see your face, lad. People do the most absurd things for beauty, you know. I've been involved in several wars that were to satisfy someone's vanity."

"All of them," Jack muttered.

"For the glory of the Empire …"

"And what's that but vanity of a community?" Jack's tone wasn't as cynical as his words, and puzzled me almost as much as the discovery that the limestone caves deep in the Arguty Forest produced some kind of luxury cosmetic that I'd never heard of. Here I'd thought the only thing worth smuggling in the Forest was illegal booze.

Then again, I'd already fallen afoul of things I thought I knew about the people and secrets of South Fiellan.

How naive I'd been, coming home and expecting nothing more exciting than the Dartington Harvest Fair.

"What do you reckon?" Jack said, stopping before a wall. We ranged beside him and contemplated the barrier in front of us. The tunnel ended in a flat, obviously constructed wall, about fifteen feet wide, with four ornately carved wooden doors set in a row across it. "This is the boundary of the troglodyte kingdom."

"You don't know?" I asked.

"It's different each time. How's your luck?"

"Abysmal," I replied, but I'd had time to register the carvings on the doors, so I was able to add: "But I am tolerably proficient at puzzles. Where do we want to go, exactly?"

He blinked at me, single visible eye making it seem a deliberate wink. "South towards Arguty and Ragnor Bella."

I examined the markings closely. A fair thread of excitement was displacing the gnawing dislike of the close dark tunnels. This *was* an adventure—and how Mr. Dart would regret missing the troglodyte kingdom, to say nothing of the tippermongeramy!

"The second door," I said at last. "If you trust me."

Chapter Four
The Hunter in the Green

"ALL RIGHT," SAID Ben, some time later. "I'll bite."

It was a curiosity of Alinorel society (or so suggested the few books I had read that were from elsewhere in the Empire) that one almost always gave face credit to self-professed expertise in a subject. It was my youth, not my background, that I expected to give pause. I did not have the decades of slow mastery in a subject for the simple reason that I had only just entered into my third decade of life.

We were wending our way now through what were both much more constructed and less used passages. Only their darkness proclaimed us still underground and not in some warren of a palace or public building. Some deep and savage tension had slightly relaxed; my mind was no longer quite so frantically running through all the poems I had ever half-memorized.

I smiled into the wavering dim circle of light and the multiplicity of shadows cast by the werelight Jack held before him. "I don't know much about the troglodytes, but the carvings were all in Early Fourth Calligraphic and Second Synthetic-Nominalist styles, which were parallel philosophical movements of the first half of the reign of the Empress Dangora IV, to the end of whose reign is usually ascribed the boundary-line between Old Shaian and Modern."

The Empress' successor had overseen a major overhaul in the bureaucratic system, which had included a revision of the chancery scripts in order to reflect changed habits of speech and pronunciation. The use of classical ideographs up to that point in all formal documentation—and the fact that the complicated script meant that only highly-trained scribes were literate—had masked what had presumably been major shifts in how people actually spoke. Certainly when they started to write in the phonetic system derived from the ancient Tarvenol script used by those educated in Tara and its successor universities—which had been conquered the century or so before by the Empire—the difference was marked from the phonetic transcriptions the first Alinorel recorders had made of the Shaian spoken by their conquerors.

"Some good poetry came out of the Fourth Calligraphic period," Jack observed. "Let's rest here for a nonce."

I was grateful to sit down and drink from the water bottle Jack offered me. I was feeling slightly shivery from the damp chill— all right, *underground*—tunnels, which added to a certain ominous scratchiness in my throat and eyes.

"So, Late Second what-have-you," prompted Ben.

"There was a fashion that ran through the whole of the Third and Fourth Vertical Calligraphic periods for puzzle poems. At the Empress' court these merged with a parallel development in the visual arts, chiefly painting and architecture, which culminated, in the latter days of the reign, in a highly sophisticated and quite widespread system of common symbols and tropes that were—well, for the most part were used just as part of elaborate court games, especially the allegorical masques that were then in fashion. There were also several intrigues carried out by the artists and poets, including the entire Gainsgooding Conspiracy."

"Which, of course, marked the end of the Empress' reign."

"Er, yes."

Mr. Dart and I had written a spirited series of letters between Morrowlea and Stoneybridge on the topic. He'd been studying the conspiracy—nearly the only successful assassination attempt on an Emperor of Astandalas—and I had just about mastered the language enough to attack the puzzle-poems.

Together we had traced out the whole plot, which had been conceived, elaborated, and plotted entirely by means of the esoteric symbolism. Several of the poet-conspirators had never been caught, and others had successfully argued that the surface or exoteric symbolism was all that they had intended and that whatever some people might make of subtexts, that wasn't their fault.

Several schools of literary criticism dated back to that legal trial. One had eventually formed the core of the much-respected Department of Philosophy at the then-new Imperial University in Astandalas. This was much to the disgruntlement of the older schools of Philosophy in the great universities of Alinor, who believed that talking about signs was a lesser branch of Logic and that only the study of things-in-themselves could truly be called by the name of the Queen of the Sciences. The ensuing debate was the fifth great iteration of the insoluble Nominalist-Realist Controversy recorded by the Scholar-Archivists of Oakhill, who kept track of such things.

"But what has all this to do with the troglodytes' magical

doors?" asked Ben, after a slightly stunned silence.

"Oh; Mr.—that is, a friend of mine is a keen historian, and he's told me of these tunnels, and that they used to be called the Dancing Rooms, from an old story. I won't bore you with that now, but as soon as I saw the doors, I recalled the tale, which ends with a moral that the second and fourth are always the ones to choose. That was corroborated by the symbols carved on the doors. In the exoteric language—that is, in the common symbolism developed by the poets at the Empress Dangora IV's court—the fourth door said, 'Pass, friend, home daffodil'—which is obviously a reference to Yellem, whose emblem that flower is, and the second said, 'Pass, friend, home oak', which is Arguty. The other two were 'Pass, stranger, adventure wolf,' and 'Pass, stranger, adventure circle', which I would guess would take you on the one hand to the mountains and the other to an entrance to the Kingdom, but I could be wrong there."

"And in the esoteric language?" Ben sounded fascinated, which pleased me as it meant I could keep explaining without feeling like I was talking their ears off.

"They spelled out four stanzas from the great bard Lachlan Dart—who was one of the companions of Tarazel when she went to found Tara, you know—namely:

> *Spring winds bear me onward*
> *Calling me to the wide world*
> *Speaking of a foreign star.*

> *Summer winds bear me homeward*
> *To my love in the singing woods*
> *Polestar of my compass.*

Autumn winds bear me ever farther
To the wide world spinning faster
The stars my heart's ransom.

Ah, my lovely winds of winter
Home by my fire you cradle me
In the love that holds the stars.

It's a rough translation," I added gruffly, for a moment my voice sounding thick as Jack's. I'd always loved that poem, one of only a handful to come down from the bard. I had forgotten he was a distant ancestor of my Mr. Dart's. I wondered if Mr. Dart knew that fact, which was not well-known and which I had only discovered late in the winter term of my last year at Morrowlea, when I was horribly sick in the hospital wing and Violet had brought me ancient poetry to occupy my mind.

"Do you always talk this much?" Ben asked. Jack had risen brusquely to his feet and set off again, but not before I'd caught a glimpse of tears on his beard. Both sides, which meant his eye was injured or merely hidden, not gone.

"Oh," I replied belatedly, blushing, "I'm afraid so."

***

There was no treasure; there were no troglodytes; there were no trolls.

I was not particularly disappointed.

I was still cherishing that off-hand comment about Mad Jack Greenwing *boasting* about his son.

I walked around the dusty tunnels, seeing without particularly noticing the few relics the tunnel-builders had left ('troglodyte' referring in this case to a group of people from before the coming of the Empire who had built the tunnels for shelter and, presumably, to harvest the tippermongeramy). I had never doubted my father's love for and pride in me, his only child. But still.

But still, there was something so marvellous about the unexpected benediction, this tiny glimpse of the man who had been to me simultaneously my beloved 'Papa' and the heavy burden of an infamy I did not believe but could not disprove.

I had a friend, however, who *could*, and was powerful enough in his own right to see justice prevail against these with reasonably fat pockets and the local constabulary on their side—to wit, my uncle Sir Vorel, who was the only one who stood to lose by the vindication of my father's reputation.

At this point in my reflections the tunnel ended unceremoniously at another door. Jack gestured to us to stay back, set his ear to the door, and listened intently. I reflected that it seemed imprudent of the troglodytes not to have provided for a method by which to ascertain if the way outside was clear; and so, when Jack at last essayed the door, it proved.

***

The fight was over before it began. I had no weapon but a branch I had immediately dropped my bedroll to collect. I brandished it and discovered that no one else was fighting.

Ben was grinning. "Nice effort, lad, but unnecessary at the moment."

I felt uncommonly foolish.

There was something in the world of mortal danger that called to me, that made decisions easy and my actions sure. Coming out of it into the ordinary world always left me a little confused and muddled.

Against a chorus of laughter and rude comments I set my chin, relinquished my stick, and picked up my bedroll. Well, it was certainly not the first time, and likely would not be the last, where I felt foolish in the extreme. Why, a month ago I had launched myself at a fire-breathing dragon armed with nothing more than a cake-knife and an off-set spatula.

There was nowhere particular to stand, or rather, no one to stand with. Ben and Jack were speaking to a man and a woman by the cliff, and the half-dozen others were still grinning maliciously at me.

I recognized none of them by sight, though the fading light made it hard to tell. We had spent an entire day traversing the tunnels, I realized incredulously, and felt obscurely better about not knowing enough poetry by heart.

It was cold, and felt like snow. We were presumably in the Arguty Forest, though I had no more precise location than that. I didn't know whether Ben and Jack were friends or foes.

And I was still on the lam.

A whiff of woodsmoke set me sneezing. From the scratchiness in my throat I was fairly certain I'd contracted a cold. I blew my nose. Of course I had.

"What's this?" a new voice said suddenly. "A guest in discomfort? Friends, friends, what are you about?"

A powerfully built man in a full face mask bounded into the clearing. He was dressed all in green, from hood (of course he wore a hood) to boots, via several items of clothing I had never seen outside of a play, including a codpiece in embossed green leather. I did not look at it closely enough to determine what the pattern was, but it might have been the same as the leather mask, which was done all in leaves.

His voice was pleasant, his enunciation sharp and precise, and his accent very strong and from very far away. I looked again, but his clothing hid every clue to ethnicity, down to gloves hiding his hands. He was big and he was bouncy and he was, it appeared, the leader, for everyone started to move as soon as he spoke.

Green for the Lady of Summer, I presumed, and green also for any number of woodland ballads. Somehow I doubted he was the Hunter incarnate—though to be honest I was nearly at the point of believing actual divinities would start to show up. Mr. Dart would have that we'd met the Lady in the woods two months ago, but I had my suspicions that the lady in question had been the Lady of Alinor, a great mage and a mysterious figure, to be sure, but still human.

The Hunter in the Green—I might not grant him divinity, but that was obviously what he was going for—chivvied us away from the cliff, over a small stream, and eventually up into another cliff with a door set in its face. I sighed.

"This one's better," Jack rumbled.

"'Pray believe that I would never impugn a man's hospitality, sir.'"

The line from *Aurora* made him creak out a laugh. It sounded as if the motion hurt. He put up his hand to his cravat, which had come askew. "Will you instead offer us tales to while away boredom?"

I gave him a half-court bow, which Hal had been making me practice. "If you'd like, sir."

"I'd rather have a cup of coffee and a game of Poacher," he said wistfully. "Ben doesn't play."

Ben laughed. "Not well enough for you. Come, lad, I see a spark in your eye. Fancy a game for that quick wit of yours? I presume you play?"

"Learned to cast at my father's knee," I replied, as I usually did, and smiled mendaciously.

***

Poacher is a game much like life, where a fortune or a reputation can be made or lost on the interpretation of a card or the turn of a narrative.

The thing about Poacher that beginners don't realize is that it's a game not of secrets but of revelations. I should have known Lark by her game, but we had in three years never faced each other across the two decks and the tall tales.

I had played with Hal, and could hardly bear to do so a second time, he was so easy to beat. I had played with Violet, and in the tall tales and competing narratives found a silver fish of such rarity I could not bear to disentangle myself from her net.

After a cursory glance around the room—for room it was, complete with tables, chairs, bunks, and a wood stove someone was, in fact, making coffee on—I sat down across from Jack.

From a pocket he produced two exceedingly battered decks of cards, the Fish and Happenstance decks from different sets. He set them on the table between us and silently indicated the choice was mine.

The cards were merely a prop, my father used to tell me. The true game is wit against wit, soul against soul.

Soul? I had protested in confusion. I was nine and had no inkling beyond the natural of metaphysics.

"Soul," my father said firmly. "How you play shows what sort of a person you are, and that is your soul."

Deep stuff for a nine-year-old, but I had committed it to memory, as I had committed everything my father told me to memory.

I smiled a thank-you at the man who brought us our coffee. I presumed he had adulterated mine; it was traditional. And then, like any poor schlub of a mid-rate Poacher player, I chose the Happenstance deck to deal.

People bet on us, as was also traditional, while we attended to the preliminary skirmishes. I shuffled the deck with the would-be flashy moves of an over-confident young man, keeping my face deliberately set in imitation of the Honourable Roald Ragnor's most irritating vacuous bonhomie.

I watched like an eager puppy as Jack shuffled his deck, dealt the Fish. Sipped my coffee, sighed happily at the unmistakable taste of whiskey—that, at least, unfeigned pleasure, as I was still cold and woefully inclined to congestion, and it was the superb type that one could not simply buy from any legal merchant—and finally picked up my hand to see what I had been dealt.

The first hand didn't matter except to poor players. I pretended to study it as if Two Small Pike, A Sudden Squall, A Bobcat, and Three Minnows was something better than what sounded like a truly unrewarding day's fishing, while actually watching how Jack's own attention barely flickered from his own cards. Of course, the eyepatch did camouflage his response.

He sighed, set his cards down. Drank his coffee, ignored the other men's keen interest, and said desultorily, "I'm weak in my coffers just at present. Tell you what, I'll wager you my belt knife."

One played differently against a master than a beginner or a middling player. There were codes for the higher levels, layers of exoteric and esoteric symbolism like the deep games of the Late Syncretic-Nominalists.

A belt knife, to the beginner, sounded what it was: a friendly wager, nothing very serious, nothing to take seriously.

At the exoteric level—that is, to those who knew of the existence of a code, and that said code could be had for a fairly reasonable price in most bookstores (*The True and Neglected Art of Poacher* cost five bees in mine)—at the exoteric level, the belt knife stood to indicate that the one facing you considered himself a sharp player, and this was your warning that you were about to be fleeced.

At the esoteric level, together with the comment about the coffers it meant that the man facing me was one of the Seven Masters of the Game.

I took another sup of my laced coffee, feeling the warmth in my core. I was good at Poacher—very, very good, in fact, better than most. Good enough to beat one of the Seven Masters?

No; not yet. But that didn't mean collapsing like a wet cravat the first time I faced one.

"I'm afraid I find myself without any possessions but for three handkerchiefs and a ring that is, unfortunately, only on loan to me. I hope you will understand if I place my one of my handkerchiefs as my wager."

I spoke lightly, as befit one placing one inconsequential ante beside another. A used linen handkerchief against an old belt knife.

That I had personally woven the handkerchief at the Morrowlea looms (the relative neatness of its hems showing how late in my university career I had made it), and that its monogram had been embroidered by that same Violet, was irrelevant to everyone but me.

In the exoteric language, a handkerchief was a good-natured indication that the lessons about to be taught would be willingly, if undoubtedly ruefully, learned.

Jack stared at me out of his one good eye for a solid half-minute. I did not squirm, merely continued to smile and sip my coffee.

In the esoteric code to offer one out of three items was to accept the challenge.

Chapter Five
The True and Neglected Art of Poacher

I LOST, NATURALLY, but I may say that I lost *well*.

Our game, initially the object of a flurry of bets and interested commentators, soon sent the stranger men muttering away in boredom.

We did not play with any of the usual gestures, comments, bets, flash. You do not need to, past a certain level. By the time we were at Setting the Scene only Ben and the Hunter in Green were still watching.

Poacher is a game of nerve and chance, of swift calculations and topsy-turvy odds. Neither Jack nor I looked much at our hands, though I'm sure he was counting what cards had come and gone as much as I. The dance of Fish and Happenstance and skill and luck, which like an allegory reveals even as it hides the souls of the players.

I'd been in games of Poacher that lasted ten minutes, and one that lasted four hours. This one took perhaps forty minutes from the first warning to the last stand.

Quite how it happens I don't know. How is it that a man can reveal his soul so well picking up a card, discarding another, creat-

ing a story by what is taken and what is left that is almost always
not the one described at the end? I don't know. I only know that
of my last three games of Poacher with a skilled stranger, one had
left me soiled, one with the conviction that my opponent was the
most dangerous person I had ever met, and this one …

I sighed with regret that the game had to end as it came time
to turn over the Emperor card and see what alchemy it wrought on
one's hand. I knew that the Emperor card was the Holy Grail; I also
knew that excellent though my hand was, Jack's beat it.

"Well?" he said.

"Friend, Local Boy, Vengeance, and the Salmon of Wisdom. I
hope you find the last, sir."

There was a perfect silence. Then Jack started to laugh. He
turned over his cards to show they were the ones I had named.
"And here I wondered what you could possibly do with Two Fat
Carp, A Mysterious Letter, A Stranger, and A Storm."

"You forget the Holy Grail, sir."

"Oh, indeed not," he said, and exchanged one of his deep
glances with the visibly nonplussed Ben. "*That's* how you play the
game, Ben." Jack offered me his hand. "Thank you, lad. It's been a
long time since I enjoyed myself so much."

I shook his hand, wishing for a way to ask how I might—
well—learn more? Sit at his feet? Help him with his mission? Why
at every moment I wished for something I could not even begin
to say?

He smiled crookedly. "Time for some food."

***

"It's rare to find someone so young so skilled," Jack said once we'd sat down again with the bowl of stew one of the strangers had given us. Venison stew; the more usual result of the game in real life.

"Hardened gamester, are you?"

Rough though his voice was, I could now hear the approbation in it. One *could* be a bad man and a fine player of Poacher, I knew, but my father had told me, and life so far had not disproved, that past a certain level the the faults of the soul were on display quite as much as one's wit. The Tarvenol duellist who remained the most dangerous person I had ever met puzzled me because the danger had been matched with iron honour; but then again we had not finished the whole game on that occasion.

Jack did not think me a hardened gamester. They did not tend to play Poacher; they bet on other people's games instead.

"My father taught me as a boy."

It was difficult to talk about my father. It was very close to the anniversary of his death, and I had started to wonder if he had been murdered, and he seemed to be present all around me. All the past fortnight, since I slew the dragon, I had been dreaming of him. It had been years since the last time that had happened.

"He was very good."

"Yes."

I remembered the evenings spent learning the cards, how he would spend an hour, sometimes the whole evening, on each. How they'd made their way into the decks we now used, why they were pictured as they were, the obvious, coded, deeply hidden, and wild-card meanings of each both separately and in all their many conjunctions.

The early mornings spent literally fishing or tracking or meeting the other inhabitants of the decks of Happenstance and Fish.

My father had taught me how to shape a fly, bait a hook, how to find the holes where the great pike lurked, how to lay ground bait for a school of bream.

And while we waited, the wide-ranging conversations, instructions, stories, tall tales, always circling around the game he loved so well. He had taught me to understand the world through two decks of cards and a few not-so-simple rules. He had shown me my soul … and his.

I ate stew until I felt composed. Smiled at Jack, who had been eating his own meal in thoughtful silence. "May I ask what your plan is? Against whom are you seeking vengeance?"

He looked startled. Scratched his beard. "Those were the cards I was dealt, lad."

I arched my eyebrows at him. "Naturally."

Ben, who'd been sitting quietly beside us, snorted. "Got you there, Jack."

Jack grinned. "Not buying it, are you?"

"When I have had the honour of losing to one of the masters? I was not taught that the game is one of reacting to what one is dealt, sir."

"Point." He let out a noisy breath. "You were playing the carp."

I regarded him solemnly. If he knew that my uncle was devoted to his fish ponds and their fat golden carp—well, and so what? That might mean nothing more than that he had a friend who was interested in fish and knew the names of those who shared his passion. It was common enough.

"He's the acting chief magistrate this session," I said. "While out for a run in Ragnor barony, I was seized and delivered to Yellton Gaol under a false charge of murder designed to create as sensational a trial as possible. He has reasons to dislike me."

I stopped, jarred by flash of memory streaking across my mind like a meteorite. It was gone as quickly, leaving only the briefest flash of illumination. I had *seen* something—but what?

What, indeed? I wondered. And what did it have to do with my uncle?

The Hunter in Green came over to our table. "Done your stew?" he asked, accent as nearly-impenetrable as before. "Good, good. We're clearing out. Watch the ways south, there's plenty looking for trouble along your route."

"I am well acquainted with the dangers of the southern Arguty Forest," Jack said in a brittle tone.

The Hunter in Green nodded. "Merry hunting."

"Merry hunting," Ben replied.

"*Merry* is not the word I'd use for it," Jack said in a low voice.

I could not think when I had ever seen another human express such emotion, unless it was the look on my mother's face when she saw my long-reported-dead father come through the door of her new husband's house.

Ben obviously saw it, too, and perhaps he knew what emotion it was (which I did not), for he spoke with urgent cheerfulness. "We're safe enough to sleep till the morning, anyhow."

Jack said nothing, face settling into grimness.

I lay down on one of the bunks, far away from Jack. I was exhausted, and despite my congestion fell asleep quickly.

My night was full of dreams in which all three iterations of my father's death figured prominently.

***

I awoke disgruntled, a feeling which the dull weather did nothing whatsoever to mitigate.

Jack had made some sort of porridge, which was filling. I yearned for some of the fabled Noirell honey to spoon across it, but quite apart from the lack of such amenities in the hideout, the bees had been cursed until a fortnight ago and there was no expectation of honey for this year. After the meal I completed my toilet as best I could in the washbasin, which wasn't very.

"A few more days and you'll have the beginnings of a respectable beard," Ben said encouragingly.

I glanced at his scurfy facial hair, which went every-which-way, and decided (not for the first time) that a bow was always better than words you might regret. He grinned.

Jack had gone outside while I ate. He returned, blowing on his hands. "Cold wind, I'm afraid. Let's hope all the sensible people stay indoors."

"I presume we are not to be counted in that number?"

He cocked the eyebrow over his eyepatch at me. I could not help wondering how severe the injury to his eye was, really.

"I have not known you long, lad, but very little of what I've seen you do falls under the heading of 'sensible'."

"Point."

"Here's one you might find more useful." I turned, confused at the pun until I saw that Ben was pointing at several weapons he'd laid out on another table. "The—our friends said we might arm ourselves. We've chosen our weapons, so you may have your pick."

So Jack had seen something trustworthy in me, playing Poacher. Not *sensible*, mind. The comment stung a little, for I usually considered myself a sensible, practical sort of man, reining in the wilder extravagances of my friends.

Nevertheless it had to be said that neither Hal nor Mr. Dart had ever found themselves breaking out of gaol with two ex-soldiers of uncertain current profession (revenge presumably not paying one's regular bills) after being accused of murdering Fitzroy Angursell in the form of a dragon.

Lady preserve me.

I focused on the weapons. Three swords; four daggers; an axe.

Not the axe. I'd never learnt more than to chop wood with one—though that, thanks to Morrowlea's views on sharing the work, I could do better than most young gentlemen.

This was a test.

One sword was adequately-made but flashy. One was made of something only slightly better than pot-metal. And one was … superb.

I picked up the third. Smallest, lightest, plainest, dullest in appearance. But like Ragnor Bella, vaunted least interesting town in all of Northwest Oriole, it had its secrets.

"Are you sure this isn't someone's?" I asked Ben, watching Jack watch me. "This is too fine a blade to be someone's cast-off."

Ben and Jack exchanged one of their glances. Jack rumbled, "Not everyone has your eye."

"Surely—" I stopped myself, attending instead to the feel of the blade. Surely anyone could tell? Even *Hal* would be able to tell.

"Your father teach you this, too?" asked Ben.

"A little. One of my professors at—at university used to be an armourer, and he taught me what to look for."

I was still reluctant to identify myself as Mad Jack Greenwing's son. Why, I wasn't quite sure. I did not really think that Ben and

Jack were wicked, and they had already made it clear they respected my father's memory, but … but I felt I had exposed myself too
much in that game of Poacher, in the dark tunnels, in these past few
minutes looking at the weapons. I did not want to hand them all
the keys to my heart in one fell swoop.

"May I take a dagger as well?"

"Please."

The daggers were none of them so fine. One fit best in my
hand and had a belt to go with its sheath, so I took it. Belted, I
felt a little less ramshackle; fussing to get the rapier's scabbard in
position felt good and right and almost inevitable, although to tell
the truth I'd never gone about armed before for longer than the
length of a class.

The rules were different in the Arguty Forest.

Rules were always different in the green, I thought: in the
Woods Noirell, where magic waited around every tree and thicket,
and in the Arguty Forest, where the perils were mundane but very
definitely still mortal.

And in all the very many layers of metaphor the word *green*
could bear?

Chapter Six
Cutting Counter

I HAD BEEN deceived in the weather by forgetting we were underground, I found when I followed Jack and Ben outside. The door had seemed obvious last night; this morning a curtain of dying vines hung down over the entire face of the cliff, obscuring all evidence of human work from the outside and most sunlight from the interior.

I wondered for a brief moment how the Hunter in the Green's men had done the trick. Not releasing the vines down from the top of the cliff, which only required one person up there, or failing that a long rope; but getting them up there in the first place to be so released. Jack set off at a brisk pace to the southwest, so I left that enigma to stay with all the many other small mysteries in my life and set off after him.

Mrs. Etaris, my employer, had told me that we never do find out the whole story, whether of an adventure or of a life. I was finding it hard going to resign myself to that fact.

It was cold and clear, and frost rimed the branches where the sun had not yet touched them. My spirits raised. I was back in my own clothes, I had a magnificent sword belted on my hip, and all the puzzles of my current predicament seemed this morning as answerable as any poem or riddle. I had merely to determine what code or key lay below the surface, and which below that if necessary, and then it would all make sense.

Easy as pie.

We walked carefully, Jack again in the lead, Ben behind me. They were more alert than the previous day, which infected me with wariness. I did not have the experience what to look for, but I did my best not to let my mind wander.

The Forest did not *feel* dangerous, not in the crisp November air, even with the occasional bitter gusts of wind. Little was stirring: a few titmice in gay blue and yellow plumage, a handful of robins, a rabbit or two. Then we flushed a flock of grey jays.

The jays screamed alarums, their cries echoing through the cold woods, against unseen cliff-faces, returning garbled to our ears.

"Loosen your sword, lad," Ben said in my ear. "Everything with ears knows we're here now."

"We'll cut counter," Jack said, a phrase I puzzled over even as it clearly meant leaving the path we'd been on and haring away from the screaming jays. We left them behind, but it soon became evident that we'd left Jack's knowledge with them. He slowed his pace and moved his head after landmarks that, from his accompanying scowl, he did not find.

Half an hour or so after we'd left the jays, he left the trail we were following to guide us into the heart of a thicket of junipers. They were scratchy and resinous and I got tangled with my unaccustomed sword, but the centre was out of the wind and roomy enough for us to sit upright on our bedrolls.

Jack and Ben looked at each other; Ben shrugged. Jack sighed.

"Do you know the Forest, lad? You've not said, but we've not asked, either."

"I've never been far from the road or the southern fringes, I'm sorry to say. When I was a boy we never went in too far, and since the Fall it hasn't been safe."

Another meteorite flash of memory, or—not a memory, but the inkling of a memory, that something I said was *important*—but what?

Jack grunted. I wanted to say that over the last month I'd run nearly every road, lane, bridleway, and footpath between the Woods Noirell and the Forest, all the Vale of the Rag between East and South rivers. Ask me who had dogs, overgrown stiles, early-crow-ing cocks, late crops of kale, cabbages, parsnips, or mangels—ask me where the ruts were worst or the mud deepest or the odd patches of saffron crocus that Hal was trying intermittently to map before they all withered—ask me who else was out early in the morning as the late autumn sun rose—

I blinked. That was it. I'd generally been running before work, sometimes again in the early evenings, though more often Hal and I sat in our little parlour talking, reading, having our lessons on magic or *noblesse oblige*. That morning I had gone for my run, a twelve-mile circuit of the barony, north to the White Cross first to pay spur-week respects to my father's unhallowed grave.

And there I'd seen someone who shouldn't have been there.

Who eluded me. I twisted the ring on my finger, wondering. It was not the first time this year that magic had caused me to forget.

Jack shared out some sort of hard biscuit sandwiched together with beef dripping. It was surprisingly tasty.

I thanked him. "I'm new to the business of adventuring; I'd

forgotten the need to bring refreshments."

Ben chuckled softly. "Soldiers learn to sleep and eat and be prepared at all times."

"I was planning to go for soldier, before the Fall."

"Your father?" Ben asked politely. Jack stirred, but only to rearrange items in the bundle that had contained the biscuits.

I very much did not want to talk about my father there in the Arguty Forest where he had either committed suicide or been murdered. I nodded shortly. I was glad to be interrupted by another outburst of grey-jay alarums and warning cries, and was far slower than Ben and Jack to realize what the distant cries indicated.

Something else was out there to disturb them.

Or some*one* else.

***

The Arguty Forest is known for its dangers.

Along with sizeable component of highwaymen and other scofflaws, wolfs heads, and people at the lower fringes of society, it also contains bears, boars, wolves, deceptive terrain, sudden sinkholes, and somewhere or other, the Magarran Strid.

The great oak woods and mixed thickets are host to a large quantity of game, including the famous Red Stags (which the Honourable Rag had spent most of an uninvited evening visit telling me about the week before), so that mixed in with the rest are daring hunters, charcoal burners, woodsmen, and any number of illegal stills where people turn sunlight into moonshine by way of apples, pears, barley, and yeast.

I had learned yesterday about the Tufa and their tippermongeramy. As a kind of companion piece to the Hunter in the Green, there were also the rumours of the Wild Saint. No doubt there were also people doing disturbing rituals to the Dark Kings that had once been proscribed and heavily punished by Astandalas.

I wondered how many people lived in the Forest.

The jays accompanied us and whoever else was out there like a ranging dog. Now off in the distance, now disturbingly close, they set off their alarums at irregular but frequent intervals.

"Quiet as you can," said Ben, as we prepared to leave the juniper thicket. "Jack's the leader; he's the experience."

At sneaking? At scouting? In the Forest? All of them, I presumed, and rather wished I'd taken Mr. Dart up on his occasional offers to go picking mushrooms in various parts of the barony, which was his preferred euphemism for the version of poacher that was not played with cards.

I'd been trying so hard not to make a stir.

The jays cried again, over to our right this time. I froze. Jack said, "No, this is when we move, when they're already disturbed."

So we moved. We went along game trails that more or less led us south and west. I had no idea how Jack was guiding us. Perhaps he had some magical means of direction. Such things had been commonplace before the Fall. Since then … I'd heard of more than one person who'd used such a compass and found himself in the Kingdom between worlds.

Bowing to my reluctance to put myself deliberately in more trouble, Mr. Dart had given up poaching and come instead to the little flat above the bookstore where Hal was staying with me. We were friends; no one thought twice of his visits. Mr. Dart had a gift at magic and needed to be taught even more discreetly than I.

I was discreet because magic was out of fashion and I needed desperately to get safely to the Winterturn Assizes. Mr. Dart's gift was a wild magic, and that was not only unpredictable but had once been a sentence of exile or death.

I disentangled my scabbard from an ivy-enveloped bush. So much for good intentions.

***

After two hours of the jays, we'd started to take them for granted. There was something almost fun in the way we moved, in the sense of those mysterious other movements marked out by the local grey jay population, in the cold, clear air, in the path a little more human-made and from the sun definitely going the right way that Jack tentatively led us onto. I had nearly figured out how to walk without getting the sword stuck on everything.

That, of course, was when I walked straight into a trap.

***

My first thought was an inarticulate profanity; my second and third progressively more pungent. Then I picked myself up off the ground and determined that nothing much hurt but my pride.

"Pit trap," Ben said conversationally to Jack. "Haven't seen one of those in a long time."

"No," Jack agreed. "You hurt, lad?"

I brushed off bits of the dead leaves that had cushioned my fall. "Not to speak of, thank you. I'm sorry to be so presumptuous, but would you terribly mind helping me out?"

Jack and Ben exchanged glances, then disappeared. I hoped my estimation of their characters was not entirely wrong and considered my predicament.

On the lam in the Forest in the company of two ex-soldiers bent on a mission of revenge and now also stuck ten feet down in a sheer-sided pit previously covered with a lightweight framework of branches disguised by leaves.

Oh, yes, and all this was on the cusp of winter; I'd forgotten that part earlier.

This did not inspire me to poetry, either.

I stamped my feet, tucked my hands under my arms, and wished I had spent more time with other sports besides fencing and cross-country running. Pole vaulting might have been helpful; acrobatic gymnastics certainly.

Not, alas, my sport.

Ben and Jack were out of range, potentially for good.

It occurred to me to wonder what Mrs. Etaris would do in such a case as this. It was no use letting her general appearance and demeanour of a respectable middle-aged middle-class woman of South Fiellan occlude one: she was far too much like the barony, and had deep reserves of mystery, mischief, and possibly even may-hem below that seemingly placid surface. There was a lot more to Mrs. Etaris than met the eye.

I had in my possession: myself; a dagger in its sheath; a fine sword in its scabbard; a belt for said weapons; a blanket; miscella-neous brush and forest litter; two consistently successful spells (to light candles and shoo away flies) and a smattering of magical the-ory; a head stuffed full of poetry and Poacher and the symbolism of many centuries; and a magic ring that, as far as I knew, did nothing but more or less suppress my sneezes.

I stamped my feet some more.

Over the past month, while I worked during the bookstore,

Hal had occupied the portion of his days not given to scouring the barony for strange plants by systematically going over my new flat. This appeared to give him great pleasure; as I knew it was hardly an activity he (being an Imperial Duke by trade) indulged himself in at home, I was glad enough to let him run with it. He was theoretically staying with me to teach what it meant to have an Imperial title in these post-Imperial days, but I had received the strong impression that he was delaying his return home by every reasonable means. Quite why he felt the need to this I had yet to determine.

Last week he had reached the back of a wardrobe in the attic and there found a stash of what we somewhat incredulously determined to be old adventuring items: well-worn leather boots and an even-more well-worn woollen cloak, both of foreign style, a small roll of leather that held a set of pen-knives, a second of artist's brushes and inks, and a third of what we realized (even more incredulously) were picklocks.

"They must be Mrs. Etaris'," I said.

"Could belong to the former owner of the building," Hal said. He had yet to become convinced as to Mrs. Etaris' more exotic skills, though he'd been the one to discover that she'd been at Galderon during that university's protracted rebellion from its provincial governor.

Mr. Dart was visiting for an evening drink, as he often did, saying the six-mile ride home in the dark to Dart Hall was nothing. I was starting to be a little worried about Mr. Dart, truth to be told, for a number of ill-defined impressions that did not go away no matter how I tried to rationalize them. He poked at a set of metal prongs and fabric strips that were bundled on top of an old and very battered leather bag. "What do you reckon these are?"

We spent a while drinking wine and coming up with increasingly salacious and silly uses for them. None of these were close to the truth, or at least not to the tale Mrs. Etaris spun for us the next morning.

"They belonged to a friend of mine—oh, that bag! That was his, too." She smiled foolishly at the battered old thing.

"Was this by any chance the friend that sang going into battle?" I asked suspiciously. He was the only 'friend' of her university days Mrs. Etaris had so far mentioned, but from the very little she'd said I would have believed nearly anything of him, except possibly that he existed.

"Oh, that brings back memories.... I do beg your pardon, Mr. Greenwing. Yes, indeed it was he. Would you mind if I left the bag here? He asked me to look after it for him, many years ago. Not that I expect him ever to call for it, this late date, when probably he's been dead since well before the Fall, and anyway there's nothing much to it, but I did promise."

I looked wonderingly at her. Her voice was brisk, her words light, her eyes full of a long wistfulness. It must have been a good twenty-five years or more since she'd been at university.

I hoped I would never be put to it, but that if ever I was, I would keep a promise to a friend long past any sensible expectation.

"And these?" Mr. Dart asked, lifting one of the metal prongs. "You must know we're very curious about their purpose, Mrs. Etaris."

***

Without practical demonstrations the climbing equipment was

more than a little baffling. The bands one apparently looped around the pole or tree and used to provide leverage as one climbed, as if one were creating a sort of mobile clove-hitch the way up. The metal spikes, like unsharpened knife blades, one used as handholds, jabbing them into crevices and then walking oneself up the wall or cliff or—theoretically—ten-foot-deep pit face.

It had seemed straightforward when Mrs. Etaris explained how to do it.

I considered my available tools. Unfortunately I had only the one dagger. The sword, apart from being too long, was also far too good to use for such a purpose. I dared not call out to Ben or Jack for fear of other listeners.

I scrabbled around in the bottom of the pit for a while. None of the branches were stout enough to bear being shoved into the earth, let alone bear my entire weight thereafter. The only one that was remotely strong enough I managed to break off trying to pull out again.

Well, it would provide a footrest. Maybe.

The walls of the pit were vertically cut earth, claggy in the bottom sections, a little sandy higher up. The only rocks visible were either pebbles or bigger than my head and firmly embedded.

For want of any better idea I scoured around some more, and eventually discovered a narrow rock sticking out of the pit wall down near the floor. I pried it out with the help of the dagger, figuring the blade was shortly going to be much worse abused, and closed my hand around the stone. It was about an inch wide, tapering from a wider section, rough-edged, and harder than sandstone. I decided not to wast time puzzling over geology (for instance, why was there sand, and not limestone, just here?). It was too cold, even out of the wind.

I went back to where I'd broken off the stick. That was about chest high. Clearly I needed to start as high as possible so I could swing myself up and out before my strength gave way. I was reasonably strong after years of fencing, archery, garden-digging, and wood-cutting, but I had neglected most of my exercises but for running the past year. First from illness, then from heartbreak, then from lack of opportunity, and finally from lack of habit.

I resolved to remedy this as soon as I'd resolved my more urgent legal affairs. Mr. Dart would fence with me if I asked him, surely; he was trying to learn to accommodate his stone arm.

It was a pity that Ben and Jack appeared to have absconded. They surely knew what they were doing with a sword. They might conceivably have been willing to give lessons once their efforts at vengeance were completed.

Without further ado I put Mrs. Etaris' theory into practice.

It would no doubt have been easier with the proper equipment.

But it worked, albeit slowly and with much difficulty. I shoved the stone into and heaved it out of the earth. If I plunged the dagger angled slightly downwards, my weight bound it into the soil. Then I could brace my feet to swing up the other side, stone forced in—

Yes, I really needed to work on the strength of my arms and shoulders. Hal wouldn't be much use, he had to be reminded to leave his plants, books, and food alone to do anything more energetic.

Except for polo. Hal did love polo.

I didn't have, nor could afford to acquire, a horse.

I was feeling very proud of myself, and very thankful to Mrs. Etaris, when I rolled over the lip of the pit-trap and discovered I had an audience.

Ben and Jack had dragged a dead tree onto the path for me to use as a ladder. For a moment I was so glad they hadn't abandoned me to my fate I didn't register any of the other people.

I was still on my knees, catching my breath, when someone pushed me down onto my stomach and stepped onto my back.

"Very pretty," an unexpected voice said. "I'll have to remember that trick. Hans, disarm him."

"Aye, m'lady," said a gravelly voice, and in short order my sword, dagger, and bedroll were gone and I was trussed neatly as a pheasant. Hans then turned me over so I could look up at 'm'lady'.

I felt, as I rolled over trying to place the voice, a moment's annoyance that the jays had not warned of us any near intruders. Then I saw that the young woman facing me had a grey jay on her shoulder and another come to her hand for the seeds she held out for it. I blinked at her. "Myrta?"

Chapter Seven
The Hanging Hill

MY FIRST, STUPID thought was that banditry must pay far more than I'd imagined, since Myrta had been in my year at Morrowlea and therefore could not have been the Rondelan scholar. My second, third, and fourth thoughts were none of them much better.

Myrta frowned meditatively at me. She was a strong, handsome woman, her hair a rich auburn like Mr. Dart's, but her eyes hazel-green to his blue. We had not been particular friends, since Lark and she did not get along, but I had liked and respected her intellect in the classes and work we'd shared. She'd studied weather; she was very good at archery, needlepoint, and carpentry; she had no sense of the absurd; and that was about all I knew of Red Myrta, as we'd called her to distinguish from Dark Myrta in the year above us.

"Jemis," she said at last, unsmiling. "I see you're recovering about as poorly as I expected from the lovely Lark."

Had *everyone* known what was going on except for me and the professors?

I replied with what dry insouciance I could muster. "Thank you. Is this new, or a family profession?"

I reminded myself again that she had never demonstrated a sense of humour when she just stared at me. "Family." She surveyed me again, more slowly. "What about you? I'd not figured you one for the wild lay."

It was flattering, in a way, to be taken as sufficiently ruthless; but then again, Red Myrta hadn't exactly said she figured me for a *successful* highwayman. I tried to maintain suavity. "It has been suggested to me as appropriate, but at the moment I'm afraid I have a much more bourgeois occupation." I reflected for a moment. "Presuming my employer doesn't fire me for being absent due to a slight misunderstanding with the law."

"What do you stand accused of?" Myrta asked politely.

"Wrongly accused. The murder of Fitzroy Angursell in the form of a dragon."

"How strange," she said, giving the words face value.

I tried not to sigh. "May I ask what you intend with us? You can see we haven't much in the way of worldly goods."

"You do not presume very much on our shared alma mater."

"Ought I?"

She did smile. "Up until the last day of the *viva voce* examinations, I should have said *not on your life*."

She paused, presumably to give me the opportunity to appreciate the full import of that phrase.

"That was before you had the guts to perform one of the most spectacular break-ups I've ever heard of. My favourite was always the story of how the warlord Tzië Hu chose to announce her break with the Emperor Eritanyr by way of sending him the governor of West Voonra's head in a barrel of rice wine, but now, when I reflect on splendid and stupid gestures, I visualize you standing up to Lark."

Myrta had not cast the first stone. I knew that; she'd been sitting on the other side of the room. "Thank you," I said, which was weak.

"So now that you have broken with the lovely Lark, I am more inclined to consider you a potential ally. You understand I cannot let you have your weapons?"

"Naturally not."

"Will you vouch for your companions?"

They had been returning with a way for me to climb out; and one had to start trusting somewhere. It had to be said I rarely found it difficult to decide on the characters of strangers. It was my family whose motivations I distrusted.

"Yes," I said firmly, "if you will take the assurance of a man once besotted with Lark."

Myrta smiled bitterly. "You were not the only one besotted with the lovely Lark. You *were* the only one who broke with her before she was done with him. Jack Ready, untie our—guests."

The faint emphasis reminded me not to underestimate Myrta's commitment to her profession. I was grateful for the chance to move my hands, which were stiff and numb with the cold. "Thank you," I said politely to Jack Ready, who glanced incredulously at me before going over to Ben and Jack.

Once they were untrussed and also stamping feet, blowing on hands, and contriving to get close enough to each other to talk, Myrta said, "Right then, onwards. To the hollow."

"Aye, m'lady." Jack Ready let out a piercing shriek, the near echo of the grey jays.

Myrta's gang moved through the forest as if it were theirs,

which perhaps it was in all the important ways. Myrta strode in the lead, followed by two of her men, then Ben, Jack, and me, and Jack Ready and four or five others behind. Someone had taken our weapons, and there were many hidden someones in the trees around us. Jay calls echoed frequently. Some of those were from the birds who flocked to Myrta; some certainly were not.

It was full dark long before we stopped. As the twilight began to gather shadows I began to stumble. The third time I nearly fell one of the gang appeared at my side to take my elbow. I was embarrassed, but she held me as gracefully as if for a ball, and I needed the guidance too much to demur.

The route took us through an increasingly elaborate series of obstacles: along a tree-trunk bridge, through a narrow cleft in a stone ridge, up into a hidden tree-top structure of rope and wood bridges and platforms that I was a trifle embarrassed to be grateful was hidden by the heavy twilight. At one point below us I heard the sound of a great river, but could smell water only briefly. I wondered if it were perhaps the fabled Magarran Strid.

The Magarran was a major tributary of the Rag. The Strid was a section of its route through the Arguty Forest, where it passed through a limestone gorge. This was the special haunt of the Red Stags; it was also the most dangerous topography in the Forest.

My elder uncle had died there when his horse stepped into a sinkhole and threw him. No one knew how many lives the Strid had claimed.

According to Mr. Dart's stories it was best described as a river turned sideways: six or eight feet across; at least a hundred down, though no one had ever measured it. It was said it was the most dangerous stretch of water in the world precisely because it didn't look it.

Magarran Strid or not, we passed it by in the darkness. We left behind the rope bridges; descended again to the ground; and came at last to the Hollow, which was anything but.

***

In the darkness it looked like what they called 'fairy hills' in South Erlingale—South Erlingale being far enough from the countries that marched along the Kingdom not to worry over-much about naming the Good Neighbours. The Hollow was a smooth-turved low dome, bald of trees, likely to be some ancient pre-Astandalan kinglet's burial mound. Perhaps it was that of the legendary Bloody Queen.

I could see it so clearly because of a line of torches that spiralled around its foot. This should have seemed imprudent but some trick of topography meant I did not see the torchlight until we were close enough also to see the sentries.

Myrta spoke a few words to one. She was answered with ges-tures, and led us around the bottom of the hill to what did seem more accurately called a hollow. This was a grassy dell tucked under an overhang with a huge old oak tree on the crest above us, its dry leaves clacking faintly in the wind. Here there was a bonfire, and many more people.

"Stay here," she said, pointing unceremoniously to a log well on the hillside side of the fire. "Food'll be along in a minute."

"Thank you, Myrta." I bowed; she sniffed and stalked off.

I sat down on the log between Jack and Ben. If they were tired they didn't show much sign of it. I was tired. I'd considered myself fit, but I did not generally spend all day on a forced march.

"I'm not sure I fully relish the vagabond life," I murmured. The bonfire had been burning long enough to throw a great heat, but the log was hard and cold and there was an icy draught coming down the hill at our back. We were facing southwest; I could see a faint reddish-green tinge remaining in the sky to our right. It could not be that late, after all; possibly seven or eight o'clock. I hadn't heard any bells all day.

Ben snorted agreement. "I'm getting too old for this shit. I want something fiery to drink and a warm bed."

"If I've not mistaken the place," Jack replied, "We're at the old hanging hill, so the drinks should be available, if nothing else."

"The hanging hill?" I did not like how sharp my voice was; but no one had ever said exactly *where* they had found my father.

Jack spoke without any concern for my megrims. "Did you see the oak? The king oak, the old folk used to call it. Not a savoury place, certain times of the year. Even when I was a boy there were still rumours that people were making sacrifices there."

"The Dark Kings," I said, heart sinking.

Ben started. "Here? Out west, yes, but this far into the Empire?"

"Ragnor Bella's always been a little backward," Jack rumbled.

My turn to snort. "Yes; and there is, or was a month ago, an active cult to the Dark Kings in the barony."

Mr. Dart and I had—mostly inadvertently—flouted several of the cult's activities. I felt an undercurrent of unease at the thought. We were at one of the turning times for the year, from autumn to winter, when both Schooled magic and the old cults held high ceremonials. Although we had seen the arrest of two of the three priest-ringleaders, both the identity and the whereabouts of the third were unknown. We had not been able to identify *any* of the good citizens who had been participating.

I could only hope I had not been recognized for my part in the affair. I'd been in disguise—

But it wasn't exactly a difficult guess to suppose me neck-deep in the thing, one way or another.

I shivered against a gust, pulled my jerkin closer about myself, and wished for a hat, scarf, gloves, and coat.

That I did not keep imagining my father's body swinging from the king oak on the crest of the hill above and behind us.

I sneezed. From a dozen yards away or so Myrta turned at the noise, then shook her head in resignation when I pulled out one of my remaining handkerchiefs. I was almost certain that my father had not taken his own life. He had not been a traitor, was anything but a coward.

I sneezed again. My throat was scratchier than that morning, which suggested the cold was fast developing.

Surely the man who had held a mountain pass so the rest of his party could escape—surely the man who, trapped on the other outside of the Empire during the Fall, had not only survived but made his painstaking way home—surely that man would not have taken his own life. Not even when he was faced by the wife who had remarried, the brother who denied him, the community that thought him a traitor, the son who … still worshipped the ground he walked on.

"Bless you," Ben said beside me.

"Thank you," I replied.

It was very difficult to face the thought that my father might have been murdered.

"Bless you again," said Jack, from my other side.

"Thank you."

But at least with murder there was something I could *do*. I could find out the truth.

It was such a pity I was on the run from justice.

"Anyway," said Jack, ignoring my following series of sneezes as unworthy of attention, "since time out of mind there's been a distillery here."

I caught my breath. "Surely if it's known to be here that would lead the authorities straight to it?"

"People knew exactly where the Gold Fort was, but that didn't mean anyone ever reached it."

Mr. Dart was far better at history than I; he had written to me about the infamous fastness of the Trigoon Wastes on Voonra. The people there had flaunted their gold mines by coating their hilltop fortress in it, so that it shone as a beacon across the foggy wastelands in the middle of which it was situated.

Astandalas was always hungry for gold. Seven armies had tried, and failed, to capture the Gold Fort.

"Point taken," I replied. The Lady knew I'd never be able to find my own way back through that tangled obstacle course traversed at speed in the dark.

Ben stretched out his gnarled hands. "What do they distill out here, then? That rotgut pearjack?"

"That and even more rotgut whiskeyjack," a new voice said. I looked up. An older woman had walked over to us, Red Myrta and another stranger at her side. The latter carried a tray of bowls and tankards, all covered with wooden lids in the Charese fashion.

I examined her as best I could in the shifting light from bonfire and torches. It didn't take much to see that she was the gang's leader—nor that she was Myrta's mother. I rose to essay a bow. "Ma'am."

"This is Jemis," Myrta said. "He's always like this."

I bowed to her, too, for good measure, then sat down for what turned out to be stew and whiskey.

"I'm Myrta the Hand. My daughter tells me you made the traverse well enough for a beginner to the wild lay."

I presumed that was a compliment. "Thank you." Decided after a moment I should perhaps clarify. "I'm not seeking, ah, new employment at the moment."

Myrta the Hand gazed at me. "You're Mad Jack Greenwing's son, I presume? Heard he was back from university."

Red Myrta knew my first name, and it was not as if three questions in Ragnor Bella wouldn't identify me. "Yes, ma'am."

On either side of me Ben and Jack shifted position; probably exchanging a meaningful glance, I thought with some amusement.

"There are at least three different—let us call them *opportunities*—for those of us on the wild lay concerning you, Master Jemis."

"Mr. Greenwing," I corrected politely.

"You don't sound surprised, Mr. Greenwing."

I sipped some the 'rotgut whiskeyjack', which was the smoothest and smokiest whiskey I'd ever tasted. It was even better than what the Hunter in Green's man had laced my coffee with.

"Ma'am, I am merely surprised that there are only three. My life is the stuff of melodrama."

She smiled slightly. "I've seen the play. It was somewhat histrionic but very well done."

"It was entirely false."

My voice came out flat and cold, not quite intentionally. Jack and Ben froze beside me. Every one of the bandits/distillers/smugglers I could see except for Myrta the Hand moved into some variation of the *en garde*.

Myrta the Hand continued to regard me solemnly. "Didn't your father teach you not to pick fights?"

"My father taught me to pick the right ones. Ma'am. I am fully aware you could make this my last day if you so wished. Nevertheless, I will gladly defend my father's honour."

"He's a bottle covey," Red Myrta said after a moment. "I told you about the final exams, Mum."

"So you did," said her mother, still watching me.

I decided that given the fact that I was already well in their power, there wasn't any reason not to ask, so I did: "Would you be willing to tell me more about these opportunities you mention?"

She looked as if I'd asked the right thing. "Disruption, distress, delay. Not, at present, death."

I didn't know quite what to say to that, so I bowed to indicate my thanks. Red Myrta rolled her eyes; her mother smiled again.

She did not say anything more, for a commotion had broken out to our right. I did not at first think too much of it, until I realized first that the commotion was a man bringing in a struggling child, and secondly that I knew her.

If I had been willing to fight for my father's honour, the sight of my little sister made me understand for the first time the pure desire to kill.

"What are you doing with my sister?"

I did not ask anyone in particular. I had snapped immediately out of the ordinary world into the world of mortal danger, which was terrifyingly attractive and in which I felt even more terrifyingly at home. Not that the terror came until after; which was part of the joy.

The man holding Sela leered. "Hostage, ain't she?"

Three different *opportunities*, Myrta the Hand had said. Well, not this one.

"Jemis!" Sela cried. "Jemis! Make the bad man stop! I don't want to play any more!"

"Hey, stop crying, you, or you'll be sorry."

Sela responded to this by sinking her teeth into the man's hand.

Even in that state I fully approved.

He yowled and fetched her a backhanded blow, and that was it as far and my rational mind was concerned.

In retrospect I moved fast. In the moment I unhurriedly stood up from the log, unhurriedly made my way past Red Myrta and her mother and half-a-dozen other whiskey-distilling highway-men, unhurriedly reached Sela and her captor—

—And most unhurriedly indeed took aim and landed my right fist in his throat. He dropped. I put knee to chest and hands around his gasping throat.

I turned my head so I could see Sela as well as him. She looked so surprised she'd forgotten to cry.

"J-Jemis? He hurt me."

She rubbed her arm. My heart congealed.

"Did he touch you anywhere else?"

Below my hands I could feel the raising, slightly bubbly breath catch. The man's eyes rolled frantically, but I saw no guilt there, only horror.

Sela smeared snot all over her face. "N-no. But I don't like this game! I want to go home."

So did I, with a stabbing longing for a home that no longer existed.

I stood up. Turned back to Myrta the Hand. "Well, ma'am?" My voice rang clearly through the Hollow. "You have my sister and myself and my two companions. You hold our weapons. You know our worldly belongings. You could hand me over to the Yellem Constabulary or the Knockermen or the cult of the Dark Kings or the Ragnor Constabulary or the Indrillines or whoever else is looking for me or kill me out of hand. What do you choose?"

Myrta the Hand closed her mouth. "A bottle covey, Myr? More like a hundredweight cask."

I waited. At my feet Sela's captor rolled over to his stomach, where he continued to gasp, but less frothily. Sela skirted his head to run towards me, then ran back and kicked him in the side.

I picked her up when she came back. "It's not nice to kick a man when he's already down," I said to her.

"I couldn't kick him before," she said, sticking out her tongue.

I couldn't argue with that, and transferred my attention back to Myrta the Hand.

"You're Mad Jack Greenwing's son, all right," she said, shaking her head. "This game has too many players as it is without throwing a wild runner into the mix." She nodded sharply at someone out of my sight. Then her face changed.

"Wait. You mentioned the Indrillines?"

Chapter Eight
Refuge

FOR THE PRICE of explaining everything I knew about the Indrilline and Knockermen activities in Ragnor barony—or at least everything I was willing to describe, which meant I did not discuss Violet by name—Myrta the Hand got some of her people to lead us back through the obstacle course.

They let us go on the highway. They did not give us back our belongings, but that was probably too much to ask for. I shifted Sela, whom I was carrying, and wished—not for the first time!—that life made sense when the mortal danger had passed. The highwaymen melted back into the forest like shades into shadow.

"Well," I said, and stopped there.

Ben snorted softly. "Well, and a scientific punch that was indeed. Where did you say you worked?"

I smiled involuntarily. "A bookstore."

"And you're Jack Greenwing's son."

Jack cleared his throat. "Where did you go to university, that a daughter of the wild lay was there?"

"He went to Morrowlea," Sela said proudly, wriggling in my arms so she could look at them. She focused on Ben, visible in a stray shaft of moonlight. "Who are you? You look like my friend Hal. Do you know him?"

Ben looked politely baffled. "I'm Ben. And you, miss?"

"I'm Miss Sela Buchance. Jemis is my brother but we have different papas." She clutched at me suddenly. "Promise you're not going away, Jemis? You're staying now, aren't you? I don't want you to go anywhere."

She seemed fair set to work herself into hysterics. I soothed her as best I could, smoothing her disordered hair and discovering that her skin was alarmingly clammy. I set her down, where she grabbed my leg, so I could undo my coat, then reversed it around her before picking her up again. "There, that's better, isn't it?"

"*Promise* you won't go away again?"

Her voice was terribly anxious. Why would she worry that I would *go away*? And then I realized that to her life must seem a series of people *going away*, and not coming back. First our mother, to the influenza (though I did not think Sela remembered her), then me, to university; and now, this summer, her papa, my stepfather, to the wasps that had stung him to death.

I could not bear to lie to her, even at the risk of a very bad reaction. "Sela, love, I can't promise that I'll never go away again. But I've come back, haven't I? I can promise I'll always do my best to come back."

"You came back this time," she said darkly. "People don't always come back when they go away. My papa didn't. We went to visit his grave."

"Yes," I replied solemnly, not sure what else there was to say.

"I asked Mama but she said your papa wasn't in the churchyard with everyone else's. And then Liza said that that was because your papa didn't stay buried the first time, and I was worried that my papa would be unhappy about being buried and what if he comes back? Then you're not with us anymore and when the man came to say we were looking for you I wanted to *help*."

It was too dark to see her face as more than a pale blur, but I could fee her trembling in my arms. I pushed down my own feelings, made my voice as calm, as warm, as matter-of-fact as possible.

"Your papa won't be coming back, Sela."

"*Your* papa did."

I swallowed. "That was because he hadn't really died. He was far away from home, you see, and when they sent us a letter it had the wrong details, so we thought he had died but we were wrong."

And thus it was that my half-sisters were not legitimate, and I had for ever branded in my memory the look on my father's face when I opened the door and he saw coming behind me my mother with the infant Lauren in her arms.

And I was stuck having a conversation like this is in the dark menace of the Arguty Forest, where he had taken leave of his life for good—whether by his hand or another's—in the spur weeks between autumn and winter, on the ancient Fallowday when the spirits of the unquiet dead might walk. I sneezed again, and Sela nearly giggled. "Bless you!"

"Thank you," I said.

"Why isn't your papa buried in the churchyard?"

Her voice, thank the Lady, was losing some of its sharpness, but she was still shaking.

"That had to do with the mistake in the letter. Some people believed the wrong things about my father, and … and they wouldn't let us bury him there."

"But—"

I did not want to talk about why my father was buried in an unhallowed grave under the White Cross. I suppressed another series of sneezes. "But nothing. It's too late to talk about this. What I want is for you to try to fall asleep as we walk."

"But Jemis—"

"Hush. We need to listen very hard in case there are any nightingales."

Any nightingales there might have been would long since have flown south or through the green ways into the Kingdom, but thankfully Sela was not quite at the age to argue with logic, and that, mercifully, kept everyone quiet as we put one foot in front of another down the long dark road. I kept my mind firmly on that.

We came at last to a single brightly burning light.

I realized I'd been leading us there unconsciously but to excellent purpose. Where else could I expect refuge in the middle of the night? Not my uncle's, that was certain, and Ragnor Bella itself was another six miles on.

"My friend lives here," I said vaguely to Ben and Jack, who had walked silently along beside me the whole way. "They'll make sure my sister is taken care of, at least."

It was late, but the candle-lantern at the stable-side door suggested someone was still up. Indeed, our timing was impeccable, for as I neared a familiar dark shape emerged from the other side of the shadows.

"Mr. Dart," I said politely.

Mr. Dart checked, swung around wildly so that the poacher's lantern he was carrying sent shadows and illumination danced even more wildly around us. I shut my eyes against a wash of dizzying exhaustion.

"Mr. Greenwing. And whom do you bring to my door this fine midnight?"

"Jack, Ben, my sister Sela."

"Even more adventures than I suspected are afoot. Will they keep until the morning?"

"I sincerely hope so. Though I should inform you that you—or rather your brother—will be harbouring felons."

"Oh?"

"They were arrested for loitering, I for murdering Fitzroy Angursell in the form of a dragon, and we escaped out of Yellton Gaol."

"That explains your last few days."

Sela made a murmuring noise of protest as I shifted position. Mr. Dart laughed.

"Or no, it doesn't? I can feel the disgruntlement radiating off you. Welcome, gentlemen, please enter. I ask merely that you respect my brother the Squire's hospitality while you are on his premises."

"We can manage that, I believe," Jack rumbled gravely.

"We're not entirely felonious," added Ben.

"Very good," said Mr. Dart. "In that case, you should feel quite at home."

***

Sela had insisted on sleeping with me, a fact I recalled when she started bouncing on me far too early the next morning.

"Wake up, Jemis, it's time to get up."

I wrestled my arm free of the blankets pinned by her weight. Rubbed my face; resolutely did not open my eyes. "I'm sure it's still time to be asleep, Sela."

"It's not! Wake up, Jemis, everyone's awake!"

I opened my eyes at that. "Really? Who's everyone?"

She began describing the people she'd seen crossing the yard below the bedroom window. I recognized the descriptions as various members of the Dart household: housemaids, stableboy, and finally Sir Hamish, whose presence suggested that it probably was time to get up.

At least the Darts had the newfangled unmagical plumbing, and thus when I levered myself out of bed I could lead Sela to a quite luxurious bathroom for her morning ablutions. I had to dress her in yesterday's clothing, of course, but someone had managed to clean and dry most of it. I always admired the efficiency of the Darts' household staff. I was more than glad I hadn't had to do laundry between midnight and morning.

"Is it time for breakfast now?" Sela asked hopefully when I sat her down to do her hair.

"Hold still." I wrestled with her fair flyaway hair—inheritance from Mr. Buchance, as our mother was a dark brunette—and finally got into into an acceptable braid. "There. Let me get myself ready."

"Or you'll have a beard like Mr. Dart!"

This struck her as exquisitely funny. She was still laughing about it when I emerged clean (and clean-shaven) and dressed in my own proper clothes. After far too many of Mr. Dart's *adventures* since my return home had ended with me obliged to borrow his clothing, I had finally begun leaving a suit in my room at the Hall. It was summer-weight, but I couldn't help that. I didn't have enough winter-weight clothing to bestrew it across the barony.

I felt much more that young gentleman, Mr. Jemis Greenwing (technically Lord St-Noire), once I was dressed in fawn breeches, green waistcoat, midnight coat, a cravat tied in the Subdued Mathematical, and six fresh handkerchiefs in my pocket.

"Ready, Miss Sela?"

"I've been ready for *ages*, Jemis. I'm so hungry I could eat a whole sheep."

"A whole *sheep*? Not a cow?"

She giggled as I opened the door. "Cows are very, very big. I'm still very, very small."

"That's true."

Jack was coming along the hall towards us, face more than a little troubled. Possibly that was just the effect of the beard and the eyepatch; he was clean and brushed, but had not chosen to shave. He was wearing the same style of clothes as I, but one or two rungs down in terms of quality. People seeing me had trouble believing I was on speaking terms with the nobility; people seeing him would have trouble believing him on speaking terms with the gentry. I wondered if his were as misleading as mine.

"Good morning, Jack."

"Good morning," he rumbled. "Look, lad, I must talk with you."

"Maybe *two* sheep," Sela said, swinging my hand meaningfully.

I smiled at Jack. "Can it wait? She didn't have anything to eat last night, as far as I can make out,."

"Or a pig."

Jack looked dissatisfied. "Yes, but I—it's very important, lad."

"I'll gladly speak with you once I see my sister settled. Why don't you come down with us?"

He seemed ready to say something more, but I was being tugged along by Sela and might have been mistaken on the point.

He did follow me along to the stairs and down to the breakfast parlour, where we found Master Dart, Mr. Dart, and two house-maids setting out platters of food. I was reminded that I had been too busy sparring with Myrta the Hand to eat more than a few mouthfuls of my supper. Sir Hamish was coming along into the room from the other direction with Ben behind him.

Mr. Dart looked up. "There you are, Mr. Greenwing. And Miss Sela, how lovely to see you this morning."

Sela was suddenly shy. She did a minuscule curtsey and then clung to the back of my leg. I smiled apologetically at the Squire and Sir Hamish. "Thank you for your hospitality, Master Dart, Sir Hamish. I'm sorry to have arrived so importunately at your door in the middle of the night."

Master Dart harrumphed but did not appear displeased. Sir Hamish actually grinned. "What else are friends for? I trust the explanations will be both forthcoming and fascinating."

"But first breakfast, before Miss Sela quite faints."

This was Master Dart, who smiled so kindly at her she let go of her death grip on my leg. He gestured at the seat next to him-self, and Sela climbed up eagerly when I nudged her, although her eagerness probably also had something to do with the housemaid proffering her a plate of food.

Sir Hamish sent Ben along the table next to Mr. Dart before turning to Jack. "What an interesting face you have. I should like to paint it."

Jack advanced into the room, but stopped at these words. I sympathized. I found Sir Hamish's occasional painterly regard dis-concerting.

Sir Hamish was staring at him with deep intensity, expression shifting from polite welcome to something I could not decipher. Then he started to smile.

"I *have* painted it. By the Emperor, Jack, only you would manage the trick of returning from the dead *twice*."

Chapter Nine
First Draw

—NO.

***

My attention, my whole world, focused on him.

The rueful amusement, the lopsided half-apologetic smile, the one visible eye.

I had not inherited much of my physical appearance from my father, everyone said. I looked like my maternal grandfather instead, lean and a little short and inclined to fret when I wasn't busy being a bottle covey and revelling in mortal danger.

The gravelly voice, the eyepatch, the beard.

—The hands clenching at his side.

I wanted to sneeze but my body felt far, far away.

My ears were roaring.

Someone touched me lightly on the arm; I jumped as if shocked by static.

"Why don't you two go next door," Master Dart said. It was not a question.

His words seemed to come from very far away. I understood

them, but they did not rouse any response. He tugged my arm gently. I followed passively, staring at nothing.

The door closed behind me. Jack stood before me, face working.

"I tried to tell you," he said. His voice was still rumbling, but—O Lady, now it was *familiar*—"I couldn't when you were telling your sister—"

He stopped, for I'd made a gesture. I didn't really mean for him to stop talking. I didn't—I couldn't—I had no way to think what I could possibly say.

Saw the wariness in his face.

Could not say anything.

I could barely breathe.

I walked forward out my silence, into his silence.

He held still. I reached forward out of my silence, into his silence, and I embraced him.

My head rested on his shoulder. He smelled of soap and woodsmoke and fresh air.

After a moment his arms curled around my back.

***

"You did try to tell me," I said at last, backing up so I could pull out two handkerchiefs. My father—my father!—Jack took one, wiped his face. He was careful around the eyepatch.

"It's almost healed," he muttered, gesturing at it. "I didn't lose it."

"Oh."

A thousand years ago I had wondered if it were simply a disguise, if there had been a real injury there at all.

We stared at each other some more.

Feeling was starting to come back to me, washing over me in great crashing waves of confusion, elation, fear, euphoria, wonder, doubt.

He reached out and ran his hand down my face. "Jemis."

His fingers were callused, but his touch was very gentle. I wanted to smile; instead I sneezed.

He laughed as I brought up the handkerchief, the sound still hoarse but echoing painfully in my memories.

I used to dream regularly about my father miraculously not being dead after all. But every time I called his name he disappeared or transformed into something … not him. After a year the dreams had stopped … and started again a month ago, after the Harvest Fair when I slew the dragon.

O Lady.

"I am confounded," I said, aiming for nonchalance and failing my target abysmally. "Shall we go into the other room so you don't have to explain twice?"

He nodded. "Sensible."

"I thought you'd decided that wasn't one of my notable traits?"

He laughed again. "These counter-characteristics come out at times in the best of us."

In the breakfast parlour Sela was squirming around on her chair—in agitation about my disappearance, I presumed, until I realized she was describing to a bemused Sir Hamish how Hal and I had promised to make her a cake for her birthday.

"The same one they were making when Jemis fought the dragon," she concluded.

"Your birthday isn't for months, Sela," I pointed out.

"You might need to practice."

Ben cleared his throat. "So, er, you were serious about there being a dragon."

"Didn't you hear the rumours of it as you came south?" Sir Hamish said. "It's the most exciting thing to happen here since Jack came home last time."

"Jemis *killed* the dragon!" Sela cried proudly. "Just like in a story. Except that you didn't have a sword or a lance or anything proper."

"I'll try to remember for next time."

Sela described the fight gleefully but probably with very little coherence for anyone not present. We all watched as her thin face blossomed with excitement. "And finally he jumped on its head and stabbed it right in the eye and it went all over the place and finally he landed in the cakes and it was dead, just like that."

"What was your weapon?" Ben asked. For no particular reason the cadence reminded me of Hal and I knew who Ben must be.

"A cake knife—it was in the middle of the cake competition at the Dartington Harvest Fair," I added for my father's—my father's!—benefit. "My apologies, sir: I've just realized who you are. Your great-nephew Hal was my roommate at Morrowlea. He said he thought you'd be coming to Ragnor Bella."

"Oh!" cried Mr. Dart, jumping up so he could bow. "You're General Prince Benneret Halioren? I am honoured, sir!"

Sir Hamish and the Squire murmured equally welcoming, if more bemused, responses. Ben snorted. "You gave us hospitality unquestioned despite warning we were gaol-breakers."

"Oh, well, when it comes to Mr. Greenwing's affairs gaol-breaking companions hardly merits a raised eyebrow," proclaimed Mr. Dart, which did prompt several raised eyebrows from everyone else.

"Let's leave me aside for now," I said.

They all looked at me. Master Dart murmured, "Of course," and briskly walked around the table to clasp Jack on the shoulder. "Welcome home. Will you tell us what happened?"

"What I can," he said bleakly, glancing at the maid bringing in another dish of toast. I could not bring myself to sit down. I went to the sideboard to prepare coffee for Jack and Ben, wishing I knew the small details of taste and preference.

My hands shook on the silver coffee pot. It clattered against the cup. "Sorry," I whispered, unable to be flippant, but no one seemed to hear.

The maid went out again with a wink at me. Jack said, "The short version is that after I came home last time to find my reputation destroyed and my family situation complicated, I resolved to go to Nên Corovel to beg the Lady's advice and support." He smiled lopsidedly. "I got there this summer."

"And between?" Sir Hamish asked, sipping his coffee. *His* hands were trembling slightly as he set it down. This puzzled me, until I recalled that he was my father's cousin, and he and Master Dart had been—were—by the lady, *were*—his close friends.

"Ay, there's the rub." Jack sighed. "I was waylaid in the Forest."

Master Dart leaned forward. "By whom?"

"Does it matter? Nobody I knew. One of the many gangs of people displaced by the Fall. I was unsuccessful in my efforts to escape."

He waited while the maid came back in with another pot of coffee. I was still standing by the sideboard, and she poured me some into my cup. She added the cream I liked without my asking and swished away again. She was new this past month, but I was sure I'd heard Mr. Brock mention her name … Ellen, I thought, or Elinor. She looked vaguely familiar, but I couldn't think why. She couldn't have been much older than sixteen. Perhaps a relative of hers had been in the kingschool at the same time as me.

"Did Jemis rescue you, too?" Sela asked suddenly.

We all looked at her. "I'm sorry, Miss Sela?" Mr. Dart replied politely, when it appeared no one else was going to.

"Jemis rescued *me* from the bad men in the Forest."

Jemis had not rescued his father from the bad men in the Forest. Jemis had been nearly catatonic with shock and horror and grief and rage and guilt at his father's suicide. Jemis had eventually spent the better part of a month under daily attentions from Dominus Gleason and Doctor Imbrey, the now-dead local physicker, until finally he had been able to hide the telltale signs and been pronounced well enough to go out in public again.

Jemis sneezed, and was brought once again into the present tense. I turned to look out the window while I blew my nose. Behind me Jack said, his voice a little odd, "This was when he was younger, Sela."

"How did you get away, then? You must be very brave and very strong."

I could hear the smile, and the regret, in his voice. "That's not always enough, I'm afraid."

"What happened?"

"The … bad men travelled … went further north and west, until along the coast past Ghilousette we came across some pirates on shore leave. By then they were tired of my efforts to escape. They sold me to the pirates, and on the galley I stayed. This spring it was boarded by a ship of the Lady, who freed us … slaves … and

I made it at last to the Lady's door. I was surprised but pleased to find Ben there, too. It seemed wiser to come quietly to see what was toward this time, especially once he told me about that play."

"Where did you meet Jemis?" Mr. Dart asked quietly. I turned around to see Jack glancing away from me. Behind him the maid (who was clearly intently interested in the story; as who wouldn't be?) glanced out the open door to the hall and, looking annoyed, went out. Jack ignored her.

"In Yellton Gaol. We'd been taken up for loitering while looking poor. Not wishing to be press-ganged into the Rondelan navy, we took our engaging young cellmate up on his suggestion of how to break out."

They all looked at me again. I flushed hotly. "They put the hinges on the *inside* of the cell door."

Mr. Dart smiled. "A fact I shall try to remember if ever I find myself locked in a gaol cell somewhere. Come now, Mr. Greenwing, whatever were you doing in the Yellton Gaol?"

"I told you," I said, "I was arrested on charge of murdering Fitzroy Angursell while in the form of a dragon."

Sela giggled. This seemed the most appropriate response. Everyone one else just stared at me, arrested. (As it were.)

"That seems very obviously contrived," began Sir Hamish.

I half-bowed, which seemed to amuse him. "Yes, contrived to make the most sensational gossip since—" I stopped.

"Since Jack came back from the dead the first time," Master Dart agreed. "While I cannot condone gaol-breaking as a *regular* practice—"

"I assure you, Master Dart, I have every respect for the law possible."

His lips quirked. "Yes, I well believe you do, Mr. Greenwing. Oh, and good morning, your grace."

I glanced over at the door to see that Hal had followed the maid in. He'd already divested himself of hat and gloves, but held a small collection of letters. He smiled broadly at everyone. "You've been leading us a merry chase of questions, Jemis! Mrs. Etaris says I am not nearly so competent a clerk as you. I told her it was because you spent all the time you weren't running in the library, while I was doing more useful things. Fortunately she was equally happy talking about gardens."

"Oh yes?" I said weakly.

"Good morning," he added to the others, sweeping a bright smile along the table. "Thank you for summoning me—oh! Uncle Ben!"

He produced a half-bow of evident respect to his great-uncle, who shook his head and snorted. "Rapscallion."

"A graceful one," murmured Jack, which was a pun I'd somehow not yet myself made.

Hal looked quizzically at Jack. "One of your old comrades-in-arms, Uncle?"

Jack smiled crookedly. "You could say that."

Hal stared at him, then swung around to frown intently at me. Ben was half-smiling, and did not seem at all surprised when Hal returned his now very sharp gaze to Jack. Hal, I reflected, was good at recognizing relationships in more than just plant families.

"Surely not," Hal breathed.

Ben was definitely amused now. He spoke formally, the words rolling off his tongue in an accent I now surmised might be Astandalan court: "Your grace, may I present my good friend and former comrade, Major Jakory Greenwing of the Seventh Army? Jack, my great-nephew Hal, the Duke of Fillering Pool."

"I am honoured," said Hal, bowing very deeply.

Jack stood so that he could bow back. "Thank you."

I did know Hal's preferences, so I made him coffee. My hands barely shook this time. My stomach seemed to have taken up the quivers, but that was to be expected.

He thanked me and sat down beside his great-uncle. "I've some letters for you, Jemis; they seemed like ones you might want as soon as possible. I was glad to meet the Darts' messenger this morning, I must say. Mrs. Etaris and I have been quite concerned about your whereabouts, especially once Miss Sela disappeared last night."

"Jemis rescued me from the bad man, Hal," Sela informed him. "He hit him in the throat and he fell over."

Sela, I reflected, showed definite signs of a bloodthirsty streak. I wondered at what age it was appropriate to start teaching one's little sister how to fight.

Hal did not like physical violence, though he was one of the most morally courageous people I'd ever met. "How, er, efficient of him. So, what have you been doing with yourself this week, Jemis besides hitting bad men in the throat?"

I sighed. "Most of a day in the Yellton Gaol, then a day and a half in the Arguty Forest. We got here last night at midnight."

He made an encouraging gesture. "And for the rest of the week?"

I blinked at him as this, and a few other things, fell into place. Their pattern of meaning confounded me utterly. "What *day* is it?"

Chapter Ten
Correspondences

IT WAS MID-MORNING in Dart Hall, and my father was alive.

I had somehow lost two and a half days of my life, and my father was alive.

I was on the lam, a gaol-breaker and a wanted man: and so was he.

"Walk us through what you remember," he said intently. "You were out running?"

He did not seem to care that I participated in the poor man's steeplechase. Perhaps years as a slave on a pirate galley wore off the sharper points of pride.

"Yes. I left early, for I was intending to make a twelve-mile circuit."

Everyone looked at me. I tried not to flush, thinking firmly instead that I liked the gold-on-blue brocade of the curtains. After a moment Master Dart asked, "How long did you expect that to take?"

"About two hours. I'd not gone on a long run for a while, and I was feeling restless."

"Not my response," Mr. Dart muttered nearly under his breath.

Master Dart nodded. "Very well. You left at—?"

"In the pre-dawn. I've been running the barony the last month. I am tolerably well acquainted with the condition of the roads. I wished to be back in time to bathe before work."

"Work?"

I found it very difficult to look at my father as I described my life. My throat felt scratchy with the burgeoning head cold. And ... my life was surely so different from what he had hoped for his son ...

"I work as an assistant clerk to Mrs. Etaris at her bookstore in town. I have rooms above the store. Hal's staying there with me."

Ben guffawed. "That must spite the noses of half the town."

"The Baron finds it exceedingly difficult to comprehend," murmured Master Dart.

"The Baron finds most things exceedingly difficult to comprehend," Sir Hamish responded. "Do continue, Mr. Greenwing. You set out for your exercise in the pre-dawn, heading—?"

"I went up along the highway to the White Cross, and—that's it. It's as if I stepped directly from the cross-roads into the Yellton Gaol. I didn't even see the gaoler clearly."

Mr. Dart passed the sugar to Sela, who was gazing adoringly at him, or possibly his beard. "There must be *something*—some clue or key. Perhaps if you describe it?"

I might be talkative, but I was not used to talking about my private impressions of a place, a moment, a situation. Certainly not the White Cross in the grey light before dawn.

I sneezed, muttered an apology. "It didn't take me long to get there; it wasn't yet light." I closed my eyes to call up the memory; or perhaps to hide from it. "It was quiet. I could hear a rooster starting down the road—Mrs. Hennessy's cock is always the first to crow. There was mist in the river-valley. Not too much on the highway.

"It was thicker on the Borrowbank Road and—yes, and along Spinney Lane, too, because I was planning on going that way and I remember wondering how difficult it would be along that soft spot by the Wester Marsh. It had been very muddy the last time I went down it."

I drank a few sips of coffee to clear my throat and to distance myself from the eerie dawn errand. It did not help at all to have him sitting there across the table from me. He did not *look* as he had in any of those dreams, but—

I cleared my throat again. "An owl hooted just as I stopped before the waystone. I jumped, and—and I was in Yellton."

"Again. Refine your vision."

Jack's voice was the brisk commander's, as if I were a young soldier giving his report.

I tried again. "I stopped running where the Borrowbank Road comes up to the highway, where the surface changes. I walked up to the waystone. The owl hooted as I came past Spinney Lane."

"Why did you stop running?" Ben asked intently.

I felt piercingly embarrassed. Could not meet anyone's eye. I traced a spill of salt on the table before me instead. "I was … wanting to make the spur-week offering."

Jack said, "Why on earth would you—"

He stopped abruptly, hearing the shocked dismay in his own voice that a son of his would be doing anything around a cross-roads before dawn.

We had had a few classes in Philosophy and Theology where we were invited to imagine having a glimpse of how our reputations fared after our deaths. I had found it a very difficult exercise, knowing firsthand how painful that realization could be.

It did not appear any easier the second time.

"I'm sorry, Jemis," he said quietly.

I had been feeling numb, except for the raw throat, but the quiet dignity of that apology woke some fire within me.

"Need you be? Did you stage your own suicide?"

"Jemis—no! Never—I would *never* have left you—I would *never* have pretended that!"

His voice was raw, his visible eye horrified.

I had had too many dreams when he said that to me.

—No. I would not let those dreams govern me. I would not. I *would not*.

I spoke with precision, not so much for him as in defiance of those dreams. My throat was thick, with tears or phlegm or both. "Then let us find out who did."

***

All the things we did not know could have filled several books. After a struggle to return to some semblance of normal conversation I was relieved to be reminded of my letters by the arrival of the second post for the Darts.

I had three letters. One was marked Tarvenol, one South Erlingale, and one bore no postmark at all.

I couldn't help myself, and opened the Tarvenol one first. I felt such a crushing disappointment that it wasn't from Violet that it took me several moments to realize what it *was* about.

"Shocking news?" Mr. Dart asked lightly. "Are you summoned to attend the Last Emperor?"

"I've been offered a place at Inveragory."

They were fulsome with their congratulations, so it took me a while to explain my shock. "I haven't *applied* there yet." I looked at my father, whose expression was unreadable. "I was planning on writing to them, but I haven't yet heard from my tutor about sponsoring me."

"You did come First at Morrowlea," Mr. Dart pointed out. "Faculties seek out the top students from other universities for advanced degrees, you know."

"That's right—you said Tara had offered you—"

Too late I realized that this had not been something Mr. Dart had shared with his brother and Sir Hamish. They both frowned, the Squire profoundly. "Perry—"

"Of course, you wanted to come home," I added hastily, knowing it was lame, knowing I had unwittingly betrayed a confidence. I had thought Mr. Dart *had* truly wanted to come home to be his brother's land agent and learn to steward the estate.

Looking at their faces now I had the sinking sensation that I was wrong.

Mr. Dart had managed to hide a gift at wild magic from everyone for most of his life.

Mr. Dart was always the one starting adventures.

Mr. Dart smiled easily at his brother. "What would I want with Tara? I've already been to Stoneybridge. Look at the quality Tara's putting forth nowadays."

"Roald Ragnor went to Tara," Sir Hamish said for Jack's benefit. "He's the Baron's son, and rather wild, too," he added for Ben's.

I looked down at my letter. A full scholarship to Inveragory for Law. That made so many things easier … and others so much harder. …

The letter from South Erlingale was from my tutor, and explained, at least, that the Dean of Law from Inveragory had been visiting his brother, one of the other professors at Morrowlea, and had been in the Senior Common Room when my letters arrived.

"Letters?" enquired Mr. Dart.

My correspondence was none of their business, except for all the ways in which it was.

"I wrote to ask about Inveragory." I wouldn't explain everything about the spring's disastrous examinations, I thought, though I had also written to explain that my defence of the virtues of scholarly rigour and logic—in the form of meticulously taking apart Lark's final paper—had not been fully disinterested. She had written a brilliant rhetorical argument for why Major Jack Greenwing's name should not be recorded in the House of Fame. I had not said then that I was his son; but I could not bear for the university senate to think I was not.

I cleared my throat. "I also wrote about the dragon and to ask if any of the Scholars wanted to come examine the carcass."

The Squire harrumphed. "Do they? I shouldn't mind having the old granary back sooner rather than later."

I focused on the letter. "Ah—yes. They're coming as soon as possible, Dominus Lukel from Morrowlea and a couple of other Scholars he knows from other universities. He's the Master of Arms."

"He spent a full month on dragons in Self-Defence," Hal said brightly. "He must be overjoyed to think his best student actually met one."

***

The rest of breakfast passed with innocuous conversation. Hal carried most of it; neither Mr. Dart nor I said much. I was tired and emotionally overwhelmed; Mr. Dart seemed ... shadowed, or perhaps he, too, was just tired. He had been coming home as late as we'd arrived. I presumed he had been out picking mushrooms, but he might not have been.

"Why am I here?" Hal asked rhetorically after Ben said something.

"It seems a reasonable question."

"First it was to find some Noirell honey, and then since I found Jemis along with it, I decided to stay a while and see if you turned up."

Ben snorted, but I could see he was pleased. "You thought I'd come?"

"I was sure you would once you learned about that play. You did know about the play, sir?"

"Yes," Jack growled.

My father. I sneezed. Everyone ignored me except for Sela, who said, "Bless you!" with amazing condescension.

"We went to see it this spring with Jemis—they didn't advertise it with the subtitle. I wrote to you, Uncle Ben, then decided I'd come visit. When I heard you'd gone off I presumed it was here, after the truth of the story, and came myself."

Ben regarded him shrewdly. "Cruel of you to leave Elly to your aunt's list."

Hal whooped, startling everyone as his laughter usually did. "The list of eligible parties," he explained. "It's my aunt Honoria's masterpiece. Every possible good match itemized and ranked according to elaborate criteria. I shall have to send you a copy, Jemis."

I looked up from my toast crumbs. "Er, why?"

"Reference. It's pretty well the same list for you, though I believe Aunt Honoria would permit you to consider regional nobility. She thinks I ought not look below a ruling countess."

I stared at him some more. "Hal, I am currently under allegations of murder. I work at a bookstore. I am probably going to end up a lawyer. I don't think *anyone* on your aunt's list—"

"Wouldn't be interested in the son of Mad Jack Greenwing, Viscount St-Noire and heir to the Marquisate of Noirell? Don't be absurd, Jemis. You must see the appeal to more than the criminal element."

I ignored this slight on Lark and Violet (I did not think I had yet mentioned Red Myrta, who anyway had never shown any indication of romantic interest in me). "You can't be seriously thinking of choosing a bride off a list?"

Hal shrugged. "I shall marry either for love or dynastic succession. It would be best to do both, of course, but the second is far easier to attain, and then again there's the difficulty in finding the truth of emotions when a title and a fortune are involved. Elly's marrying for love—" He smiled quickly at his great-uncle. "Not that anything's official yet! The betrothal will be announced at our Winterturn ball. I in my turn shall, no doubt, be expected to seriously consider the young women produced to attend the various festivities."

"The Ironwood heir and so on?" I enquired lightly, though I felt sick to my stomach in a way difficult to describe.

"Precisely. One of them will doubtless suit well enough, or if none of them will do at all—or will have me, though any unattached young woman who comes to my house this winter will be well aware of what's toward—then my sister's wedding in the spring will bring the rest, I shall choose one, and that will be that."

"Seems cold-blooded," Sir Hamish ventured at last. I looked up at a note in his voice; he was gazing with a mild frown at Mr. Dart.

Mr. Dart himself was smiling cheerfully and unabashedly. Hal shrugged again. "I have been the duke since I was seven, Sir Hamish, as you know. I have always known my duty. At least the circumstances since the Fall have changed so that I am not obliged to entertain a purely arranged marriage, as would have been the case a dozen years ago." He grinned at me. "Don't look so troubled, Jemis. Your grandmother probably doesn't know the fashion is for marrying young nowadays, so you have a few years yet to study Aunt Honoria's List and make your acquaintance among the *beau monde*."

I struggled with a great many sentiments, none of them helped by the presence of the stern-faced man sitting across from me. I pitied Hal's matter-of-fact acceptance of his duty; I envied him it; I wished I understood my place in the world with such unshakable confidence.

Eventually I managed a pretence of nonchalance. "It may be that I end up with one of my dashing criminals unless I can clear my name of these bizarre charges. No one of gentle birth will want to wed such a scandal."

"I think you underestimate the upper-class ladies of Northwest Oriole."

I had not met many besides any other incognito ones at Morrowlea (whom I had, of course, not recognized as such) and the Honourable Miss Jullanar Ragnor, who was decidedly uninterested in scandal after her abortive attempt to elope with an itinerant knife-sharpener who was actually the Earl of the Farry March in disguise.

"Perhaps your final letter will be of assistance," suggested Mr. Dart.

I slit open the third envelope, not expecting anything but a local's anonymous gossip. I had already had a few such missives, which Hal and I had been ceremoniously burning during magic practice.

It was not a crank letter of support or condemnation.

It was from my mother.

Chapter Eleven
The Third Letter

—MY DARLING JEMIS:

It is my dearest hope that you will never read this letter.

—I must start again.

How can I not hope to speak to you across the years?

If you are reading this it is because my worst fears have come to pass. My darling, I'm so sorry to leave you orphaned. I cannot shake the belief that I will not see another spring. I will never see you grow up to your full potential ...

My love, I am weary. I must not delay—there are too many things that you must know, if all that I see comes to pass.

First: I have the Sight, much good it has ever done me. I can see that you have a gift buried deep. If it wakens, know that our family's line holds magic from and for the Woods. It comes out sometimes in the Sight, sometimes in healing, and every once in a long while in what one our ancestors called the 'wild green luck', which was half affliction and half glory.

The blood of the Good Neighbours runs in our line, my son. That always has strange and mysterious effects. Part of ours is that the farther we are from our Woods the weaker our magic ... If you never return across the boundary stream your magic may never awaken. You may find you have the odd dream that comes true; that is as much as most of our family has ever had of the wild green. You will certainly find that honey from the Woods helps you.

That is one thing. The second concerns your father.

Oh, my darling, I hope so much that I am able to resolve this before the Lady calls me to her garden. My vision is so uncertain …

I have seen you (I know it is you, a young man coming into his own, in a fine red hat I wish I might see you wear). I have seen you dancing the Lady in, for the bees. I have seen you standing before the Lady … and I have seen you standing before the White Cross looking so angry …

I no longer have the letters that came from the Seventh Army before the Fall. They were taken by your uncle that he might write. I know you dislike him: distrust him also. When one looks at it coldly you stand between him and his heart's desire, which is to be a man of consequence. He believes the trappings of estate and wealth and title are what grants consequence. His wife has only encouraged those pretensions. She is half-deluded by her own lies.

Do not be deceived by the folly of the world, Jemis. Those are mere ornaments. Your father was a far greater man standing destitute on the doorstep than his brother will ever be.

I can see so clearly still the expression on your face, my son, when you opened the door to him.

In my vision he had gone.

Oh, Jemis. I hope you have forgiven Mr. Buchance for being there when Jack came home. Please try, for my sake and your sisters'—and your own. You need a family. You have so much to fight against ... remember always what you are fighting for.

I loved your father more deeply than I could ever say. No matter how far he went I rested sure in his love, that I was his lodestar as he was my hearth. I waited for his return as the limes of the Woods wait for the bees. Believe me when I say when I would have waited for ever if I had not seen him dead in a vision.

Forgive me.

I did not realize until it was too late that the Fall gave me twisted visions. Before I always knew when the vision was true. During the Interim that, like so much else, changed.

I was afraid for your future, son of ignominy and glory, and Benneret Buchance was a kindly man who loved me and promised to cherish you as his own. I have always been afraid I would not live to see your majority, and I wanted to make sure you had more than the accusations of traitor to sustain you.

So much for why I remarried. When I think to that scant month between Jack's return and his death—oh, Jemis, my heart breaks again for you, for him, for myself. I was so afraid he would ask to take you—and so afraid you would just go.

I did not want him to leave my life again, but that is a hurt and an injury deeper than I have ever inflicted, and he is gone past my living ability to make my amends. My apology will have to wait until we are both in the Lady's garden.

—I must continue while I still have the strength. I am weary, so weary ... this influenza is stealing away my life.

(I am sorry. Know that I am facing my death as befits a daughter of the Woods. Before the spring there is the winter ... but after the winter there is always the spring. In the spring of creation we will dance in the Lady's garden together, my son ... and though my heart cracks to leave you, let it be many years from now before you join me there.)

My son, painful as it is, I must write about those three horrible weeks. I cannot imagine what you were thinking. You were so quiet—you, my chatterbox son—quiet, and bewildered, and so very angry.

Hold on to your anger, Jemis, and control it. Anger is like magic: uncontrolled it can do terrible things through your agency. Controlled, well-directed, *known*, anger can be the fire that changes the world.

Remember that only if it is just does that lead to a better society.

My love, seek justice.

Your father came home to find himself misdoubted a traitor, his son disinherited, his younger brother in Arguty Manor. His wife married to someone else. We spoke of what he should do—what *I* should do, unintentionally a bigamist with a new family.

We decided, your father and I, that he should go to seek the Lady's justice in Nên Corovel. He spoke of a friend there who knew the truth of that last battle at Loe ... He spoke of his plans to no one, I think, but myself. I had a strong presentiment of danger; could feel disaster pressing every closer. One did not need to have the Sight to see that ... not when the rumours and accusations in the barony were so vicious, so continuous, so manifold. We knew someone was spreading them on purpose.

Jack did not believe it was his brother Vorel, but who else stood to gain?

Jack left one night to seek the Lady Jessamine. I prayed that the

Lady of Spring would grant him safe travels and safe homecoming.

His secrecy and my prayers were in vain, as you too well know.

Jemis—there was a note in your father's hand (how well I know it!) for you. All the evidence pointed to suicide caused by despair, but—

Oh, Jemis, I am loath to lay this on you.

He was found hanging in the Forest.

He left you that note.

He was a proud man accused of the worst calumny. A loving and beloved husband who came home to a wife forsworn and married to another. A loyal soldier devoted to his comrades accused of betraying them for the meanest reasons.

I have no proof whatsoever except for the certainty of my heart.

But I write you this with all the certainty of my heart: *your father did not kill himself.*

You will ask why I let you believe him a suicide when that disgrace capped and crowned the rest. You will ask how I could bear to let the bravest and truest man I ever knew be buried in unhallowed ground under a crossroads. You are right to ask.

My dear son, I wanted you to live.

Whoever killed your father did so because he threatened them—and the only way he threatened anyone was to stand truthfully the *hero* of Loe and not attainted of treason.

I can imagine how angry you must be. With me, with yourself possibly, with the world. Jemis, my son, disinherited and the stepson of a Charese merchant you are not a threat. Your father is gone past the need for human glory—

—And when I see him in the Lady's garden I shall have this to beg his pardon for also.

No matter that we agreed to let the accusations and slander go without legal response until we had evidence and proof of the true state of affairs. No matter that the last thing he asked of me was to see you safe. Until I die I shall regret my complicity in that unhallowed grave. I see that vision of you before the White Cross, a splendid figure of a young man … surely the pride of his family … looking at the stone that pins down the most shameful slander onto the father he so deeply loved.

Oh, Jemis, I am weary. I fear this influenza and I fear that I will see no spring. I shall leave this letter to be delivered in the case of my death, knowing it is a heavy burden to lay on you … but knowing also that you would rather a mystery than a platitude. My dear son, I am so proud of you.

Seek justice, not vengeance, and remember that you are loved.

I remain always your loving

Mama

Chapter Twelve
Murder?

"YOU'LL HAVE TO come down," Mr. Dart called.

I nearly fell out of the tree. As I recovered myself, I laid my forehead on the cool, damp, earthy bark of the branch I was laying on. I was in what had always been Mr. Dart's favourite thinking place when we were younger, the great oak tree on the north side of Dart Hall. I'd fled there because I could think of nowhere else to go. I'd wanted to run, and run, and run, but was tethered by prudence and the desire to stay close to my father and the sorry sensation of a head full of congestion.

After a few minutes I recovered from the spike of terror sufficiently to make my way safely down to where Mr. Dart stood.

He looked in all ways the proper young gentleman, and quite as if he'd long since given up climbing trees.

I brushed ineffectually at my garments. "That wasn't very dignified of me, was it?"

"Stuff and balderdash to that. I can't get up that gap to the first branch with my arm. Perhaps by the spring."

"Oh, has Hal had an idea for how to disenchant it?"

He didn't say anything for a moment. His left hand was brushing the top fold of his sling; a breath of air washed over me, cold and damp and promising inclement weather. Finally he said, "No. I meant that by the spring my left arm might be strong enough to compensate."

"Perry—"

"*Don't* make a fuss, Mr. Greenwing."

I met his eyes squarely. "Mr. Dart. Friendship runs both directions. You keep supporting me through my various tribulations."

"Which are considerably more significant and interesting than my own. Jemis, *your father is alive.*"

I turned away to sneeze and gather my thoughts. Was it the action of a friend to keep pressing when he so obviously did not wish to be pressed? Yet ... I did not know, had no idea, what was wrong, except that something was. "I'm sorry for saying that about Tara offering you a place. I hadn't realized you hadn't told your brother."

He played with the tassel on his sling. The one today was a dark brown, matching his waistcoat. "You don't let it go, do you?"

I raised by eyebrows at him. "I follow the examples set before me."

"My place is here," he said precisely, letting go of the tassel to gesture at the well-tended fields and pastures spilling around us, the handsome house at our backs, the stables and the orchard and the distant banks of the river and the grey edge of the Forest. "I am well content."

He sounded much more pugnacious than content. He had given up a fellowship at Tara—and he could not have drawn the boundary of what he was willing to discuss any more clearly.

"Did he read the letter?" I asked, giving in. I'd thrust it at my father when I abruptly excused myself from the room, to his and everyone's astonishment.

"Not out loud. He said it was from your mother ... I'm amazed that you were able to read it through at the table."

"Indeed, I am verily a watering-pot." I pulled out one of my handkerchiefs, decided I needed the retiring room and a mirror to even begin to repair the damage, and said nothing about how Mr. Dart relaxed as soon as I left the topic of himself.

***

Returning more-or-less tidy from the retiring room, I was directed into the library by Mr. Brock before he wafted off in the general direction of the front door, where someone was knocking loudly. I hastened out of the hall, not wishing to speak to whoever might be calling on the Darts that morning.

Hal began, "Should Jemis perhaps—"

But his advice went unspoken, for in loud vociferation my uncle strode in past the unhappily protesting butler. "Don't be a gudgeon, man, where else would he be?"

At home in my little flat above the bookstore; in a brigand's camp in the Arguty Forest; in gaol ...

"My dear nephew," he boomed, and fell upon my neck.

I extricated myself with difficulty. He began searching his pockets for a handkerchief, to no avail. I supplied one of mine, reflecting as I did so that I had been using them at nearly my winter rate. My uncle daubed his eyes and blew his nose and if he were acting his relief it was the best performance I'd ever seen.

Mind you, I could think of five reasons for him to be relieved that had nothing to do with my actual continuing safety.

"My dear nephew, I have just received the most *extraordinary* communication from Sir Mattrin Terrilee, my fellow magistrate in Yellem."

My heart sank. "Oh?"

"He said you were to be arrested on charges of murder!"

I did my best to feign total shock at this pronouncement. "Murder? Sir Vorel—"

"*Uncle* Vorel, my dear boy, we've spoken of that disastrous formality I inflicted on you when I thought my poor brother ..." He choked, had recourse to the handkerchief again, and bowed to Hal, who was haughtiness personified.

Sir Vorel sighed heavily. He crumpled my handkerchief in his hand, face a study in woe. "If only I ... oh, my dear boy, if only I had *listened* to my brother when he returned ... If only I had ... But I have spoken of this already, I think."

Yes; and I did not for a moment believe him. There were too many years of snubs and snideness to wash over in over-emotional apologies that came only once an imperial duke was there to stand beside me. I said, "I find this question of murder somewhat more pressing at the moment, sir."

He chortled, good humour suddenly restored. "An entirely absurd matter. Sir Mattrin is a fine angler, a sound man for trout and salmon, but in this case he has entirely the wrong line. Why, you saved my life from that dragon!"

I affected puzzlement, which was not difficult. "The dragon?"

"Someone has alleged that you *murdered* the dragon, which is impossible under the law even if it were provable that the dragon was really an enchanted human being."

"Was it?"

He patted me on the arm, jewelled rings flashing. "My dear nephew, how on earth do you imagine I should know? My dear brother—" He choked again. It occurred to me that this was a convenient method of implying emotion without having to actually say anything of import. "I am mourning his loss anew, you know. It will be seven years next Wednesday … but of course you know that."

"Yes," I replied blankly, not looking away from my uncle. *Seven years gone …*

He showed signs of imminent departure, from the subject if not the room, so I added hastily, "Sir Vorel—"

"*Uncle* Vorel."

"Sir, what do you think I should do?"

I was merely trying to keep his attention from straying to Jack, but at my question he swelled: literally swelled out his chest, put back his shoulders, and gestured expansively with my handkerchief like a flag in his hand.

"My dear nephew, you may leave it *all* to me. Rest assured that these allegations are absurd to the point of mischief. I don't know what Sir Mattrin is about countenancing them for an instant. Let him keep to his trout, that's my advice. He can tie a very nice artificial fly, you know—"

"And me?" I pursued.

"Your father taught you to fish, did he not?"

Out of the corner of my vision I caught Mr. Dart (safely behind my uncle) rolling his eyes expressively. I tried to marshall my features into deferential eagerness, which made my uncle pat my arm in genial avuncularity again.

"I tease, my boy, I tease. Do avoid Yellem. They had a gaolbreak this week—a trio of highwaymen from the gang that's running the whiskeyjack ring, I hear. Degenerate criminals, the lot of them. Sir Mattrin's got to have *some* success to show before the Winterturn

Assizes, and if he can get you …"

He left it there. Bowed to Master Dart, Sir Hamish, and Hal, squeezed my arm painfully, and swept out past his dear brother without according him a glance.

I looked at my father. He was smiling twistedly. "Same old Vor—though hasn't he run to fat!"

I had never before heard any nickname for my uncle. It rattled me unexpectedly. Blustering, jovial, hypocritical, possibly murderous—all those I could see and, seeing, comprehend. But 'Vor', my father's little brother?

The betrayal crashed over me with sickening force. I turned aside, stared hard at one of Master Dart's Collian scrolls. When I had composed myself and turned around again, my father was sober-faced and serious.

Sir Hamish gestured us all vaguely to seats. I sat next to Mr. Dart, who pulled out his pipe to fuss with.

"I have had a thought," Sir Hamish said.

My father chuckled. "Surely not?"

"G'way with you, Jack. My thought is this: we cannot presume every visitor will be as magnificently inattentive to our guests, those degenerate and and dangerous criminals, as Sir Vorel, Magistrate."

"And so?"

"And so I think we should all—most especially young Mr. Greenwing—take care to call you Jack, and identify you as the General's aide."

I felt a shameful rush of relief. I could only hope it did not show on my face; and, recalling my thought about my uncle, for once unnecessarily blew my nose.

"Very sensible," Ben muttered. "That being sorted, what next? A story?"

"Perhaps it will help to come up with a plan," I said diffidently.

Mr. Dart blew a smoke ring, then grinned. "How very organized of you, Mr. Greenwing."

"Thank you, Mr. Dart."

He ignored this essay into sarcasm. "Well, what do you see as the central concern? Your uncle appears serious about disregarding the allegations—I am a little disappointed you are not truly felonious."

"Not enough whiskey."

"There's not enough whiskey in the woods to turn your head, Jemis," Hal put in.

"The Forest," Jack, Mr. Dart, and Sir Hamish all corrected at once.

"It's honey-wine in the Woods, and Mr. White's is potent enough to turn anyone's head."

"That just led you to riddle-answering and dragon-slaying."

I considered the carpet below my well-polished boots. I had laid the base polish myself, though this morning's gloss was courtesy of some one of the Darts' servants. Mention of the dragon's riddle had placed the beginnings of a clue in my hand, like figuring out the first word of a crossword puzzle.

"It seems possible, at least, that everything is connected to—to Jack's apparent suicide," I began slowly. "Yet—it might not be. Strange things have been occurring all autumn."

Mr. Dart blew another smoke ring. "Since you came home, in fact. Before that all the talk was on the distillers in the Forest and the new inheritance laws being mooted in Parliament."

I brushed aside the inheritance laws, which were only likely to affect the Baron and the Honourable Rag, if them. "To say nothing of your ducks. Things precipitated when I arrived, but apart from the dragon their *existence* had nothing to do with me. I hadn't anything to do with the Talgarths or Miss Shipston."

I was not at all certain what Mr. Dart had told his brother about our activities, and didn't want to misstep again. Mr. Dart frowned, but did not bring up the cult.

Jack said, "When did you come back?"

"End of September. Hal and I went on a walking tour from Morrowlea to Fillering Pool with another friend, then I kept travelling alone through to Ghilousette before I received word that Mr. Buchance—my stepfather, that is—had passed away. I came as quickly as I could, but missed the Midsomer assizes."

"You only have four more days to get through before the Winterturn ones start," Hal said encouragingly.

"Daunting thought."

There were an awful lot of servants at Dart Hall. Ellen or Elinor came in with a tray of fresh coffee and sweet biscuits, as if it had been ages since the start of breakfast, then stayed to mend the fire. The Darts did not precisely *ignore* her—Sir Hamish murmured thanks and Mr. Dart winked at her as she passed—but they did disregard her human curiosity.

I waited till she shut the door behind her. No one else spoke; the sounds were the crackle of the new wood on the fire, Mr. Dart's soft puffing, clinks of porcelain on plate. I had a headache and a sore throat and a deep feeling of malaise and … and my father was alive, and my mother was dead, and one sent me mysterious letters and the other simply *was* mysterious.

"Point one," I said finally. "The Assizes do start next week. As a named party I must be present so the will can be read."

My father looked at me with a veiled curiosity. I wanted to tell him—I wasn't even sure what. My feelings for Mr. Buchance were muddled and I was too tired to figure out how to sort through their contradictions, all of which seemed highlighted by my father's appearance. It seemed a betrayal of my father to say how I had eventually come deeply to respect Mr. Buchance ... it was a betrayal of Mr. Buchance to pretend I had not ... it was a betrayal of myself to lie ...

Mr. Dart blew a smoke ring. "So no gaol or gaol-breaking or other criminal activity between now and then. Should be simple enough."

I raised a tired smile. "Point two: as my uncle pointed out, it is very nearly seven years since my —since Jack was reported dead. The second time. Isn't—Surely seven years is significant under the law?"

Everyone looked at each other.

Sir Hamish cursed.

Chapter Thirteen
The Embroidery Circle

HAL AND I took Sela home to Mrs. Buchance. She refused to leave my side; I had had to accompany her to the privy before breakfast was over, to my embarrassment if not hers.

Well, that was the easy explanation, anyway. I was not yet ready to look any deeper at the waves of emotion that were sloshing away below the surface of my thoughts.

Ariadne nev Lingarel had had what almost amounted to an obsession with the ocean in her poem. I had thought this reasonable enough for someone imprisoned for life on a cliff-top prison. As I sat through that interminable breakfast, the awkward leave-taking, the settling of an excited Sela in the Darts' carriage, fragments of the poem spun through my mind.

There were a lot of winter gales and bitter north winds in that poem—as was, to be honest, reputed to be the case in Orio City. The occasional descriptions of sunlight on waves (or whales or ice floes or schools of herring visible from the barred windows) broke through the relentless structures and strictures like—

O Lady, I thought. They broke through all those endless ways of describing the ocean as 'grey' like the flashes of joy that could be felt even within the doors and walls of that most famous of all Alinorel prisons, the one no prisoner had ever escaped from.

"What's wrong, Jemis?" Sela asked urgently. She squirmed in my lap until she could touch my face.

It was only then I knew I was crying. Soundless, my chest and throat and jaws aching, the sun coming in the carriage window blurred brilliantly.

I bent my head over Sela's soft wispy hair, which smelled a little of violets from the soap we'd used that morning, and mumbled reassurances that I was all right, really I was.

> ... *On the wave-road*
> *the whale-road*
> *The white crests crescent and collapse*
> *Cast between leaf and leaf*
> *And the eye of heaven*
> *When the shadows of our dreams*
> *stand between us*
> *and knowledge ...*

There had been a total eclipse of the sun the year that Ariadne had committed her crime; so said the commentators.

***

Hal did not say anything at all to me, all that way to town. He spoke to Sela, telling her the names of trees and asking her about what she liked and disliked. By this I learned that Sela loved motion much the way I did, and regarded Lauren's more placid interests as unfathomable. She also *noticed* far more than I had expected. I felt quite sure that she would be able to identify her captor again—and probably be ready to bite him again, too, if she could.

The coachman—Mr. Brenning, I recalled after a blank moment—let us out in the square before the Ragnor Arms. Before I could do more than begin to thank him he'd set the horses off at a pace a little too fast for town. I looked around but saw nothing that seemed likely to have alarmed him, unless it was Dominus Gleason looking smug and smarmy outside the post office.

That was reason enough, I reflected.

Fortunately the magister was not facing our direction. I turned sharply away. Hal strode briskly off towards Mrs. Buchance's, still without comment; I found I was beginning to find his silent compassion irritating.

Not enough to start speaking, however.

Sela gripped my hand tightly. Her face was again anxious, but not out of fear of her reception, for she pulled me ahead once we came in sight of her house. I could not walk much faster without running, and tugged her into a slightly more decorous pace so as not to arrive red-faced and breathless.

She danced impatiently as I rang the bell and then opened the door without waiting for a response. Mrs. Buchance had made it clear I was to consider the house ... well, if not *home*, then at least a friend's.

As soon as the door was wide enough, she cried out, "Mum! Mum! Mum!" and raced down the hall towards the parlour, where a gentle clatter of voices could be heard. "Mum! Mum! Mum! Jemis rescued me from the bad man! And then I met his papa and he's a pirate!"

Dead silence greeted me as I halted in the doorway to the parlour. Half a dozen women looked between Sela, enfolded in Mrs. Buchance's arms, and me.

Mrs. Inglesides, Mrs. Kulfield, Mrs. Henny the Post, Mrs. Buchance, and Mrs. Etaris. All of them were ... friends ... or friendly, at least, in memory of my mother.

I don't know what they saw in my face, but Mrs. Kulfield—my mother's good friend, our neighbour when my father came home the first time—Mrs. Kulfield said, "Oh, Jemis, you poor boy."

I nearly started to cry again. Hal's hand came heavy and comforting on my shoulder. I'd forgotten he was behind me and started, and that broke my paralysis.

"He's not a pirate," I said, and why that was the first thing to come out I probably would never know.

"He has an *eyepatch*, and he said he was on a pirate ship."

Hal gripped me more tightly. I locked my eyes on Mrs. Etaris' steady gaze. She did not look surprised, or if she was it had already faded before the relentless curiosity and relentless interest in ramifications I abruptly knew were two of her defining characteristics.

Her eyes narrowed. Without looking away she inclined her head.

All of a sudden I could hear my pulse thundering in my ears. My chest was tight, my breath shuddering as if I'd been sprinting at the end of a long race. I let my gaze leave hers then, slide away around the room at the puzzled and sympathetic and curious faces. I cleared my throat several times.

"On his way to seek redress from the Lady, my—my—my father was caught in the Arguty Forest by brigands, sold into slavery which included a stint on a pirate galley, from which he was rescued by a ship of the Lady this summer."

The bald facts rattled them. I felt Hal's hand again, radiating warmth and possibly magic. After a month of lessons I was starting to feel a faint tingle in the presence of magic. Today the over-whelming emotional circumstances and the quickly-developing cold made it almost impossible to tell. I breathed shallowly, trying not to cough, to cry, and looked around the room again. This time I saw the coffee cups and sweet biscuits, the embroidery frames and the strange hooked knitting Mrs. Etaris sometimes did in the store. My throat felt very tight.

"Someone betrayed my father and pretended he had died by his own hand."

Mrs. Kulfield was a large, comfortable woman. Acid shock did not sit well on her face. I felt as if my heart were trying to strangle my throat.

"I do not know a great deal about your ... I know you are interested in more than simply embroidery ... I cannot ask you ..."

I did not beg.

I did not know whether I wanted them to act or not to act.

I knew I did not want them to gossip about this through the town.

I wrestled with the knowledge that it was folly not to exact a promise, but I did not *want* to demand, based on—what? My rank? A month ago I had had none and worse than nothing for a repu-tation, and Mrs. Buchance had taken me in without question and Mrs. Etaris given me a job without hesitation.

Mrs. Kulfield had believed me when I told her I had not missed my stepfather's funeral on purpose.

Mrs. Inglesides was Mrs. Buchance's sister-in-law, and always smiled kindly on me when I passed her in the street or the book-store or her husband's bakery.

Mrs. Henny the Post, the oldest of the group, sat there knitting in a cloud of soft wool, blue eyes twinkling like the epitome of a warm-hearted grandmother. My own grandmother was acrid and eccentric; and Mrs. Henny, my father had once warned me, was the best player of Poacher he'd ever met.

My father was one of the seven masters, I thought, watching Mrs. Henny's wooden needles flicker in the air. What did that make her?

Her twinkling blue eyes watching mine gave nothing away at all.

"Thank you for telling us," Mrs. Etaris said. "You may rest assured in our discretion."

And I recalled her, that first day in her bookstore, making a wide gesture at the shelves of poetry and philosophy and cooking and history and saying that if there was anything she knew how to do, it was how to have an adventure.

What a gift it was to know I *could* rest in their discretion.

I bowed.

Chapter Fourteen
Fairy Blood

"THIS IS STUPID," I said, not for the first time.

"It's an adventure, Mr. Greenwing," Mr. Dart replied, laughter threading his voice. I could only look at him in scattered, petulant (I could admit it to myself) glares. *He* was properly dressed, from hat to boots every inch a young gentleman. I was wearing—

"Sheets."

"They're *robes*, Mr. Greenwing."

"They're sheets."

"You look very distinguished."

"Yes, like a madman."

"Or the Wild Saint," Mr. Dart agreed with placid good humour.

"Pshaw," I said, tugging down the *sheets*. Hal came back into the room with a wreath made of twisted holly and ivy. I eyed this with revulsion.

"Pshaw?" he said, grinning at me. "This is all for you, Jemis, you know."

"Will you please explain what we're doing?" My voice came out alarmingly plaintive.

"Discovering what magic you have, of course; I said that."

His silent forbearance as we walked (slowly) back to Dart Hall had finally broken through my reticence. I had braced myself to talk about my father, almost to tell Hal about the dreams that had finally stopped, only to come crowding round in life.

It had taken so *long* to convince myself that my father was dead, truly dead, and buried under the White Cross as a suicide and a traitor and a disgrace.

But I had not been able to begin with that discussion, had instead begun with my mother's letter, with her comments about my uncle and those about her family's magical lineage.

I had argued unsuccessfully that I should stay in town, as I would need to be back for work the next day. Hal had stared at me with too much comprehension before stating firmly that as it was still only Saturday, no, I didn't, and that as we did have an afternoon more or less free ahead of us we could do one of the spells he'd just thought of.

And so we were standing in the middle of the bare room Mr. Dart had found for us, which he (it appeared) had been using to practice exercises to compensate for his stone arm and which once upon a time had been the workroom of some distant Dart ancestor who had been a wizard.

And somewhere in the house was my father.

"Someone sent me that letter," I said abruptly.

Mr. Dart nodded. "I've been wondering that, too."

"I forgot to ask Mrs. Henny. She was at Mrs. Buchance's when we brought Sela home."

"Later," Hal said. "I promise I'll remind you. Mr. Dart, will you pass me that pitcher, please?"

Hal arranged items on a wooden tray he'd brought in. A branch of red rowan-berries, a coil of blackberries with the fruit green and red and purple, several feathers—white, grey, blue, bronze, peacock. A rounded white stone and a rough reddish one. A glass bowl he filled with water from the pitcher. An unlit beeswax candle. And finally, a tiny silver spoon.

Mr. Dart tilted his head, staring mesmerized at the tray. "They're … humming …"

"Hush. This ritual isn't for you. Jemis, will you take off your ring, please?"

"I haven't been sneezing anywhere near so much—"

"You're nowhere near normal, either," Mr. Dart replied.

"I have a cold."

"That, to be sure, explains all."

The laughter was still in his voice. His face, when I glanced suspiciously at him, was bright, eager, intent, unshadowed, focused on the tray.

I caught my breath. I could not remember, literally could not recall, when I had last seen him look like that. There was always a faint reserve, even when he was focused on a history book and dreaming—well, it behoved me to believe him when he said he dreamed of his brother's house and the land he would one day inherit.

"You don't want to be dependent on that ring, surely?" Hal asked.

I was spinning the ring with my thumb, as had become my habit when I felt anxious.

I did feel anxious. I did not understand Hal's insistence that I learn magic, *now*; I did not understand my own reluctance to do so, when I found it so delightful; and I really did not understand why I had to keep explaining how wonderful it was not to sneeze all the time.

I thought of my father when I'd started that morning at breakfast, and as if on cue, sneezed several times in succession.

Without saying anything I took off the ring, laid it next to the tray, and stood a few steps back from the table so I could be racked by many tiny sneezes all by myself.

Hal cast me a severe glance, but he knew they were involuntary. "We are here," he said, in a more formal tone of voice, "at this time of transition between the autumn and the winter, in the spur weeks between seasons, when the moon turns in her phases and the sun in his. We bring a life in transition, a soul in transition, a young man between the second and the third age of his life, between *undaura* and wizard, between the past and the future. In this cusp of the moment as the world turns, let the symbols of his power call him that he may come into his own power unfettered by fear. I, Halioren Isidorus Leaveringham of Fillering Pool, descendant by blood through many generations of the Sun and the Moon through the line of Linara, do ask the magic this in the name of the Lady of the Green and White, the Emperor of Astandalas, and the Prince of the White Forest whose name is blessed."

I did not know who the Prince of the White Forest was; I had not realized that Hal was a descendant by however many generations of the third of the Imperial lineages; and I was only vaguely aware that *undaura* meant something like 'one who is untrained'.

I felt the magic move.

It began as a tingle that grew to a strange beautiful humming, very like the song of the bees of the Woods Noirell when I woke them from their curse. Was that, I wonder, what Mr. Dart heard when he heard the voices of the inanimate?

It was, perhaps, inevitable that the humming came from the candle, symbol of my mother's inheritance and also my father's. He had always sought to 'hold the Sun', as it was called, holding the Sun Banner firm on the edge of an embattled cliff in Orkaty, holding the Border firm at the Gate of Morning on the other side of Loe.

The bees were my mother's. She had always said that was our family's inheritance: honey, stings, light.

"Take the one that speaks to you," Hal instructed softly.

I stepped forward. The candle was calling me to take it and call forth its inner fires into light. Out of the corner of my eye I saw the dark mass that was Mr. Dart step forward beside me. I half-turned my head so that I could still see the candle and also see his face. It was still eager, intent, unshadowed. My heart leapt with gladness to see him so and something I thought just perhaps was pure magic coruscated golden-white-and-green in the air around us.

The scent of honey rose up strong as the Tillarny limes of the Woods, who waited like brides for the bees of Melmúsion to visit them.

I touched the candle and Mr. Dart touched his object, and the magic exulted.

***

I woke to long slanting sunlight and the unusual sensation of my hand being held.

I lay still for a while. I was in my room at the Darts', with its green and gold striped walls and the comfortable bed and the view over the stable courtyard.

The room wavered, as if it was not really there, but only an image on fabric, and the fabric was billowing. I watched it calmly, unworried about this.

From somewhere the thought floated into my awareness that usually I would be very alarmed and upset to see the fabric of reality rippling.

Yes, I thought, usually I would be, but that didn't mean I *was*, just now. The ripples were pretty, my mind and my body were both very calm, very relaxed, and the person holding my hand had a deep rumbly soothing voice.

Another thought floated by: that perhaps I might like to look at the person holding my hand, stroking it rhythmically in fact, and murmuring those soothing words.

It was followed slightly more quickly by a third: that perhaps I did not, after all, want to look at the person holding my hand and murmuring, in case it was who I had dreamed far too many times it was.

I lay there, the room rippling, someone rumbling, until I fell asleep again.

***

I dreamed three things in succession:

My mother, dancing the Lady in, in our garden at the dower house. Except that it was not our garden; this was another garden, lovelier, richer, more resplendent. It gave me an inkling of why Hal liked gardening so much. The bees were there, golden-bright circling around my mother, who was fearless moving in and through and with them.

She danced: the bees sang: and she caught sight of me. She smiled with her whole being. She stood poised for a moment, arms lifted as if to take flight or offer thanksgiving to the Lady of the Green and White.

"Jemis," she said, "my love, be not afraid."

She danced on then, into the sunrise, and as I blinked and worked my eyes the light dazzled me and fell away into the dazzling ripples of brilliant water.

I squinted, turned from the glare, and saw Violet sitting on the side of a large rock on the sea. She was singing, her voice contralto, a song as sad and lonely and beautiful as the waves washing up to her feet. She was dressed in pale lavender, with a green cloak pulled across her shoulders.

The colours of the Lady of Alinor, my conscious mind said, and the dream turned before I could walk into her notice and see what she said.

The song turned into the cries of seabirds.

The sea here was darker, greyer, ominous, the waves great steady swells that did not break into foam. I had seen the sea on my journey into Ghilousette, but never waves like that.

Open-ocean waves; Ariadne's whale-road; my dream-mind was full of dark water and dark sky and brilliant white birds with black-tipped wings and heavy yellow beaks. They dove, plunged into the sea, the water fountaining up white and delicate like silver-lace embroidery.

A ship came into sight. Long, low, lean, with a curved prow and a dozen long oars a side. Its triangular sail was black; many figures in blackened armour stood crowded under a shelter to the stern, looking over weapons well-used and cruel. Before them stood

someone with a heavy drum, beating out a rhythm that cut counter across the waves.

One large man stood behind the drum, a long carriage-whip
in his hand, lashing the oarsmen to go faster, faster, faster.

His face was cruel, a light in his eyes of sadistic enjoyment in
the pain he was inflicting. I shuddered away from it, following the
line of the whip as it flicked forward and landed almost delicately
on the oarsmen's knotted backs. They were half-naked, their backs
lines of weals and scars, the sweat sheening as it cut runnels through
grime.

One of the men in the back shouted an alarm. The whip
cracked out over the oarsmen as the drumbeat picked up urgency. I
looked away from the straining ropes of tendons, the blood joining
the sweat, the dumb and desperate concentration.

There was another ship. She angled across the waves, casting
up spray like the diving birds, her sails white as their feathers, as
brilliantly gleaming. She was bigger than the oared galley, but not
as fast; she was cutting across the waves and the wind seemed to be
not fully behind her; and she did not have the oars, nor the oarsmen, nor the drum and the whip.

In the dream suddenly I heard golden-voiced horns. Loops of
light—magic—rose from the new ship. The whipster bellowed in
anger and turned his whip to the sky, licking the loops out of the
air before they could land on the galley. He was impressive in his
defiance, in his mastery of the magic; but I was glad that he could
not prevent the horn-calls from reaching the oarsmen's ears.

Then I saw their faces as the horns rang out again. Blank despair, blank terror, blank resignation—blank, blank, blank.

They were slaves, ankles chained to their seats, feet sitting in vile bilge.

They were still rowing, their tendons stranding out, their skin almost washed clean by the sweat of their exertion, their faces set, as the whip cracked above them and they rowed away from their salvation.

The horns rang out again. They were just slightly fainter this time, slightly more distant, slightly less triumphant. As if it were a signal he'd been expecting one of the oarsmen held back his oar.

I could see in his back, his shoulders, his arms, his neck, what strain it was, the brute force it took to break that rhythm, that pattern, that binding. Dark fired flickered around him as he swung his heavy oar into an angle that fouled the next three oars on his side.

The galley lurched, juddered, yawed wildly as it swung broadside to the waves. The oarsmen screamed in a terror more primal than the fear of the whipster. *Wait,* I whispered in my dream, *hold on—*

The slave-driver snapped his whip forward so the tip of the long cord lashed across the face of the man who had so thoroughly thwarted him.

The trumpets rang out in all their brilliance.

One of the golden loops dropped down, spitting sparks as it landed, and draped across the shoulders of the oarsmen, who no longer looked so blank in their despair.

The whip came down again and again in frenzy on the shoulders of the one who slumped over his oar. The trumpets cried. The unchained warriors in the stern cabin shouted and brandished weapons and boiled out of their shelter, and the golden magic floated down to bind and to free.

Chains unravelled from the oarsmen and bound the pirates.

The freed slaves leaped around, and if there were injuries meted out it was a form of justice I could not deny the desire for.

There was one still figure in the galley, one man who had not leaped to freedom when his chains fell away from him. He slumped over the misaligned end of his oar, back a mess of blood and raw flesh, face welted across his eye, dark hair black with sweat and blood and grime.

Someone in green walked through the violence as if all the rest were ghosts and touched the still figure on the hand.

Hers meant nothing to me: for I knew the hand that she touched.

Even as my heart broke the dream dissolved into long slanting sunlight and my old room at the Darts' and the sound of my breath as I woke myself sobbing.

No one held my hand this time; but there was a chair beside my bed.

Chapter Fifteen
The Gift

A GLANCE OUTSIDE showed that it was already coming on to evening. The Darts kept the old hours for meals, so I did not have long to make myself fit for company.

I had all the summer clothes to mark me out as a fine young gentleman. My stepfather had given me an allowance for Morrowlea, despite my protests that he hardly owed me anything. I had not spent it while at university, for Morrowlea prided itself on its radical egalitarianism, so that no one was to dress out of the uniforms or the clothing we made ourselves. I had actually quite liked the classes on sartorial arts; my favourites had been the ones on weaving and tapestry needlepoint, which was hardly something I felt comfortable broadcasting at large in Ragnor Bella. The only clothes of my own manufacture I had kept were my exercise wear, which was unsurprising as they were what I had put the most effort into.

After the disastrous spring, Hal and Marcan and I had set off afoot from southwest South Erlingale up to the borders with Ronderell and Lind. We had all worn our Morrowlea clothing, until Hal and I reached Fillering Pool and Hal stepped back into his role as the Duke Imperial. I had looked at the money from Mr. Buchance and decided to spend some of it on clothes appropriate to the gentleman I felt, at the time, I was beginning to cease to be.

I dressed now in breeches, shirt, waistcoat, coat, stockings of my own knitting, boots of my own polishing, cravat of my own tying. Not for me the wilder fashions of Stoneybridge (if I could believe Mr. Dart's accounts of them; he himself had never shown any inkling towards the particoloured hose and slashed doublets and codpieces—codpieces!—he swore some of the dandier set were sporting). I liked good tailoring and good colours, but I also liked the sort of clothes I could still run in, if it came to it.

And now I was the heir to a marquisate that had no money, and my father had come home, and if I occasionally felt impoverished in comparison to Mr. Dart, for instance, that was nothing.

I was earning enough at the bookstore to pay for the flat and my food and a few other essentials. I had enough left from what I had saved from Mr. Buchance's allowance to pay for a few reasonable if not first-stare clothes for the winter months.

Mr. Buchance had told me in the spring, the last time I saw him, that he would see I wouldn't starve, but that as I had never wished to be formally adopted by him, his fortune would go to his daughters. I had agreed: I had kept my father's name and I kept its inheritance. I had asked only that he not distinguish between his daughters by his first wife, my mother, and those by his second.

What a curse it was on Mrs. Buchance that the reading of the will had to wait for me. The only, very minor, good thing was that it was not a full six months between the Midsomer and Winterturn Assizes, as the latter went on for the better part of three months. The reading of the will was, nevertheless, set for the very first possible day, which was the coming Thursday.

I set aside the cravat, which I'd spoiled, and picked up another.

Whatever riches were still in the Castle St-Noire—mostly, I believed, my grandmother's personal jewelry—would have to go to restoring the castle and its community. A comment or two by Hal had made me realize that the villagers would have to buy in most of the winter's food, as they had been under a curse through three growing seasons. I did not, as of yet, have any idea how they, or I, would manage. There was no honey, their main income now that the highway to Astandalas no longer went anywhere.

My mother's inheritance was long since spent apart from a few items more precious to me than money: her jade honey crock, the letters from my father, a few of his gifts to her.

They'd have to go back to him, I thought distantly, watching my hands fail to make the proper creases in the cravat for the third time, and picked up a fourth.

Usually I did not care so much about the perfection of my cravat.

My father could have no conceivable source of income. He'd been a pirate slave; he was considered in the law not only dead but dead a suicide and a traitor. There were no army pensions for traitors, so it was not as if we could go to the court … I did not actually know of whom we'd ask such a thing, with the Empire fallen, and perhaps there would have been nothing; I knew no other officers whom I might have asked. There were reasons so many of the highwaymen in the Forest knew my father's name. Far too many had served with him.

First we had to sort out the accusations of treason. Once we knew how that had come about, we might be able to figure out why—and, of course, there was always the nagging curiosity of *who*—and once we knew that, we might be able to counter it.

The deadline—the word caught me up in wry appreciation of its aptness—was the seventh anniversary of my father's apparent suicide. It fell on the day before the Assizes began, three days from today.

I flubbed another crease and set aside the ruined cravat just as someone knocked on the door.

"Come in," I said, bracing myself.

Mr. Dart slipped in and immediately shut the door behind him. His expression was cheerful as usual, but the faint shadow of reserve was there, where I had not noticed it until its absence. He smiled easily when he saw the pile of cravats on the back of the chair next to me.

"I had not realized you carried so many cravats with you, Mr. Greenwing. I thought your attention given wholly to the supply of handkerchiefs."

Perhaps because of the audience, this time my hands made the folds faultlessly, and the Subdued Mathematical, my favourite knot, took swift form.

"Only six; they are easier to stockpile than hats." Not to mention far cheaper, but that was not a gentlemanly thing to discuss.

"Very true. I find in myself a tendency to the acquisition of stockings, which I presume has much the same impetus. There is something glorious about the first wearing of a new pair."

"One stands upon a foundation of simple wholesome pleasure?"

"Oh, very good!"

He said nothing more, came to stand to look critically at himself in the mirror and the picture he made beside me, with his left hand on the back of the chair, right arm in its sling. This evening's colours echoed my dream of Violet, deep green and purple. It was not quite a light enough purple to proclaim employ or close allegiance with Lady Jessamine, but it certainly invoked the association.

"Did you dream also?" I asked.

I was watching his hand in the mirror, not his face, and I saw the way his fingers dug into the chair back. His voice betrayed no tension, however.

"Just now? I didn't lie down. Had a bath instead."

He'd once told me, in jest as I'd thought, that he did his best thinking in the bath.

And he might as well have been brandishing 'no trespassing' signs about his person, for all he wanted to talk to me.

I moved to pick up the spoiled cravats, and saw how his hand relaxed. Too soon, I thought, and said: "What object called to you?"

That *did* spark anger. I saw it in a flare of brightness in his eyes, in the lines of his face, in the hand digging again into the chair. "I think you mistook what you saw—I was leaning to watch your choice, Mr. Greenwing!"

"I chose the candle—or it chose me," I said levelly. "I was not so absorbed I did not see that you were reaching towards—what?"

I waited. There was a brace of candles on the ledge below the mirror. I hadn't lit them, as when I'd begun my toilet there had still been enough light coming through the window. The sun had set now behind the bulk of the stable and the wooded ridge on the other side of the grounds, and the light inside was fading.

Or it had been: and then, without either of us saying anything, the candles lit.

Mr. Dart's fingernails gouged through the varnish into the wood.

I waited. Two could play Hal's game; and it had worked.

"My brother doesn't know I have magic," he said finally, tensely, voice very quiet.

"There seem to be many things you have not told your brother, Mr. Dart."

I left it there. I folded the cravats carefully, knowing that Mr. Brock would nevertheless take them away to be starched properly. He had scolded me roundly on another occasion for aspiring so high as to presume I could out-valet a man of his experience and genius. I had smoothed out the fourth, and had another moment or two to reflect on Hal's method of insistently not asking the questions that were so obviously there, and—

—And Mr. Dart broke. "Please will you not tell him? He'll be so disappointed in me."

I found it hard to imagine anyone being particularly disappointed in Mr. Dart, let alone his brother. Then again I could see there were fissures between the brothers that I could not fully account for. If I had seen Mr. Dart occasionally during our university years, and corresponded with him often, I had not seen the Squire and Sir Hamish until my return to Ragnor Bella. In his letters Mr. Dart had rarely mentioned more of them than the occasional amusing anecdote.

"Please," Mr. Dart said again, and his expression was, now, genuinely pleading. "Please. I don't want to tell him about the wild magic."

That, at least, made a certain amount of sense. Wild magic had once been a sentence of madness, exile, or death, and the dangers to both practitioner and community were in half the books to have come out of Astandalas and in half the warning tales told by those who had come of age during the Empire.

Mr. Dart and I were of the generation who had been children of Astandalas but were adults of the new order. Magic of any sort was unfashionable to the point of taboo (I, as it happened, found it fascinating; others did not). Our early adolescence had disappeared into what was euphemistically called the Interim, which equally euphemistically was held to have spanned three years. My mother and I had tried to count the days during one storm that kept us within the dower cottage; we had not even been able to tell when night fell or the day broke.

I could comprehend the horror with which the Astandalan world had regarded wild magic. I had only to think of the Interim to know why they had feared the powers that could not be bound by Schooled magic.

But all that was in the general and abstract. In the particular was Mr. Dart lighting candles without speaking and hearing the voices of the silent world.

"Which item called you?" I asked again, pursuing here where I had not dared or desired to push on other areas. I did not want to talk about the dreams for which I had wakened nightly for over a year after my father was buried at the White Cross—or not buried—and who *was* buried there, if he hadn't been? There had been *witnesses*, surely—

There was a story in the Legendarium, which I had been studying the past fortnight. In some places, it was said, there were such a thing called kelpies, water-spirits who often took the form of horses. Beautiful, strong, attractive horses, grazing peacefully by a river or a lake. Any traveller, seeing them, would be stricken with wonder and desire. The kelpie would prance up to the traveller, snorting and whickering and acting delighted, loving, tame. Their victim, overcome now by that wonder and desire which the sight of the horse had woken in them, would mount with ease.

The rider would have a few minutes, maybe even a few hours, to marvel at this magnificence, at the communion between man and beast.

But it was not, of course, any communion between man and beast, but between mortal and fairy.

At some point off the kelpie would run, over water and under, never stopping, never resting, until the rider was dead of exhaustion and drowning and the drain of his magic.

In my dreams, in every one of them, at some point I would give into my better judgment, and over and over again the kelpie had ridden me to death.

This was the waking world, not a dream. This was not the Interim, when magic twisted dream and shadow and imagination and reality into strange and disturbing permutations.

This was Dart Hall, and my oldest friend, and my problems were not the only ones looming unacknowledged in the room.

"The candle, the water, the peacock feather, the ivy crown," Mr. Dart said dully, the flare of anger gone, the intensity faded. The candles behind him burned brightly.

"The four elements," I said, the imagery clear as any poem. "That's the sign of—"

"Don't say it."

The plea was very soft, and all the more powerful for that.

I did not hesitate, not this time. I moved my hand to touch his, which was cold. He jumped. I said, "I won't say anything, Perry. We'll just say it was the spell interacting with my magic and your stone arm that caused the fuss. I'm prone to over-exaggerated physical responses to magic anyway, we all know that."

He stared at me searchingly. I smiled confidently, the require-ments of friendship sounding out clear as the next move in a game of Poacher. I might have picked up the Grail or the Salmon of Wis-dom or the Book of Secrets: in such a case one had to pretend that neither the game nor one's understanding of the world had been upended for the third time in a day.

Finally he nodded. Unbent enough to say, "You can tell Hal, if you think it necessary. And—Jemis—about your father—"

I just looked at him. He flushed.

"When you wish to talk of it, I'm here."

"Likewise," I replied lightly. "Shall we go down?"

After a moment Mr. Dart began talking about Farmer Bean's lovesick mule, and I retorted with a story I'd heard in the bookstore about Mrs. Jarnem's four cats, and by the time we reached the bot-tom of the staircase we sounded almost normal.

And if I were Ariadne nev Lingarel, writing of the ocean?

I knew from my studies in literary symbolism and my one term's worth of classes in the History of Magic that a wild gift called to the four elements of *old* magic—Astandalan magic, drawn as it was from Zuni traditions, held there were five—such a person was not a wizard, but had the makings of a magus, and potentially one of world-shaping power.

If, that is, he survived the learning process.

If, if, if.

Chapter Sixteen
Dinner Plans

THE LAST DINNER party I had attended was the one hosted by Dame Talgarth my first weekend back in Ragnor Bella.

I had not been invited to that party, had in fact been given the cut direct by Dame Talgarth earlier in the week, but for various reasons had ended up at it disguised as a much-powdered footman. This deception had been made possible by Dame Talgarth's ill-fated but very deep fondness for the Late Bastard Decadent style of dinner parties. Traditionally they ended with an orgy; I had been grateful that the cult using the house to hide their wireweed and the criminal gang who wished to steal it had precipitated matters slightly before that dénouement.

There was absolutely no reason to compare the Darts' dining table that evening to Dame Talgarth's. The only common elements were myself, Mr. Dart, and the fact that I was uncomfortable and out of my depth but also quite competent to the manners involved, having been well-trained at Morrowlea for any position between second footman (my position at the Talgarths') to the seat opposite an Imperial Duke (that tonight). I had been more appropriately dressed for the former, but that, alas, is life.

Neither Master Dart nor Sir Hamish had much truckle with the changing fashions in dining (or in anything else, for that matter, besides possibly portraiture and agriculture). They ate the way they had always eaten, with silver dishes, two removes, evening dress, and service in the old Fiellanese country style. This meant that the butler poured the wines for each remove and departed, the maids placed a round dozen dishes on the table and departed, and we were, theoretically, private. The only difference between the evening and any of those the room had held over the two hundred or so years previous was that the room was illuminated by candles, not werelights, and no magic kept the food warm.

Perhaps it was Morrowlea or perhaps it was working as a bookstore clerk or perhaps it was spying on Dame Talgarth's guests while waiting on them that made me so acutely aware of the eyes and ears and minds of Mr. Brock the butler and the two parlour maids whose names I didn't know. No one else paid any attention to them, not even—especially?—Hal.

Whatever explanation Hal had given for the magical alarums and my sheets seemed to land on my clumsiness and general propensity to mayhap. Sir Hamish asked after my health, then started teasing when I declared myself well.

"Come, now, Hamish," Jack growled after a rallontade in which my sneezes figured prominently. "Leave him be."

I flushed at this rescue. "Oh, I am well used to it," I assured him, "my life is one odd episode after another. Why, last week all the gossip was split between whether anyone besides Mr. Pinger saw the twa-tailed vixen in the commons and whether I might contrive to—what was it again, Mr. Dart?"

"I believe it was a matter of wagering as to whether you'd be able to see out Winterturn at the bookstore."

"What are the odds?' Ben asked, leaning forward intently. He was dressed in what must have been clothes borrowed from Sir Hamish (who was closer to his size than the Squire), and with his chin clean-shaven and hair combed and pomaded he looked now like the old politician in a comic play.

Mr. Dart laughed. "Two bees he'll end up in the Woods, four in the Forest, five up before the king, and a gold Emperor both ways for destroying the store or staying on."

"Roald?" I asked, not having heard this last.

"Who else? He must do something while they wait to hear about the inheritance law. He doesn't seem all that interested in the whiskey tax."

"He'd do better to do something other than simply waiting," I muttered, taking the plate of macerated fruit I was offered and then staring at it blankly. I supposed I did have to eat something, to show willing. I put a small spoonful on my plate, where it did not look likely to go all that well with the wood snipe.

"Did you hear about that, Jack?" Master Dart asked, giving Mr. Dart a slightly reproving glare which Mr. Dart entirely ignored.

"The liquor tax? Everyone's talking about it! And talking about the efforts of the kingdom's gentry to avoid it. Not that you would know anything about that, Tor."

The Squire snorted. Sir Hamish laughed. "Ah! There's the Jack I remember. Tor has hopes he'll be a Justice of the Peace come the end of the Assizes. Naturally *our* cellars are fully in order."

"I spent a week in August moving all the contraband to the stables," Mr. Dart agreed cheerfully, then quickly added, before his brother could say anything, "About the inheritance bill. It's not going to get through, surely, after all this time. The king …"

The king has inherited over his older sister, I finished silently, and would hardly want to cast doubts on his own legitimacy.

"Ah, but the Duke of Ronderell's son is simple," Hal said, "and his daughter one of the most competent leaders in the four duchies. Fiellan's always permitted ruling duchesses, so there's no trouble there, and the Earl of the Farry March appears to be a supporter of the idea, though I'm not entirely sure why unless it's a true conviction of its merits."

Mr. Dart set down his fork so he could reach for his wine. "I wouldn't be surprised if he were doing it to spite our baron. Baron Ragnor forbade a marriage between his daughter and the Earl on account of the Earl's magic—and if the new law passes, she'd inherit over Master Roald."

I wondered whether this prospect actually bothered the Honourable Roald Ragnor. Once I might have known, but even if our social classes had not diverged in the way I'd believed a month ago, we were no longer friends. Sometimes I regretted that, but I knew my weaknesses, and I did not wish to become intimates with a man whose major—perhaps even sole—occupations were gambling, drinking, and hunting.

Drinking had taken my grandfather, hunting had taken my uncle, and gambling had more than once very nearly ruined the estate.

The maids came in to clear dishes and bring the second remove. I watched them take my plate in surprise. There were remains on it, so I had eaten, but I could not name what I had taken and not tasted. I could not even say what liqueur the fruit had been macerated in. Quails, rabbits, wood snipe, sweetmeats, trout, and even a few vegetables went by in their sauces, all of them equally mysterious.

As was the Darts' custom, the second remove consisted of cheese, nuts, fruit, and various sweet offerings. When Mr. Brock had given us all our choice of dessert wines, port, and coffee, and ghosted out again, Master Dart said: "Now, let us make some plans."

***

There were seven us at table and three days before the anniversary. It seemed fitting that we come up with seven tasks to accomplish. We were not quite so symmetrical as to contrive one task each on each day, but life does not always imitate poetry—which is probably just as well, for those sort of symmetrical deeds are usually found in terrifyingly logical ballads about fairy curses.

Over the course of our fruit and cheese and whatever else was on the table, we decided first of all that Master Dart would speak to Sir Vorel about who had laid the allegations on me. When I mentioned that Mrs. Etaris, as the wife of the Chief Constable, might also be of assistance, the Squire looked astonished and a little affronted that I would suggest speak to a woman of her class.

My father shook his head. "You've grown into a great snob, Tor. Her father was a physician, you know, and she's always struck me as an intelligent and sensible woman."

"May the Emperor defend me from intelligent and sensible women!" Master Dart replied, but he did desist from further comment.

"That should take care of your little problem, Jemis," said Ben.

I forbore stating that I trusted Mrs. Etaris' intelligence over my uncle's in every conceivable respect. Whether she had more sense than his sensibility was a slightly different matter. I smiled gratefully instead and inwardly promised myself I'd ask her for what she'd heard, whether from her husband or the Embroidery Circle. On the whole I'd put my money on the women.

"I'll undertake to spread the gossip of your mysterious disappearance," Sir Hamish said cheerfully.

"Do you really think it's best to tell the truth?"

Mr. Dart laughed at me. "Still unconvinced? Come, Mr. Green-wing, someone enchanted or drugged you to cause memory loss. If Hamish goes around decrying the state of affairs on the public highway, why, your enemy will be reassured."

I remained unconvinced of the wisdom of this tactic. Jack was scowling, for a different reason: "And everyone else will think him half-cracked."

That surprised a chuckle out of me, to his evident surprise. "Oh, that will surprise no one, sir."

Sir Hamish nodded and poured himself more port. "Indeed, there is nothing anyone likes better than discussing young Mr. Greenwing's affairs and trying to guess what calamity or good fortune will land on him next."

"Why, he is already becoming known as a great eccentric."

"Thank you, Mr. Dart."

"Oh, it's entirely my pleasure, Mr. Greenwing."

Third was the question of my mother's letter. I was to ask Mrs. Kulfield about it; privately I decided to involve Mrs. Etaris in this as the rest. The Embroidery Circle contained Mrs. Henny the Post, after all, with her twinkling eyes and her hidden talents at Poacher and her iron grip on the last forty years of the mail.

Those three tasks sorted, or at least began to sort, my major concerns. I wouldn't have focused on any of them except for the looming spectre of the Winterturn Assizes and the knowledge that my shames no longer redounded solely on myself, but also on my father.

I stole a glance across the table at him. He was talking to Master

Dart about some adventure they'd shared in their university days, and as he laughed, for a moment uplifted, I felt a shock of recognition expand through me.

He still *looked* the rough piratical stranger, but his laugh sounded now my father, the papa of my cherished memories, with a sore throat from shouting too much the time he'd come home from the Yrchester races with a bad cold.

He turned his head so he could see to refill his wineglass. His good eye caught mine as he did so, and I smiled. His expression faltered, flickered, then something fine and tentative started to blossom.

The haze of unreality, of dream-sodden fear, finally lifted. I leaned forward to say something, I knew not what—perhaps about the vision or dream I'd had of the ship, perhaps to say I had his book of haikus at the flat, perhaps simply to call him by name— and then Hal, reaching inattentively to a bowl in the middle of the table, knocked against the candlestick. I reached to right it; something singed sent up a thin column of black smoke; and I sneezed and was once more back in the muddled world.

Hal said: "Can we go over this burglary idea again, please?"

I sighed, and sat back, and found a handkerchief, and retreated hastily into a mood more appropriate to planning the restoration of my father's good name and legal standing, which were the next four tasks and probably much more important.

But I wished I hadn't lost the opportunity to say whatever it was I had wanted to say.

Chapter Seventeen
Hollow Ways

OUR FIRST ORDER of business for Sunday was to burgle Arguty
manor.

We'd decided that we needed to find out if the letters about
Loe still existed and acquire them if they did. My uncle being the
prime suspect for everything, this required a stealth mission into
Arguty manor, and that had to be under my father's auspices.

That was the first task.

The second was to find out who had been the witnesses for the
suicide, and figure out why they had said what they had.

"Your mother wasn't called to the identification?" Sir Hamish
asked me, frowning. "I always thought she was. That was why I
didn't make a fuss when I came back."

"You weren't here?" Jack asked.

"No, I wasn't."

"I should remember," he said apologetically, "but I wasn't in the
best of minds then, I'm afraid."

Sir Hamish shook his head, smiling ruefully. "Jack, my friend,
you need not apologize. I was in Kingsford and Fillering Pool,
painting his grace here, actually, and his sister, for their sixteenth
birthday."

I had entirely forgotten that Hal's birthday was coming up. I frowned at him; he seemed unconscious of the hint. Was he not turning twenty-one? Should there not be some sort of coming-of-age ball planned for him back home? He had been duke since he was seven ... and his sister wished to marry an unsuitable party ...

I wondered briefly what I could possibly give him. When were students at Morrowlea our own efforts at learning new arts and crafts had been sufficient and welcome. To a Duke Imperial on his twenty-first birthday ...

Plants, I thought, plants were always welcome to Hal. I'd make the time to go to the Woods and talk to Mr. White the innkeeper, whose friendship I wished to cultivate and who would know the gardeners of the village. Perhaps I could pot up a sapling of a Tillarny lime for Hal.

By the strange chains of reflection and association in the mind, thought of the Woods opened up a memory connected with the Forest.

"Hagwood," I said aloud.

"The Arguty factor?" Mr. Dart said politely after a moment.

"Yes. He's—he was involved. He was the one who came to tell us ... the news."

"Hagwood would *never* betray me," Jack said.

His confidence was so absolute I could think of no reply. Hagwood *had* been the one to tell us, my mother and me and Mr. Buchance, that my father had been found hanging in the Forest. I had not consciously remembered the expression on the factor's face, but now I did, how he had been grey and sweating with nerves, his eyes white around the rim like a frightened horse's.

Sir Hamish had none of my qualms. "Like your brother? Jack,

someone *did* identify the body to your family as you."

And my mother had believed him; but not believed it was suicide; but let me believe it was suicide, that my father had taken that route out of his disgrace. In some places and times and situations such an act would have been considered noble, even praiseworthy; not here, and then, and in such a collocation of circumstances.

I cleared my throat against the burgeoning cough. "This sounds a task for myself. It will be more or less understandable if I go asking about the story."

"It would have made more sense to do so when Hal came with the story of Loe, or you came first back from university," Mr. Dart objected. "Why now?"

"Because too much happened that first fortnight I didn't have a chance to think about it, and now it *is* the anniversary coming up. And perhaps I read something about it in a book at the shop," I replied promptly.

"We'll come with you," said Mr. Dart.

Hal smiled with a disquieting edge. "Yes. No more opportunities for mysterious disappearances until the first one is cleared up."

To that I could not voice my objections, which were mainly along the lines of injured pride and a desire to go on long solitary runs with only my thoughts for company. My thoughts this week would not be very good company, I thought with black humour. "Very well. And the order of things?"

Ben had not spoken much through the course of our deliberations, instead leaning back with his eyes closed as if half-asleep. I saw the occasional glance he exchanged with my father, however, and knew he'd been listening, and considering, and weighing our plans with the experience of a lifetime as one of the noted generals of the late Astandalan army. He leaned forward, and immediately gathered all our attentions.

He chuckled. "I was only reaching for a piece of cheese ... No?"

"I'm sure you have some ideas, Uncle Ben," said Hal. "You always do."

"Naturally; I have always been noted for them. I shall resume my proper persona as an eccentric old general and tell everyone the truth, which is that I am come to see the truth of the return of Jack Greenwing after Loe. I shall stay here as a guest of Sir Hamish's, who has painted me and most of my family, and—" He grinned, even more disquietingly than Hal. "And we shall see what my stirring the muck brings up."

"Someone is willing to murder," Master Dart said quietly, his voice a little troubled.

"In the past," I said, not convincing anybody.

Master Dart moved his shoulders in what was not really a shrug. "Given what has been happening to young Mr. Greenwing, I fear whoever it is is still here in Ragnor Bella. He—or she, or they—will be only the more determined to keep their secrets after seven years of success."

Mr. Dart smiled at his brother. "And that is where you come in, Tor. Doing the official researches in the constabulary's records and making sure it is widely known that you are doing so, and that you support Mr. Greenwing in his efforts to clear his father's name, and rejoice in the General's presence."

The image of the White Cross as I had last seen it flashed into my mind: the pale stone, wreathed in mist in the pre-dawn, tall and stern and uncompromising in its various roles as waystone, ley-anchor, linchpin, and marker of dark deeds punished by law.

An owl had hooted, the cock down the lane had crowed, and—

And that was it.

Except for all the many ways in which it wasn't.

***

Master Dart, Sir Hamish, and General Ben went to church in the morning in order to begin performing their tasks. I could have begun mine the same ways, but that would have meant missing the opportunity to burgle my ancestral home. Mr. Dart and Hal were determined to come with my father and me, of course.

"Four is a lot for a mission," Jack said, surveying us.

"I'd thought scouting parties were usually sent out in groups of five?" Mr. Dart replied.

Jack smiled suddenly. "Never lost your love of history, eh?"

"No, sir."

"Nor of adventures, I reckon."

"I'm quieter than Jemis in the woods."

"Better at Poacher?"

"Not with cards!"

"You make me feel old," Jack murmured, but I could see it was a false complaint. He was moving more lightly this morning, his eye brighter and more eager; and he made no further objection.

"We'll go—" He stopped, looked speculatively at me. "You've been running all round the barony, you said. What do you reckon's the quietest path between here and the manor, Jemis?"

Was that the first time he had called me by name? It might have been. I coughed against a reflux of emotion.

"Unless Mr. Dart knows a better, I'd say the old sunken lane that starts in the bluebell wood."

Mr. Dart nodded. "Yes, and to get there we should go along

the nuttery. That'll be new to you, sir, it's where my mother's old glasshouse and gardens were."

"Right enough. Everyone dressed for dust? I don't want us to be fighting, not in my brother's house, no matter what we might suspect him of. No weapons past a belt-knife, please."

His voice was crisp, easily commanding, easily obeyed. I had no problems whatsoever falling in behind him and Mr. Dart as they led the way past the stables and into the nuttery. Hal came along behind me, murmuring softly to himself what turned out to be the botanical names of the plants he'd been out in the gardens at dawn that morning to look at.

What Mr. Dart had failed to mention about the nuttery was that it was his ducks' favourite haunt. I say 'haunt' advisedly, for while there was a plentitude of circumstantial indication for their presence, there was no actual *proof.*

Half-listening to Hal's muttering, half-watching my father, altogether trying not to sneeze, I stepped down a slight incline and skidded on something that didn't bear closer inspection. I windmilled—unlike the last such experience, did *not* fall into a moat—and pitched upright against a not-very-stable shrub. I used my handkerchief, since it was already to hand, to flick at a bit of wet grey-green matter I did not wish to enquire too far into.

Pale buff down danced in the air like mayflies, catching the bright air and making the air feel sparklingly cool. I followed the progress of one piece of fluff down to where it landed softly next to a significantly larger fawn-coloured feather.

"What are these? The feathers of the proverbial golden goose?"

"Was it golden, or merely its eggs?" asked Hal. "What variety of hazel are these? What's your frequency of coppicing?"

"Nine years, Eraclian Cob, and these are my ducks."

I made a great show of looking around. The shrubs spread on either side of us in a diamond-patterned grid, rough-edged leaves mostly on the ground but a few brave remnants flying like banners on the ends of the long straight rods the coppiced shrubs had created. I couldn't see any cobnuts; and, despite all the feathers and down and grey-green matter, no ducks, either. "Are they invisible?" I enquired. "They're so well-discussed I had thought them likely to be much more prominent."

"They're down in the drainage ditch," Mr. Dart responded haughtily, and strode off.

My father said, "Each to his beloved," and I, reminded, took Hal by the arm so that he would actually come along with us.

***

The old sunken road was as ancient as the Greenway leading to the Green Dragon, although as it did not lead anywhere but between Dark Hall and Arguty manor, it was much less travelled. Even Mr. Dart's ducks did not appear to have penetrated past the edge of the coppiced hazel; the new quince and medlar plantation, where we nearly lost Hal, showed no sign of them.

In our childhoods, Mr. Dart and I had spent a great deal of time along the old sunken lane. It was secluded enough to be appealing and near enough were rarely late home for meals. In its time it had been haunt of unicorns and highwaymen and fairy princesses and dragons: for in those days none of them were at all likely to appear but between the pages of storybooks.

Hal managed to discover three new species of fern in the first ten yards.

"It could be worse," I said to Mr. Dart. "It could be high summer."

"How did you ever manage to get anywhere this spring? You can't have gone many miles a day."

I laughed. "We didn't. We *walked* ten or twelve—then I would go for a run while Marcan chatted up the cooks and Hal begged names and seed off all the gardeners. Come along, Hal, it'll be easier to collect when next you visit."

"Next time I'll be encumbered with a wife," he muttered.

"It will be 'encumbered' if you go into marriage with that attitude."

He abandoned that line of thought, although not the ferns, whose spores he was carefully shaking into a paper envelope. "If it were a bookstore with a good Classical Shaian section you'd be just as long."

"I spend a sufficient amount of time at the local bookstore, thank you."

"Jemis, you *live* in the local bookstore. Bookish folk the province over would swoon at the thought."

"Perhaps we might continue in the hopes we will be able to complete our errand before the good folk return from church?"

We jumped a little guiltily, but my father (my father!) was smiling. His expression was faintly puzzled, faintly wistful, more than faintly amused. Friendly bickering could not have been much of a part of his recent life, I thought, and remembered with brutal clarity the vision of the pirate galley. My answering smile faded. His turned more puzzled, more wistful, more … sad.

I took a breath, wrongly, for Hal had stood up and brushed against a branch liberally festooned with musty-mildewy honeysuckle. I backed hastily away to seek out a second handkerchief. Hal ignored me apart from a blithe benediction, attention moving from stowing away the envelope of fern seed to my father. "You will have gathered, major, that I am a botanist, whereas Jemis took a slightly circuitous route to tortuously symbolic poetry in Old Shaian."

"The mind boggles," Mr. Dart added with a mock shudder.

"I have already been impressed by my son's knowledge of antique symbolism."

My son!

"Mind you," Mr. Dart continued, "I admit Mr. Greenwing's insights into the Gainsgooding conspirators' poetry were fascinating and very different from the historians' accounts."

"Where did you go, Perry? I've heard already that Jemis and his gr—"

"—Hal."

"—Hal went to Morrowlea. I apologize that I have yet to ask Tor or Hamish about you, though clearly you did exceptionally well."

"Oh, I didn't do so well as Jemis in the Entrance Examinations. I went to Stoneybridge."

"You came seventh," I said, not liking this.

"I am surrounded by the overly intelligent," Hal said, and threw up his hands. Unfortunately he was striding forward at the same moment and did not see the large rut his foot was just about to land in.

"These boots!" he cried, which was not what I thought when I saw his face.

I grasped him by the shoulders and moved him bodily onto

the bank and out of the mud so we could have a look at his ankle. "Hal …"

"Let me, Jemis," my father instructed. He knelt down heedless of the mud and moved to the boot. "How badly does it hurt, your grace?"

"Neither graceful nor gracious at the moment," Hal said breathlessly. "Ah, major, I think I'd prefer to leave the boot on for now. As Jemis can tell you, I am at present limited with respect to my boots, my coachman having most inconsiderately driven me and all my belongings into the Otterburn, and since I prefer my boots to fit more than I care for their polish, I decided to wait until my return home for their replacement."

"If it's broken …"

"Hardly that!"

Jack looked at him. "Do you say that because you don't *wish* it to be so, or because you don't *feel* it to be so?"

"I do like your distinctions between *wishing* and *feeling*, major. I broke my ankle once, in a fall at polo. This isn't nearly so bad."

My father seemed to consider this a suitable sentiment (or reason?), for he sat back on his heels and contemplated Hal's face. "I think you should sit with your foot elevated and cool for a bit, rather than come in with us. The secret passages are narrow at times, as well as dark, and we may need to exit quickly."

"I do apologize for the delays, major."

"You will listen?"

Hal flashed him a brilliant smile. "Major, I may be a duke, but I am not entirely a fool. This is your party; and I have been raised in the admiration of your skills as a soldier and leader of men."

My father (my father!) nodded. "Very well. It's warm enough

out down here out of the wind … you can sit on my coat."

He began to remove the garment. I said, the protest jumbling incoherent emotions together, "No, here, he can have mine."

Jack stopped and looked at me for a long moment. "Jemis, I have spent most of the last seven years on a pirate galley on the North Seas. I am, if anything, overheating."

Once again the dream filled my vision. The ragged breech-clouts, the scarred and bleeding—and above all, *bare*—backs. I stepped back, unable to express in words how much I admired his dignity, his sense of humour, his ability to smile; and how angry I was that he should be subject to even so minor an indignity (and for so excellent a reason!) as laying his coat down for Hal to sit on.

And I felt very unworthily aware of the fact that I had already lost one of my two coats that autumn, and that I needed to acquire a winter one … and so would he (for this one, even now being laid on the mossy bank for Hal to inch himself back on and arrange himself with his foot higher than the rest of him and, as he said, several new ferns and an exquisite example of something-or-other close to hand, was thin and obviously second-hand) … and that it was one thing to dress according to one's wealth when one was sliding down the social scale in the public estimation, and another thing entirely to do so when everyone seemed deeply committed to forcing one to behave like the heir to an imperial marquisate. The Empire didn't even *exist* any more.

We settled Hal in his patch of sunlight with his ferns and his notebook and a newfangled reservoir fountain pen Mr. Dart had in his pocket, and set off again along the sunken lane towards the bright circle ahead of us where the woods became garden.

Jack said, "So, Stoneybridge and Morrowlea, and you said

Roald Ragnor went to Tara, didn't you? You're all so much smarter than we were."

"Well, Roald and I did have to pay," Mr. Dart said self-deprecatingly. "Jemis was the one who went on merits."

I wanted to shout that I might have gone to Morrowlea on merits, but Mr. Dart was the one being offered fellowships to Tara.

But I said nothing, because there was naked pride on my father's face.

The last thirty yards of the sunken lane were muddy and rutted. Mindful of Hal's mishap, I kept my eyes down at the road below me, pretending I had not run this way four times in the past week and did not know exactly which tufts of grass or lumps of leaves were the safe ones to step on. There was not going to be a pit trap on this path; or if there was, I had already fallen into it.

I fell back behind Mr. Dart at a convenient narrowing of the way. No. I was not going to retreat again. As I had in the pit trap, before I was sure of Jack and Ben's benignity, I had to analyze the situation and decide how to extricate myself. Mrs. Etaris and I had had a number of oblique conversations about emotions, on a few rainy days at the bookstore when Hal worked away above us with comforting thumps and scrapes and snatches of song, and she and I sorted and arranged and talked about books and through them, life.

What had my father called her? A sensible and intelligent woman? Yes, and one who had read both widely and deep, and who watched the movements of the people in the town with an attitude I had hitherto only understood insofar as it related to literature or history. (Or botany.) She said very simple things, did Mrs. Etaris, but a nonchalant proverb or an absently-placed book were counterpoints to her courtesy. On first meeting her I had laughingly thought she might write the 'Etiquette Questions Answered' col-umn in the *New Salon*; after a month's acquaintance I now thought that if she did (and I did not yet discount the possibility), she was probably also running a country-wide espionage ring at the same time.

I was pretty sure someone was.

—And all that was seductively interesting, and not very rele-vant to my uncle's sordid misdeeds, and every time I brought up even a hint of the topic, Mrs. Etaris would find that somehow we had miss-shelved *The Undercurrents of Thought: the History of the Understanding of the Self* or *The Eternal Metaphysical Quandary of the Mind and Body* or—and this one had hurt—*The Correspondence of Love and the Soul.* This last was renowned for being the most piercing effort to understand one's own heart ever to be written in modern Shaian. Some said the *Correspondence* was written by Fitz-roy Angursell after his mysterious disappearance; others that it was a work out of the Emperor Artorin's court; still others that it was no one anyone else had ever heard of. I had read its ninety-nine perfectly constructed sonnets and wished for a small box to go hide myself in that I might find within its impenetrable darkness the inexhaustible centre of light the anonymous poet had.

I could not write an ode, let alone a sonnet, but I could, at least, look at the mud below my feet and know that the hollow hungry feeling in me was not only, or perhaps even chiefly, left over from the addiction to wireweed.

It was blindingly obvious to me that it was precisely his es-teem I craved. The problem was that it felt as dangerous a joy to acknowledge it as it was to sit down at table seeking the thrill of risk that came with the bets and the cards and the efforts of wit and skill pitted against chance.

It had seemed so safe a gauge of my behaviour and accomplish-ments, that imagined benediction or disdain. What better standard to judge my actions than to ask myself what my father, Jakory Greenwing, winner of the Heart of Glory, might have thought of them?

To have him right there looking at me was—was—it was too much, that was what it was.

I stepped with exaggerated care over a fallen tree. Someone caught my arm; I looked up and was dazzled by sudden bright light. We had come to the edge of the woods.

"Right," said my father, letting go as if I'd burned him. "Here's the plan."

Chapter Eighteen
The Burglars

MY UNCLE HAD twice invited me to dinner since Hal's revelation that father was very definitely not the traitor of Loe, but since the invitations had also come after subsequent reflections—also on Hal's intimation, as it happened—that I therefore stood between my uncle and his current estate, I had so far declined.

"We'll go in through the Beacon door and head by way of the Third Closet to the Wardrobe passage," my father said.

He might as well have been speaking another language.

He was evidently surprised at my blank stare. "Didn't someone tell you the names?"

"I haven't been inside the house since I was ten," I replied.

His turn to stare blankly, brows slowly furrowing. How lucky he had been not to lose the eye with a whiplash like that, to direct blow or subsequent infection.

"You haven't been inside since ..." He trailed off.

I leaned against the sturdy tree next to me, tired already despite the relatively early hour. I could not clearly recall the night's dreams, but my sleep had been unsettled, and I knew there had been some recurrences of the ancient nightmares. My eyes and nose felt dry and sandy, my throat scratchy, my lungs starting to be depressingly congested.

"The last time I was inside was for Uncle Rinald's funeral. On our way out Lady Flora told us it was inappropriate for us to come into the family portions of the house any longer."

"Vor—"

"My uncle said that of course he would see that we did not starve."

"You're still angry," he said, watching me closely. If he was himself he hid it better than my ability to detect it.

"We'd received the letter saying you were a traitor, Uncle Rinald died out hunting, and Mama lost a baby, all within the space of a month. Yes, I'm still angry at how they treated us. At least Uncle Rinald had made sure in his will that we could stay in the dower cottage—"

He wasn't attending to that. He'd frozen. "There was a baby?"

I did not often think of the baby brother, born six weeks too soon—from the shock of the news, the midwife said—tiny, perfect, and not in the world long.

"Jack," I said numbly. "A boy. He didn't … He died after only a few days."

"I didn't realize you'd named him," Mr. Dart said softly.

I looked away, in the vague direction of the dower cottage and the hawthorn tree we'd buried him under. "He died before the naming ceremony," I said; whispered, really, throat tight. "But yes, that was what Mama and I called him."

After a moment I felt a firm hand clasp my shoulder. I knew it was my father's; his hands were much bigger and much warmer than Mr. Dart's. And if the look on his face had been too much …

"Right," Mr. Dart said briskly. "Do we need more directions, sir, or shall we just follow you?"

***

Unlike, say, the Talgarths' house (famously one of the three interesting features of Ragnor Bella in Tadeo Toynbee's *Guide to the Kingdom of Ronderell*; the other two were, naturally, my grandfather's famous racehorse, Jemis Swiftfoot, and the increasingly tortuous history of Major Jakory Greenwing), or indeed the baron's so-called castle, or even Dart Hall, the Arguty manor house—called variously Arguty Manor, Arguty Hall, or The House, depending on whether one came from Dartington, Arguty village, or the wider barony—had no pretensions to architectural merit or even coherence.

The central block was a pre-Astandalan fortified farm, the east wing a brooding gothic thing reminiscent of the Castle Noirell, the south wing (there being no west) a mishmash of whimsical ornaments of seven conflicting periods overlaying a former barn, and in the back there was a kind of tower with a double spiral staircase and a belvedere courtesy of a not-very-distant ancestor who had had a theory about the health benefits of climbing up and down a certain number of stars each day. It was, in a word, a jumble.

I loved it.

According to local gossip it was riddled with secret passageways. These did not owe their existence to fashions for hiding servants (as was the case in the Talgarths' house), nor merely to whimsy (as I suspected accounted for most of those in the baron's castle), but because certain Greenwings past had wanted to hide priests of forbidden cults, smuggled goods and occasionally people, and, according to my father as he sketched out a rough plan for the benefit of myself and Mr. Dart, at least three illicit lovers.

"What were they smuggling?" I asked, dividing the question between the both of them.

"Back then? Practically everything." Jack gestured south towards the Woods and the old Border with Ysthar. "The Noirells made their money on taxing everything and everyone coming through the Border in return for managing this side of the crossing. Any luxury item would double in price with each Border crossing—and that's without getting into questions of merchants and other middlemen." He glanced at me. "Your grandmother …?"

I shrugged. "The Marchioness only acknowledged my existence after I broke the curse on the bees and slew the dragon that had been summoned out of the magic of the Woods to test my suitability as heir."

He blinked. "I thought the dragon was at the Harvest Fair? That was only a month ago."

"Precisely," I agreed, and resolutely walked on.

The Beacon Door (did it need capitals? I decided it did) was a concealed entrance on the end of the east wing, which faced us. I blinked in the general direction of the sun and wondered whether I or the builders had gotten turned around; both, I supposed. We faced the end gable through a screen of huge Arcadian cedars. These were convenient for our purpose but seemed a trifle malaprop for the house's security. Certainly they hid us from observers while Jack took out a stiff wire from his sleeve and poked into a tiny hole in the wall between two apparently unnecessary buttresses.

Something clicked. My father removed his wire, pushed on a stone, and an irregular section of the wall pivoted smoothly on a central axis.

"Wonderful," breathed Mr. Dart. I was stifling an attack of sneezes as the cool, dusty air billowed out of the passageway in front of us. I lowered the handkerchief to determine they were well ahead, my father waiting with an odd expression his face. I don't sneeze on purpose, I wanted to tell him, but saw, as I hastened into the passage, that his attention was turned inward. More to himself than to me he murmured, "Welcome home."

***

The passage reminded me of the troglodyte tunnels. After leaving History of Magic under the encouragement of Lark (who in retrospect obviously did not want me learning about what she was doing), I had begun to study architecture as a subsidiary interest to complement the Classical Shaian poetry. I had gravitated to the puzzle poets and their elaborate symbolic language, and found an understudied niche in what I called architectural poetry.

What Scholars usually meant by the term was either poetry that was *about* architecture (the most famous of these is probably "The Ode to the Stars," a very lengthy description of the Palace of the Emperors in Astandalas) or that was so structurally informed that it was somehow akin to architecture as an art (the infamously complex *Tikla Dor*, beloved of children who missed all the allusions). I had read poems about buildings, fascinated in the inexplicable way one becomes enamoured of a certain thing by the idea that one would spend one's poetic genius on describing other people's artefacts.

It had seemed as pointless as describing a painting, I'd thought at first. Those poems existed, too; but most of them were boring unless they were really about something else. Then I discovered the concept of memory palaces, and diverted my attention for a time to studying those.

Possibly I was a flibbertigidget in my heart of hearts and doomed never to focus on any one thing; or perhaps it was the wireweed beginning its work. It was unpleasantly hard to know. I had studied the memory palaces, those imaginative constructions intended to assist the memorization of vast quantities of data, and begun wondering about what else might lie behind or between the lines of a poem on the surface merely laudatory of a building programme.

Then Mr. Dart had written me about the Gainsgooding conspiracy, which he was studying, I had turned to the books of the poets, and there discovered the exoteric symbolism of the Second Perpendicular School of Architecture and that of the Third Late Calligraphic poets, and that was the first time I had felt the world open up to me.

I followed Jack through the secret passages of his family home. I supplied us all with (clean) handkerchiefs against the thick dust. I considered the ways in which a poet might translate the jumbled structure of the Arguty Manor into a poem, and what it would be worthwhile to say in so doing. Some poets seemed content to let their poems simply to be, beautiful at best, solipsistic at worst, but I liked my poems both to be and to mean, preferably on several levels.

My thoughts seemed excessively loud even to myself. I thought that, and another thought flashed by, that perhaps my newfound dislike of small dark enclosed spaces had something to do with the wireweed withdrawal.

Except it was recent—

I couldn't remember the last time I had been so anxious at being in such tunnels and narrow passageways between walls that were *not* actually narrowing as I pushed along behind Jack and Mr. Dart.

I breathed deeply through my handkerchief. Who was I fooling? A the moment I couldn't remember the last time I'd been *in* a passage this narrow, dark, dusty, and enclosed. At the thought I sneezed.

I muffled it with the habit of long practice (and many hours in the Morrowlea library). Jack didn't move from his position, which was kneeling on the floor with his eye pressed to a crack. I blinked at him, only then discerning the dim light just barely illuminating the space. Mr. Dart spoke softly into my ear. "Nicely contained, Mr. Greenwing, especially as that can't have been the first."

But it *was* the first, I thought. My thumb went to where the ring was that seemed to suppress my sneezing. I wasn't wearing it.

Hal, I thought. Hal hadn't given it back after that strange magic-divining ritual that had not gone quite as planned.

"Here we are," Jack said quietly. "Perry, the door. Jemis, the window. I'll search."

I nodded, then felt foolish in the dark, then realized it didn't matter, since he had spoken in his officer voice and obviously expected no response besides obedience.

The door on this side was a carved section of the sported oak panelling (for which the manor was locally noteworthy). It opened and shut without any difficulty at all, which I confess I found surprising. The door up to the attic room in my flat over the bookstore made significantly more protest at use, and that was very frequent since Hal was staying there.

Jack gave me a sharp look. I started, realized I was woolgathering again (what was *wrong* with me?) and moved over to the window. The drapes were half-drawn, so I stood within a fold where I could see outside but remain mostly hidden.

There wasn't much to see, as a line of evergreens had grown up to block the view. We were on a half storey above the ground, the window seven or eight feet up. A few lesser titmice were busy in the branches, pecking at Lady-knew-what. I hoped Hal wasn't too cold and damp where we'd left him. He'd professed himself content with the array of plants about him, but a fog seemed to have settled in while we were traversing the east wing.

"Yes," Jack hissed softly. I turned to look at him: he was at the great wooden desk in the centre of the room, fiddling with what I guessed were the hidden latches to secret compartments. One had opened; he was pulling out papers.

He sorted through them as quickly as shuffling a deck of cards. Stopped thunderstruck at the end; then smiled with grim satisfaction.

This seemed far too easy.

"Someone's coming," Mr. Dart said abruptly from the door. He stepped over to the panel by which we'd entered, which had closed, and began to fumble with it.

The drawer that had revealed its secrets so readily did not want to receive them again anywhere so quickly. After a frantic motion that only served to snap the empty compartment shut, Jack cursed and handed me the stack of papers so he could open the door that Mr. Dart was still struggling with.

As I took them a motion from the window caught my eye.

The titmice, I thought first, before realizing the flash was grey and white, not blue, and too large for the little birds.

Grey jay; and a hand gripped the windowsill.

I pushed behind Jack and Mr. Dart. I brought the panel door to latch as quietly as possible. The papers were an unwieldy mass in my hands, and the dust tickled my throat.

The bastard offspring of the marriage of curiosity and prudence, said Fitzroy Angursell in one of his poems about what you learn as a trespasser who becomes privy to secrets for fear of being revealed by moving.

We waited while noises occurred in the room on the other side of the wall. I held the sheaf of papers and wondered what Myrta the Hand's people wanted with my uncle, or his study at least.

There was a sharp rap, seemingly right in front of me. I tried instinctively not to jump, and crackled the papers slightly.

"There," said a voice I half-knew. "Did you hear that?"

"A mouse," a very familiar voice replied dismissively. "Lady Flora can't abide cats so the place is overrun with 'em."

Roald Ragnor, I thought, sounding almost like a normal person for once.

"Cats?"

"No, mice—don't be a round fool, we've only got a few minutes before everyone gets back from church."

"It's not that late, surely?" That was Red Myrta—I thought it must be her—echoing my own thought.

"Short service, the week before the Fallowday. Surely to the Lady your folk would pay heed to that?"

Red Myrta, alas, did not find that as bemusing as I did, for she asked nothing about it. There was a sound of moving items—

papers rustling, soft clicks or thuds as other things were set on the table or blotter or shelves.

"Good enough?" she asked after a moment.

Roald spoke after a pause, presumably of inspection. "Yes, I think that will do. Now, you'd better be off."

"Yes; I shouldn't want you to miss your lunch."

A soft laugh followed, dying away as if she'd gone back out the window. I was near perishing of curiosity but prudence, along with a foot fallen asleep, kept me still.

The other voice, or rather its owner, made a few further sounds. These seemed to me to be mostly throaty noises of amusement. Then an audible count to seventeen—and then he opened the door on us.

The Honourable Roald Ragnor, currently—if no longer *definitely*—heir to the barony, blinked in what I was pleased to see was genuine surprise. "Jemis?"

Chapter Nineteen
Factors

ROALD FOLLOWED ME back through the secret passageways. I gripped the papers to my chest carefully and did not have to think too hard about poetry to stop the walls being too close, the ceiling too low, the dust too thick. My imagination was too busy spinning theories for why the Honourable Rag could possibly have been there, and the explanations he might conceivably choose to give us.

I felt incredibly happy at the discovery that there was, in fact, something going on with him beyond dissipation.

He had not seen my companions, I realized when we spilled out into the fresh air in the dull shade of the Arcadian cedars. The mist swirled around us, revealing stretches of still-emerald grass studded with decaying leaves in rich umbers and burnished golds.

A glance at Jack led me to taking the lead across to the edge of the Forest where the sunken road. Once under cover I turned to Roald. I did not try to hide my amusement. "Well?"

He glanced from me to Mr. Dart, who was also grinning, and at my father, whose scowl was formidable. He did nothing like a double take, so I presumed did not recognize him.

For a moment Roald looked actually concerned. I raised eyebrows expectantly, and, as I expected, the concern slid away to the usual smirk. The Taran drawl re-entered his voice.

"And here I'd thought you were one of the good boys," he said. "This is, what, the second house you've been in under false pretences in the last month?"

Life is a game of Poacher. I smiled deprecatingly. "I believe this would count more as burglary, but I will have to leave the nuances to Inveragory. What of you, Master Roald? I do believe that's the *second* member of a criminal gang I've caught you consorting with—and come to think of it, both times were in other people's houses."

"Hardly do to meet them at m'father's. Speaking of, I'm due for luncheon."

"Ready for the Fallowday?"

He glanced at my hand, where I felt the absence of the ring. His face flickered, as if a bird's shadow crossed over its wide sunny blankness. Then he grinned, touched his hat to Mr. Dart, bowed with mock formality to me, and strode off, whistling an air I recognized a few minutes later as the comic relief's song from *Three Years Gone*.

The Honourable Rag was annoyingly good at Poacher.

***

Hal was sitting on the bank where we'd left him, leg stretched out with his hat as a cushion. His notebook was in his hand, but he was listening with an excessively patient expression to a man talking at him in a solid monotone.

With a curious sense of inevitability I recognized his interlocutor as the Arguty factor.

Hal looked at me with glad relief. "Jemis!"

Mr. Hagwood spun around. He was narrow, weedy man, with a narrow, saturnine face. Of melancholic disposition, his monotonous voice and dull features hid a skilled understanding of the lands of the estate and their yields. Everyone always assumed he was smuggling, but he was good enough at minding the estate that no one looked too hard into it.

I opened my mouth to greet him. He looked past me and screamed.

***

It was a good scream: long, high-pitched, bloodcurdling, totally unexpected.

I could not help myself. I turned around to see what was behind me, expecting—I don't know. Another dragon? A basilisk? A manticore? A sphinx?

My father, looming out of the mist.

I swallowed and turned back to the factor—or rather to Hal, as Mr. Hagwood had run off into the woods. The echo of his scream lingered.

Jack frowned at me. I wondered what he saw on my face, or if he were thinking of something else. He said, "I am more easily recognized than I anticipated."

My insides churned. Easily recognized by Sir Hamish and Harry Hagwood: totally unknown to his son.

Hal said, "He was just telling me how he'd cut down Mad Jack Greenwing's corpse from the Hanging Hill, seven years ago, and all the stories his grandmother used to tell him about those who were cursed for handling the dead. And 'she had the green sight and the white, so you know what she said was true'—" Hal made a good imitation of Hagwood's drone. "He was belabouring the eeriness of the grim task and trying to make me feel uneasy: he might well have scared himself into expecting the sight of a ghost."

I had avoided the White Cross ever since—well, ever since my father had been buried there, but even more so after I had heard a few whispered ghost stories about the unquiet dead who were bound under crossroads. Three days ago I would have believed in my father's ghost.

It was easier to imagine him a ghost than to accept that he was standing right there, alive, beside me.

"Come," Jack said brusquely. "Let us return to Dart Hall and confer. Give me your hand, Hal."

***

"Have we ever a plentitude to tell you—Hal? What's this? Hurt?"

Hal smiled at his great-uncle, who had come striding into the hall at the Darts' to greet us. "An unlucky step and a strained ankle is all, Uncle Ben. I'll be right in a trice."

"Found a new plant, did you?"

Hal laughed. "Three new ferns, and one of them with the most splendidly plumoso-cristatum fronds …"

Ben threw up his hands. "Now, lad, you know my rule: I didn't listen to technical details about the evolutionary habits of finches from my sister, nor to technical details of the magical properties of sheep wool from my nephew, and certainly not to the special characteristics of ferns from you, duke-me-lad."

"And yet *we've* heard your analyses of all your battles seven times over."

"Privilege of age, me lad. When you reach mine you can say whatever you like to your over-entitled relations, too. Now come along, Jack, boys, there's food on the table and plenty of news to be shared."

Mr. Brock came out of one of the side doors, saw the situation, and gestured sharply at an underling behind him. In short order a pair of brawny footmen had taken Hal in hand and borne him off to find a washbasin. Mr. Dart and I went to our rooms to wash and change for the meal. I had only the outfit from yesterday to exchange for my practice gear, which I'd worn for our excursion. I made quick work of my ablutions and entered the dining chamber a moment or two before Sir Hamish.

"Well?" said my father.

"Well!" replied Sir Hamish.

"Hamish," Master Dart said in admonitory toners, rather as he might have used to Mr. Dart or myself. Mr. Dart, coming in, suppressed a smile and sat down beside me. Sir Hamish merely winked at him and applied himself to his food.

Pigeon pie, grapes from the cool room, cheese, crayfish, cornmeal cakes, a lightly spiced soup … the Darts ate a wider variety of dishes at one meal than Hal and I had managed to cook in two weeks. Possibly even in the whole month Hal had been staying with me.

I wondered how hard it would be to make the pigeon pie, and whether Mrs. Brock, the cook, would be willing to share her recipe. There was a faint warm spice and some sort of liqueur in the filling—nutmeg and brandy, conceivably, and perhaps a hint of orange zest, too.

"There," said Mr. Dart impatiently, setting down his fork. "*Now* may we hear what has wrought you to such a pitch of excitement?"

Master Dart shook his head magisterially. "I shall leave you to your deliberations. You may use the library—I shall be making a call on Sir Vorel."

He sailed away, dignified as his butler, to my surprise and my father's but not, it appeared, to anyone else's. Sir Hamish grinned at Jack. "It was borne in on Tor this morning that given the general situation he may very soon be in a position to realize his ambition as the chief magistrate."

"Plausible deniability?"

"It seems to work for most things. Let us remove ourselves to the library, Brock will send our coffee there—but tell me, as you know we are perishing to know, did you find the letters?"

"We did," Jack said, rising. He patted his waistcoat pocket, which crinkled.

Ben held himself very still. "And?"

"We haven't had a chance to look at them yet. Too many distractions along the way."

He told Ben and Sir Hamish about the interruption of Red Myrta and the Honourable Rag and the even more extraordinary response of Hagwood the factor to seeing him.

Ben looked speculatively at me from where he'd enthroned himself in the best chair beside the fire, but did not express his thought. "That is very curious indeed. Major, what's your report?"

"Besides what I've told you? A puzzle with too many pieces at the moment. It sounds as if you have more to add. Shall we hear that first or look at the letters?"

He withdrew the sheaf of papers and placed them on the del-

icately carved table between the lot of us. Sir Hamish sat next to
Ben, then Jack, then Mr. Dart, then me, and finally Hal on the
other side of the fire facing his uncle. We all leaned forward as if
the blankness of envelope and fold would tell us all their secrets
without the bother of reading.

What *did* Mr. Dart hear when he heard things speak?

"A lot of pages for an official letter—or even two—from the
Army," Ben said at last.

"Pish." Jack fanned them out. "I was holding the whole stack of
Vor's secrets when we realized company was on its way."

I looked at the papers. Accounts … letters … what looked like
a will … an itemized list that was upside-down to me but seemed
to be a reckoning of barrels of something-or-other … Pages in the
thin paper and elaborate inks of the Army notices, which I had
only seen once but apparently had never forgotten, given my instant physical reaction to them. I pushed back in my chair, breathing hard, feeling my heart thunder. That first letter …

"How did you know where to look?" Hal asked.

"My brother was always fascinated by that desk. He loved that
it had a secret compartment."

"You knew about it."

Jack chuckled. "Of course. He was never as good at keeping his
secrets as he thought he was."

"Or his accounts, it looks like," Hal said, frowning at the top
set. "I'll need to go over this more carefully, but I'd say he's been
fudging them."

Of course he was, I thought, anger kindling again. Not for my
own sake—the Arguty estate had never been an expectation of
mine. I was angry that my father should have come home to *this*—

and, a little more distantly, angry that my uncle had so abused the legacy left by Uncle Rinald, who had worked so hard to redeem the estate from the situation that my gambling-mad grandfather had left it in.

"Too bad my sister's not here—she's a fine practical mathematician, sir."

"Don't listen to him, Jack. Hal's been running the largest private estate on the continent since he was fourteen."

"I have excellent advisors," Hal rejoined.

Ben grunted. "Speaking as one, let us leave aside the finances, intriguing though they indisputably are. Hamish—you know the people."

Sir Hamish smiled at our rapt attention. "We put a cat among the pigeons by showing up today with the General. At first I thought it might have been better had Mr. Greenwing been there as well, but as events turned out—"

"Hamish, you've never been concise but for the love of the Emperor, spit it out."

"I'd forgotten how patient you are, Jack. Your son resembles you there as in so many other aspects of his character."

"Hamish."

I doubt my father's growl had any real effect, but Sir Hamish did resettle himself into his chair, sardonic smile glinting, and begin.

"I shall tell you this in order and with details," he announced, "so that you may fully appreciate it. We decided to walk, it being a fine day."

"It was foggy," I objected.

"It was a fine day to walk along the Teller Road."

"That's not the way to the church," my father objected.

"Must you keep interrupting? We were going to the Big Church. It replaced the Little Church by the Lady's Cross down by the Ragglebridge, which was damaged in the Fall. It's up on the knoll above the White Cross, which was convenient for the Baron."

"What about the Dartington church?"

"We do not attend under the current priest."

"That's changed the barony politics a trifle, if everyone goes to the same church nowadays."

Hamish's smiles could be very edged, sometimes almost malicious; this one was. "You will have a grand time of it, Jack, discovering all the changes in society since the Fall. Not to mention all the many, ah, challenges, your son is making to what had been the new status quo before he came home from university."

"They're not *all* on purpose," I muttered, a little indignant and considerably more embarrassed.

Sir Hamish shook his head in a manner very like the Squire's when he'd taken his departure. "If I may? Thank you. We walked to church, accompanied by some of the local families, including a few of the servants from the house. After we crossed the bridge we began to meet more and more people. We thought it very odd that so many were still on the road—and then when we came to the crossroads we discovered why."

He paused there for effect. I refused to play into his theatrics, but Hal felt no such compunction. "Yes, and?"

"And there at the White Cross was the itinerant knife sharpener who nearly eloped with the Honourable Miss Jullanar Ragnor."

It was Mr. Dart's turn to object. "He turned out to be the Earl of the Farry March, though. What's he doing back here in disguise?"

"Ah! A question you were not the only one to ask but one which the man could not at first answer."

I glanced at Ben, who had steepled his hands and was smiling at them. He had very knobbly joints, I noticed again, swollen beyond what I thought happened with arthritis.

Hal had said something about his great-uncle's hands ... he'd been telling me the true story of Loe, as he'd had it from Ben. That was it. Betrayed, captured, imprisoned, General Ben had also had his hands broken. He'd been placed in a cell at the edge of a cliff, with a way out he could not pass with broken hands and freedom taunting him with every breath ... and from which my father had rescued him.

I shivered and smiled at my father, feeling shy in his presence, in the still-rough exterior and the towering reputation that had nearly been able to withstand false accusations of treason without shattering.

He did not see. He was still looking enquiringly at Sir Hamish. Hal leaned over and placed another log on the fire, casting up a spray of sparks and smoke. I coughed, sneezed, and sat back out of the way. There would be ... O Lady, there would be a lifetime to spend time with him.

I hugged the thought to myself. We just needed to disentangle all these mysteries and make it safe for him to take his rightful place.

Sir Hamish said, "It turned out that this man was the *real* knife sharpener. The Earl had borrowed his face."

Chapter Twenty
Introductions

I RAN THE six miles from Dart Hall to Elderflower Books as slowly as I could manage, and wished it were longer.

It was past dawn, but not long past, and there were people out-and-about as I loped into the market square and fumbled with my latchkey. I found the early inhabitants of the town fascinating: maids and footmen on their way to their work if they lived out, or on early errands if they did not; Mr. Inglesides the baker and his assistant, getting ready for their first customers (very often those same maids and footmen); fishermen heading out and carousers heading in.

I was holding my boots in my hand and probably looked like one of the carousers. I had not been one of their number; I had, in fact, gone early upstairs, pleading a headache to account for my disinclination to cards or drink or cigars or any of the normal gentlemanly after-dinner pursuits.

How dull the life of leisure was.

I had had a bath, and tried to read one of the books in my room, and lain in bed, and all the while a cold sludge had crept along my veins as I thought about wizards borrowing faces.

Ben didn't care two sticks for the current prejudices about magic. He described the mess of crimes, impostures, and shocking revelations that had run through Fillering Pool during the first year after the Interim. He did not explain exactly how it had been stopped, only that Hal's mother had somehow figured out the way. I had not realized quite how skilled a practitioner of magic the Dowager Duchess was.

The knife sharpener, it appeared, had been met by the Earl of the Farry March and offered a summer of living like an earl in return for the tools of his trade. He had not learned until after the gold and the jewels and the fine clothes had faded away into dead leaves and dust that he had given away much more than his sack of whetstones and grit. He had lost years of his life, the respect of his fellows, and half the knowledge of who he was.

"Oh," I'd said, but no one had looked at me or my father.

Sir Hamish said, "His point about losing a summer let us ask about young Mr. Greenwing's bout of memory loss."

"Oh," I'd said, even more weakly. This time they did laugh at me, as Sir Hamish listed off the various improbable activities people had given (apparently straight-faced) for my missing time.

I wished I could be certain I had not been dancing slowly in complex circles through the Taylors' winter wheat. Or fishing along the East Rag, the Raggle, the Tennerbeck, and the Magarran at various points of the day and night. Or doing barbarous things with Mr. Pinger's twa-tailed vixen. Or dancing again, this time around the White Cross, which everyone agreed was a very bad idea, even if they did do strange things down in the Woods.

The only unusual dance I knew was the one my mother had taught me, to dance the Lady in, which I had danced in the cellars

under the Castle Noirell to break the curse and waken the bees. I
had not been afraid of the dark and the enclosed spaces then.

And all that was superficial froth, as was the incessant questions
of *why* everyone cared so much about me, and just how I had managed to make multiple mortal enemies without intending to, and
what I had actually been doing in the period I could not remember, and even what precisely I had found there by the White Cross
in the pre-dawn.

It had been misty around the White Cross, the sun invisible in
the east, the sky lightening but not yet light. Over in the east the
morning star shone like a beacon. Down on earth the pale stones
of the highway were almost the same colour as the mist. Sight gave
the wrong impression: made it seem as if every step should sink
into cloud, should be insubstantial beneath the feet as the air was
to the hands.

The air cold on my face, though I was still warm from the run
up to that point.

The waystone, taller than I, white limestone etched with ideographs to warn and to inform and to bind.

The concentric circles of black basalt set in iron bands marking
the crossroads itself, like a spill of ink in the mist, so the tall waystone looked like one of the stones at the Lady's Pools. *No offering
stone*, I'd thought, looking for a place I could leave my paltry spur-
week offering. I'd looked around, I remembered now, to see if there
was a loose stone anywhere nearby I could use for the offering. I
did not want to put it down on the ground, my flowers and wheat
and candle. At a proper grave there was a shallow stone dish before
the headstone. I hadn't thought that there would not be such a
thing at the White Cross.

I'd stopped, my silk-wrapped package in my hands. Seen off on the Spinney Lane side a white lump I'd taken to be a chunk of limestone, but when I'd reached it I'd seen that it was—

—And I was in Yellton Gaol two days later.

—And—

And those fairy-trained wizards of Fillering Pool had been able to borrow (steal, surely) the faces of those who had willingly (if unwittingly, like the knife-sharpener) given permission, or those who were dead.

No one else seemed to register this when Ben said it. There were no startled motions or stillnesses, no glances at me or my father, no awkward words or expressions. The conversation had flowed on without pause, widening to take in the various effects of magic since the Fall, and from there to current politics, to the pirates, the press-gangs, and how everyone was waiting for the whiskey-tax assessors to show up and discover what everyone else was hiding in their cellars.

And probably it was stupid.

It seemed incredible—surely it *was* incredible?—that a wizard should have found my father's body and taken his face and gone off for seven years only to return *now*.

Except that seven years was long enough for memories to fade, for a wife to die, for close friends to overlook any doubts in the surprised gladness of seeing a beloved friend alive again after all.

For a son to lie awake the whole night through as doubt coiled cold and slimy through his every thought.

Six miles was not far enough to run. Six hundred wouldn't have been far enough.

It was chilly, so I lit the wood stove in the front room of the bookstore before going upstairs to wash and change. I looked for a long time at the laughing man in Sir Hamish's portrait, and did not feel any better at all. Made coffee and brought it downstairs at a quarter to nine so I could sip it between the steps involved in opening the store for the day.

"They will not fit that direction no matter how hard you push, Mr. Greenwing."

I looked at Mrs. Etaris, who stood by the door so she could hang her coat on the hook. Looked back at the shelf where I was trying to stand up a handful of books a good two inches too tall for the space.

"Put them on the counter, please. Perhaps one of today's customers will realize they are his heart's desire."

I was skewered by the words—by the idea—oh, for a heart's desire so easily attained!—by the wish that the doubts were wrong, that the dreams were wrong, that this news was *true*.

"Oh, Mr. Greenwing," she said in a softer voice. I remained crouched where I was, one knee on the floor, hands on the too-tall books, racked.

A few steps, not exactly light, a swish of cloth, a creak of the floor and a faint murmured complaint, and then her arms came around my shoulders. She smelled a little floral and more like nice soap. I felt a stab of envy for her children and hoped they were grateful for her.

After a few moments she tugged me upright. "I'm sorry," I said, fumbling for a handkerchief. My heart quailed at saying anything else. "I'm sorry."

She deliberately misunderstood me. She was so good about that. "Mr. Lingham was not a wholly terrible replacement, although I believe I'd prefer to hire him for my garden over my store any day of the week."

I smiled weakly at her, trying to convey my gratitude for all the things she said and did not say. What had my father called her? A sensible and intelligent woman? Yes: and a kind, warm, and funny one, too. I wished my mother had known her better.

That reminded me of one of my tasks, and I turned my thoughts even more gratefully to them. "Mrs. Etaris, I received a letter from my mother on Saturday. Hal brought it to Dartington with him. Do you happen to know anything about it? Or how I might go about finding out who sent it, now, and not four years ago? In the letter my mother said she was leaving it with someone in case of her death."

She was checking the fire, and straightened with her face composed, if ruddy from the heat. "A letter addressed to you was left on the counter during the course of the day on Wednesday. I had been intending to speak to you about it, for of course there are numerous unpleasant reasons someone might send you anonymous mail—"

"Yes, I've received some. Hal and I have been burning them."

"There are always a few, alas. I do apologize: you were missing, and I forgot to mention anything about it to Mr. Lingham, who must have presumed it should go with your other post."

"He brought it with a letter from Morrowlea saying they're coming to look at the dragon, and one from Inveragory offering me a place."

"Congratulations, Mr. Greenwing."

I set up the till, stacking the coins inside much more precisely than was required. Mrs. Etaris left me for a moment to do the little

things that made the space cozier and more inviting: fluffing cush-
ions on the chairs near the wood stove, running a dust cloth over
the shelves, straightening the rug on the floor, evening out a row of
books that had tilted. I fussed at the counter and waited forlornly
for something to happen that would take my mind off the cold
hollow core of my existence.

"Have you eaten anything today, Mr. Greenwing?"

I picked up my coffee. "No, thank you, ma'am. I left Dart Hall
early."

"Running six miles before breakfast is admirable but not a
substitute for eating, Mr. Greenwing, and you do not need to lose
any more weight. Go and fetch something from the bakery, then
you can mind the shop this morning, if you'd like."

This was the downside of a maternal figure, I supposed, but I
had found it easier to obey Mrs. Etaris on such matters than stand
up to her. I wasn't hungry in the least, but I did want to ask Mr.
Inglesides what he'd heard about my mysterious absence.

The bakery was full of the second wave of customers, children
on their first break from the kingschool and those of the town's
professional class who began their work at the leisurely hours of
9:30 or 10:00. Ragnor Bella was a small town in a barony with a
much smaller population than once upon a time, but there was still
a branch of the Imperial Bank of Scholarship and Trade, even if it
only boasted three employees, and there were the usual complement of lawyers, physicians, independent scholars, and clergy.

I waited patiently while Mr. Inglesides' assistant, Polly, dealt
with a gaggle of children, and while Mr. Inglesides himself chatted
with Father Rigby, two men in legal gowns whose names I didn't
know, and Dominus Gleason, professor emeritus of magic.

When this last came in I faded back as best I could against the shelves of confitures and jams on the side wall of the bakery. Alas, it was not a large store, and when the children cleared out not a noisy one, and my sneezes sounded forth clearly as a trumpet.

"Excuse me," I said in resignation as all four men turned to look at me. Mr. Inglesides, who had winked at me earlier and not addressed me, winked again.

I would have bowed to Mr. Inglesides out of respect for his person, and to Father Rigby out of respect for his office, and to the lawyers as a salute to their positions and possible future relevance, but I intensely disliked Dominus Gleason and would have preferred not to give him the time of day.

My mother had dinned into me that courtesy was a far greater thing than pride. After the past month of acquaintance with my grandmother I knew more of why that had been so vital a lesson. The Marchioness was proud beyond sanity, and had never reconciled with her daughter after a break whose cause I did not know.

A flicker of memory came shooting across my mind about Hal's Aunt Honoria's list of eligible brides, and that mine would be the same as his except that as heir to an imperial marquisate rather than a dukedom I could *perhaps* look as far down the social scale as regional—i.e., provincial—nobility.

The second son of an impoverished county baronet would not have been on any such list for my mother in Astandalan days.

All this flashed through my mind in the space between sneezing and excusing myself and then I realized it was the next hand in the game of Poacher that was life, and I smiled and said, "Mr. Inglesides. Gentlemen," and bowed once to them all.

"Mr. Greenwing," Mr. Inglesides replied, his smile warm, genuinely welcoming, and ever-so-slightly malicious. He's heard something, I thought immediately, and was pleased my guess had been correct.

"Lord St-Noire," said Dominus Gleason a bare moment later, at his most unctuous.

Father Rigby looked blank, but he always looked blank when he saw me. The two lawyers exchanged glances. One said delicately, "Mr. Greenwing?" and the other, even more delicately, like a sigh made speech, "Lord St-Noire?"

I looked at Mr. Inglesides, giving him tacit permission to make the introductions, which was quite against the rules. I did not, however, wish to be indebted to Dominus Gleason for so much as an introduction, and I remained unconvinced that Father Rigby remembered who I was between one encounter and the next.

Mr. Inglesides blinked twice, slowly, and then his face smoothed into his professional courtesy. With as much punctiliousness as the Etiquette Master at Morrowlea could have wished he said, "Mr. Greenwing, may I present Mr. Morres and Mr. Tey? Mr. Greenwing, the Viscount St-Noire, gentlemen."

Mr. Tey was the one who'd spoken like a sigh. His voice matched his appearance: he was tall, willowy, delicate, dark-skinned, and fussily dressed at an expense I wondered he could afford. He was perhaps in his late twenties. Family money, I deduced, though of course it equally well have been crime.

Mr. Morres was older, middle thirties I guessed. He was average in all respects—build, features, skin tone, hair—except for his eyes, which were a sharp blue that put me in mind immediately of Mrs. Henny the Post's. He's the one to watch, I thought, smiling, as he said, and Mr. Tey sighed, "How do you do." Their expressions suggested that the many irregularities of this introduction were not lost on them.

"Good morning," I replied with the closest to pleasant neutrality I could manage with a head cold. Dominus Gleason watched me steadily, with a tiny smirk and a delighted gleam in his eyes. I did not like to think I had done something to please him so excessively.

Father Rigby harrumphed, but said nothing when I glanced enquiringly at him. Finally Mr. Morres said, as delicately as he'd initially commented on my name, "Mr. Tey and I have been sent from the chancery court in Kingsford. We've been asked to assist with certain cases at the Winterturn Assizes here, including, I believe, one making official the inheritance claims for the Imperial Marquisate of Noirell."

I stifled a sudden wild hope that I was not, after all, going to be eligible for the title. Between the dragon and my grandmother I feared I had very little choice. I smiled politely again. "I expect I shall be seeing you again on that matter, then, sirs."

Mr. Morres took off his spectacles and examined their lenses against the light, and put them on again, and I thought, very clearly: he is here for another reason, too.

It needn't *necessarily* have anything to do with me, but too many other things had, this past month, for the hope that it didn't to be anything more than a mild, wistful, wish.

"I've just been telling our visitors about your exploits with the dragon," Mr. Inglesides said chattily, and once again attentions sharpened behind deliberately vague expressions.

Dominus Gleason was still delighted, as if I were his excelling student or pet; Father Rigby was good-natured and blank, a flicker of dismay or distress rippling the blankness only momentarily; Mr. Tey showed well-bred amusement; and Mr. Morres's face was vapidly curious and his thoughts well-hidden.

I laughed self-deprecatingly as if slaying dragons were a common and minor feat (far better than being treated—or still worse, *demanding* to be treated—as a conquering hero). "I've had a letter from Morrowlea. Several Scholars are coming to examine the carcass."

"Morrowlea?" Mr. Morres murmured. "The carcass?" Mr. Tey said faintly. Dominus Gleason's smirk narrowed into a frown, then widened again to a yet-more-self-satisfied smirk. Father Rigby sighed. "Poor creature."

"It tried to eat my uncle," I pointed out a little snippily, and was abruptly fed up with all the games and jockeying. Mr. Morres made me uneasy. Not in the way that Dominus Gleason's predatory and possessive air did, but uneasy at the danger he represented. I could like and trust him, but.

But: the Indrillines, the Knockermen, the cult, my uncle, and the Yellem constabulary were almost certainly involved *somehow* in the arrival of these two lawyers. I could not afford to be so profligate with my trust as I had been till now. Someone had paid Myrta the Hand's gang to abduct my sister, and that was without adding in the complications my father brought with him.

"Could I please have two cinnamon rolls and a Wardrider pastry, Mr. Inglesides?" I said, and, in a tone of voice that I feared was almost insolently indifferent, added to Mr. Tey: "I went to Morrowlea, sir."

"Of course," Mr. Inglesides replied, while the two lawyers exchanged glances. I watched Mr. Tey move his hands delicately in the air as if batting away invisible motes of dust and revised my opinion of him. He, too, was hiding something.

I nearly smiled at the thought. I was learning that almost everyone was.

Mr. Inglesides set the pastries on the counter for me. I realized then that I'd left my money at the bookstore, but before I could say so the baker added, "I'll put it on your account, Mr. Greenwing, and you can settle up with me later."

This was the first time that option had ever been offered to me, and I knew why. "Thank you," I said, bowing again, and took my comestibles and my head cold back to the bookstore that was rapidly and disquietingly coming to feel like home.

Chapter Twenty-One
Face Cards

MRS. ETARIS STAYED while I slowly and unenthusiastically ate the Wardrider pastry. The potato and onion filling was delicious, I knew at an intellectual level; at a physiological one I was disinterested to the point of nausea.

She did not exactly hover, but every time I looked up to see if I could safely get rid of the rest of the pastry she was there with a comment about new books or a little piece of gossip.

By such means I learned about the middle class of Ragnor Bella. I did not truly belong to it, with my title and my family, but in terms of wealth and status my mother and I had long since joined its numbers. Her second marriage to Mr. Buchance had added another dimension, for he was not only commoner-born, but foreign, and, over the years, increasingly wealthy. After my mother's death he had married the nursemaid hired for my infant sisters, Mr. Inglesides' sister and my putative stepmother.

There were far too few customers this morning, I thought balefully, nibbling at the crust. Mrs. Etaris asked what area of study Mr. Dart had specialized in.

"Late Astandalan military history," I said, though his interest was catholic and his range extensive. "What about you, Mrs. Etar-is?"

She was petting the cat, who lay in feline ecstasy on the chair beside the stove. "At Galderon? Political philosophy."

That surprised me. I glanced involuntarily around the store. There *were* books on political philosophies, two shelves of them in fact, but they did not have the air of love I should have expected from such a longstanding interest. The romances in prose and verse took up much more of the store.

"Interests do sometimes change, in much the same way as fortunes," she said. "Thank you for the cinnamon roll."

I went back to the pastry and thought about the changing fortunes of barony families. The Darts were gentry, though untitled: Sir Hamish's knighthood was for his painting, and he was, anyhow, a Greenwing on his mother's side. Master Dart was the Squire, an arrangement older than the barony itself.

Go back a thousand years, to the patchwork of universities and small fiefdoms before the coming of the Empire, and you would find the Ragnors, the Greenwings, the Woodhills, and the Kul-fields—once a great family—listed in parish and post registers. Go back seven hundred and fifty years again, to the days when Tarazel was marching across the wilderness of Oriole to find knowledge and found learning in the form of the university of Tara, and the Darts of Dartington were there: and one of them was marching at her side.

When the pastry was at last reduced to crumbs, by which time the town clock had struck numerous quarters (and there *still* hadn't been any customers), Mrs. Etaris stirred. "Very well, Mr. Green-wing. I shall leave you to mind the store while I do some errands;

my husband may have some news of you for me. I shall be back before lunch."

"Very good, Mrs. Etaris," I replied, trying to sound cheerful and not succeeding. I did feel a little better for the food, less inclined to faintness of muscle, but the cold sludge and hollowness were, alas, merely cast in greater relief.

I wondered, not for the first time, why she'd married her husband, who was (I supposed) reasonably handsome, but that couldn't be it, surely, for her? Perhaps he had changed over time … or she had … or perhaps behind closed doors there was a joy that made up for the public dissonance he barely tried to hide.

I would not, myself, like to spend my life married to someone I could not respect.

As soon as Mrs. Etaris left people started to come and go for books and belated copies of the *New Salon* and to consider me with narrowed eyes and smirking mouths and half-intended-to-be-heard comments. This was all very much as usual; only the subjects changed. The range included how long it had taken me to get home from university (occasionally); how appalling it was that I'd missed my stepfather's funeral and the Midsomer Assizes (more frequent now with the reminder of the Winterturn Assizes coming up); the dragon (with disbelief, as if half the barony hadn't witnessed its demise); my father (always); and now, also, my disappearance and the Yellem accusations, which someone had deliberately let slip.

I sighed inwardly and smiled outwardly and wondered fleetingly from time to time what my father would have thought to see me, which was also as usual. When two giggling schoolgirls had finally taken their leave with their new novels and I looked up for the next customer to see him standing there, I was for a moment utterly confounded.

He had drifted in unnoticed behind the schoolgirls and taken up a station in the corner by the cookbooks (and political philosophy), where he could warm himself at the fire and gently fondle the ears of the cat, an activity that I had learned could keep people in the store indefinitely. He must have been watching me at work for some time, I realized, and thought about those sidelong comments.

I wanted to smile but the cold sludge of doubt leaped into my throat and strangled my greeting with horrified uncertainty.

I had dreamed this too many times. Imagined speaking to him, man to man, too many times. Doubted that my life was anything like what he'd approve of and hoped fiercely and desperately that at least he'd approve of my efforts to live with honour and courage—oh, every livelong day.

"Jemis."

"J-Jack." I cleared my throat. "Were you looking for a book?"

An idiotic question, for all that we stood in a bookstore. He stared at me, brow furrowed and mouth set, as it had not been in the split second I first looked at him.

"Jemis."

I stared mutely, at his mouth, not his eyes. Eye. The doubt was *there*: that this was a dream, an illusion, a hallucination, a cheat. That standing before me was *someone else* wearing my father's face and trying to step into his shoes, his place, his life.

A distant rational part of my mind said that this was absurd, that of all people to choose a disgraced war hero with no money and a reputation as a traitor and a suicide made no sense. That voice was too distant to make any difference to the doubt or the hollow certainty that this bright dream would turn into betrayal with all the rest. I did not have good luck with those I loved.

"Jemis," he said a third time, and then, when I still stared at him, fighting with the heavy tentacles of doubt and fear and desire, his voice burst out: "For the Lady's sake, will you not *say* something?"

The dragon had flung me into a table: that had been nothing. Nothing.

But yet the doubt was there, suffocating, treacherous as a bog, as Lark, as the Magarran Strid.

Something clattered. I looked at the counter dumbly, astonished to see that I had knocked over the pen-stand. I was trembling with emotion. My heart felt as if it were convulsing, my pulse throbbing, and the cold heavy serpent coiled in my gut and my breast and my mind.

His face was pale, good eye brilliant, muscles working. Something broke there as I watched. The intensity slid away, a dullness rising in its place. His voice when he spoke next was flat, barely audible. "You thought I was a traitor."

"No!"

The denial made it out past the stranglehold of doubt. It had all the fervour of truth, all the steadfastness of one of the rocks of my life. I had never believed the accusations, never even countenanced them.

The expression on his face did not ease.

I felt sick. I wished Mrs. Etaris had not made me eat the pastry.

The reasonable part of my mind was screaming at the pain I was inflicting on my father, my father, my father.

And like blood in the mouth, metallic and sickening, the doubts moved.

"Then why?" he whispered, expression flattened with shock

and hurt and grief and a thousand other emotions. "Did you not—
Do you wish I had not come back?"

I was drowning.

I could barely think of anything but the heavy certainty that
this was not true and that it was true. That it *was* my father, standing
there while I rejected him out of fear that it was not him; that it
was *not* him, and I would have to live through the next several years
trying once again to persuade myself that he was dead.

I tried. Again and again I tried to pull common decency out of
my silence if I could not find anything else. I had not let the dragon
kill my uncle, even though I hated my uncle and I thought then
that he might have murdered my father—if I had saved his life how
could I do this to someone who might be the person I loved best
in all the world—might be, might be, *might be*—

"Jimmy," he said, and his voice was alarmed now. The old nickname that no one else had ever called me pierced just enough of a
hole in the doubt so my struggling rational mind was able to grab
control of my tongue.

"Tell me something only you and I know," I cried desperately.

His face went totally, completely, almost hilariously blank.
Mystification presently began to turn into comprehension, of more
than I could see or comprehend myself. Certainly his face lost its
rigidity.

"When you were nine I took you up into the hills to jump the
Leap."

My hands were shaking. I placed them on the counter before
me, leaning my weight down hard. The shakes passed up into my
shoulders, down into the rest of my body. I shook my head. "I told
people."

He smiled, though I did not think this was amusing. I leaned on my hands and fair shook like a—a *blancmange* and felt overall as I had in the first horrible weeks of the summer when betrayal and wireweed withdrawal had hammered heart and mind and body and soul.

He hesitated for a moment longer, then began to speak, more fluently as he went on.

"I was home when you were born. Did you know that? We lived in the dower cottage then, your mother and I. We paid a rent to my brother Rin. He always said that for a few years there that rent was all that kept him from bankruptcy. He was a good man, Rin. I'm sorry he's gone."

So was I. I did not remember that much of the sad procession bringing him home, but I remembered how tightly my mother had gripped my hand.

"When it was Olive's time he called me over to the Manor and we drank the last bottle of good wine. He'd hid it from the creditors so we could. I came back in the early morning, the last day of February. There was a patch of snowdrops I'd seen going over to the manor. When I stopped to pick some for Olive they were surrounded by primroses. The first ones I'd seen that year. If you'd been a girl we'd've called you Primrose, our gift from the Lady of Spring."

Instead I'd been named after my grandfather's favourite racehorse.

"Olive knew you best, of course, as a child. I was called up to the Orkaty campaign when you were just over a year. There wasn't enough money for me to sell out—and once I was there I loved it, always, the camaraderie and the fighting. Knowing I'd left you behind ... I'd always wanted to be heroic, I think we all do, one way or another. We all want our chance to shine."

To shine ... oh yes, we did.

How nervous I'd been, going to the post office to see the results of the Entrance Examinations. For a moment I hadn't been able to find my name and been so terrified that something had gone wrong, that my results had gone astray—that my *exam* had gone astray—and then I'd seen my name way up at the top of the page in the separate list for the top ten students in the whole kingdom, and there I was, second. No one could remember the last time someone from Ragnor Bella had placed up there.

And I remembered so clearly how I had thought: *My father would be so proud of me.*

Was he?

He was still talking. I was still shaking. I still felt literally sick to my stomach with doubt. Any moment now the fight against my emotions would lose—

"Knowing I'd left you behind ..." He shook his head, staring past me at something long ago and far away, like Mrs. Etaris thinking of her long-lost (why did I keep thinking he was imaginary?) friend. "I'd always wanted to be heroic," he said again, his voice that low rumble that I could not even begin to understand how I had not recognized it before, the deep soothing sound of my father talking to my mother in the next room.

"I'd always wanted to be heroic. We came to the end of the canyon, and Ben sent me with the colours up the cliff into the teeth of the enemy, and I planted the Sun Banner and I thought of my wife and my son and I held the border for you. As if the only way I could protect you, way back on the other side of the world, was to hold it."

I pressed my hands on the table as if the pressure would press down the doubts, the cynical voice that said that all this could have been learned or invented, that it was not *proof.*

"After Orkaty there were a few short campaigns. The triumph to Astandalas."

Upstairs on the wall of my little parlour hung the Heart of Glory, the highest award for courage in the Empire, which my father had won for holding that cliff.

Every person who had ever heard his name would know of that. In all the years of his reign Emperor Artorin had presented five: one for each world of the Empire, Mr. Dart had said was in one of his history books. For Alinor it had been my father.

"I was able to spend a few months each year at home, with you and your mother. Rin was well on his way to mending the family estate by then. It began to seem possible that I could sell out sooner or later. Emperor Artorin was not the expansionist his uncle had been, and there were fewer active fronts."

All that was in the history books.

He sighed, looked straight at me. "I still loved it. The army. Soldiering. I wasn't ready to do something else. I didn't have anything else to do … I hadn't even gone to university. I didn't come second on the exams!"

That would be in the records. This was not—

"Rin was supporting Vor through a legal degree—the estate wasn't profitable enough to justify a steward. And I … I did love it. The glory. I was still hungry for it."

All of this, part of my mind told the rest firmly, could be pure conjecture. *None* of this was provable; it was too long ago and too many people were dead.

And part of my mind wanted to sit down on the floor and cry

as I had when I was a little boy and he came riding up the lane from the road and I was too happy for words.

"Ben wrote to tell me he was going on one last mission and would I come. We were to go in the autumn to the muster at Eil and from there to the front. It was a silly time to start a campaign into the mountains, I thought, even in the southeast, but I decided to go on one last campaign. It didn't mean crossing the Border between worlds ... and since Ben offered me a promotion to sweeten it, with the better pay, Olive and I decided, we'd be able to live different lives. And so—"

At this point, of course, the door opened, the bell jangled, and Mrs. Etaris' sister swept in for her *New Salon* and the gossip.

I pushed back from the table. My wrists ached from how hard I'd been pressing on them. I nodded brusquely. "Good morning, Mrs. Landry. Your *New Salon*?"

She laughed complacently. "I'm not much of one for books. Never have been, not like my sister. *She* always had her head in a romance."

Not political philosophy?

Mrs. Etaris and Mrs. Landry were visually fairly similar, but not at all in character. I would not have believed anyone who told me that Mrs. Landry was successful at espionage. All the gossip of the barony that didn't go through Father Rigby went through her.

"I hear you had a mischance last week?" she began, fishing in her pockets for her change purse.

I did not want her to ask about the piratical stranger in the corner. I smiled wryly at her. "You could say that. Have you heard anything?"

She pursed her lips. "My dear Mr. Greenwing, I have to admit that when my sister hired you I couldn't *imagine* what she was about. Between your father and your university, I told her, you were the *last* person to put to work. The *last.*"

"Beyond even Master Roald?" I asked curiously.

She tipped the change onto the counter, along with a quantity of fluff, bobbins, and a tiny piece of quartz. I caught an errant pin and passed it back to her. "Thank you, Mr. Greenwing. One would not expect Master Roald to want to," she added, which put me into my place.

"Oh, indeed."

She began counting the money for her paper in the smallest possible coins. I could see at a glance that she did not have enough, and reached into the till for the change necessary for the combination that would get rid of the majority of them.

"I expect you were out with Mr. Dart, eh? He does seem to love his fish. Oh dear, I'm sorry, I shall have to use the wheatear—"

I collected the half-dozen small coins and the wheatear and passed the paper and two bees. "Here you are, Mrs. Landry."

She blinked down at the coins, and did the math agonizingly slowly over again twice. She had a reasonably thriving business in the form of a small parlour-café, I thought in exasperation; surely she could do basic math?

"How quick you are," she said at last, and began collecting her various items with even more agonizing slowness. I presumed she wanted me to drop some sort of *on-dit* or other juicy item of gossip, but as I had no intention of telling her the juiciest piece of gossip ever to come through Ragnor Bella (for the *second* return from the dead of Mad Jack Greening surely eclipsed everything, dragon, cult, criminal gangs, mermaid, and all), I merely smiled with clenched jaw at her until she finally left.

She gave me a parting shot: "You're looking peaky again, Mr. Greenwing. Do take care of yourself—it would be unkind to your uncle to lose his last family!"

I sneezed as she shut the door behind her: three times in succession, which was unfortunately familiar from the lead-up to the worst part of the spring's illness. I sighed. Possibly the doubts were all to do with physical malaise.

I turned back to my father, and they leapt up into my mind as if I hadn't for so brief a moment forgotten them.

He said immediately: "I used to take you fishing in the mornings. Cards in the evenings. I taught you to read Old Shaian ideographs from the book of haikus your mother gave me. Do you remember? We spent ages and ages on the poem about houses and frogs because you never got tired of the pun on 'house' and 'heron'."

He smiled suddenly as I stared at him. "No wonder you're good at puzzle-poems."

Someone else came into the shop just then, a stranger who wanted three copies of a Temby poet's new book. I wondered briefly if he were the poet, there was something so odd about the way he asked for the books, but then again all the oddness might have been in the way I spoke to him, for I was very close to throttling him for the interruption.

"Tell anyone else who comes in I'll be right back," I said abruptly to my father once he'd taken his books ("wrapped in brown paper, if you please") and left. Jack appeared baffled but willing. I did not wait to explain, ran upstairs into my rooms via the back staircase.

Found, in its place of honour beneath the Heart of Glory, the book of haikus. I did not hesitate, not this time, not though the cold doubts were infuriatingly still *there*, still coiling in my stomach. What else can you want? I snarled at then. What more proof can he give?

Even more infuriatingly, that was the end of the slow period. I thrust the book into his hands and even before he could begin to react the bell jangled, and jangled again, and I was obliged to deal with a dozen customers, some of whom, alas, wished to chat.

Jack faded into his corner and was almost entirely ignored except by the one person who wanted a cookbook. I thought it a little odd that no one seemed at all curious about a stranger with an eyepatch, but as I was also sneezing with springtime regularity I could not bring my thoughts to bear on that puzzle. After a while I ceased to be so sensitive to his presence, which was just as well given the normal run of conversation in the bookstore.

I fielded questions about current novels, old poetry, local history, and that splendid new melodrama, *Three Years Gone*, which was to be put on in Yellton starting the next week, did I know? I eyed with dour suspicion the three people who gaily introduced the play, but as I did not know any of them personally I could not decide if they were needling me on purpose. To each I smiled sweetly and firmly denigrated the play as melodrama built on lies.

The last customer to bring it up was a stick-thin older matron dressed in rich woman's clothes. She was accompanied by a quiet man in quietly comfortable clothes who did not seem to be either groom or relation or total stranger. When I smiled and denigrated her comment the matron said: "Oh, but Mr. Lindsary is feted for his factualness."

Her accent was Kingsford, and I wondered what she was doing all the way down here. Touring the location where the dramatic events had taken place?

"Major Greenwing was a man of this barony," I replied with dignity.

Her laugh was as thin as the rest of her. "I'm surprised to hear you defending him. You can't rejoice to have such a *traitor* besmirching the reputation of your community."

This was something I had heard too many times this summer. I had ripostes. Of course I did.

But fury started to burn in my toes and began to tingle its way up my body.

It was not *my* shop. I could not simply ask her to leave.

She gave me a tight little smirk. "Such a pity that he turned out to be so weak and cowardly in the end. Suicide, and all that."

The fury had reached my chest. It burned. It shouldered out the cold sludge: for a moment my mind was clear, my heart undivided, the heavy dragging unpleasantness only a suspicion of familiar illness.

I had a lot of practice smiling and speaking with courtesy as fury burned ever higher inside me. "I find it curious, madam, that you would believe a play over the word of General Prince Benneret Halioren, or indeed that you could find it possible to describe a man as weak and cowardly who was awarded the Heart of Glory by the hands of the Emperor himself."

"That's not possible. That is, you must be mistaken. All the countryside hails him a traitor."

The fury was ringing bell-like in my mind, white-hot and clear and invisibly powerful as foehn wind.

"All the countryside is wrong."

My voice came out flat and certain: so I had spoken a few days ago to Myrta the Hand; so I had spoken a few months ago to Lark; so I had spoken, over and over again, in the mornings to myself when I put away the doubts and suspicions of the night.

Some inner certainty was crumbling in her. Even in my fury I thought this very strange, for why should she care so much about the matter? But I did not care about her megrims; I cared about my father's reputation.

She said, "But this is *impossible.* Why would he have killed himself if he wasn't the traitor?"

There were a thousand and one reasons someone might kill himself in such a situation. I had spent most of a dismal year counting them out.

And they were all wrong.

"Why, indeed?" I replied ironically, but inside my heart was singing. They were wrong—wrong—wrong! My father had *not* killed himself—

The thin woman jerked back. "Who do you think you are, young man, speaking so to me?"

I confess I very nearly rolled my eyes, but I managed to turn the desire into an even more ironic bow, with every curlicue gesture I had ever devised. "I have no idea who you are, madam, but I am Jemis Greenwing."

Her mouth opened, but the quiet man behind her grunted in satisfaction and silenced her. "This is the Baroness Temby, Mr. Greenwing, and you are under arrest."

I just managed not to say, "Again?"

Chapter Twenty-Two
Research Questions

BARONESS TEMBY CONTINUED to appear totally astonished, though whether this was due to my identity or the arrest I wasn't sure.

"I beg your pardon?" I said finally.

"You are under arrest," the quiet man repeated. "Please come out from behind the counter. Keep your hands where I can see you, and there will not need to be any unpleasantness."

I instantly thought of three different ways I could use the objects on the counter in front of me to immobilize the quiet man and escape. The pens were weapons ... so were the two books remaining of the too-tall ones from that morning (for I had managed to sell one of them to a hopefully gratified customer) ... and this was not at all an occasion in which the response of violence, however tempting, was correct.

Behind the quiet man and Baroness Temby I could see a party of darkly-garbed persons approaching the shop. The imperfections in the glass meant I could not identify them, but out of a vague idea that the more witnesses there were the better, I waited until they opened the door to speak.

I had had several days of intermittent pondering on what I ought to have done on my last arrest—though my magically-induced amnesia meant I was not *entirely* certain what exactly I *had* done—and I intensely disliked making the *same* mistakes twice.

I bowed therefore to the quiet gentleman, with fewer curlicues than I'd bestowed on the baroness but equal irony. The door opened: four Scholars and Mrs. Etaris came in: and I said: "Please forgive my confusion, which surely is born out of ignorance, but who are you, under what authority do you operate, and under what charges do you propose to arrest me?"

"Murder," said the quiet man imperturbably, and grabbed my wrist.

Behind him the Chancellor of Morrowlea raised one perfectly groomed eyebrow. "Most dramatic a delivery. I am sure we are all deeply curious about the answers to the young man's other questions."

The quiet man appeared startled. He half-turned without letting go of my wrist, and together we considered the party who had entered.

Behind the Chancellor (and what was *she* doing there?) was Dominus Lukel, the Morrowlea professor of Self-Defense, and with them two other Scholars whose hoods proclaimed their affiliations to Oakhill and Quance. From the quiet man's angle he conceivably could not see Mrs. Etaris, who was shorter than all of them and stood closest to the door with unabashed amusement on her face.

I ignored the quiet man as haughtily as I could and performed a necessarily abbreviated courtesy. "Chancellor, Domine Lukel, Scholars."

"Jemis," said Dominus Lukel, his voice a little distressed. I felt a stab of shame that he saw me in such a situation, which was hardly what any university, let alone one of the Circle Schools, desired of its students.

The quiet man was unmoved. "I am Cornelius Quent, Detective Inspector on the Flying Murder Squad out of Yrchester. And you, young man, are charged with the murder—"

On these words the door banged open again. I looked away from Inspector Quent to see quivering in the doorway a vision of late Astandalan aristocratic privilege in all its glory. Mrs. Etaris stepped out of the way without losing her smile.

She was not tall, was rather thin, and had probably never been particularly beautiful, but the Marchioness of the Woods Noirell had *presence*.

"Who are *you* and what are you doing with my grandson?" she demanded with no preamble whatsoever.

"I am Inspector Quent, ma'am," said Inspector Quent again, with commendable patience. "This young man is charged with the murder of Fitzroy Angursell in the form of a dragon."

He said it with no indication he had noticed the absurdity. I could not see his face clearly, so I watched the audience, whose number was even now being swelled by the arrival of Hal, who went over immediately to stand next to Mrs. Etaris, out of the way of my grandmother's exceedingly wide skirts. His ankle must not have been sprained at all, I realized, merely twisted, if he was wandering around town without apparent discomfort.

The Scholars all appeared half-amused, half-shocked; Mrs. Etaris and Hal were entirely amused; I could not see my father behind the bulk of Dominus Lukel; and my grandmother lifted her elaborately coiffed head and stared gimlet-like at the Inspector.

"And what authority have you?"

"I am a Detective Inspector on the Flying Murder Squad out of Yrchester, ma'am."

His voice was still polite; I was impressed.

"Rondelan police?"

"Yes, ma'am."

"Then you are three times a fool."

He did blink at this round condemnation; I'd decided to watch him instead of the audience. "I beg your pardon, ma'am?"

"One cannot *murder* a dragon. It is in the laws."

Why, I wondered, did both my grandmother and my uncle know this fact? It hadn't even occurred to me to look it up, let alone that there would be some sort of precedent in the laws to deal with the (in fiction, at least) heroic slaughter of supposedly mythological monsters.

I was never going to make a good lawyer.

"Moreover, that dragon was not Fitzroy Angursell. It was drawn from the wild lands to test my grandson for his suitability as my heir."

That was what the dragon had said. It seemed a likelier thing for my grandmother to know. Inspector Quent's face was discomposed. I sympathized. An elderly gorgon dressed in a wild late court style from her iron curls to her be-panniered incarnadine skirts was not what anyone expected.

"And third, and by far the most important: as a Rondelan policeman you have no authority to lay hands or charges on a person of Imperial rank."

For the first time Inspector Quent appeared genuinely perturbed. "Mr. Greenwing is not—"

"Mr. Greenwing is not his title, Inspector," said my grandmother with enormous majesty. "He is the Viscount St-Noire, and
he is not to be touched by the likes of you."

I had no idea if that privilege still held after the Fall, but the
mere thought of it made my blood boil.

"One moment," I began.

"Now is not the time for radical politics," Hal said firmly, and
with even more splendid grandeur stepped forward in his full ducal
mode and swept a court bow to my grandmother. "Marchioness."

Everyone stirred and rearranged around this new figure, like
iron filings on the introduction of a magnet. I caught a glimpse of
my father's smile as Dominus Lukel shook his head (Hal, I feared,
had never been one of his favourite students). It was hard to tell
whether amusement or disbelief was foremost in anyone else'
minds.

My grandmother unbent enough to produce a taut, but perfectly correct, curtsey. "Duke."

The general rearrangement had brought Baroness Temby into
my grandmother's line of sight. The Marchioness, to my awe, managed to rise to a still greater height of offended pride.

"If you have come on an errand to marry off that daughter
of yours, rest you assured that I will never grant the Viscount my
blessing to court her."

To my even greater astonishment, Baroness Temby actually
blushed. Behind her my father raised a hand to his mouth to hide
his expression. Inspector Quent's face was a study in professional composure and human amusement. I decided I liked Inspector
Quent, even if he let go of my wrist but did not move away from
his position, which kept mine firmly behind the counter.

I decided it was time to add a stir to the pot. "My lord duke has mentioned that his aunt Honoria has been compiling a list of eligible ladies." I presented this without further comment, and was delighted by Hal's subsequent fight to retain his equilibrium.

"Honoria Leaveringham always was a great snob," the Marchioness said with great satisfaction. "I am pleased to hear you taking an interest in your duty, Viscount. I came into town today to discuss your coming-of-age ball."

The only thing that occurred to me to say was the truth: "My birthday isn't until February, Marchioness."

"What of it? To do things correctly takes time. It is all too unfortunate that you cannot be presented at the Imperial court."

She made this sound as if it were my fault. I wondered briefly what she would make of my father's reappearance, and rather looked forward to that revelation when it came. I gave her a half-bow, as I was still obstructed by the counter. "I comprehend, Grandmama, and am grateful for your solicitude, but perhaps we might discuss it another day? The Chancellor of Morrowlea has come with her fellow Scholars to see the dragon, and I would feel most remiss in courtesy to keep them waiting even for so, er, joyous a cause."

If I recalled my lessons correctly, the Chancellor of one of the Circle Schools was of equal rank to an Imperial Count, and rumours at Morrowlea had made our elegant Chancellor to have been originally a Ystharian princess of very high degree and delightfully scandalous activities.

"The sentiment does you credit," my grandmother said at last.

I remembered something my mother had once told me, that some people loved nothing so much as having others indebted to them. Knowing that I would probably regret it in future, but fairly sure that my grandmother was one of that number, I smiled as winningly as I could. "Grandmama, did you by any chance come in your coach?"

"Of course I did. I am not some flighty young debutante to *ride!*"

This was said with a glance at the Chancellor, whose smile now was faintly appreciative. The stories passed down from student to student at Morrowlea had the Chancellor escaping an arranged marriage to run off with a troupe of acrobats, which was *surely* not entirely true.

"It would be most gracious and generous of you to permit us to borrow it, as the dragon is in Dartington and I'm sure the Scholars will have certain tools with them."

I larded on the compliments for—I swear—several minutes. Eventually I persuaded her to come herself (for she was not going to let her carriage go off without her, and dismissed the idea of visiting any of the townspeople with a magnificent snort of disdain) to see General Ben, whom she recalled from the year they had been presented at court, some time in the halcyon days of the Empress Anyoë.

Everyone finally filtered out but myself still behind the counter, Inspector Quent still blocking my exit, and Mrs. Etaris holding the door. She shut the door behind my father, who contrived to give the impression that he'd been stuck in the corner as an uninvolved bystander that whole time, and looked at me. "May I expect you tomorrow morning, Mr. Greenwing?"

"Presuming I am neither waylaid nor arrested, yes."

"You need only send me a message if another claim on your time appears."

"Thank you, Mrs. Etaris."

Inspector Quent said, "You are quite certain, I presume, Mrs. Etaris, that the dragon was not an enchanted human being?"

"I am no wizard, and certainly no expert in such metamorphosis, but insofar as can be reasonably adjudged, then yes, I am quite certain."

"Not even Fitzroy Angursell?" The inspector pulled out a leather-bound notebook from his pocket and made a note in it.

Mrs. Etaris hung up her coat on the hook behind the door and pulled out a long hatpin from her millinery. I eyed the eight-inch spike with respect. Now *there* was a usefully hidden weapon. It wasn't needed for a man's tricorner, alas, unless it was as liberally bestowed with feathers as the one Violet had sported on her visit. Mrs. Etaris' confections seemed to need the spike to balance. The question occurred to me whether she favoured the abundance of decorations in order to warrant the hatpin.

"I can't imagine why you should think that would make a difference, but I am convinced it was not the infamous poet: the dragon demonstrated no indication of a sense of humour beyond dry irony, which was hardly Fitzroy Angursell's style."

"I do defer to your literary judgment, Mrs. Etaris, as you know. Mr. Greenwing, will you permit me to accompany you on this scholarly mission to examine the dragon? Quite apart from completing my assigned task—which is to see justice prevail, I assure you—I am curious."

Mrs. Etaris seemed to know him, and moreover, like him; even respect him, if I read the look in her eyes correctly. I smiled and half-bowed. "I have no objections, Inspector, though I fear there will be insufficient room in the carriage."

He was not quite composed enough to hide his relief. "I shall fetch my horse from the hotel stables. You go towards Dartington?"

"It's in the old granary at the edge of the five-acre field," I said.

Mrs. Etaris nodded and promised to give directions. Inspector Quent laughed and said he might prefer a map, if past results were any indication. I left Mrs. Etaris laughing, and wondered what their shared past was for a few pleasant moments before the complicated present once more overwhelmed me.

***

There was not enough room in the coach for everyone, for all that it was an antique falarode drawn by six horses and theoretically seated ten.

The male Scholar was not a small man; neither (for the opposite reason) was Dominus Lukel; and one glance at the Marchioness' pink skirts was sufficient to know she wasn't going to share her seat very well.

"I shall ride with the coachman," I announced. Jack had already made his unobtrusive away around the horses' heads to speak with him.

"What, like a commoner?"

I was ready for this. I gave my grandmother my best court bow, in the form appropriate for heir to incumbent of an imperial title between count and duke, which I had practicing under Hal's tutelage for just such an occasion. Hal's lips twitched; so did the Chancellor's.

"Madam, it will be an honour to guide such a noble assemblage on its way. A Duke Imperial—a Marchioness Imperial—the Chancellor of Morrowlea—three Scholars of three of the most superlative universities of the Nine Worlds—there is, I assure you, nothing common about it."

"Harrumph," said the Marchioness, but Hal was a good teacher (as had been the Etiquette Master at Morrowlea), and in morbid curiosity I had looked in the books to determine where my putative rank stood in relation to the rest. I had not yet come of age, nor been officially recognized by the law in my title, and under those conditions Scholars of the Circle Schools outranked me.

Hal made a face at me as he climbed the stairs after the Chancellor. I wished him well of the monologue my grandmother would likely inflict on them, shut the door, and climbed up on the box seat.

The coachman spoke morosely. "I am surrounded by Greenwings, one not to be called by that name, and t'other ought not be."

The coachman had, in my opinion, some relation to the Good Neighbours whose boundaries were folded through the Woods like the cream in a blackcurrant fool, and seemed to take great (if somewhat subterranean) delight in gnomic pronouncements and strangely-obtained knowledge. "Mr. Fancy, can your horses bear eight?"

"Eh, they've had a long rest. Ain't had a full load since your mother's marriage."

"Isn't that the time everybody but the wedding party got lost?" Jack said.

"Eh, I wasn't coachman," replied Mr. Fancy, flicking his long whip to start the horses off. I glanced at my father, but his face was uninformative. Perhaps the whip bothered him; perhaps it didn't. "How's your driving, young sir?"

I watched as he took a far tighter corner than I would ever have tried with six horses and a falarode. Several pedestrians scattered; more stared after the monstrous assemblage. Jack slouched and tugged down a shapeless felt hat. I settled mine on my head, wished for Mrs. Etaris' hatpin, and found a discreet handhold. "Not good enough to drive a coach-and-six through town, Mr. Fancy."

"Not many as can," he replied complacently, and touched the horses up to a rolling trot. We had to go directly down the centre of the road, as there was no room for us otherwise.

The horses (I guessed) saw a relatively open route ahead of them—occupied as it was merely by a handful of schoolchildren, several women with baskets, Mr. Kim the fishmonger's assistant with a barrow, said barrow full of fish and what must have been either the last or the first ice of the season; someone's wandering rooster; a small white dog; and a flock of pigeons. Apparently disdaining all these as obstacles, the six black horses set forward at a dead run down the slope towards the old humpback bridge over the Rag that all the waggoners complained about.

"You're, er, not going to try the humpback bridge, surely?" I asked.

"Eh, it's not exactly the Leap," said Mr. Fancy, and sprung the horses.

I gave up on remonstrance and looked for something to hold on to.

The carriage hit a small bump before the bridge and launched itself into the air. It landed on the crest, bounced up again to miss the entire awkward dismount of the bridge, and the horses, encouraged by Mr. Fancy, cantered on up the hill to the highway.

"That'll clean out the cobwebs," said my father. He was grinning in wild delight: and my heart clenched at the way that his face was lit like the portrait of him as a young man.

"Too right," said Mr. Fancy. The horses settled down to their rolling trot again, a plume of dust from a sudden gust of wind catapulted me into a series of all-too-familiar sneezes, and my father laughed aloud. The coachman carefully put his whip into its holder. "Now then, lads, tell me the news from outside the Woods. I heard tell as the young lord was found naked as a babe in a barrel at the edge of the Forest?"

Chapter Twenty-Three
Anatomy of a Dragon

"WE SHALL HAVE to go back into the Forest," my father said.

I nodded, unable to speak through convulsive sneezes no less odious for being familiar. I had recovered from the dust, but then we had turned onto the main highway and into a cloud of thick smoke from someone's bonfire.

"We shall have to consult the Wild Saint, if we can find him. There's the Hunter in Green to consider."

I nodded again through my sneezes, though I was mystified. Was it possible they were the same person? But I could not speak through the smoke, and my father moved on to chat with Mr. Fancy: old stories of when Jack had been courting my mother the Lady Olive, and battle stories, for Mr. Fancy had, it appeared, gone on one of the shorter campaigns for an 'adventure', which he seemed to have more than found.

I watched the road unspooling ahead of the six black horses and sneezed intermittently and felt physically awful and emotionally down. The edge of doubt was still there, though now directed to my father's views of my life.

It was as irrational to dread his ability to comprehend as it was to dread his imposture. The repeated inward argument did not melt the suspicions or worries. Too many times I sneezed and caught him looking wonderingly at me. It might have been a trick of eye-patch, hat-shadow, dark beard, that made those glances seem tinged with disdain, dismay, disapproval, dislike.

It might have been: but the cold sludgy doubts would not let me rationalize those fears away.

So I watched the highway with blind eyes, and sneezed, and shivered, a felt a deep malaise very much only partially physical. I was glad withal when Inspector Quent cantered up to join us just before the White Cross and the Dartly Road.

I turned away from the waystone, hoping the movement was masked by the need to grab hold of the seat-back as the coach made the turn. My father reached at the same time along to grab the rail and clasped my hand instead.

For a moment I felt an almost physical pain as my heart tried simultaneously to leap with joy and congeal with horror. Then we were around the turn, and Jack let go to resettle himself, and Mr. Fancy asked me for directions to the old granary, and I tried with all my might to be the aloof and nonchalant young gentleman I ought to have been.

***

In death as in life the dragon was compelling.

The old granary was on the edge of the five-acre field given over to the Harvest Fair. It had been the tithe-barn for the region back when Ragnor still gave its taxes to the Empire in the form of grain and other produce. That practice had ceased with the development of better forms of agriculture and the annexation of better grasslands. Dartington and the rest of the barony had come to pay their taxes in gold and their tithes in art and service, and the old granary was thenceforth used for extraordinary surplus, for winter assemblies, and for occasional musters or other storage.

The dragon lay outstretched down the centre of the room. It was a wooden hall, with a beautiful hammer-beam roof, exalted as a church and far lovelier than the baron's new one. It had a band of windows the whole length of each wall, high up under the eaves. It was not far off midday when we arrived, and even the low November sun slanted down golden as summer, catching thousands of dust motes sparkling.

The air smelled of bitter saffron and honey of the Woods and the rich warmth of the hay that had been in here last. There was no hint of corruption to my nose, for all the dragon had been dead a month.

Its head faced away from us, oriented towards the north wall. That was the way corpses were laid out, with their faces towards the pole. I was glad that someone had decided to honour the dragon that way, and wondered who it had been.

It was the colour of green jade, the colour of my mother's honey-crock, and of the well-head between village green and white-washed inn in the village of St-Noire, which between them had held two answers to its riddle.

Its tail narrowed, then flared at the tip to a flattened portion shaped like the spade in a deck of cards or one of the heart-shaped leaves of the Tillarny limes of the Woods. Golden spikes ran the length of its spine, culminating in the great crown of golden horns around its head. One wing was folded tightly against its side, the other outstretched until the spine on the end of its leading rib touched the far wall.

The dust motes eddied in the draught from the open door. They passed through the shafts of light pouring in from the high windows, now brilliant, now invisible. When I had run through the Woods in the hours before midnight, running to reach the village of St-Noire to answer the dragon's riddle, fireflies in their hundreds of thousands had filled the darkness around me in a river of light like the River of Stars famous from the poets.

"It is very definitely a dragon," pronounced my grandmother, and with that I recalled the party at my back.

I sneezed, half out of habit, and beckoned the Scholars and Inspector Quent to follow me to its head. My father said, "I'll tell the Darts and the General that we're here," and departed. I wrestled with an incongruous hurt that he did not want to examine the dragon his son had slain. We did ought to tell the Squire we were here; and he could not say what he thought with so many strangers present; and … and I was disappointed.

"Who *was* that man?" demanded the Marchioness: a better question than she knew.

"My great-uncle's companion," Hal replied easily. "Will you take my arm, Marchioness?"

I turned back to my little group. "This is Inspector Quent," I said, and looked hopefully at Dominus Lukel.

"Dominus Vitor of Quance, Professor of Anatomy, and Domina Enory of Oakhill, whose specialties include magical creatures and curses."

She smiled reassuringly. "Just in case. There are stories about dragons and their effects."

I stared with sinking heart at the dragon. All I needed was for it to have been exerting a baleful influence across the barony.

"You do not seem to have inflicted any injuries back here," Inspector Quent said thoughtfully. "Will you—that is, if the Scholars are amenable, would you please take us through the battle as it appeared to you?"

"Certainly," I replied, trying to sound enthusiastic, and led them to the head and the ruined eye. I stared at it for a moment, then transferred my attention to Dominus Lukel, whom I knew best. "We were, as you heard, in a large pavilion out in the field. Hal and I had entered the cake competition. We'd just finished our entry, I was still holding a cake knife and a spatula, one in each hand, when I noticed that part of the roof was on fire."

I paused there while Hal and my grandmother joined us. Hal smiled at me. I felt relieved to have him there with me, as he had stood beside me on other occasions. "The dragon was silhouetted against the canvas when we looked up. Everyone froze. It climbed down through the hole its fire had made." I made a vague gesture to indicate its motion. "It stopped in front of my uncle, who was petrified with fright. The dragon smiled at him and said something about him being a fine rabbit for the eating. No one else did anything so I said 'Hey!' and the dragon looked at me."

I wouldn't mention that Mrs. Etaris, of all present, had been the only other person to grope for a weapon. Dominus Lukel smiled with eager interest. "What did you do then?"

The side door of the grange opened. Ben and Sir Hamish came in, half-hidden by the folded wing and out of my direct line of vision. I swallowed disappointment (was my father not coming at all?) and turned back to Dominus Lukel.

"I asked it what it was doing. Coming for its payment, it said.

Then it opened its mouth and started to go back towards my uncle."

"Yes?" Inspector Quent's voice was all mild encouragement. "You saw the dragon turning with open mouth towards your uncle, and?"

"I didn't want him to be *eaten*."

"Of course not."

No need to go into all the details of my vindictive desire for him to pay for what he had done, which at the time I was half-convinced was the murder of his brother my father.

"There was no time to think, nor any *need* to. All I thought was that Dominus Lukel had told us that a dragon's three weaknesses were its eyes, its armpits, and the very base of its jaw, at the top of its throat. All I had were the spatula and the cake knife, so I—" I stopped, frowned. "I can't remember if I threw the spatula first or vaulted the table."

"Vaulted the table," said Hal.

"Right. I vaulted the table—our table, that was—then jumped onto the one next to my uncle, and then I threw the spatula into the back of its throat to make it swallow." I started to act out the motions, finding my memory clear with the movements. Dominus Lukel was nodding with great encouragement. "The dragon swung its head at me. For a moment its jaw was exposed but I could see a glow and I thought, I didn't want to stab *into* its fire, and then there was the palate—I suppose we can see if it's really asbestos? We had a debate in class about that, and I didn't want to chance it in the moment."

"Dear Emperor," said Inspector Quent faintly.

"Shh," said Dominus Lukel.

I gestured with the hand that had held the knife. "So when it came towards me, I jumped and grabbed hold of one of its horns— I'd thrown the spatula, did I say that?—and got my knees to grip on either side of its snout, and stabbed down into its eye with the cake knife. I was worried I would miss the optic nerve opening … we had talked about that, too."

Inspector Quent walked up to peer at the knife. Its hasp was barely visible in the congealed jelly of the eye; the bent tip stuck out about an inch at the base of the skull.

"I was worried I would miss the brain," I said, a bit lamely.

Dominus Lukel said, "Jemis is one of the finest students I have ever had."

"He clearly inherited his father's battle-courage," murmured Inspector Quent, shaking his head.

The Chancellor inclined her head to me. "We are very proud to have had Mr. Greenwing as a student at Morrowlea."

"Oh yes," breathed Dominus Vitor, but his attention (thank the Lady) was on the dragon. "May I?"

"Please," said Sir Hamish, coming forward to introduce himself. Domina Enory drew from her reticule a handsome pair of hand-held spectacles made of wood, silver, and crystal.

I found Hal beside me, and behind him Mr. Dart (and when had he come in?). "Zauberi glasses," Hal said, indicating the spectacles. "To show magic in visible form."

We watched the Scholars at work. Domina Enory continued her examination through the glasses. Dominus Lukel, Dominus Vitor, and the Chancellor began measuring various external features of the dragon. They quickly drew Hal, Mr. Dart, Inspector Quent, and me to assist with this task.

I was vaguely aware of other comings and goings. Someone brought chairs for the Marchioness and General Ben, so they could sit in estate to watch us work and gossip of times, people, and places long since gone. I rather wanted to listen to their tales, half-hearing names out of poetry and history. I consoled myself that there would be other occasions. Tales from the Astandalan court were something I could ask my grandmother about next time I had a dining engagement with her.

Eventually they ran out of externalities to measure. The rest of us drew back to allow Dominus Vitor and Domina Enory to discuss the best way to anatomize the dragon without indissolubly soiling the broad wooden planks of the grange floor. I found myself this time next to my father, who had returned who-knew-when in the proceedings. Perhaps he had been the one to bring the chairs for the General and the Marchioness.

We were a little apart from the others, close to the wall, not far from the great curve of the haunches. I wondered vaguely about how dragons reproduced, whether like basilisks they were made by magic and intent, whether they truly were mere (mere?) manifestations of chaotic magic, or whether they could mate and procreate like any other animal.

"I am glad you didn't let it eat Vorel," my father said softly. He leaned back against the wall, out of the slanting shaft of light. The dust motes were still still brilliantly dancing; the saffron-and-honey scent of the air was stronger. I sneezed, my throat thick, the malaise roiling my insides as the air grew heavier. It had been so much better when I'd been preoccupied with the numbers of measure and ratio.

"I was tempted," I admitted very quietly. "That was right after

I'd first begun to wonder if he had … murdered …"

"Thank you," he said even more quietly.

My nose and throat ached. I turned my gaze firmly back to the activity around the carcass. Domina Enory had her glasses up again, to examine everything in the room—looking for traces of a blood curse?—including us as part of the audience.

I wished in fierce defiance of my constitution's stupid weakness to magic and the hollowness left by the wireweed that I could shout out my father's name, that he stood right there beside me. I turned my head at the thought to tell him that I was so glad that he was alive that I could almost not bear it—

Out of the corner of my eye I saw swift movement. I turned my head sharply. Domina Enory had crossed the space between us—and the moment was, once again, lost.

I took refuge in a clean handkerchief. She still had the glasses up; they made her eyes appear huge, the pupils distorted.

It was no surprise, really, when she said: "Young man, did you know you were cursed?"

Chapter Twenty-Four
Two Sticks and a Stone

"THERE IS ALWAYS the question," wrote one of the poets of the 'Two Sticks and a Stone' school, "of what, precisely, is being revealed by being hidden in a code. If known to none it is dumb and pregnant of inaccessible meaning as an animal and not to be considered language; if known to one and one alone it is solipsism and worse than inaccessible, for it is as deliberately exclusive of all the rest of creation as a suicide; if known and knowable to all it is taken for granted and inaccessible through its lack of mystery. It is the code known by a few that creates an inexhaustible mystery in the space between sense and significance and sign. In short, it is the *intimation* of esoteric meaning that creates the poet and reveals through the commonplace the divine."

Lady Pinel was generally held to be a better poet than theorist, but the passage had struck me and stuck with me. In the game of Poacher the signs of cards and sequence and interruption had a layer of sense, of meaning, that was accessible to anyone with half an hour's instruction in the game. The deeper level of significance was built out of the doubled and redoubled encodings of the cards and their conjunctions.

The poems of the Two Sticks and a Stone poets were often read as simple, even naïve, descriptions of everyday objects, situations, and people. Unlike the more famous Voonran puzzle-poets whose works had inspired the school, the poems were not immediately and unabashedly difficult. The art of the Gainsgooding conspirators was cheerful, popular, even celebratory: only once one stumbled into an incongruity between sense and significance and sign—most often by seeing in a grouping of images or objects (or, still more, subjects) the echo of another style or school's celebrated symbolic meanings—that one began to realize there might be a mystery in what had seemed opaquely and complacently bland.

Ariadne nev Lingarel wrote a lengthy narrative poem about her experiences in prison. For centuries it had been read as a fine example of a minor poet of the Entrian School, who were much given to autobiographical narrative poetry that at its best rose up into extraordinary acts of communion between one naked soul and its audience.

On Being Incarcerated in Orio Prison had a few such passages. These were excerpted in anthology collections of regional or period poets. Appreciative readers who turned to the full text were usually daunted by the thousands upon thousands of lines of beautifully turned poetry whose insights into nature or architecture or society were disappointingly never as powerful as those three or four passages where the poet cried out the state of her soul.

Paging through the volume, looking for the context of my favourite one of these, fresh off the correspondence with Mr. Dart about the Gainsgooding conspirators and the Two Sticks and a Stone poets, I had come across a sequence describing the furnishings in the fair Ariadne's cell—and noted one odd, old-fashioned word for the fabric of a cushion.

If I had not just written a letter to Mr. Dart explaining why the word *ebraöni* was used by one of the conspirators not only because it was a much better metrical fit in the line than the usual word in Antique Shaian for wool but also because the literal transla-tion, 'mountain-cloud', was used by a very famous Voonran haiku poet—the very one, indeed, whose book my father had carried with him everywhere—to refer not only to wool but to having the wool pulled over one's eyes, like fog rolling down a mountainside.

Well, if I had not just written all of that in a letter, I, like all the rest of her readers, would also have passed over the fair Ariadne's use of the word as metrically convenient and a pretty echo of Lo en Tai.

Half joking to myself I had begun to examine the poem using the tools I had learned for the Gainsgooding conspirators. Entire-ly to my amazement the competent, lovely, and mostly undistin-guished poem began to reveal dizzying chasms between sign and sense and significance.

I had fallen steadily more ill as I tried to unfold even the be-ginning layers of meaning. I had gone on long runs; I had told Violet my half-baked theories that the poem was, first, an answer to the conspirators (who had never been connected with Ariadne's near-contemporaneous treason; but then again some of the prima-ry conspirators had never been identified except by the pregnant absences of certain key links in the games of the poets); and, sec-ondly, a reflection of, even a revelation of, the secrets of the prison.

Not that any of this had been coherent to anyone but me.

Domina Enory took me to the back corner of the grange to work through what she described as my 'most incredibly fascinating' magical signature. My father was called over by Dominus Lukel to apply his strength to flipping over the dragon. As Mr. Dart's arm prevented him from being of much assistance to this (considerable) effort, I waved him over to join us.

When I introduced him, Domina Enory gave him a cursory, mostly inattentive glance halfway through and halfway over her magical spectacles. Then she did a classic double take and lifted the glasses to examine him more carefully.

"And *you*," she breathed.

Mr. Dart looked alarmed. "I say, domina!"

She lifted an ironic eyebrow. "You must expect some reaction to your arm?"

Relief flitted very quickly across his face. "Most people have not said anything, ma'am, except for how bad a break it must be to be so long healing."

"It appears stable for the moment, so if you will concur I shall continue to examine Lord St-Noire first."

"Certainly," he said.

"Mr. Greenwing," I corrected. I glanced across automatically at my father, who had set his shoulder to the dragon's chest. *Surely*—

My thought went nowhere as Domina Enory moved her arm and an eddy of air brought saffron and sneezes to my nose.

"Excuse me," I said when I could, smiling apologetically at her.

Domina Enory regarded me gravely through the Zauberi glasses. I felt as exposed and uncomfortable as when Sir Hamish turned a painterly eye on me. I should grow a beard, I thought inconsequentially; and wondered whether I would look more like my father if I did.

"Is there, Lord St-Noire—"

"Mr. Greenwing."

"My apologies. Is there a reason, Mr. Greenwing, why a curse would coil more and more tightly around you every time you look at that man? The one introduced as the General's companion."

Mr. Dart reached out and set his hand on my shoulder. I was grateful for the touch. I felt dizzy.

"The dragon …"

"It is not the dragon."

Domina Enory's cool academic dryness almost masked her intense desire to know and to understand. Her regard was unwavering. "Mr. Greenwing, you appear—unsurprised, I might say, that there is a curse; deeply shocked that it is to do with that man; and yet almost immediately resigned to the fittingness of its being so."

My face was far too open.

Mr. Dart's fingers dug into my shoulder. One connected with a knot of tension, causing a kind of almost-pain to sproing through my system.

"Yes," I said finally, dully, confused, and, yes, resigned, and, again, yes, expecting something else to happen.

"Please would you expand?"

She must be a good tutor. I wondered briefly whether I could conceivably go not for Law but instead for magic … but at the end of a degree in Law I would have a useful profession. Lawyers were never out of fashion.

Mr. Dart said, "Perhaps the professor will be able to help you."

I stepped back, and back again, away from his touch and her intensity. The back of my legs hit a chair and I half-fell into its seat. Domina Enory said nothing about any irregularity of conduct, instead coolly and composedly drawing another chair from the line along the wall in which to sit. Mr. Draw drew a third out to close the circle, which gave an illusion of privacy, if not security.

I took a deep breath. "Domina, may I have your word that you will keep these matters to yourself unless I tell you otherwise?"

She considered for a moment before nodding. I could see her regret for a lost paper (or, who knows, a monograph; I would not have been entirely surprised if I had a fascinating enough magical signature, by this point of the year, to warrant one). It took a moment, but I was able to make myself say, "I hope some of it, at least, will cease to be secret soon."

"I shall not betray your trust."

She did deal in curses. Presumably she had a vested interest in not becoming the subject of one herself.

"I have a number of—it sounds so histrionic, I'm sorry—enemies, or people whom I seem to have made enemies, and could easily imagine a couple of them cursing me. Mr. Dart and I fell afoul of a cult to the Dark Kings about a month ago … in rescuing me from a fascination cast by one of the priests he received the stone arm."

She lifted her glasses to inspect first him and then me. She set them down again in her lap, her fingers stroking the rich wood. "It is possible the same wizard was responsible for both, but your curse is much older and much subtler, Mr. Greenwing. Its physical effects are obviously different, and its signature may only indicate that the one who cursed you also dabbled in the forbidden arts. The touch of the Dark Kings infects all who try to deal with them."

I nodded as if this made sense. "The second possibility is that I … while I was at university …" I squirmed in my seat, flushing with shame at the whole episode with Lark. "I was … beguiled and

... and drugged by another student who ... I thought ... She was using wireweed to—" I could not bear to say 'enslave'— "to endear me to her and to steal my magic. I didn't know I had any, but that's what people have said ... I have been sick from the ... She stopped in the spring, we had an argument and I broke from her then, and all the summer and autumn I have been ill from the ... the process of ... ceasing to be ... on ... the drug."

"The last time you took any was this spring? When did you begin?"

I winced. "Nearly three years. Since Winterturn of the first year."

Mr. Dart shook his head in a sympathy that for once I found reassuring.

Domina Enory said, "Does the Chancellor know?"

"I haven't told her," I replied sharply.

She regarded me through her glasses for another few moments. Acutely uncomfortable under her huge-eyed gaze, I shifted my feet and glanced over her shoulder at where my father now was standing next to Hal. Both looked at us, concern visible in their bearing; and I thought with a queer wrench in my heart how marvellous and incredible it was that those two people should stand there caring about me.

"Your relationship with that man is of more than three years' duration."

I sneezed; as if that were going to hide anything any more than my uncle's blustering emotion did.

"Mr. Greenwing?"

She was a professor, that was certain; she had that inexorable patience of questioning.

I shifted position again. "Yes," I said, and it was an admission, not the triumphant acclamation it ought to have been. Too much of my soul was still angled out defensively to protect the man I had thought buried under the White Cross.

"How long, Mr. Greenwing?"

My throat was sore from my earlier bout of coughing; my chest felt tight, heavy with frustration and a grief I did not at all understand and those encircling doubts that came crowding into my mind every time I relaxed my vigilance. The air was heavy with an acrid scent I did not recognize, tinged now with corruption like rotten meat.

They must have opened the dragon's stomach, I thought vaguely, automatically lifting the handkerchief.

Domina Enory was implacable. "How many years have you known him, Mr. Greenwing?"

I was so tired of being sick, at being at the beck and call of every passing whiff of magic or incense, at trying to fight off the thickness in my throat of grief and resignation and disbelief.

Mr. Dart laid his hand on my shoulder again. He shocked me and himself; we both jerked and exclaimed at the static discharge. In the strange way of things sometimes the accidental seemed pregnant with meaning, like one of those domestic poems used to plot apocalyptic revelations or revolutions.

A Scholar and two students seated in an old tithe-barn: figures hunting knowledge into whatever coverts it might be found.

Mr. Dart smiled in apology at the shock. I smiled back as he laid a comforting hand once more on my shoulder. I could not think why I had not yet answered what was not a very difficult question.

"All my life," I said simply. "He's my father, you see."

Domina Enory turned with her glasses trained now on him. After a moment she gave a grunt, turned back. "I think I begin to. Mr. Dart, was it? Will you ask Mr. Greenwing senior to join us, please?"

"Major Greenwing," Mr. Dart corrected, and strolled unhurriedly over to him. I swallowed down phlegm and felt acutely miserable.

"I'm sorry for sneezing so much," I said to the professor, feeling a strong need to say *something.* "Ever since this spring I've been fighting illness … and I seem to have some sort of adverse reaction to magic; it makes me sneeze. The dragons's smell doesn't help, either. And in addition I appear to have contracted a bad cold over the weekend."

"Mm," she replied with scintillating interest.

"You asked for me, domina?" my father said politely.

"Yes, ah, major. Your son has asked me to be discreet, which I assure you I will be. One does not live to be a curse breaker without the ability to keep one's counsel."

"Very good. What can I do to help release my son from his curse? Is it from the dragon?"

She dismissed the dragon with a wonderful shrug. "No, it appears that particular legend is not realized in this instance. Young Mr. Greenwing here has given me part of what I need to know. A second portion I would be grateful if you were to explicate."

He smiled with grim humour. "My variously reported deaths and reappearances?"

She nodded. "I am afraid all my knowledge beyond your heroism at Orkaty comes from the play."

"*Three Years Gone.* Well, to begin with, I was not the traitor of Loe—you may ask the General for the truth of that, if you will. I was instead trapped on the far side of the Border and was still there when the Empire fell. It was more or less three years later that I returned home to …"

He glanced at me. I nodded tiredly, pressing the handkerchief against my lips as if the pressure could offset my interior turmoil.

"I came home to a reception not too different from that described in the play. This was entirely to my shock, for I assumed I had been reported missing presumed dead. I was expecting to be greeted with astonishment and … joy … not to find my reputation destroyed, my son disinherited, and my wife married to someone else."

Mr. Dart gripped my shoulder firmly. It was still more or less comforting. But no one, I thought dismally, was holding my father's shoulder.

"What happened then?" Domina Enory asked with placid implacability.

"You might need Jemis or Perry to describe their side of the story. On my end I set off to Nên Corovel to ask the Lady's assistance. In the Forest I was waylaid, captured, enslaved, and eventually sold to a pirate galley. This summer I was freed by a ship of the Lady and made my way here."

Domina Enory nodded gravely. She glanced between me and Mr. Dart. "And your impressions?"

I was fighting back a pain in my chest that might have been more phlegm in my airways. It was conceivable, at any rate, that it was the developing cold.

Mr. Dart said, "About three weeks after Major Greenwing's

reappearance we heard that his body had been found in the Forest. My brother and Sir Hamish were good friends with the major, and Jemis and I have always been close … so we heard … the death was ruled a suicide."

"What was the general response?"

I could not, simply could not believe Domina Enory had asked that with my father and me right there.

Mr. Dart's hand stayed reassuringly warm and tactile on my shoulder. "In the community? Disbelief and dismay from most people. Nobody had wanted to believe all the talk of treason, despite all the rumours. Lady Olive was very pale and silent, I remember that, and Jemis was so overthrown he was sick in bed. Everyone was worried about him."

I flushed with shame—no, with *embarrassment*—at the weakness. I would not, I did not, feel shame for loving my father.

Domina Enory said, "Did something happen that had to do with your father this spring, Mr. Greenwing? I realize you did not know him to be alive at that point."

If I had felt embarrassed mentioning the wireweed it was nothing to describing what had happened with Lark at the end of the term. Making the whole thing worse was the fact that at some point over the past few weeks I had begun to wonder if Lark's betrayal of my confidence had extended to finding a pet playwright. If that were so it was *my* fault that the story of my father's terrible return had achieved the circulation it had with the success of *Three Years Gone*.

Even so I explained how I had one day broken Morrowlea's rules to tell Lark about my family, justifying it to myself at the time that I had wanted to marry her. How even as I grew progressively

sicker from the wireweed (or so I now understood my spring illness) she had written that stunning philippic; and how at the very
end of things I had stood up against her in the *viva voce* examinations and refuted her every point and process as intellectually and
morally bankrupt.

"And at what point did you collapse?" Domina Enory enquired
politely, as if she were asking about the state of the croquet lawn.

"Shortly after Lark whipped up the other students to the point
of stoning. Hal—did I say that Hal came down to stand with me?
That is, the duke—he and another friend, Marcan, took me to the
hospital wing and when I was a little recovered we went off on a
walking tour up to Fillering Pool."

Domina Enory made another quite wonderful shrug. I kept my
eyes on her. "Please correct me if I am wrong. The pattern appears
to be this: your father, who had been reported, falsely, twice dead
for contradictory reasons, returned to your joy and many other
people's consternation. He was then reported, again falsely, dead by
his own hand. Did you believe this?"

I bit my lip; had to drum up my courage to look my father in
the eye. "Yes." The eye closed in silent pain. I coughed wretchedly.
"I did not, then or ever, believe him a traitor, and I found it ex-
tremely hard to believe in his death." I coughed again, the tightness
not easing in the least. "I dreamed for months that he was not dead,
that he would come back again."

The eye opened in startlement. Please understand, I begged
him. Please understand that I would do anything for this to be real,
to be true, to be not a dream ...

"And you fell very sick. Did a physician attend you?"

"Yes, Doctor Imbrey and the local magister."

She nodded. "How long did it take you to recover?"

I wondered bleakly if I had ever recovered. My behaviour this past week suggested I hadn't. "About a month, I think."

"What can you tell me of those who attended you? The physician and the magister?"

I was frankly baffled, and accordingly spoke rather brusquely. "Dr. Imbrey is dead—it couldn't have been long after that, actually, because he wasn't there when my mother fell ill with the influenza the next winter."

"I think he fell into the river trying to save someone around Winterturn," Mr. Dart supplied. "My brother will remember."

"And the magister?"

I tried to affect nonchalance. "Oh, Dominus Gleason? He's still here, in town. He used to be a professor of magic in Fiella-by-the-Sea, but came back after the Fall."

"That's impossible," said my father. "He's dead."

Chapter Twenty-Five
The Importance of Being Earnest

THE WILD SAINT of the Arguty Forest was to me little more than a rumour, as unsubstantial as children's tales of smugglers' caves or dragons.

I looked at the very corporeal dragon whose body lay down the length of the old grange, jade green of scale and dark maroon of blood where Dominus Vitor had been cutting into it.

And the caves had been there, courtesy of ancient troglodytes and modern tippermongeramy-hunting Tufa.

As for the Wild Saint … the very name evoked faint thrills of excitement and trepidation and wonder. One did not—*I* did not—expect the irruption of the divine into ordinary life. Mr. Dart's eyes shone with delight every time the words were said.

Mr. Dart, I reflected (not for the first time), seemed halfway to a vocation as inconvenient to the heir of a prosperous family as his unexplored and inadmissible gift at wild magic.

The Wild Saint's name keep recurring because Domina Enory was starting to be baffled by the curse.

"I'm sorry," she said, each time she tried something new that did not work; and she was still trying to disentangle its components, not even to undo them. "The wizard who cast this is both skillful and subtle."

"He keeps wanting to teach me magic."

My father looked at me worriedly. "He's *not* the real Tadeo Gleason."

"Whoever he is, he makes my skin crawl."

"Your instincts are good," murmured Domina Enory, pulling out yet another magical implement from the box she'd brought with her.

Sir Hamish and Hal came over at this point to join us. "What's toward, Jack?" Sir Hamish asked in a low voice.

Jack said, "Did you ever notice a … change … in Tadeo Gleason's behaviour?"

Sir Hamish accepted the apparent non sequitur with sardonic equanimity. "Recently? No, except that he's been sniffing around Jemis, and he usually skulks in the background—which he always did."

"And before? Years ago, maybe."

"I was never friends with him, Jack. I know you used to visit him in Fiella-by-the-Sea when you were up there, but I always thought there was something unwholesome about his fascination with the Good Neighbours. All that just got worse after the Fall. Mind you, everybody with magic found the Fall disturbing. I suppose he was a little cracked by it. So many were."

Domina Enory was listening intently. She seemed to be waiting for something more. After a moment I awkwardly cleared my throat. "Yes, Mr. Greenwing?"

"Dominus Gleason bound the waystones. After the Fall, I mean, so their magic wouldn't keep … coming out. People say South

Fiellan was the least affected region—magically affected, that is, by the Fall. No one knows why but he's tolerated as an open wizard because of that."

Sir Hamish frowned. "How could he have done that? You're right that he does claim to bind them—he certainly does some of the old ceremonies at them—the final autumn ones this week, for instance—but now that I think of it he didn't come here till after the Interim was over. They closed the faculty of magic at Fiella and he came home to retire."

"Family?" Domina Enory asked delicately.

"His parents had died, his father before and his mother during the Interim—the Pestilence, I think it was. His father was a drunken oaf, no one missed him. I remember, the house was empty for a while. Not that we came into town much until the end of the Interim. Once we started coming in regularly he was well established." Sir Hamish sniffed. "I remember now, he snubbed me badly the first the time I saw him after he'd moved back. I'd gone to call on him out of respect for your old friendship, Jack, rather than any sense of my own, and he was so repellently nasty I never tried again."

Domina Enory nodded as if all was becoming clear to her. I wished I felt less stuffed-up and achey, for it was hard to govern my mind to think of anything but my sore throat and the tightness in my chest.

"Will you explain your earlier comment, major?" the professor asked.

Jack's face was grim. He watched Sir Hamish as he spoke. "Tadeo Gleason died before I went on the Seven Valleys campaign. I'd gone up to meet the General in Fiella-by-the-Sea, as we were sailing from there to the muster at Eil. I called on Tadeo, as I usually did, and found him dying of a cancer in the lungs."

"Were you with him when he died?"

He shook his head. "No. The General had arrived that day and I had to report to him and ask for leave to wait until—he never had many friends, Tadeo, and even though I never really *liked* him, we were countrymen and I didn't want to leave him to die alone. When I went back one of his fellows from the university was there—a woman professor, I think—I didn't think much of it at the time except that I was glad he wasn't totally alone. We buried him the next day in the churchyard of Saint Fiella's. The day after that I left for the front."

I realized I was gripping my chair-seat to the point of making my fingers ache. I unclenched them one by one, very consciously.

Mr. Dart was the one to speak my thought. "Keeping that secret is a fairly good reason to want to murder someone."

***

For a moment everything made sense: and a moment after that everything returned once more to confusion.

"But he *wasn't* murdered," I said, not quite able to address my father directly. (And why *not*? I demanded fruitlessly of myself. Why could I not shake this strangulation?) "We all thought he killed himself … but then he wasn't dead at all."

Domina Enory nodded. "Surely you have theories regarding that?"

Sir Hamish uttered a kind of bark of humourless laughter. "Our theory focuses on the person we'd thought had the only motive for getting Jack not only out of the way but also disgraced and attainted—his younger brother, who currently holds the estate."

"Whereas it should have gone to Jemis," said Hal.

Domina Enory put up her hand to stop Hal from continuing. "Please, your grace, one moment so I can have all the facts. Because you were held to have committed treason, Major, your brother took control of your estate instead of seeing that your son did? Did your wife not object?"

"My elder brother held the estate when I left for Loe. He was still in possession of it when the letter falsely announcing my disgrace came."

Sir Hamish nodded in turn. "Yes, and he died before the second letter—the true one—came."

Of course—the *second* letter *was* correct—For a moment the puzzle shifted as if about to be resolved, but—

"Forgive me for opening old sorrows, but how did he die?"

I couldn't hold on to the insight. "He broke his neck out hunting."

"Yes," said Sir Hamish. "He'd gone into the Forest—there's excellent game—and his horse missed a jump down in the Magarran gorge."

"Were there any witnesses?"

I took a sharp breath and coughed long and hackingly before I could catch my breath again. Sir Hamish said quietly, "No. Rinald liked to hunt alone. It was only when he didn't return for dinner that people started to worry. I was part of the search party that found him the next day. We didn't wonder about foul play. The Magarran limestone is treacherous to man and beast."

"Someone could very easily have disguised their activities, in short," said Mr. Dart.

We all knew who had the most to gain. I stared glumly at the dragon. That was another victory hollow in so many respects.

"Might they have bene working together?" I said at last.

"Tadeo and Vor never liked each other," my father began.

"Except it wasn't Tadeo," Mr. Dart finished. "If they were working together it makes sense why Jemis would be cursed to, well, if I have understood you correctly, to have a physical revulsion to certain thoughts or sentiments regarding his father."

My mind was too slow. Was this—all this physical malaise—the *curse*?

Domina Enory nodded gravely. "It explains many of the symptoms: that the three great illnesses were after his father's first unexpected return and subsequent appearance of suicide, when he—how old were you then?"

"It was after the Interim … about thirteen or fourteen," supplied Mr. Dart. I was speechless, my chest so tight I wondered that I could still breathe, my stomach roiling.

"Old enough to make a great deal of fuss seeking out the truth," suggested Domina Enory. "But young enough that no one would be shocked at so extreme a reaction. Then this spring, when the need to defend his father's honour overwhelmed every other consideration, enough to break free of serious enchantment and to waken a slumbering curse, whose effects would slowly subside only to gain incredibly in strength when his father returned *alive*—"

"Excuse me," I said abruptly, and fled outside.

***

I knelt behind the old grange until everything conceivable that could come out did so. I had, however, not eaten very much that day; and what I most wished to eject was not actually in my stomach or lungs at all. It felt very physical, nevertheless, and my body did its best to oblige.

At last I sat back on my heels. Fishing wearily for a clean handkerchief I discovered I was clean out.

"Ah! Have I the opportunity to supply the inexhaustible Mr. Greenwing with a handkerchief? Please, take mine."

I was too weak and dishevelled to do more than accept it gratefully, although I was not much in the mood to be grateful to the Honourable Rag.

"Here," he added; when I turned, aching in my ribs and heart and unable even to pretend I was glad to see him, he handed me a dipper of water.

I took it slowly, and sipped even more slowly from it. The dipper was battered old tin, the water cool and fresh and exactly what I needed. I cleared my throat. "Thank you."

He reached out a hand and pulled me easily to my feet. "You have not been eating enough, Mr. Greenwing."

This was said wholly earnestly. I was shaken. The Honourable Rag and I did not have a relationship of earnest friendship, or even earnest indifference. Earnestness, in point of fact, was nowhere evident in the Honourable Roald Ragnor's personality.

He was still holding my hand, I realized. He wore tan kid gloves, but I could feel the hard line of the ring he wore underneath. It was the match of mine, gold with a stylized flower-pattern in garnets—except that I was not wearing mine, as he could see; I had no gloves.

"You're not wearing the ring."

I gazed up at him. Tall, blond, muscular, and today, this moment, earnest as well as handsome. *I wonder*, I thought, and asked without pressure: "Why should I be?"

He seemed to have forgotten all his usual tricks of misdirection and bluff. He frowned. "You wouldn't have joined Crimson Lake if you didn't believe in the mission."

He put a faint emphasis on *you*, as if to indicate he thought me a man of great principle and honour. I stifled an inward hollow laugh to the effect that though I *tried*, I really did, I seemed always to end up making everything personal. By the Lady, I was *curious* about Crimson Lake.

"I won the ring in a game of Poacher," I said as neutrally as I could.

"Whom were you playing?"

"A Tarvenol duellist."

The most dangerous person I had ever met. That core of utter ruthlessness the game had revealed ... and the deeper core of iron honour that the game had so tantalizingly been beginning to show.

Never had I regretted a game of cards being untimely halted as that one.

The Honourable Rag narrowed his eyes in speculation. 'Tarvenol duellist' meant something to him, clearly; equally clearly he didn't feel like sharing his thoughts. I waited patiently. I could feel all the thick sickness hovering around me, waiting sluggishly but inevitably to envelop me again. I felt sluggishly resistant. I did not even try to draw my hand away.

Roald himself did not move. His eyes were narrowed, his attention turned inward, his face intent and thoughtful.

It wasn't long that we stood there like that. Not even a full minute, I supposed. It was long enough for me to think two things about the Honourable Roald Ragnor: One was that for the first time since I'd come home from university there was not even the hint of alcohol on his breath.

The second was that I always saw him either with his family or alone. Oh, I'd often seen him *talking* to people, and a few times out dining, but never with people our own age, who might conceivably be called his *friends*.

Abruptly he let go of my hand. I bent to pick up the dipper from the ground, which was a mistake: I gritted my teeth as nausea rose and stuffiness descended, and more slowly stood up again.

There had been only a dozen students in our year at the king-school (which anyway Roald had not gone to, the baron having preferred private tutors). That was not many for a community the size of Ragnor Bella. For whatever reason there had not been so many our age to begin with, and several had been lost in the Interim or moved away shortly thereafter. If you looked only at those who sat easily within the category of 'gentry' there *was* only the Honourable Rag, Mr. Dart, and me among the male persuasion. Roddy Kulfield was down a step, and he was anyhow away at sea, and Mr. Kim down another; and that was it. There were not very many girls; none of gentry rank in our year at all.

"Do you have any friends coming to visit over Winterturn?" I asked.

His face slid into its customary pleasant vacuity. "Been invited upcountry a ways for winter hunting. Boar's good this season, you know."

"I'm not much of a hunter," I replied, disappointed and a little puzzled, and then even more puzzled when intensity returned in one brief skewering glance.

"No? There's a fine trophy in yonder hall that says otherwise."

The dragon. Was he giving me *clues*? Or was I just reading too much into what I wanted to be true?

"I'd like to know more," I blurted. "About Crimson Lake."

"'Tis a paint colour," he said, grinning. "Ask Sir Hamish; I am happily ignorant."

And that was that. I sighed and watched him saunter off at a deceptive pace. I returned the dipper to the nail next to the well, fussed fruitlessly with my clothing in the hopes I didn't look a total mess. Glanced around the deserted area behind the old granary one last time.

Over by the bushes something white gleamed. One of my handkerchiefs, or Roald's, I thought, and went over to reclaim it. The way it was crumpled on the ground reminded me of—O Lady—

At the White Cross had been my *aunt*.

Chapter Twenty-Six
Anatomy of a Curse

"BUT WHAT ON earth was Lady Flora doing there?"

I grimaced.

Mr. Dart, who had met me at the door and thus received my blurted discovery, nodded sympathetically. "That is the question, isn't it? At least your memory's starting to come back."

I nodded, which set up a throbbing in my sinus cavity. I must have looked particularly green around the gills, for Mr. Dart grasped me firmly by the arm and drew me over to where Domina Enory and Hal were deep in conversation.

"Ah, there you are back again," said Hal, quite as if my disappearing to be sick in the bushes was commonplace—which it *wasn't*, thank the Lady. "Domina Enory and I have come up with an idea, Jemis, but we'll need to go back to the workroom in the Hall. Will that be acceptable, Mr. Dart?"

"Of course. I'll tell Hamish. Do you want, ah, the major?"

"I don't believe his presence will be necessary," the professor replied. I looked across the dragon's body. My father stood next to Ben, who seemed to have finally been able to trade his place next to the Marchioness with the Chancellor. The waves of roiling sickness churned. I put my hand on the back of Hal's chair, hoping my dizziness was not apparent.

"Go on," said Mr. Dart. I blinked at him. "To the house," he added, and frowned.

"It's to be expected," Domina Enory said briskly, standing up. "Come, Mr. Greenwing, will you take my arm and show me the way?"

"Yes," I said, grateful to have a simple and clear task to do. It seemed longer than usual to get to the Darts' house, even though Hal paid no attention to any of the flora we passed. I even pointed out a patch of saffron crocus.

"Thank you, Jemis," he said, barely glancing at it. "Domina Enory, are you *sure* he should be reacting like this?"

"We have been waking the magic. Curses are strange things, half-alive at times. It will know, at some level, that we are trying to remove it."

They continued to talk. I focused on not losing my footing on the road, and not losing my bearing, either. The fog had come back, but this was one of the most familiar roads in the barony, and I shouldn't lose my way. I felt dizzy and was grateful to the need to guide Domina Enory, as it kept my mind off everything else.

We did eventually reach Dart Hall. Mr. Brock opened the door. He bowed courteously. "I believe everyone is out, Lord Jemis."

I was too dizzy even to wonder where Mr. Brock had pulled that particular address from. Hal nudged me. I swallowed down a thickness in my mouth. "Mr. Dart will be by shortly. He asked us to meet him in the workroom."

"Very good," said Mr. Brock. "Shall you want refreshments?"

"Yes, please," I said, since it seemed proper to have them. Mr.

Brock nodded and set off down the hall one direction. I blinked stupidly for several moments into the relatively dim light, then turned to Hal. "I'm feeling very turned around."

"We're in the entrance hall of the Darts'," he said neutrally.

I closed my eyes. "Oh yes. Uh, upstairs first, then I think it's left."

"Do you want some directions?" a cheerful voice asked. I opened my eyes again to see the parlour-maid—Ellen, that was her name, I remembered now—looking at us with bright eyes.

"Mr. Dart's workroom, please, Ellen," I said. "He's joining us later."

She smiled at me, as if to say she didn't particularly care one way or another whether Mr. Dart was or not. "This way, sir." I followed along behind her, Domina Enory still holding my elbow, Hal showing his injured ankle by a very slight limp. Why did I see those things so easily, but yet feel completely turned around in a house I had been in and out of since I was a boy? Ellen held open a door for us. I smiled gratefully, for I would never have found it on my own. She was several years younger than I, perhaps not much more than fifteen or sixteen. I could not think why she looked even the least familiar, but she did.

"I thought it was upstairs," I said, puzzled, when we finally landed in the room.

"Why don't you sit down, Mr. Greenwing," Domina Enory said. "This would be a good chair."

I sat down obediently where she indicated. "Hal, is your ankle hurting?"

"Nothing to speak of," he said. "No, don't get up, Jemis, you can't do anything to help at the moment."

I sat down again. My head felt wrapped in thick wool, inside and out. Things jumbled together for a while; I'm not sure I didn't fall asleep. Certainly I opened my eyes and there was a tray of coffee and water, but when I looked again the tray was full of the objects Hal had laid out for me during the ill-fated attempt to find out the nature of my magic.

"Can I have the candle?" I asked sleepily.

Mr. Dart was beside me. "The candle?"

"The one from the Woods. On the tray."

He glanced across the room where Hal and Domina Enory were deep in discussion; and then he was back again, seemingly without having moved. "How did you do that?" I asked, taking the candle from him. "I love the feel of wax."

"I walked across the room and back," he replied. "Yes, it is a pleasing texture, isn't it?"

"And beeswax smells so good." I inhaled deeply, expecting to pay for it with a tithe of coughing and sneezes, but instead the honey-scent seemed to work to clear my mind. I frowned at him. "Perry, I'm sure I'm missing something … it's the *ebraöni* again …"

"The what?"

"You remember, when we were writing letters about the Gainsgooding conspirators. *Ebraöni* was the word that started to unravel the mystery."

His face cleared slightly. "Yes. It meant … cloud, didn't it?"

"Mountain-cloud—wool—pulling the wool over your eyes—"

"Jemis, I'm sorry, but you're not making any sense."

"My mind doesn't make any sense," I said in frustration. "And I can't breathe."

"We're working on it," he said soothingly.

Time jumped, both directions.

Domina Enory made me stand in the middle of the room, where she drew a circle made out of salt and iron filings and lavender petals.

I was hovering in the sky over the pirate galley: cruel white birds, golden-throated trumpets, the pirate whipping good magic out of the air, my father turning his oar to turn the ship.

I was on the dragon, knees clenched, wishing I'd spent more time riding instead of running so my thighs would be stronger for gripping. It threw back its head and laughed and fire came through its laughter and all I could smell, so incongruously, was cinnamon and lavender. Mrs. Etaris would know whose cake recipe involved lavender.

Hal pricked each finger on my right hand with a small golden pin. He was speaking words in Old Shaian, the language after Antique Shaian and before Modern, the last one still written in the old ideographs, the one the Gainsgooding conspirators had spoken. He spoke words of cleaning, of purifying, of healing. I hoped it would help his ankle.

Violet and Lark stood on the battlements of some building at the edge of the sea. Lark was smoking the long ivory pipe with which she'd drugged and enchanted me. She looked even more beautiful than I remembered her, even more desirable. Beside her Violet looked diminished, smaller, lesser: and anger kindled in me.

I laughed with my father and set my old pony over the Leap.

My uncle grabbed my hands in his and told me intensely that he had loved my mother and only married Lady Flora because he could not have her.

Poor Lady Flora, I thought compassionately.

Dried flowers fell down around me, lavender and marigold and larkspur and heartsease, and the words that Domina Enory was chanting were from a very old poem whose meaning teased at my mind. I should know those words—I should be able to understand the lines—but they hovered like a fading dream just outside my consciousness.

The Morrowlea bell rang the hour, and I said to Hal, "One day we'll be glad to know how to bake," and he, who I did not yet know was a duke imperial and one of the highest-ranked people on the continent, grinned at me and said, "You never do know where the road leads."

And a scent of saffron burning made me sneeze, and I was back in the workroom. The dragon reared up suddenly in front of me, no longer green and gold but grey and maroon. I reached out for a weapon, any weapon. My hand closed on a handful of petals and salt and iron filings like grit.

"No, here!" cried Mr. Dart, and threw me the beeswax candle.

My mother had told me in the letter that my magic was dependent on the Woods, and that honey would help. The wax, too?

The grey dragon coiled cold and dank and loathsome around me. It smelled like corruption, like bitter saffron, like the sort of glue made from dead things. I cried the first spell I had learned, calling fire to the wick of the candle, but it did not light. How could it not light? The grey dragon was cold and slimy, oozing between its scales. I felt my body want to vomit from disgust at the corruption, the maroon blood seeping through the squamous hide.

It spread its wings and cut out the light around me. I did not want to be in a box—*No more boxes!* I cried in my mind, and as in the tunnels, in the narrow secret passages, my thoughts turned to poetry. This time I pulled out an image from those perfect sonnets of the *Correspondence of Love and the Soul*.

The anonymous poet had found, in the infinite darkness and tiny space of his situation (her situation? No one knew; and no one knew whether the prison was the body around the soul or the stones around the body), a centre of light that nothing could put out.

Airo was the central metrical foot of the central line of the central sonnet. *I am. I exist. I am here.*

I am here, I said to the grey dragon; I exist; I am.

And I am not going to let you *win*.

In my mind I held that line from a poem, and I drew on the images of light that were everywhere in the *Correspondence*, fascinated as the poet was with the light and the dark and all the possible variations that might be rung on their symbolisms.

The dragon coiled.

The candle lit.

I held the fire with my mind and my hand and *pushed* with all my might, and everywhere the scent of honey grew stronger, and stronger, and I held it like that until I could smell no more saffron and no more corruption and no more glue and then in the heart of the blazing light I saw the darkness open like a doorway and the dragon burned at my feet to a line of white salt and black iron and silver-glinting scales.

The Morrowlea bell rang the end of curfew and Hal and I, who'd spent the entire night on the roofs rather than climb back down and risk being caught, looked at each other and laughed at the wood-doves flocking up out of the woods to the east and the way the campanile vibrated under our feet with the bell and the light that streamed red and gold across the sky to burnish us.

I blinked, and summer sunrise turned to autumn sunset, red and gold and cold and clear coming through the doorway open to the garden and beyond the garden the fields and the trees and the river and all the wide world.

I breathed in air that nearly hurt with its purity.

I stood in the centre of the inscribed circle, with Domina Enory, Hal, and the doorway at the points of the triangle around me.

The sunset receded, the doorway closed, and both somehow became Mr. Dart, and like the dragon's riddle life closed into secrets around me. I took a deep, clear breath, and I met Mr. Dart's eyes. His blue eyes held brown and gold and green and sunset and all the colours of the four elements sparking like Winterturn lanterns.

I smiled at the magic in him, warm and golden and rich and life-giving as the song of the bees of Melmúsion. The air was full of honey.

He smiled back at me. "Welcome home, Jemis."

Chapter Twenty-Seven
Literary Criticism

SINCE DOMINA ENORY and Hal not only rejected my offer to help clean up but actively ushered Mr. Dart and me out of the door, we went to the library so I could spend a few moments trying hard not to cry.

"I'm fairly certain this is a normal reaction to disenchantment," Mr. Dart said when I surfaced to apologize.

"They don't mention it in the ballads," I said, fishing in my pockets.

"Are you out of handkerchiefs? I don't believe it!"

I laughed. "Roald said the same thing. Come to think of it, I still have his." I pulled it out, remembered I'd used it after throwing up, decided my sleeve was probably the more hygienic option, and realized gratefully that Mr. Dart was offering me his. "Thanks."

"When did you see the Honourable Rag?"

"When I went outside to be sick behind the grange."

"What was he doing there?"

I reflected. "I have no idea. He gave me his handkerchief and a dipper of water, told me I wasn't eating enough, asked why I wasn't wearing that ring, and when I asked him why I should told me I should ask Sir Hamish about what Crimson Lake was. It's a paint colour, apparently."

"How odd."

"He is." I contemplated Roald's handkerchief, which was a huge cotton square in an unusually loud paisley pattern in an even more unusual shade of puce. It hid the mess I'd made fairly well, which I supposed was a good thing.

Mr. Dart reached over and tugged on the bell-pull. "He is right on one count, anyhow; you need to eat more."

"I've been feeling so—I need to talk to—" The door opened and I shut my mouth with a snap as Ellen the parlour-maid came in. She must have been hovering outside the door.

She bobbed a curtesy somewhere in our general vicinity.

Mr. Dart said, "Ah, Ellen, could you fetch us a snack, do you think? And maybe some drinking chocolate. Unless you fancy coffee, Mr. Greenwing?"

"Do you fancy anything particular, Mr. Dart, Lord Jemis?"

"Muffins with lots of butter," Mr. Dart said promptly.

"*Lord* Jemis?" I added faintly. "Mr. Brock called me that, too. Do you know why, Ellen?"

She turned her grin at me. "Mrs. Brock said to."

"And did Mrs. Brock give a reason?"

"My mum came to visit from the Manor. She said Sir Vorel told all the staff that was what everyone should call you."

Possibly my mind wasn't as clear as it had initially seemed. I frowned. "And your mother is ... ?"

"She's Mrs. Bellfrey, the cook at the Manor. My dad's the chief groom there."

"That's why you look familiar," I said, glad to have that cleared up. Although talk of her family at Arguty Manor made me—what had I been doing to *my* father? I gathered my straying thoughts as Mr. Dart frowned at me. "Did—did my uncle say *why* he'd suddenly decided on this?"

"He said that as your mother was Lady Olive, and you were her heir, you should be Lord Jemis. Mum said he was very pleased to have thought of it. You know how he gets: all full of pomp and virtue."

Mr. Dart tried hard to suppress his snort. I bit my lip. "Well, thank you for explaining."

She nodded, satisfied. "Your uncle is ever so proud of you. He keeps talking about how you saved him from that dragon, you know. It's about all he talks about these days, Mum says. He keeps coming down with ideas for special dishes for when you come to dinner. It drives Lady Flora half to distraction. Anyhow, I'll bring you something in half a trice, sirs, *and* there's more apricot jam, Mr. Dart, don't you worry." She bobbed another curtsey and took her leave.

I looked at Mr. Dart. "I find myself feeling slightly guilty for putting my uncle's dinner invitations off so often."

"This could all be a ruse to cover up your murder, you know. If he knows the dishes in advance he could prepare a little something to slip inside."

"Where would he get poison from?"

"If he's in league with Dominus-not-really-Gleason, he would have access to all sorts of things. The magister's got more than the complete works of Fitzroy Angursell in that house of his."

The last time I'd been in Dominus Gleason's house had been to deliver a box of books and to ask about the stargazy pie I'd found in the town square. That time I'd sneezed so much I'd fainted from lack of air, which in retrospect probably should have given me more of a clue that something was up.

"I need to find my father, Perry," I said.

"They'll be coming here soon." I shook my head and went towards the door, unable to express the jumble of emotions in my heart. He followed to take hold of my shoulder. "Jemis. I know you want to talk to him."

"I've not been *able* to talk to him. I have to tell him—what I—how I—"

"Mr. Greenwing."

I stopped straining against his hand at his tone. "Mr. Dart."

"Mr. Greenwing, you have just had lifted a curse of seven years' standing. Your father is in the midst of any number of people who don't know who he is and whom he does not wish to tell. You are in no fit state to be going anywhere at the moment. Your skin is clammy and you are shaking with reaction. You need to eat something before you faint."

"I need to tell him how—how glad I am he's here."

The words were so weak.

Mr. Dart looked oddly at me. "Jemis, he knows."

"I've been so suspicious and—and I didn't *recognize* him! Not even when we were playing Poacher!"

"That, of course, is exactly when you should have."

"Yes," I cried, grateful he understood, and turned in his grasp only to find the door open upon me. I jumped violently. It was Hal, dusting off his hands and smiling cheerfully as he entered the room.

"Welladay and—Jemis, what's wrong?"

"He's now feeling guilty for all the effects of the curse," supplied Mr. Dart.

"Oh, Jemis, you must understand that your emotions are muddled at the moment from the magic? Also you need to eat."

"Why is everyone so concerned with my diet?" I asked, exasperated. "How can you not see that I must go find my—my father and tell him—"

I stopped.

"Ah," said Mr. Dart. "Not all the doubts were from the curse."

I sank down before the hearth. The fire was well along, the bed of coals throwing off a fine heat. "I need to talk to him."

"Jemis, I hate to say it but it has started to snow and you are nearly certain to catch ill if you rush off into it to tell your father things better said indoors and in private. They'll be on their way back by now, anyhow. It's nearly dark."

It felt wrong to submit, but what they said made a certain amount of sense. I did feel shaky; and even hungry, dammit.

I added another log to the fire. From behind and above me Mr. Dart said, "Ellen will do that when she comes back."

"I like mending fires," I said, watching the lines of fire etch themselves across the duller coals. There was *something* I was missing, something that would turn smouldering coals into bright fire … If I left aside my anxiety to apologize to my father, that left—well, everything else. I sat back on my heels, twisted to look up at Mr. Dart. "What am I missing, Perry?"

Relief flickered across his face. He must have thought I was about to ask him about one of his forbidden subjects, I thought wryly. That would come at some point, but not when we were with Hal, in a room where we might be interrupted at any moment. "In the room just now you said something about *ebryony*."

"*Ebraöni*," I corrected. "Mountain-cloud. Wool."

"Having the wool pulled over your eyes," he added, and flung himself into one of the wing chairs on either side of the fireplace.

I seated myself more slowly in the other one. "The key to the Gainsgooding conspiracy, to Ariadne nev Lingarel's poem, and, possibly, to our situation."

"You've had an intuition," said Hal.

"An intimation of *something*, anyway." I frowned at the fire, at the flames licking the smaller logs I'd placed over the coals. "Let's think about this in a scholarly fashion."

"Like our letters back and forth about the Gainsgooding conspirators?"

"I hadn't realized you'd found that so memorable a correspondence."

He looked at me a little incredulously, laughing. "Mr. Greenwing, we wrote at least a letter a day for two months. You must have known I was much taken with the matter. Surely you were?"

Mr. Dart, I reflected, was never going to open his heart to me if I did not show him the reciprocal trust. "Yes, I was, but I was also riding very high on wireweed, and I have to admit that between that and this curse I am no longer very confident about my memories of what was actually going on."

I spoke lightly, but it was honest, and he saw that. Hal frowned at both of us, then sat back in his chair as if to pretend he was invisible. Mr. Dart was visibly torn about how to respond. I took pity on him—again thinking of how insistent Hal's silence on obvious topics had been—and turned back to the day's more prominent concerns. "This is a library; have you paper and a pen anywhere in it?"

"Here," said Hal, drawing out Mr. Dart's.

"I still haven't asked Roald for my pen," I lamented, going to the desk so I could fetch paper. Glancing out the window, I discovered it was earlier than I'd thought, though the dim heavy clouds made it dark. Certainly not the sunset whose echo and glory I'd seen reflected in Mr. Dart's eyes. "Mr. Buchance gave it to me."

Mr. Dart leaned against the desk to watch as I checked the nib and arranged the paper on the blotting pad. "You always call your stepfather 'Mr. Buchance'."

"So I do. I am rather muddled about it, I suppose."

"Your sentiments?"

"Are we, or are we not, gentlemen?"

He picked up a spare pen and twiddled it in his fingers. "Meaning I should not ask to plumb the depths of emotions? We ought leave that to the poets, I suppose you would say."

I raised my eyebrows at him. I am really not as patient as Hal, alas. "Do the histories never involve the hearts of those making them?"

Mr. Dart stared at me. The pen was motionless in his hand; the tassels on his sling waved in some draft from the window; the fire crackled behind us. Hal closed his eyes in some baffled thought. I drew three lines lengthwise down my page. The scratch of the pen sounded very loud, as did the click of the door.

"Your refreshments, Mr. Dart, Lord Jemis," announced Ellen, and set them on the table to one side of the desk. "Would you like me to pour? If you need anything else, just ring. I've brought another cup for Mr. Lingham."

"Thank you," I replied. "We can serve ourselves."

"Of course we would ring," muttered Mr. Dart as she went out again; "and that's her job."

"She's still a person." I gazed at my three lines, added a horizontal one at the top as a header, and swivelled in my seat to contemplate the tray she'd bought. "Good heavens, I'm hungry."

"Roald wasn't wrong. You have lost weight."

"Try eating when your stomach feels as if it's trying to strangle you," I replied, choosing two muffins dripping with butter and adding a liberal dollop of honey. Not honey from the Woods, alas, but that would come in time and in season. "Mm, these are good. I must do some more baking. We keep forgetting to, eh, Hal?"

"The skill of the local baker makes me less inclined."

"He doesn't make muffins. Or crumpets."

"Too true, alas."

Mr. Dart shook his head and pointed at my page. "Why do you have three lines?"

"It's the way you begin analyzing a puzzle-poem. I thought it might help for our puzzles. On the left goes the word or the line— usually it's three to seven ideographs a line, of course."

"Of course."

I smiled fleetingly. "I'm sure your historians have their conventions and styles."

"I am wondering ever more if there are ones I have missed. I was looking for the patterns in the histories, not in the historians, despite all that I learned from you about the Gainsgooding conspirators about how much the form can reveal—or hide. Anyhow, go on. On the left goes the word."

"For instance, *ebraöni*." I wrote the ideograph with a flourish. One chevron pointing up, with slightly flared curves at the ends of its open sides; one pointing up, centred upon it, and a dot in the centre of the diamond made by their crossing.

"Very good: mountain cloud, and wool, and the wool pulled over your eyes."

"The primary meaning goes in the first column." I wrote *wool* in modern Shaian lettering in the appropriate space. "In the second column goes the secondary meanings." I wrote *mountain cloud* and *trickery* there.

"And in the third?"

"Third is for correspondences with other poets. In this case, I'd write Lo en Tai, who is the one who introduced the word into the lexicon, the Gainsgooding conspirators, who were caught by it, and Ariadne nev Lingarel, who wrote the poem I studied most." I wrote their names in smaller letters. Hal rolled his eyes at the mention of the fair Ariadne, whom he'd heard about at least as much as I'd heard about the habits of various shrubs in the genus *Ilex*.

"What about us? We are also caught in the games of these two sticks and a stone."

"Yes, but we have yet to write our experiences in poetry of unexceptional superfice and astonishing depths."

Mr. Dart replenished my cup with chocolate from the pot. "Do you not write poetry yourself, Mr. Greenwing?"

I shrugged, finding this an even more difficult subject than—well, than the rest of my inner life. "I've tried. It doesn't seem to be correct."

He let it go, instead gesturing with the pot at the page. "So now that we have a sense of what *ebraöni* means, or can mean, what next?"

I contemplated what I'd written. "I'm missing something."

"So we've already established. Your memory."

"Go to, Mr. Dart. Ah, that's it." In the secondary-meaning column I added *white* and *ascending fog*.

"White for the colour … why is it 'ascending' fog? I should have thought mountain clouds *descended*."

"That's how it's always glossed in Lo en Tai … and I suppose it's because fog rises, whereas clouds descend. Certainly when I was running the other morning the fog was coming up off the fields like they were burning."

"I think your next line should be 'White Cross'. Followed by 'False Colours', 'Faked Death', and 'Inheritance'."

I wrote the words in ideographs. Added the primary meaning, started in on the secondary meanings of the words. 'White' added in meanings of purity, divinity, death, winter, innocence, and hope. Cross for crossroads, for death (again; sometimes it seemed as if half the words of Old Shaian were euphemisms for a topic the ancient Shaians appeared to have been most anxious about) for the possibility of resurrection, for binding and roads and where fate met chance. Started in on 'False Colours,' which took me a moment to come up with the translation. Eventually wrote it out literally. Considered the result. "Would you look at that. The Antique Shaian for 'False Colours' is only a punctum—a dot—away from the word for 'highwayman'."

Mr. Dart snorted. "We are centred on the Arguty Forest—there are always rumours of highwaymen."

I wrote Arguty Forest in the Correspondences column. "More than rumours. I've met three separate gangs in the last month. One of them took us across the Magarran Strid, if my geography wasn't totally off. We ended up at a place called the Hanging Hill."

"The infamous whiskey distillers' headquarters," Mr. Dart

agreed. "Everyone knows they're there, but no one but them knows how to get across the Strid to get there."

"Except for whoever does evil rituals at the king oak on the Hanging Hill."

Mr. Dart looked at me. "That's where Hagwood said he found your father."

Chapter Twenty-Eight
Bull, Boar, Stag

IN THE COURTYARD before the classic elegance of the Darts' frontage, lightly veiled in new snow, there stood the Chancellor and the other Scholars with Chief Constable Etaris, Master Dart and Sir Hamish, Ben, my father, two men who seemed to have been brought for their digging abilities, my uncle, and a pile of silvered and blackened bones.

"Those are not human bones," said Dominus Vitor.

Sir Vorel said, "Oh, Jack."

Ellen had described him bustling down to the kitchen, full of pomp and virtue, to tell her mother all the dishes he'd thought of for when I came at last to dine. Vor, my father's little brother, who had treated my mother and me very wrongly, and who professed with melodramatic delivery how remorseful he was and how he wished he had not acted as he had—

And what if he wasn't lying?

I grabbed Mr. Dart's arm to anchor myself. As he stood to my left, it was his stone arm. The hard coldness of it disconcerted me almost as much as my thoughts.

We'd come out in response to Ellen's garbled message that the magistrate was there about my father. They were standing beside a pile of bones.

If my uncle *wasn't* lying—if he was, in fact, telling the truth—if he hadn't arranged for my father's death (by murder or apparent suicide)—if he truly *was* glad to restore his name, if he truly was glad he could acknowledge me—

Would he be willing to give up the baronetcy?

What if he were?

What if it was *Lady Flora* who wasn't?

The snow fell onto the bones and melted away. My uncle stared at me in dismay.

"I've been—the duke has *proof*," he said intently, almost pleadingly. "The first thing was to exhume his bones."

My knowledge of the law was admittedly minimal, but I somehow didn't think that the restoration of an accused and convicted traitor and suicide *began* with the exhumation of his corpse. Not on the say-so of the man who inherited from his disgrace, under the direction of his crony, one day off the seven-year anniversary. And where was Inspector Quent? Or even Mr. Morres and Mr. Tey, the two Kingsford lawyers? The Scholars—especially the Chancellor—were excellent witnesses, but surely there should have been more—more—more *ceremony*.

Sir Vorel said, "My dear nephew, I can only imagine the thoughts in your head at this moment."

I very nearly started to laugh.

My living father stood five feet away. The bones of what was popularly supposed to be his corpse lay at my feet. My uncle's face was white as the snowy stone behind him, his hand at his throat, the cravat twisting about his fingers.

I looked down at the bones. There were three animal skulls, the eye hollows black as if with fire, the outer bones silver-gilt.

Two months ago, my first weekend back in town, Mr. Dart and I had witnessed a cultic rite at the Ellery Stone. A cow had been sacrificed to the Dark Kings, using some magical stone the priests called the Heart of the Moon, calling down twisted power to the dozen or so people caught up into its ecstasy. The next day people had said it was a good thing I'd been with Mr. Dart all night, because they had found silvered bones, and people knew what that meant.

And did I know what *this* meant?

Dominus Vitor said, "Those are the skulls of a bull, a boar, and a stag. I expect the rest of the bones will come from those animals as well."

He glanced around, apparently aimlessly, but then walked briskly to a stick on the ground some distance away. He brought it back and used it to poke at the pile, which, I now saw, was spread out on what looked like someone's many-caped driving coat. It was drab cloth; my uncle's. The deer skull fell over and revealed a red pigmentation staining the underside of the jaw.

"Black, silver, red, and white," he said, the disgust evident in his voice. "Someone's been mucking around with the Dark Kings."

The Chief Constable found his voice. It was not an attractive one. "Sir Hamish, we found this under the waystone, where Jakory Greenwing was buried."

"You mean, where the *semblance* of Jakory Greenwing was buried." Domina Enory took the stick from Dominus Vitor and prodded some long rib-bones. "I suspect a more thorough dig would reveal frog bones, the feathers of various species of fowl, and runic inscriptions on the bones."

We all looked at her. The Squire found his voice first. "Are you familiar with this—this abomination, Domina?"

She almost smiled. "I am a Scholar of curses, Master Dart. I am familiar with certain branches of magic that are not at all respectable: I fight them. Yes, I am familiar with the spell that worked this. It is the most elaborate and the most permanent of the seemings: those spells designed to give one object the appearance of another. This one did more; it was intended to give the animal bones the very weight and magical signature of the human it replaced."

"You are certain?" the Chief Constable said. His voice was usually self-satisfied, patronizing, utterly self-confident. He bobbed along in my uncle's wake like a line trawled behind a punt. My uncle being in total shock, his lackey seemed unsure of himself.

"Certain?" Domina Enory said, and sounded every inch a Scholar of the Circle School most famously known for magical theory. "My dear sir, I do not have the library of Oakhill with me, but failing that, yes, I am sure. There was a period in Alinorel history when every wizard on the Lady's side needed to know the spells to test the dead for this semblancing. It utterly fools the ordinary eye and most magical tests. Those who saw this when it was intact would have had no reason to believe it any body but what it seemed."

That at least answered one question—to wit, whether Mr. Hagwood had been lying or not. Unfortunately it did nothing for the central one of *who* and *how* and *why* my father had been saved for the pirate galleys.

Before realizing what it might sound like to those who did not know my father stood five feet away staring at the bones that we had all thought for so long were his, I said, "But then what *happened?*"

"'Tis a good question," said Ben. "Any ideas?"

Sir Vorel exclaimed, "Oh, my brother!" and started to cry.

***

We all went inside for a drink.

Well: most of us did. Mr. Etaris and his brawny underlings stayed outside to watch over and discuss the further removal of the bones, and Domina Enory stayed with them to provide any necessary advice or warnings. I surmised she also was delighted to have another odd bit of magic to investigate; there was something about her expression that suggested she felt she'd been given a present. Dominus Vitor stayed to identify the bones. Once he stopped looking disgusted he seemed thoroughly engrossed.

I dallied slightly behind the others, trying to figure out what *else* about that scene over the pile of bones was significant, and was therefore just in time to witness my uncle striding into the library and seeing his papers spread out over the table.

He was roused from his earlier shock at the sight. "What— those are my papers! How did you come by them?"

Everyone swung around to look at me, which I didn't think was quite fair. I bought a moment of time by assiduously helping him to a chair. "Sir Vorel, I—"

"*Uncle* Vorel, my dear boy, how can you call me anything else after seeing that—that—" His face crumpled. I hastily offered him one of my newly replaced clean handkerchiefs.

A month ago he would have assumed I had stolen the papers.

I took a deep breath. "Uncle Vorel, I must offer you an apology."

This time I expected the glances aimed at me. I chose my words carefully. I had finally realized where we were in the game of Poacher that was life. We were waiting for the turn of the Emperor card, which might, if we were lucky (or possibly, if we were cursed), turn out to be the Holy Grail.

And if that were the case, the only tall tale that might work was the truth.

"Uncle Vorel, I have been unjust to you."

"My dear nephew!"

Jemis. My name is *Jemis.*

"Some weeks ago, when it became clear to me from his grace's testimony that the accusations of treason against my father were provably as false as I had always believed them, my thoughts turned to who might have stood most to gain from those accusations."

"A natural thought, my dear boy, I assure you I quite under—"

I went on relentlessly. "That is, sir, you."

His mouth opened and shut like one of his golden carp.

I was unutterably glad for my father's sake to see there was not even the smidgen of guilt in his face. Astonishment, embarrassment, anger, even a small amount of rue (if I could believe it), but not guilt.

Everyone else regarded us in total amazement.

"Mr. Dart, the Duke, and I went to see Mr. Hagwood," I went on, "who was the one who told my mother and me of my father's apparent suicide. Along the way we encountered a former class-mate of Hal's and mine, who, it turned out, had returned to take up her family profession as a highwaywoman."

Dominus Lukel blurted, "Not Violet!"

I smiled. "No, Red Myrta."

"I can see that," he said after a moment. "She's a very fine archer."

I wanted to look at the Chancellor, who had been Red Myrta's primary tutor, but I kept my eyes on my uncle. He might not have murdered my father, but I did not for one moment believe he was innocent of all the shenanigans going on in the Forest.

"She and her companion had been inside the manor," I continued.

"The scoundrels!" cried Sir Vorel. "Penetrating into my sanctum like that ... Did they give you *all* the papers?"

And thus we neatly elided what had actually happened by connecting outposts of the truth to make a sense that was not the true significance at all.

How easy it was for things to seem what they were not.

"I don't know what you had in your, er, sanctum, sir—Uncle Vorel. But this is where I must apologize again. I confess I have been suspicious of your abrupt change of behaviour towards me."

He turned shocked eyes at me. "My dear nephew, I was wrong! I hope I am man enough to admit it."

I dared not meet anyone else's eyes, especially not Mr. Dart's or my father's. "Yes, but you must see, Uncle, that I stand between you and the continuation of your status as baronet."

"Oh, *pish*." He shook his head sadly. "My dear wife cares about the title, yes, but it's only a baronetcy."

Was Lady Flora's motivation as simple as all that? Did she really do all of what I was suspecting just to be a baronet's wife rather than a mere mister's? It seemed incredible ... and I could not believe it. There wasn't enough money or status involved, surely.

And all of a sudden I recalled Sir Hamish saying to Sir Vorel, in this very room, *You cannot rewrite all the barony records to suit your fancy.* Which records? Which fancy?

My uncle met my eyes and nodded firmly, full now of Ellen's 'pomp and virtue'. "And right is, I hope, right."

I stared at him, remembering Sir Rinald's funeral, Lady Flora telling my mother and me we should not expect to come to the front door any longer. In the Interim, when we could cross the grounds to the manor house, he had made us beg at the back door for scraps of flour or yeast. After the Interim, he stared coldly away from me on every encounter. At my mother's funeral, which he had refused to attend, and at which consequently I had no one at all from any of my blood family to comfort me. Two months ago, he had wished aloud that I had not come back from university. In this very room, barely a month past, he had called me the degenerate offspring of a traitor. And he dared say to me that *right was right?*

"Yes, it is," I replied, and left it at that. I turned to Hal. "What did you find in the papers, your grace?"

He gave me an admiring smile, then turned to the table every inch an imperial duke. "My great-uncle can speak to the letters from Eil better than I, but for the rest, the only truly significant item seems to be that to do with the itemized list of the contents of the Arguty cellars."

I watched my uncle visibly relax. Too soon, of course, for Hal went blithely on: "Then there's this lovely sequence of letters blackmailing you for a certain request you made of the whiskey-jack gang oh, just about seven years ago now, it looks like. Would you care to tell us more about that?"

***

With each sentence my uncle uttered the kaleidoscope shifted. Except that wasn't quite the right metaphor. In a kaleidoscope the patterns shift endlessly, pretty, fascinating, and ultimately meaningless. I had gotten bored with the kaleidoscopes in Ghilousette quite quickly.

No, this was the arrangement of ideographs down the left of the page and their connotations unfolding in parallel lines down the right until the configurations revealed the key to unlock the significances held mutely between sign and sense.

"It didn't have anything to do with Jack."

"Seven years ago is when he returned from the dead," Hal said sternly.

My uncle was a large man, but the bluster had gone out of him. He waved my handkerchief around in small distressed circles.

"Coincidence," he protested.

Hal picked up one of the letters from the table. "'My dear sir: your request has been granted, but it has proven more expensive than anticipated, and so with the utmost reluctance I must inform you that without further reassurance I cannot promise to continue to guard your secrets.'"

"It's my wife."

"Lady Greenwing?"

Sir Vorel winced. "She has ideas above her station. She was always jealous of Lady Olive ... I started calling her Lady Flora as a, a kind of endearment, and she liked it so much others followed suit."

"It seems unlikely your wife's pretensions to a higher title than she possesses warrants seven years of blackmail."

"But it does—by the Emperor, that's what it's all about!"

To our considerable amazement he explained that Lady Flora

had what amounted to a mania for the respect and honours due an Imperial title, and this had come to centre, as she got older, on that absurdly expensive cosmetic derived from the magic-imbued algal sludge to be found deep in the limestone caves of the Magarran valley.

I watched my uncle carefully as he spoke. I had never played Poacher against him, nor any card game, but on one of those uninvited visits the Honourable Rag had regaled us all evening with an account of all the tells of the high-playing gentry of the barony. Sir Vorel's was tapping his elbow with his other hand.

As he started into the account of the cosmetic he lifted his (or rather my) handkerchief to his temple and held it there. His right hand crept over to his left elbow and set up a steady beat.

He was bluffing. Where was the lie?

Half the story was true—or perhaps all of it was, but not the whole truth. He was giving us at best the signs of the truth; not their true sense, let alone significance.

He seemed to take our silence for agreement or even belief, for he grew more animated, less despondent, as he went on. I wondered if in Imperial days people really would have paid seven years of blackmail for the Tufa-made cosmetic, whatever exactly it was. It wasn't as if it kept Lady Flora looking unnaturally young or preternaturally beautiful.

At the end of his speech I nodded without explaining the gesture and turned to Ben. "What did you find out about the letters from Eil, sir?"

Sir Vorel looked much taken aback that I did not respond directly to him. "What—my dear nephew—surely you understand—"

Ben spoke straight over him, in a tone that must have worked wonders when he was a commander of armies. "The second letter is genuine: I dictated it to a secretary after my rescue. I had promised to write Jack's family. My hands were broken, so I couldn't write it myself."

"And the first letter?"

He stared at it grimly. "Everything about it seems genuine."

"Except?"

"Except for the small matter it is under the seal of an officer who was killed by the Stone Speakers in their fortress after we were captured, and that it contains a line of poetry I've never heard of."

He passed the letter to Mr. Dart, who scanned it, made to hand it over, frowned, read it again more thoroughly, and finally said, "Isn't that a line from one of the Gainsgooding poems?"

Chapter Twenty-Nine
Crimson Lake

I HAD NEVER examined the two letters from the army in any detail. This time I was able to look at even the fateful first one with an almost detached attention. I had certainly never compared them before to see any differences.

There were not many.

The inks were the same, blue-black, still dark and crisp. The scripts were very similar, close enough that I would not have been surprised to discover they were written by the same person (except that surely any scribe would notice that there were two letters directed to the same person about the same soldier with totally different reports?). Ben murmured something about there being trained scribes in the command headquarters at Eil for just such an occasion. The dates were a month apart; the salutations the same; the words so completely different.

> *Dear Lady Olive:*
>
> *It is with extreme regret that I must announce to you the death of your husband, Major Jakory Greenwing. I assure you he died heroically on a scouting mission across the border.*

With the deepest sympathies for your loss,

General Benneret Halioren

Commander of the Sixth Division of the Seventh Army of Astandalas

"I'm sorry it was so short," said Ben. "I was very badly injured at the time and was not able to dictate a fuller letter. I was sent home immediately after that letter, and did not truly recover until after the Interim. I'm sorry I did not even suggest he might have lived. I left him holding the Gate of Morning with an army of Stone Speakers climbing up to the pass, and we had the army close the Bloodwater pass behind us. I had no anticipation whatsoever he could have survived. But I can't believe I didn't even mention he saved my life—again."

I nodded. I would have felt numb under the circumstances, perhaps, except that my father was not, after all, dead, and I—I thought suddenly—I could *ask* him about what had happened.

I dared not look at him. My face would surely give everything away, and the game was not over, not yet. The Emperor Card had not yet been turned; we still had not figured out who had saved him and why. Dominus Gleason had no apparent reason for doing so, but he was the only one with the magical skills to create the simulacrum.

Or so we presumed. More than ever I regretted a dozen years of no one talking about magic except in terms of what used to be done in the golden days of Astandalas.

I turned to the other letter.

Dear Lady Greenwing:

It was extreme regret that I must announce to you the death of your husband, Major Jakory Greenwing, as the traitor of Loe. He was shot in the back fleeing from the summons to a court martial. Under the circumstances his body will not be returned; it will be interred with the several hundred dead soldiers his action caused to be slain.

As the poet says, 'The soil of history has as many weeds as flowers.'

Lady Norcell of Westmoor

Second-in-Command of the Sixth Division of the Seventh Army of Astandalas

Despite my best efforts the pages trembled. I set them down on the table and rested my weight on my hands. Read it over again, as if it were a poem whose genre I needed to determine before I could begin the work of analysis.

"It is addressed to Lady Greenwing," I said.

"And the line of poetry? That is one of the Gainsgooding poems, isn't it?" Mr. Dart asked insistently. "I remember it because of how trite the line sounded."

"Most of their poems did," I murmured, staring at the line. "It's not quite … right … there's a word missing, or something." I ran over the poems in my mind, trying to recall which this came from. Dominus Lukel's blurt of 'Not Violet!' when I'd mentioned highwaywomen made my mind slide towards those many evenings she and I had spent researching ciphers and cracking them, when both of us should have been studying for something else. That had been my extracurricular focus before Mr. Dart had written about the Gainsgooding conspirators.

"It's odd that there would be a reference to one of those poems in here, isn't it?" Hal said. "They're not exactly learned by rote by every schoolchild."

"This is a matter of treason," I said absently, reaching for what was amiss with the line. "Perhaps they liked evoking the one successful assassination of an Emperor."

Ben snorted. "Losing an entire battalion wasn't enough for them?"

I looked up. "No. Evidently not, for they felt the need to frame my father to take the blame, as if they didn't want to soil themselves. Soil! That's it!"

"What is?"

"It should be 'The *garden* of history has as many weeds as flowers.' Not 'the *soil* of history'."

"Garden does make more sense."

"Except that the ideograph for *soil* is almost identical to that for the number *fourteen*—" I looked around for paper and pen. Sir Hamish passed me the ones I'd been using earlier. I thanked him and drew the two ideographs below the last one. "This is from a poem called 'The Fall of Rain and Civilizations'."

"Subtle," muttered Mr. Dart.

"It has nineteen verses. The fourteenth is in the form of a vocative ode addressed to the goddess of Fame—"

"Just like Lark's philippic," Hal said.

I waved that aside. "Don't introduce digressions. I'm trying to work out what cipher this is encoded in. It's not a proper game of Two Sticks and a Stone—"

"Don't ask," advised Mr. Dart. "He'll explain."

"It doesn't involve any of the cues for a prose rendering of the esoteric language, either. No, it must be a more straightforward cipher. I don't imagine it's too complicated, either, as why would anyone be expecting a code to be in it? My mother was the recipient of the letter, and *she* wouldn't have been receiving secret messages like this."

I frowned at the page in front of me. Violet had been better at divining the existence of codes than me. Once I knew they were there I was better at deciphering them, but she was always the one to realize there was a significant anagram or the first letter of each sentence or paragraph formed a clue, or—

The first letter of each paragraph spelled DIALS.

Include the two extra sentences, and you had DIHUALS.

That was not a word in any language I knew, but it *was* an anagram of HASDUIL, which meant 'fire' in Ancient Shaian and meant that if the author had been using any of the established ciphers, it was almost certainly either 'Artkey' or 'Thunderstrike'.

I read it over again. DIALS suggested Artkey, with its rotating sequence of substitutions. I frowned at the paper. Did I recall enough of 'The Fall of Rain and Civilizations' for this to work?

How likely was it, really, that someone would have all of the Gainsgooding conspirators' poetry, or an anthology of the Late Perpendicular Style of poetry made before the realization of how many of the poets were compromised? I wrote down the title across the length of the paper. This was Alinor: one never knew what book one might find in someone's library.

"What is Lady Flora's chief interest?" I asked as I translated the title into ideographs.

"The antiquity and descent of her family," my uncle said gloomily. "She's descended from the Bloody Queen, you know, from back before this was Fiellan."

"The Bloody Queen! She's the one buried at the Hanging Hill in the forest, isn't she?" Mr. Dart said.

The pattern shifted another step. Almost, almost … In the corner of the page I drew the ideograph for *ebraöni*, as if all the ramifications of meaning from cloud to having the wool pulled over your eyes would help.

"What word is that?" my father asked. "It looks almost like *kitaibë* from this angle."

Sir Vorel seemed to notice him for the first time. "Who are you, sir? You seem … have we met before, sir?"

"*Ebraöni*," I said, ignoring him. Then my father's word penetrated. *Kitaibë* meant 'thunderbolt' and, by extension, 'revelation'.

Invert the cloud and you saw the lightning.

The cipher opened up.

I scribbled words across the page, lists of how the letters shifted in their encoded patterns, matched sign to significance to the deeper layer of sense, until the words turned, and turned, and turned again, and meant—

"I've got it," I said, cutting right across whatever Ben and Sir Vorel and Sir Hamish were all saying at once.

The jumble of sounds cut out. "I beg your pardon?" Sir Hamish said carefully.

"I've deciphered it."

My uncle frowned mightily. "Just like that? Are you sure you're correct, young man?"

Not *my dear nephew*? I smiled thinly at him. "Why not? I studied puzzle poems at Morrowlea, sir. You cannot expect a cipher to be entirely alien. This one is a quite simple variation on the Artkey

Code commonly used by spies from the Imperial College of Wizardry."

Hal said, "There were spies from the Imperial College of Wizardry?"

"Everywhere the Empire was brushing up against outsider magics, certainly," Ben said. "Now, lad, what does it say? I am even more agog."

I took a breath, glanced down at my final words, and read it out.

> *Flower of Hope:*
>
> *You have done well establishing your first position. This letter supplies what you need to move to the next. Soon it will be time for our people to return to glory. The stones of the forest are older than the trees, and the water redder than the blood of empires. When the restoration comes, we will need you. Be ready at all times. You know what the red water and the white stone can do.*
>
> *We who speak for the shadows*

They were all very quiet. My father whispered something to himself in a language I did not understand; when I looked at him he repeated it in Shaian. "Stone speaks to stone, and water to water."

"The rallying cry of the Stone Speakers," Ben supplied.

"The red water," I said, and turned to Sir Hamish on the thought that this might be an opportune moment to ask the Honourable Roald Ragnor's question. "Sir Hamish, what is crimson lake?"

He appeared only briefly startled; then his eyes narrowed thoughtfully and he shifted from the sardonic gentleman-farmer to the intense, incisive, much-lauded painter of portraits. "Crimson lake is, first of all, a paint colour derived from cochineal. 'Lake' comes from the word 'lac', 'an extrusion', related obviously to the word 'lacquer'. Crimson lake is also called carmine ... it makes a superb clear colour. I'd use it to paint pale-skinned folk and sump- tuous red clothing, because it works brilliantly as a transparent wash. Vermilion is sometimes too opaque; it's an ocherous pigment."

My thought flashed to the red staining the bones that had been buried in my father's place.

"And the second point?"

He smiled slightly. "It is also, as I understand it, the name of a secret society whose mission appears the re-establishment of magic."

Hence a magic ring as a token ... although that really did not explain anything, such as why I'd been sort-of-recruited to join it. Possibly it explained why the Honourable Rag had access to were- lights. I nodded as if this was all entirely irrelevant to me.

The Honourable Rag had suggested the answer was more than it seemed, and I had decided I'd rather comport myself as if he were not a drunkard of a young man bent on self-destruction—or at least not *only* that. He had graduated from Tara, at least.

"And third?"

"Third," said Master Dart, "it's the name of a lake up along the top of the Magarran Strid, which at this time of year often experi- ences an algal bloom that colours all the water red."

"The tippermongeramy and the Tufa."

"The what?" said several people.

I ignored the discussion of the word and its meaning. My fa- ther had said that Tufa was also the word for a kind of rock. ("Isn't tufa a kind of rock?" Hal asked on cue; "I'm sure it's what we use to make stone troughs at home. For alpine plants, you know.")

My thoughts were moving almost too fast for me to think them. I waited while the others talked, as they sizzled in my mind, images jostling with each other, lines from poetry and letters and history and the game of Poacher my father and I had played what seemed an age of the world ago.

My final Net had contained Two Fat Carp, a Stranger, a Mysterious Letter, and a Thunderstorm.

Poacher did not *predict* anything; that was silly. Prognostication very rarely worked (I had gotten that far in my History of Magic classes), at least not on Alinor. It was said some of the other magic systems of the Empire supported it. What did a set of cards know?

Nothing, of course. It was all in the players and the history of meanings built up around the cards and their conjunctions. You revealed your soul as you played.

And you might, perhaps, end up showing something of the truth of the real conjunctions in the world-at-large as your unconscious mind saw them.

Two Fat Carp: my uncle and my aunt. Or, dropping down a layer of significance, the two seeming villains (for the carp meant, first, a feast, and secondly, from a famously disastrous feast once held on Colhélhé, betrayal): Dominus-not-Gleason and Lady Flora.

A Stranger: a piratical highwayman, who was my father. My uncle, whose blustering surface seemed so obviously what he was. Dominus Gleason, who was not who he seemed. Lady Flora, who was not *what* she seemed. The Honourable Rag, who annoyed me with all his misdirections. All the unfolding ramifications of the Stranger were there in its surface meaning: the potential god or demon, the potential friend or enemy, the Unknown that could open itself to trickery or salvation.

A Mysterious Letter: how many there were! From my mother; from the army; from the blackmailers.

(We should not, I reflected fleetingly, forget that small point of blackmail.)

Why had I been needed to be kept out of the way?

Why had my *father* needed to be kept out of the way?

What happened that we had seen, or might have seen, or might have interfered with? Why *us*?

Why had that letter been what was needed for the establishment of a second position?

Flower of Hope ... Lady Flora. Who had married my uncle the year before my father went to Loe.

Who, my uncle had just said, was a descendant of the Bloody Queen, that legendary pre-Fiellanese chieftain who just might (according to Mr. Dart) be buried in that grassy hill with the king oak and the hollow and the highwaymen.

Who had, as a result of this letter, become established not so much as a Personage in the barony (though there was that, too), but as the *lady of Arguty Manor*, with all its secret passageways, its proximity to the Forest and the town, and its cellar full of barrels that might, or might not, contain contraband whiskey.

I almost had it—

One more card. There was one more card before the Emperor Card was played. My last one had been A Thunderstorm.

A Thunderstorm ...

The letter had been coded in Artkey, not Thunderstrike. The whole situation seemed to be threatening *some* form of storm, from the absurd accusations heaped on me to what was going to happen to my uncle when he finally discovered my father was alive to—

My tutor's voice suddenly spoke in my mind's ear: *Do not forget the letter of the text.*

Do not forget the source of all this speculation, that was. In the game of Two Sticks and a Stone, it also meant: don't forget the literal meaning, what the words in their simplest form actually *said*. 'The garden (or soil) of history has as many weeds as flowers.' You could not fail to take the surface meaning into account when presenting your interpretation.

On Being Incarcerated in Orio Prison was, first and foremost, a poem about being incarcerated for life in a prison on the top of a cliff, with the endless ocean on one side and the city the poet could no longer enter on the other, and facing her always across the crescent of that city, on the opposing bluff the first and oldest and perhaps the greatest of all the universities of Alinor.

That was what it was *about*.

And that card was about the weather. Thunderstorms … and what was thunder, exactly?

The noise of lightning. That was the basis of half of its ramifying significances, the idea that it was the sound made by light, the sound of illumination, the sound of the air being torn in two by a bolt of pure energy.

One of the things I liked best about the Two Stick and a Stone poets was how they used ordinary everyday things as natural symbols. They did not just arbitrarily *assign* meaning, like encoding a cipher; instead they looked at things around them and tried to see what they *really* were, if you looked hard enough.

I took a step back from the table so I could take a harder look at all the people gathered round.

My glance lit on the coolly elegant and coolly amused figure of the Chancellor of Morrowlea, who was the world's foremost Scholar of Lightning.

"Chancellor," I said through all the babble, "why precisely did you come to Ragnor Bella?"

Only my uncle kept muttering after that.

The Chancellor regarded me with her usual gravity and unshakeable dignity, and then she inclined her head and smiled. "I was invited to witness the Turning of the Waters tomorrow by Red Myrta."

Chapter Thirty
Ebraöni

"YOU CAN'T TRUST him," said Mr. Dart.

I glanced across the room. We were leaning against the wall by the window; my uncle sat staring dumbly into the fire. Everyone else stood or sat in clusters around the room. Ben, Jack, Dominus Lukel, Sir Hamish; Master Dart, the Chancellor, Hal. The other two Scholars were still outside looking at the bones.

"I don't."

"Well, then. You know what Roald said about his tells. Why did you believe what he said?"

"I didn't."

"Mr. Greenwing!"

"Ssh."

"Oh, very well, explain in your own way."

"Either he is complicit or he is a blind fool. I am inclined to the latter opinion, but I haven't ruled out the former. There's still one mystery left to crack."

Mr. Dart shook his head. "Only one? Why were you taken away for two days?"

"Clearly it was to keep me out of the way. Otherwise they

could have just made up a story about how I slipped on something and hit my head."

He looked dissatisfied. "That's hardly a good answer."

I laughed at that. He looked even more disgruntled. "I'm sorry," I said, trying to sober myself. "Everything is going round and round in my head. It keeps *almost* making sense, but none of my theories account for all the facts."

"What's sticking out? That your father is not *actually* dead?"

"That's one," I agreed, then looked around hastily to see if anyone else had heard us. No one appeared to have. "Let's go outside, Mr. Dart, and see if the Scholars have discovered anything interesting."

"It might shake something loose," he agreed, and so we repaired to the courtyard.

The Chief Constable and his underlings had disappeared. Domina Enory and Dominus Vitor were standing next to the bones, both in attitudes of the most extreme puzzlement. They swung round when we arrived to frown at us.

"Is something the matter?" Mr. Dart asked. "Is there anything we can do?"

Domina Enory pointed accusingly at the bones. "These are *fake.*"

We looked down. They certainly *looked* like real bones. I cleared my throat. "In what respect? Are they made of—something else?"

"They are real bones," Dominus Vitor said. He was back to looking disgusted. "Bull, boar, stag."

I felt very confused. "Then what is the problem?"

Domina Enory folded her arms across her chest. Her mouth was tight, as if she had discovered that someone had tricked her.

"These are made to *appear* as if they were used for the semblancing spell," she said finally.

Mr. Dart understood first. "They weren't? The semblance was a fake?"

"It's not the result of cultic magic. It's all silver-gilt, red paint, and soot. It was never informed by magic."

I grabbed Mr. Dart by the shoulder to catch myself. I felt dizzy with the speed of my thoughts. "When? When would that have been done?"

The two Scholars looked at each other. "We'd have to do some other tests," Dominus Vitor said.

"Could it have been recently?"

"Oh, no," he said immediately. "These bones have been under the ground for years at least."

"Seven years?"

"Could be," he said reluctantly. "I'm sorry, Mr. Greenwing, I know this must be very distressing to you to find your father's bones disturbed."

"They're not his bones," Mr. Dart said. "That seems to be the problem."

The world spun, the pattern shaking loose so it could start to form anew.

In the Two Sticks and a Stone poets, it was the presence of an incongruous word or detail or allusion that indicated there was a meaning below the surface meaning. Find that odd poetical word for wool, *ebraöni*, and when you looked closer you might find that the wool had been pulled over your eyes.

For the Gainsgooding conspirators, it was figuring out where were the gaps in the allusions and cross-references that had permitted Empress Dangora IV's successor to identify who had been playing the game. They had never named their target: the Empress they assassinated was the absent darkness in the centre of all the present light.

Sometimes what you needed to decipher the presence of meaning was to uncover the *absence* of something.

My father's living *presence* had seemed the incongruity, the detail that indicated something else was going on. But what if it was his absence that was significant?

—If this was a *fake*, then we did not need Dominus Gleason to be connected to Sir Vorel in the matter at all. Sir Vorel could have been the one too weak to kill his brother but too fearful to let him live and take the consequences—

Then what was *Lady Flora* doing tonight?

I muttered something incoherent and rushed into the house. I doubt I would have been any more coherent in asking for her, but to my relief I discovered Ellen trimming the lamp wicks in the front hall.

"Mr. Dart, Lord Jemis. Can I help you with anything?"

She sounded hopeful. I smiled fleetingly at her. I'd always liked wick-trimming duty at Morrowlea, but then I'd only had to do it once a week. "Yes, as a matter fact, you can. I need to know who I should talk to over at Arguty Manor to find out what Lady Flora is up to tomorrow. My uncle is here and doesn't know."

Mr. Dart gave me an astonished glance, but refrained from comment. Ellen wrinkled her nose. "My mum's visiting Mrs. Brock again. Something about the cellars at home."

We went to the kitchen, where Mrs. Brock looked appalled and the sight of Mrs. Bellfrey immediately took me back to my childhood. No wonder Ellen had seemed familiar: she was the image of her mother from the dark curly hair to the cheerful smile.

"Supper will be in an hour, Mr. Perry, so don't go trying to look winsome at me."

I doubted winsome was a word anyone would ever think to apply to me, so I decided to try instead for candour. "It smells wonderful, Mrs. Brock. Mrs. Bellfrey, I'm Jemis Greenwing—"

"As if I wouldn't remember my dear Mr. Jack's boy! Our Ellen's been full of stories since you came home. She's all fired up for the examinations, thank goodness, thinking of what you did, though what she can do without a tutor I don't know."

"Oh, *Mum!*"

"That teacher at the kingschool hasn't any extra time for our Ellen or Jem's Nedling, and they're the brightest in the year, you know, and—"

"Perhaps I can give them some advice on studying for the Entrance Examinations," I said, mostly to interrupt the flow, and before she switched to the outpouring of gratitude that was sure to follow, made haste to ask my questions.

"Lady Flora? Oh, she's given me the night off. She's dining at the Terrilees' over in Yellem tonight, and staying over as she usually does."

Sir Mattrin Terrilee was the Chief Magistrate of Yellem. A good man for a fly, said my uncle; not so sound on wild allegations.

The mechanics of the past week were becoming clearer. "Does she travel through the Forest alone?"

Mrs. Bellfrey chuckled. "Good heavens, no, she takes Hagwood with her for safety." She sniffed. "Though what good he'd do in a fight I don't know. Coward to the bone, that man. Afraid of ghosts something fierce—he was gabbling about Mr. Jack's rising. As if *he* would be so inconsiderate!—I do beg your pardon, Lord Jemis."

"Thank you," I said, as that seemed easiest. "What's the matter with the cellars, Mrs. Bellfrey?"

She made an annoyed tsking noise. "Just after Lady Flora left, with barrels for the Terrilees as a gift—our cellar is better than theirs, you know, they haven't a clue how to store their liquor properly. *Or* where the best place is to get it. Everyone knows that the wine merchant in Yellem hasn't a collection worth the name. Why, I remember my father—do you remember, Mrs. Brock, how he would lay down the port for the old master, Sir Rinald the elder that was, as carefully as a mother with her babe. 'There,' he'd say, 'that will keep us through a reign or two'."

Or through one poor wager at the Yrchester races, I thought, and smiled as winsomely as I could. I didn't have Mr. Dart's charm, alas. "Lady Flora had left, you say?"

"Yes, and then who should show up but these *lawyers* from Kingsford, with a letter saying they were to search the house for contraband. I ask you! A Justice of the Peace's house! High *and* low they were looking. Can you believe it?"

I could, and, moreover, did. Even further, I was fairly certain that Mr. Morres and Mr. Tey were not only looking for contraband whiskey, and that very likely they would be most interested in the contents of my uncle's secret desk drawer. One look at Mr. Dart suggested he was thinking much the same. We hastened therefore back to the library, where my father sat alone, next to the fire, with the table full of papers before him.

He looked up as we entered. The curtains had not yet been drawn against the night, so I saw him with the fire reflected many times around him in the windows.

I saw him as if for the first time: the unruly dark hair, the now-neatly trimmed dark beard, the eyepatch, the lopsided smile.

A surge of joy began in my feet. It travelled up my body until it broke free in the form of a smile.

"We're so close," I said or tried to, for even as I uttered the words he lurched up and knocked all the papers flying and engulfed me in an embrace.

I had been thinking so much of everything else that I had forgotten that we had not been even close to private since the breaking of the curse.

"Muffin?" offered Mr. Dart, turning overwhelming emotion into laughter. He set the plate on the table, I gathered up the loose papers, and we were about to sit down when Sir Hamish joined us.

"I asked Vorel about the burial," he said. "We've moved him to the parlour," he added to us. "Easier to shut him in."

"Oh?" My father sounded remarkably blasé.

"He said it was a closed coffin. No one looked inside after Hagwood and the magister put the body in."

"He didn't witness it?"

"He was prostrate with emotion. He did manage to praise his wife's fortitude in preparing the body and sparing him that grief."

"No explanation for why *my* wife wasn't involved?"

Sir Hamish looked sympathetically at him. "Jack, I can imagine how hard this is. Harry Hagwood was a friend."

"Mama was ill," I said into the following silence. "I fell ill then, too, so she was nursing me."

"The curse," Mr. Dart supplied, nodding.

"Leaving a coffin full of enchanted animal bones to stand in for me."

"Well, there's a wrinkle in that theory," I said, and let Mr. Dart explain while I tried to think.

Tomorrow was the Fallowday of the Autumn, when the Dark Kings were most easily summoned.

Tomorrow was the anniversary of my father's apparent suicide, the mystery of which was only growing.

Tomorrow Red Myrta had invited the Chancellor of Morrowlea to witness the Turning of the Waters, which sounded like it might be something to do with the (literal) Crimson Lake and the tippermongaramy and the Magarran Strid.

Tomorrow was the last day of the spur weeks, the day before the Winterturn Assizes started, in Astandalan days the day on which the bounds of the barony were beaten and rituals designed to reinforce Schooled magic and the Lady's church and diminish the Dark Kings' cult were conducted.

Sir Hamish said that the Chancellor was supposed to meet Red Myrta at the White Cross at dawn, so that they would have plenty of time to get wherever they were going before noon, when the ceremonies started.

Noon, not to mention the Chancellor's presence, suggested Red Myrta's activities had to do with the Lady and Schooled magic and not the Dark Kings.

Lady Flora and Mr. Hagwood had theoretically gone to Yellton to dine with the Terrilees and stay over. They had taken some number of barrels with them, ostensibly as a gift, just before the two Kingsford lawyers arrived to search the premises.

I jumped when the dinner gong rang. Mr. Dart laughed. "It's been a long day. Shall we collect everyone from the parlour?"

But when we went into the room it was to a cry of surprise and pain, the crash of a breaking window, and a sudden howling wind.

I snapped into the world of mortal danger. Dominus Lukel was staggering back, hand to bleeding brow. Hal was sprawled over a chair, grabbing his injured ankle. And my uncle was three-quarters of the way across the lawn.

I was at the eaves of the forest before it occurred to me that this was not perhaps the brightest idea I had ever had.

Chapter Thirty-One
Jack-in-the-Box

I REALLY MUST practice making quick turns and about-faces at high speed.

***

I hit an icy patch of leaves, careened wildly, and skidded to a halt in a thicket where, unfortunately, people were waiting for me.

"*Tavo!*" someone cried even as I tried to recover my balance. "*Tavo! Tavo!* It's not working! Why isn't it working?"

"Because it's *Taivo*, you idiot," said another voice. "*Taivo!*"

Taivo meant 'hold', I thought semi-hysterically, and then it dawned on me that they were trying magically to bind me, and also that I felt no constraints on me whatsoever.

And also that the voices belonged to Lady Flora and Mr. Hagwood, and neither of them was a wizard, and if this was magic borrowed from Dominus-not-really-Gleason, removing the curse might also have removed any other bindings he might have put on me—

All this went through my mind to reach the conclusion that it was more strategic to *pretend* I was bound. I concluded this approximately three seconds before it occurred to them to check.

Taivo—hold—*hold still*, presumably. I held still.

Someone swung a poacher's lantern around so that its half-circle of light illuminated my face. No werelight? Ben and Jack had had a werelight ... *Roald* had had a werelight ... But these were people playing with the Dark Kings, not the magic of the Empire of the Sun-on-Earth.

The swinging light made me feel a bit dizzy. I closed my eyes. I couldn't see much anyway, in the shadows and glare, but the glimpses were enough to determine who was there.

My uncle, my aunt, Mr. Hagwood, and a large dim object I took, from the accompanying smells and sounds, to be a cart pulled by a remarkably placid horse. The horse alone, by its placidity in the face of suddenly-appearing people in the darkness, indicated that this was no new business.

I wished I'd been slightly more strategic, oh, about ten minutes earlier.

I wished I had not been quite so stupid as to run precipitously across the lawn after my uncle. One of the finest soldiers of the late Empire had been in the room: I might have waited to see what he thought we should do.

"Well, we have him," said my uncle. "Now what?"

***

'Now what' consisted of getting me to climb into a large barrel on the back of the cart.

As I continued to feel no magical constraint, I confess it taxed my capacity for subterfuge to the limit to make myself obey the command to climb in.

Eventually, with some assistance from Mr. Hagwood, I folded myself to fit the space, knees up against my chest and chin resting on crossed arms. I then concentrated on not hyperventilating with quite ridiculous instinctive panic.

"We'd better hurry," Sir Vorel said nervously. "Someone might come after us."

And why hadn't anybody? Getting me into the barrel must have taken five minutes at least, plenty of time for any of the people who had witnessed my flight across the lawn to decide on a plan of action and begin to execute it.

Unless the plan of action was to see what happened. So far all we had was the letter from Eil and a great deal of suppositions. To do anything but demonstrate my father's innocence we needed *proof*. This would surely give proof of smuggling, and almost certainly of illegal magic (for the ceremonies connected with the Dark Kings had always been against the law)—if I kept my head (the rest of the evening) and they went to gather witnesses.

—Such as the Chancellor of Morrowlea, one of the most respected people in the world. Who had been invited by Red Myrta to see the Turning of the Waters, coincidentally on the Fallowday anniversary of my father's apparent suicide.

The barrel had been used to store whiskey. The fumes were incredible.

My aunt was speaking. "There's a diversion, husband, which you might have waited another three minutes for. Once we're away no one will be able to follow us."

A cart wouldn't leave sufficient trace? Back in Astandalan days the highway might have been kept clear and clean by quite extravagant use of magic, but no one in Ragnor barony bothered to *sweep* it. It was the tail end of autumn. All through the forest would be drifts of wet oak leaves such as the ones I had just skidded on.

Someone pushed the back of my head. I jerked at the unexpected touch.

"He's not so calm as last time. He keeps moving."

Mr. Hagwood's monotone held a bit of whine, whether of complaint or nerves I wasn't quite sure.

Lady Flora replied briskly. "Hammer the lid down, that'll keep him out of trouble. Us too, if we meet anyone before we get on the grey road. Come, husband, leave off it. Your woebegone expression is inappropriate."

It was too late and I was too entwined about myself to try to jump out of the barrel like a jack-(or Jemis)-in-the-box. Mr. Hagwood had a mallet and pounded the lid firmly into place. Accordingly I missed what my uncle said, but I heard my aunt's reply: "Nonsense. By this time tomorrow all our dreams will be fulfilled!"

***

I wondered if being conscious and unenchanted for this barrel-confinement would lessen my newfound dislike of small dark enclosed places.

Somehow I doubted it.

***

My three captors did not speak much. The cart rumbled along, from its sound on one of the forest roads. My barrel vibrated and jostled a little against the others on the cart, but was securely fastened in place and I did not bang except on the ruts that made everyone jump.

I tried to listen, and, failing anything to listen to, to think, but by the time I realized I could no longer smell the whiskey it was far too late.

**

I woke with a jolt to the sound of jays screaming.

I lifted my head without thinking, cracked it sharply on the inside of the barrel, and subsided again to acute agony from my limbs, a major throbbing from several parts of my head, and the disheartening sensation of an emerging hangover.

It was particularly disheartening since I had done nothing to earn it.

Well. Apart from acting like a total idiot, that was. It served me right that no one had rescued me yet.

The jays screamed again, alarms not muffled nearly enough by the wood staves of the barrel. I could not tell whether they were real birds or the imitations of Myrta the Hand's gang.

I wondered why she was called Myrta the Hand. It had a nice ring to it. Very ballad-friendly; it was even easy to rhyme with.

"Bloody birds," muttered Mr. Hagwood. "Give me the creeps, they do."

"That's enough," Lady Flora said. Her voice sounded at a distance, then suddenly boomed closer: "How long after dawn is it?"

"Not yet an hour, ma'am."

"We have time for something to eat, then," she decreed.

I shuddered at the idea of food, then bit the sleeve of my jacket to help keep myself from vomiting at the thought. I was already going to stink of whiskey; being covered with my own sick would be the last straw of any hope for a reputation not as wildly eccentric as my grandmother's.

Mr. Hagwood muttered something I didn't catch and went to make clattering noises a little distance away.

I was desperately thirsty.

I laid my cheek along my arms to give a slight change of position to my neck and tried to identify the various sounds I could hear.

It was remarkably disconcerting to be unable to see. My senses of taste and scent were useless, thoroughly occupied as they were with the whiskey. (I was sure I would be able to identify this specific vintage until the day of my death, which would hopefully be far in the future.) I felt a pang of regret for the loss of yet another suit of clothing. This left, what, one waistcoat, one pair of breeches, and two shirts? And no coat fit to wear at all. I hoped the winter-weight outfit I'd ordered from the local tailor would be ready soon.

A string of thumps, a heavy sigh, and a bit later, crackle and spit. Mr. Hagwood, dropping an armful of wood, kneeling to set the fire, the wood catching.

The grey jays or their human imitators were easy.

A creak and a tremor coming through the barrel wood, then more creaking, soft puffs, little half-vocalized sounds of protest or grunts: my uncle, climbing onto the cart.

"Jemis?" he whispered. "Jemis, can you hear me?"

Did he honestly think I'd *answer* that?

"Jemis, I didn't know, I'm sorry."

But what he didn't know and was sorry for I was not destined to find out at that moment, for Lady Flora said, "Vorel," in pre-emptory tones.

I supposed it was good to learn my uncle did in fact know what my name was.

I could feel his guilty start through the wood. "Oh, Flora, dear, yes, what can I do for you?"

I rolled my eyes in the darkness and felt marginally cheered.

"He won't remember a thing," Lady Flora said in encouraging tones that made the statement seem remarkably sinister. "No sense talking to him, my dear. He's dumb and deaf as the barrel."

"I'm not sure about this, Flora."

Her sigh of exasperation came through loud and clear.

There followed more creaks and quivers running through the barrel into my bones: Lady Flora, climbing up to sit next to her husband, which put them at a very convenient location for me to eavesdrop.

"Dear husband, surely you're not getting cold feet *now*? Now, when we're so close? A few more hours, a few more ceremonies, and all that we have worked for will be in our grasp at last."

Had that flurry of insights been *totally* wrong? Was he complicit in the whole thing, from the cult to the imputation of treason?

"If it were only the whiskey, Flora, it wouldn't seem so bad."

Her voice was warm and sympathetic. I had never heard her sound so warm, in fact: she actually sounded *fond*. "Vorel, my dear, I know you have reservations about the tippermongeramy, but that's where the real money is."

"I know, I know." He sighed heavily.

"You wouldn't be able to play with all your friends if we weren't doing it. Not to mention those splendid fish ponds of yours—they're worth all of it, aren't they?"

"I can't like to have dealings with those … people."

"My dear, they're the ones who have the skills to make it. They need us to sell it in the wider world."

"But they use magic, Flora. Strange magic. *Old* magic."

Did he not realize what *she* was involved with? Or whom?

She laughed. "It's because it's old magic that they *can* use it. They were using it long before the Empire came, and they're still using it now the Empire is gone."

Her voice was entirely positive, even approving; even triumphant.

"I know they think you're a descendant of the Blood Queen, Flora—"

"I *am* her descendant!

"By the Emperor, Flora! You're a daughter of the Empire. You must see it's wrong. It's one thing to smuggle whiskey—even that bloody tipperma-watsit—but what they're asking for today is—"

"Are your fish ponds not worth it?" she interrupted sweetly. "Those two carp you had shipped all the way from East Oriole? The hothouse so you can have warm-water fish the year round? All those *magnificent* water-pipes and pumps and reservoirs?"

"Yes, but—"

"But nothing. You're short of sleep and you haven't had breakfast yet. That always makes you grumpy, husband. You'll feel better after we've eaten."

"But Flora, last night at the Darts I discovered—"

Her voice acquired the familiar edge. "Husband, what have I told you about them?"

"Flora, they were friends with—"

"We are not going over that old business again!" she exclaimed. "Your sentiments of guilt come rather late in the game, husband! You have lost over four hundred thousand gold emperors at table over the past five years."

Four *hundred* thousand? The number was mind-boggling. Mr.

Buchance's entire fortune might be twice that, and he had died a very wealthy merchant.

"You have not paid a penny out of pocket, my dear husband. Have I asked you to stop your waterworks? Not to order your precious fish? Give over these misgivings. They come too late. You know the only reason you're still anybody is because of me and my friends in the Forest."

"Flora …"

There were creaks and movements of the cart: Lady Flora getting up, I surmised. Her voice was a bit more distant when she spoke next. "Come, husband, it's time for breakfast. We must prepare ourselves for the rendezvous—and for what comes after."

It didn't seem as if my uncle had immediately followed her, for I could hear him breathing heavily. Then I heard a scratching sound on the outside of the barrel, and then, in a soft whisper:

"Jemis, I didn't know the truth about my brother. I'm sorry about what's happening. I can't—"

"Vorel."

Chapter Thirty-Two
Complications

HAVING NOTHING ELSE to do, I thought.

It was not the same as the day before, those dizzying flights of intuition and insight.

Those were only good for finding signs of the truth. Outcroppings, as it were. They had seen me running headlong into a trap, reacting exactly as my uncle—or my aunt—thought I would.

I should have known better.

I should have been warier of that sort of high-flying exuberance. It was obviously an effect of undoing the curse. And possibly from having a proper amount of oxygen reaching my brain for once.

No, it was time to be methodical.

If I could not contrive to free myself before the others came, I wanted at least to be able to present them with all the requisite answers to our mysteries.

I spent a few minutes gathering my mental tools together. I had no pen or paper to write a chart or jot ideas, no books for references, no friends to question or harangue.

My tutor, Dominus Nidry, had frequently harangued us (his students in the year: Violet and myself) to, above all, be *logical*.

Ascertain the facts, he had said.

Begin with the letter of the text.

Never let your flights of fancy stray so far from the text you can no longer anchor your argument in certainty.

I squirmed. I had not been following that dictum very well of late. I had been jumping from speculation to speculation as if—well, as if I were high on wireweed, or a rhetorician using every trick in the book to convince without argument.

Dominus Nidry had also frequently said to me—for Violet had the opposite tendency—*Do not be so hasty to complicate things.*

I squirmed some more. And then, since there remained nothing else to do, I thought about it.

Perhaps it was *not* the blind malignancy of fate that was making my life so complicated. Perhaps it was me.

I closed my eyes, as if that would help. The strips and spots of light from the knots and loose joints that were also providing me with air were not at all conducive to sight, and aggravated the hangover.

Ignore that.

I had been protesting all along that it was not *my* fault that all these were going on, because it seemed utterly inconceivable that it was all about me—but what if I were wrong? What if I, or something to do with me, was at the centre of things not by coincidence but by—fate?

I thought back over the past few months. No one could have expected that I would have that altercation with Lark and as a result effectively disappear for two months—

No. Back up a step. Lark had picked me out of all in our year, why?

WHISKEYJACK 341

It wasn't for any great winsomeness of my personality or appearance, surely. There were more attractive men at Morrowlea.
Marcan came to mind, and Beau Benneret.

It wasn't because I was of influence or wealth. Even with Morrowlea's commitment to egalitarianism, there were always indica-
tions. Excluding Marcan, whom no one could have imagined was
the second son of the King of Lind (I personally had thought him
a prosperous yeoman farmer's son; Hal had confessed to me he'd
thought him an archbishop's by-blow), the obvious choice for such
a quarry, if that had been Lark's purpose, was Hal, whose colouring,
accent, and bearing all proclaimed him of high family.

It probably wasn't even the capacity to be overwhelmed. Lark
had only to smile (and blow a smoke ring full of wireweed) at me
to catch me: but she had been able to make most of the rest of
the university adore her almost as easily. While I certainly had my
weaknesses, general pusillanimity of character was not really one of
them. Running headlong into danger without thinking, yes. Collapsing like a wet cravat on the slightest hint of opposition … not
so much. There were students with much weaker wills than me at
Morrowlea. Beau Benneret, again, came to mind.

But none of them were the son of Mad Jack Greening.

I frowned into the darkness. I would have sworn Lark's astonishment at my confession of identity and family was genuine.

Don't overcomplicate things, Jemis.

If that was just the bonus, the added fillip, the means to final
humiliation and revenge?

If it was not my qualities as a person, nor my attributes as a
member of my family, that left … the magic.

Magic inherited from the Woods.

Magic inherited from a distant fairy ancestor.

Magic wild enough to summon a dragon (embodiment of chaotic magic) out of the wide dreaming.

And what had happened this spring? I had broken from the
wizard who had been using wireweed to steal said magic. Over the
course of the several months following, strange things had begun
happening in and around Ragnor Bella—in and around, that is, the
Woods.

Upon my eventual return in September, the frequency and
magnitude of these odd events increased considerably, from secret
society to cultic sacrifice, from gossip to riddling dragons, from ...
from Jemis Greenwing being most notable for being his father's
son, to becoming someone the only two open wizards in the barony—Dominus Gleason and the Marchioness—almost immediately started talking about in terms of magic and the need to be
trained.

For whatever reason, I decided reluctantly, my gift at magic was
significant. I only wished I knew what it signified.

Outside the barrel the jays were still intermittently calling. It
reassured me that we were in the Forest and people were on the
move. At this point I realized that *we* were again on the move, the
cart rumbling along another bumpy road.

If point one was the still-unclear significance of my magic,
what was point two?

Don't overcomplicate things ...

Why was I here, right now, in a barrel in a cart in the middle
of the Arguty Forest?

It did not seem an undue complication to acknowledge that
with respect to my uncle and my aunt (who were neither of them

wizards), I was more than simply a source of magic.

What else had we discovered?

It seemed that Lady Flora was behind my father's disgrace.

—No. ("What is *certain*, Jemis?") She was *connected* to the person or people behind the false letter.

In the decoded message she had been told to be always ready for further communication, as if she were a spy in deep cover—

I blinked and dazzled myself with the light-spots. Of course. It was that simple. All that talk about smuggling and so on was camouflage.

Oh, no doubt she made use of the money, too. From the conversation I'd just overheard, she was clearly the one in charge of the operation. And what better cover for a spy's activities than a smuggler's load?

—Well, I personally thought the Gainsgooding poets had a much better idea for how to hide their messages. They'd conducted their conspiracy in plain sight … but no matter that. Lady Flora seemed to be working with, or for, people who thought it charming to use the letter that compromised one party to give secret messages to the one who benefited from it.

Plenty of people looked the other way in order to get the good whiskey. Probably whoever was into the cosmetic made by the Tufa did the same.

If they actually made cosmetic with the tippermongeramy. It sounded as if the Tufa were somehow connected to the old cults—

—I was getting ahead of myself again. I'd missed a connection. Giving secret messages through letters that compromised people …

What would I discover if I tried to decipher the blackmailing letters my uncle had received? Was he—could he possibly be—being blackmailed by the person or people his wife was serving?

I thought of my uncle's face on hearing Hal's story about the true events at Loe, on my translating the letter to reveal its perfidy. I did not believe him a good enough actor to feign those reactions.

And he had whispered that last confession to what he believed was his insensate nephew in a barrel …

My uncle, alas, was weak-willed and habitually under his wife's control. Even if he had cold feet about whatever they were planning, I couldn't see him doing more than make his futile protests about it.

This all suggested my insight that they were not working together was at least partially true. They were evidently in the smuggling game together—but not, perhaps, at one with the deeper betrayals.

The coded letter had implied that Lady Flora had married Vorel in order to—what? To establish herself in Ragnor Bella? To be close to Jack Greenwing? To be close to *me*?

Back up.

Various phrases from the letter suggested its writer (writers? 'We who speak from the shadows') was connected with the old cult to the Dark Kings.

General Ben had expressed surprise at discovering that the Dark Kings were worshipped here, in Ragnor Bella, when he knew them from far away at the edge of the Empire in Loe.

In Loe, where there had been a betrayal, and where my father had been sent across the Border and reportedly lost in a valiant last stand against the Stone Speakers, who worshipped the Dark Kings.

In Ragnor Bella, where Jack Greenwing was from, where

the Bloody Queen had fought an extraordinary battle against the knights of the Lady's church, where people had made unsavoury sacrifices at the king oak on the Hanging Hill during the days of the Empire, and where, after the Fall of the Empire, there was still a cult to the Dark Kings, and people still did unsavoury things in the name of the old gods.

What did I know about the Dark Kings? A few snippets from History of Magic. Rumours and gossip. What Mr. Dart and I had observed of their cultic practices at the Ellery Stone.

I went over that ceremony in my mind. It had started off so silly, so risible—and by the end of it we'd fled in serious fear for our lives and our souls. I had nearly been caught by some sort of silver-mist-borne fascination. I had been rescued by Mr. Dart, at the sacrifice of his right arm to petrification.

Back up. The ceremony.

They had focused their rituals around a stone they called the Heart of the Moon. But the stone they had been using was just a chunk of obsidian, not the true legendary object. (So said Mrs. Etaris, who had received this information from Magistra Bellamy, Ragnor Bella's resident witch, who had precipitously left town to visit relatives after the events that had followed that weekend, and had yet to return home.)

I frowned some more. I had been studying the *Legendarium* all this past fortnight. That compendium of lore, superstitions, and fairy tales did not mention the Heart of the Moon.

Mrs. Etaris had talked about it as if it were a well-known story.

The only reference I could think of was the one in *Kissing the Moon*. Fitzroy Angursell claimed that the Moon had fallen in love with him. (Now there was someone who had no problem believing that the events of the Nine Worlds turned about him!) He said offhandedly that this was because he had stolen her heart.

I liked and greatly admired Fitzroy Angursell's poetry, but that sounded pure literary conceit.

If not that, then what? South Fiellan was considered the least adversely-affected region after the Fall. What other unusual or unique magical things did South Fiellan contain?

The Arguty Forest. The Magarran Strid. Tippermongeramy. Really good whiskey.

The Woods Noirell. The old border crossing to Astandalas. A border with the Kingdom Between Worlds.

The bees of Melmúsion. The Wild Saint. The Hunter in Green. Me?

I sighed. Back a step. What else did I know about the old cult to the Dark Kings?

They had sacrificed a cow at the Ellery Stone near the autumn equinox. Mrs. Etaris had said that once they started the sacrifices, they would not long rest content with cows.

Tomorrow—today—was the Fallowday of the Autumn, once a significant date in the calendar.

The Black Priest was still on the loose and unrecognized. I had no proof, after all, that it was Dominus-not-really-Gleason.

Seven years ago the body of my father had been found dangling from the king oak on the Hanging Hill, which might or might not be the burial mound of the Red Queen, who might or might not be Lady Flora's ancestor.

Whether or not it was *actually* true, Lady Flora clearly believed it was and acted accordingly. No doubt that was why she was drawn to the cult of the Dark Kings. The Bloody Queen had not earned her epithet by being a peaceful adherent of the Lady of the Green and White.

I was really very thirsty.

It was odd I had suffered no physical ill effects from the last confinement—well, apart from the memory loss—and what had they been doing that they'd need me out of the way for?

—Or was it that they had needed me *to hand*?

If I were at the centre of the cult's activities, then perhaps the reason I'd been captured wasn't because I'd inadvertently seen something I shouldn't have, nor that I was in the way for whatever they were doing—moving contraband whiskey, I'd thought—then—

Well, I wasn't sure what then, except that I was increasingly disturbed that I couldn't remember what they'd done.

Outside the barrel noises indicated we were crossing hollow wooden planks—a bridge. As if the crossing gave permission, my uncle began to speak.

"Now, Flora, are you sure we—"

"Don't start all that again, dear husband. Think of the rewards that are coming."

He sounded unconvinced. "It seems so extreme."

She laughed gaily. I could imagine her patting his plump cheek. She'd done that once or twice to me as a boy, back before she'd engineered my father's disgrace and was still trying to pretend she liked me.

"Dear Vorel. You don't need to do anything but witness. I promised you that. And when have I ever not accomplished what I said I'd do?"

"It's not you that I have misgivings about. He's going to be missed, you know."

"My dear, I've told you time and time again, in these matters my master and I are one. As for your nephew, very shortly he will cease to be your problem. After the ceremony is complete … "

"Yes, yes, you've explained, but what about his friends? They might very well come for him. They'd be stupid not to know we're involved. What if—"

"You forget the diversion. And you forget that we were able—no thanks to you!—to prepare him properly, after all. And most of all, dear husband, you forget that today is the day the true gods walk. As soon as the sun leaves its zenith my master will open the ford. Everything is ready. The ritual is prepared, the ingredients are collected, the place is panting with eagerness for its splendour to come upon it again. We need only to arrive with our chosen sacrifice."

Her voice was so exultant I could imagine my uncle shrinking away from it. I was so caught up in visualizing his reaction that it took a moment for it to penetrate that they were talking about killing me.

Chapter Thirty-Three
The Magarran Strid

THE MAGARRAN STRID is, they say, the most dangerous stretch of water in all of Northwest Oriole.

It didn't look it.

It looked like a placid brook, actually. There was deep green moss and green ferns growing on the stones of its bank, and the sun shone in long white streaks across its glossy surface. Only the sound of a deep subterranean rumble gave any indication otherwise. Or so I thought, until my uncle tilted his head nervously. "What's that noise?"

Lady Flora was out of my line of sight, but I could hear her fond exasperation. "The waterfall down from the lake."

Crimson Lake?

"Come away from the bank, my dear, we don't want you to slip and fall in!"

He took a few tentative steps towards the direction her voice was coming from. I kept staring in the direction I'd been planted; my neck was too stiff to make movement easy, anyway, and clearly they all thought me still under the spell. He cast one piteous, guilty look at me, and then disappeared.

Mr. Hagwood came into my line of sight. He was searching the bank for something, and eventually bent to pick up a small object. He passed upstream out of my line of sight, returning at length with the horse and cart.

I shuddered unintentionally at the sight of the barrels. I wasn't sure I'd ever be able to stomach another mouthful of whiskey again. One of those four barrels was the one I'd been transported in. Mr. Hagwood kicked at the grass, picked up a long plank, stowed it on the back of the cart, and led the (truly very patient) horse off downstream. He did not look at me, either with triumph or remorse. He simply walked, humming tunelessly.

I felt a great disappointment in Harry Hagwood.

When we'd arrived at this mostly-featureless stretch of the Magarran River gorge, I had been so stiff from my night's confinement, and so stupefied from the combination of the fumes and my conclusions, that I had not even tried to escape when Hagwood pried the lid off. He and my uncle had man-handled me out of the barrel—not without a great deal of effort on their part and some additional bruising on mine. While I was still sitting on the bank in the same folded position as I'd been inside the barrel, blinking dazedly at the sunlight, they bound my hands and ankles together with thick twine.

I'd hoped vaguely that they would leave me on the bank, but Lady Flora had other ideas. Along with the barrels, the cart had contained the long plank. It was about ten feet long and a foot wide. This they slid out across the river, taking care to keep it from touching the water, until it rested on a boulder jutting out midstream. Mr. Hagwood then carried me across this makeshift bridge. He set me down, still in my crumpled-up position, and tethered me to a heavy iron ring set in the stone for good measure.

Watching him pick his way back across the plank, I realized this must be the Strid. The plank wobbled a bit at one point, and he glanced down, and went as grey as he had on seeing my father in the mist.

I waited a few moments. A few birds sang; no jays called.

I appeared to be alone, at least within my immediate field of vision.

Oh, what the hell, I thought, tied I might be at wrists and ankles, and tethered as well, but I had room enough to straighten. The exquisite pain of this process occupied me for a while. Eventually the sensations in my joints receded to ignorable levels.

Whatever the diversion had been, my father and friends would surely be on their way to rescue me by now.

I squinted at the sky. I had always assumed, from their name, the reputation of their magic, and from the events at the Ellery Stone, that sacrifices to the Dark Kings were made at midnight. However, Lady Flora's words had suggested some time after noon.

The sun was high. I was not familiar enough with the geography of the Forest to know the exact course of the Magarran. It flowed west and north out of the Crosslain Mountains towards its confluence with the Rag at Tenbridge. At this specific point of the forest?

I would presume it was getting on for noon.

My hands and feet felt bloated, my fingers like sausages.

Ignoring that for the moment … Could I be sure this was the Strid? It might be another stream. There were many of them coming out of the mountains.

I shuffled around slowly on my boulder until my view of the surface was not quite so sun-dazzled. Still nobody visible on the banks, which was something of a mixed relief.

The river was about twelve feet wide. My boulder stood in the middle, closer to the eastern (call it eastern) bank, the one we'd come from, by two or three feet. There were a few other boulders that broke the surface here and there, though mine was the driest and most substantial. Not that that was saying much: the limestone was deucedly uncomfortable to sit on, cold and with hard edges.

The water was beautifully clear. I could see other boulders, all in that fine bright white limestone, ones not big enough to rise above the water, and below them …

I very carefully sat up and even more carefully inched myself to a firmer seat on the top of what was not a boulder at all.

Still waters run deep, went the proverb. The Magarran was not exactly *still*, but its surface was calm, the only hint of its currents the odd bubble coming up from below.

Or so it seemed, until the mind realized what the eye was seeing. And then you saw that the boulders were not stones tumbled down from a rock face but the topmost tips of pinnacles that went down until even bright white limestone vanished into darkness.

I pried a loose flake off my perch. It was white, and clearly visible, for the two heartbeats before it was swept down and away and *down*.

I could well believe that no one who fell into the Strid had ever been found again.

I sat very still as I worked at the knots around my wrists.

***

I could grow to like the grey jays, I thought when half-a-dozen alarm-calls echoed through the woods around me. These were much closer than those from earlier. By the time I had laboriously changed my direction to face the bank opposite the one I'd arrived by the birds were swooping into sight.

One darted out over the water and perched on my bound hands, which I'd propped up on my bent knees. (I wasn't sure I was ever going to be able to fully unbend myself.) I looked at it, enjoying the bright dark eye alive with a kind of quizzical interest, the neat grey cap on the back of its head, the white bib and soft cloud-grey plumage.

A whistle made it flit off again. I could not see the whistler. I weighed the pros and cons of calling out. On the one hand, Red Myrta had been at Morrowlea with me, she might well have the Chancellor with her, and her mother had seemed not totally disinclined to like me.

On the other hand, they were the source of the whiskey everyone else was smuggling, they had made it clear that they were on the wild lay and behaved accordingly, and their camp was right at the base of the Hanging Hill where sacrifices were made.

I had not quite decided what to do when Red Myrta and the Chancellor walked out of the trees in front of me.

"Good morning," I called, making an ungainly wave with both my hands.

"Jemis," said Red Myrta, sighing with a gesture visible across the river. "Of course this where you ended up."

***

They disappeared back into the trees. I waited. I did not, truly, have anything else to do. My fingers were beginning to respond more naturally to my efforts to bend them, but were far from dextrous enough to deal with the knots.

After a while they reappeared. They bore a dead tree with them, trunk stripped of bark and branches and bone-white. After some muted discussion, they slid the tree out across the river awards me.

I caught it when it reached me and then sat there dumbly with it in my lap.

"Come on, then!" cried Red Myrta.

"I can't." I would gladly have pretended otherwise, but did not possess the physical faculties.

"What do you mean, can't?"

"I'm tied up." I repeated the words again when a change in the river's sound overran them.

We all looked at the water. For the first glance it appeared no different; then I saw that its former apparent placidity was increasingly disturbed. Eddies and swirls and little whirlpools were forming, chains of bubbles came up in long silver streams from deep, deep down, and now on the surface there was foam. The foam was tinged an odd pinkish colour—and the waterfall was no longer a distant rumble, but a roar.

Myrta made a very alarmed and consequently alarming gesture at me. "The turn's starting! Jemis, you have to come *now*. Here!"

I tore my gaze from the pink foam just in time to see her fling a sheathed knife at me.

Red Myrta was always good at throwing games, thank the Lady. Equally thankfully she did not expect me to be as good at catching it: it landed in my lap as neatly as a ball into a basket.

With the knife I could fumble my hands and feet free. I addressed the tether last, all the while trying not to look at the water now boiling around my rock. Finally the rope fell free.

I looked at the tree trunk. They had kept hold of the thicker base, and the topmost portion of the tree narrowed to a broken-off stump about the width of three fingers.

The water changed noise again, yet deeper in pitch and louder in volume. It was quite an extraordinary sound, as if the water was churning stones against each other.

Myrta shouted something whose sense the water snatched away. It was presumably *hurry hurry hurry*. It was not a very helpful exhortation. I had never heard anything as urgent as the sound and feel of the water around me. The pinnacle of rock I was perched on was vibrating, almost humming with the force of the water striking it.

Where was the clear world of mortal danger when one wanted it? The danger was there: where was the clarity?

I glanced at the tree trunk to see how stable it seemed.

All the foam, and there was a lot of foam now, was red as blood. There.

Now it all made sense. Now I could see how to get across the red-boiling most dangerous stretch of water in all of Northwest Oriole without adding myself to its tally of innumerable dead. My father had just come home, alive, from a death I thought had happened seven years ago today. I could not leave him alone to face the year ahead!

I shoved the narrow tip of the tree as far as it would go into the iron loop I had been tethered to. On the far bank Red Myrta and the Chancellor were holding the other end of the trunk, which made it as stable as the situation was going to permit. I took a deep breath and tried to focus on the smooth silvery-grey wood, the black knots where branches once had been, the tiny holes made by insects and the larger ones made by woodpeckers.

I could not recall when I had looked past the wood to the water, but the crimson foam was surging madly half a foot below me.

There was no way on earth I would be able to balance upright. I was too stiff to be sure I could even *stand* upright at the moment. My knees did not want to unbend, my arms barely wanted to move past a circumscribed arc.

Well, said the inner voice that knew what to do when the world outside was mad with danger, that had given me the insight not to attack the dragon's jaw where the asbestos palate and rising fire was, that had given me the reactions almost to guess what it would do before it did so. Well: if you cannot straighten, if you cannot balance upright, then use your bent, embrace your limitations, make them your strengths. That is the way of the poet, who takes the constraints of his form and turns them into freedom; that is the way of the warrior who desires to live.

I tipped myself forward, knees on either side of the trunk, elbows bent close to my sides. Crossed my crossed ankles over the log rather than each other, to keep them from dangling into the mad red foam. Leaned forward slowly, central core muscles screaming murder at having to work so slowly, until my chest rested on the silvery wood and my elbows could cup the log, my sausage hands grip.

The tree bounced.

The clarity and the slow-down of all the world around me increased considerably.

I moved forward without hesitation, without thought, without any fear permitted anywhere near the surface of my mind, any more than the surface of the Strid showed what was going on underneath. No water was visible now, let alone any of the pinnacles below; the water now was one thick cloud of red foam. It looked like the scarf or sock Mrs. Etaris was knitting out of that pouffy scarlet wool.

Ebraöni, I thought distantly. And was this colour crimson lake?

Perhaps it was Crimson Lake, the dam on its waters burst to boil into the river.

But Red Myrta had expected this, had invited her tutor, the Chancellor of Morrowlea, to come witness the Turning of the Waters.

Did this happen every year?

—Or only when a priest of the Dark Kings went to *open the gate* preparatory to human sacrifice?

The trunk was vibrating with sympathetic motion. I was sweating, the drops falling down red with the spume cast up by the Strid. The sound was phenomenal. I could barely hear myself think: soon stopped trying to, in my mind only the refrain of *Crimson Lake, Crimson Lake, Crimson Lake* to the inchworm progress across the log.

I could hear shrieks: the grey jays making their alarm-calls. Was there someone else here? Was I going to roll off the log at the other end and discover myself captured by someone else?

The air temperature dropped and with it the pressure. I found myself flattened to the log. It was wider here, my progress impeded by a stump of a branch sticking out, but I was so close—maybe three feet from the bank, and safety—

The noise had changed, I thought dumbly as I tried to raise myself against the downdraft. I could not move, my muscles weak as exhaustion.

Weak *with* exhaustion, I thought stupidly, looking down past the log despite myself.

Down, and down, and down, and—

The water dropped another dozen feet even while I tried to see what I was seeing. Leaving a scurf of red foam everywhere, coating all those pillars and pinnacles that from the surface seemed mere boulders, the Magarran Strid drained out of its gorge like water out of a bathtub.

Something deep within me propelled me forward against the downdraft and against the primal fear of depths that the fifty—hundred—hundred and fifty feet now below me inspired.

I flung myself off the trunk and rolled twice over and over to end up face-down in a pile of wet leaves. I spat one out and hadn't the energy for any more.

Someone stepped on my back.

Chapter Thirty-Four
The Turning of the Waters

I GROANED.

"Don't be an idiot," Red Myrta said briskly.

"I'm not going to run anywhere," I said, or had begun to say when the breath went out of my lungs with an ungainly *whoosh*. Whoever was standing on my back—for all I had been paying attention, all of Myrta the Hand's gang and another dragon could have arrived while I was crossing the Strid—appeared to be barefoot. I could distinctly feel toes. They walked, actually *walked*, up and down my back. I lay there with my face in the cold wet leaves trying to keep my whimpering as inaudible as possible. Everything in my body protested the walker's attentions; specific muscles in my back quivered, clenched, and released like uncoiling springs. I tried hard not to cry.

After an interminable while the person gave a bounce and then left me alone. I lay there, face in the cold leaves, breathing shallowly and too rapidly.

"Come on, then," Red Myrta said even more briskly. "We have things to do."

I rolled over and accepted the hand she held out to me. When she pulled me up, which assistance I needed, the first thing I noticed was that I was able to unfold all the way. The second was that the Chancellor of Morrowlea was sitting on the end of the tree trunk putting her boots back on.

"Er, thank you," I said, swinging my arms experimentally. My fingers still felt like sausages, but at least they were tingling with returning circulation now.

"You have a leaf on your face," Red Myrta said, not looking away from the gorge opened up before us. "Phew, you stink!

"I think that was the barrel," I said awkwardly. I brushed at my face until various bits of leaf-litter rubbed away. The Chancellor seemed entirely unconscious of the depth behind her. She stood up gracefully and came to stand next to me. "You're very welcome, Jemis. One must say that your physical courage is exemplary."

I had only had the Chancellor as a lecturer a few times, but I knew what that meant. I didn't know if my muscles would stand for a bow, so I made do with an apologetic grimace. "I'm afraid I sometimes have a tendency to act before thinking. I am trying to work on it."

"Good."

I desperately wanted to ask her if she had learned the walking-on-backs technique from her time in a travelling acrobatic troupe. She looked every inch a princess and the foremost Scholar on lightning and one of the three most important university officials in the world. But ... but I probably never would find out the truth of that particular story. I simply couldn't bring myself to ask her directly. I stared at the ground, willing my blushes to subside. I did stink, of stale whiskey and sweat and wood.

As my general embarrassment subsided, I realized that I was

behind-hand on too many points. "Chancellor, may I ask if you know what the plan is? What was the diversion that happened back at Dart Hall?"

"It was a fire in the old granary," she said gravely.

"No! That beautiful roof ... At least it was empty." She looked quizzically at me. "Usually it's used to store surplus produce for the winter."

"It did have your dragon in it."

It took a moment to realize what she meant. "I suppose it did. Does that mean the Scholars won't be able to finish studying it? That would be a pity. Dominus Vitor seemed so pleased with it."

She smiled. "I believe that having the flesh largely burned off will aid in the preservation of the bones, and indeed make it far easier to transport than otherwise. I must congratulate you, Mr. Greenwing, on the fact that your first response was for the irreplaceable beauty of the building and your second for the food it might have held."

Should I have thought first about the dragon? Or—my heart sank. "I'm very sorry it happened. Master Dart will not be happy with me."

"It's hardly your fault."

I had to look away from her mildly amused glance. (She and Sir Hamish had much the same deep appreciation for the many small ironies of life.) "Apart from, er, running straight after my uncle just as it was expected I would do, the fire was lit as a diversion to keep everyone occupied while I was carried off here in a barrel." I gestured at the river behind us. "I know that my—that Jack would have had a better idea if I'd just waited to hear him explain it! I'm sure they decided on a plan ... We need proof of crimes. So far all we have are suppositions."

"There is kidnapping, arson, and extortion," said Red Myrta. "Speaking of which, Mum wants to see you."

***

Myrta the Hand stood alone in front a door into a cliff.

It was a real door, wood painted glossy black trimmed with white, accentuated by a brass door-handle and a horse-shoe shaped door-knocker. Myrta the Hand was wearing the same sort of clothes she had when I'd first met her, which indeed were much the same as my own: breeches, shirt, waistcoat, coat. Hers had lace at the cuffs and throat, were in a wonderful deep blue cloth that went beautifully with her auburn hair, and made her look as if she were a noblewoman-in-disguise out of a play.

"Don't gape like an idiot," said Red Myrta, elbowing me. "Here he is, Mum, though I don't think he'll be much use in his current state."

Myrta the Hand wrinkled her nose. I stopped and carefully backed a few steps so I was standing downwind. "My apologies," I said, with an abbreviated bow that my entire back protested but did not make me actually fall over. The walk there had not taken much more than a few minutes, but had helped me loosen up somewhat. "I spent the night inside a whiskey barrel. You wished to see me, ma'am?"

"You are very like your father when you smile like that," Myrta the Hand observed. She was holding a pair of tan leather gloves, and now drew them on, slowly, as if the act took much attention.

"Were you acquainted with my father, ma'am?"

She smiled. "I met him on furlough a few times. He served

with my mother."

Red Myrta looked at her mother in astonishment, but I was growing increasingly aware—perhaps increasingly sober? Though to be frank I felt dizzy and dazed and not quite up to snuff—of the looming time, and I continued. "May I ask you a few questions, ma'am? They have to do with my father and with an, er, a magical ceremony I believe will take place shortly."

"The ceremonies are tomorrow," Myrta the Hand said firmly. "It is the beginning of the Winterturn Assizes. We still keep the customary rites to protect and hold our lands."

Were they not highwaymen? I decided not to ask too many diverting questions, fascinating as the answers would probably be. "This is a ceremony to do with the cult of the Dark Kings."

Her face drew into a magnificent frown of disapproval and rejection. "We have *nothing* to do with those obscenities. Why do you think our camp is where it is? We guard the Hollow from those who would pervert it."

Could I believe her? I wanted to. I decided I would trust the Chancellor's willingness to continue her acquaintance with Red Myrta into the Forest. "Ma'am, you relieve me greatly to hear that. Nevertheless, I was captured last night and transported to a perch in the middle of the Magarran Strid in order to be made a sacrifice to the Dark Kings on the Fallowday of the Autumn. Do you have sufficient guard on the Hanging Hill today? My father was found—" I stopped suddenly, remembering just *who* had told me where my father had been found. Mr. Hagwood had proved himself an untrustworthy ally.

"Mr. Greenwing?"

"Ma'am, seven years ago today my mother and I were brought

word that my father's body had been found hanging in the Forest. Do you—do you by any chance know *where* his body was found?"

No need to get into all the complications involving the bones of bull, boar, stag, and the tiny little matter that my father was not dead at all.

Myrta the Hand looked at me for a long moment. She said, "Every seven years on the day before the Winterturn Assizes the Magarran River performs what we call the Turning of the Waters. You have witnessed the first stage, I expect, where the water turns red and the river vanishes?"

I shuddered involuntarily. "Yes, ma'am."

"It is a disturbing sight," she said, slightly condescendingly.

"Yes, ma'am."

"We leave some of our number at the Hollow on guard. Since we came there we have permitted no perverse rites to be held upon it."

Was that why the cult had gone to the Ellery Stone? But then why had they brought me here?

—Wherever here was, exactly. All I knew was that it was by a cliff and not far from the Strid.

"There are three natural stone bridges where the waterfall enters the gorge. One is always above; the other two are visible in the heart of the Strid when the waters recede. Their names are Ethduil Endodon."

"'The bridges into shadows'. Dear Lady," I said, things tumbling into place. "The false letter accusing my father of treason had a coded message from 'We who speak for the shadows'."

"What was the text of the letter?" the Chancellor asked with almost incredible mildness.

I clenched my sausage fingers together, as if that would help me remember. I had a reasonable memory for these sorts of things … and that letter had corrupted my adolescence.

"It was addressed to the Flower—that's right:

Flower of Hope:

You have done well establishing your first position. This letter supplies what you need to move to the next. Soon it will be time for our people to return to glory. The stones of the forest are older than the trees, and the water redder than the blood of empires. When the restoration comes, we will need you. Be ready at all times. You know what the red water and the white stone can do.

We who speak for the shadows."

"The restoration?" Myrta the Hand said sharply. "You're certain it spoke of the restoration?"

"Yes, for the word struck me. Not as much as the red water and the white stone do, now that I've seen what the water can do."

"It's only begun. There's still the turn," Red Myrta said.

Her mother nodded, eyes on me. "The restoration, when it's a matter of those perverts with their cult, is not just the restoration of their prominence, but of the old practice of having the gods walk."

"My aunt said something about today being the day the true gods can walk …"

"Not precisely. It is the day that a certain rite can bind the Dark Kings to a human host. The Bridge into Shadows extends from—" She stopped suddenly. "Myr—send your birds to collect the others. We have to get to the stone bridge before noon."

We all looked up at the sky. I was completely disoriented, and for a few dazzled moments was sure it was past.

"East is that way," Red Myrta said in exasperation, pointing in the opposite direction. "We can't have much more than a quarter of an hour, Mum. And at least their sacrifice isn't waiting on the rock for them to fetch him."

"They don't need him to be. They'll have done all the preparations last week. The idea is that once the rite happens the host has the power of the Dark Kings and can walk the river to meet their priests."

***

Where, I wondered, was my father in all this?

Myrta the Hand led the Chancellor and me not into the cliff (for which I was cravenly grateful) but along a narrow trail that led along its foot. We walked single-file, me in the middle, and very quickly. I had to think light-footed thoughts to keep up with the highwaywoman. It didn't appear, from my occasional glances back, that the Chancellor was having any trouble. She looked entirely and thoroughly at home in the rough Forest in her Scholar's robes, her hood the green-and-gold stripes of Morrowlea, the trim on her robes in gold for her rank.

After about ten minutes Myrta the Hand stopped. I had managed to focus my attention on my surroundings sufficiently that I did not walk into her. She didn't seem to notice.

"We're a few hundred yards from the rendezvous," she said softly.

"Rendezvous?" I asked, even more quietly. "With Red Myrta?"

"With everyone," she said, nodding significantly at the Chancellor. "There are a number of people who wish to witness what is to happen here so that appropriate responses can be made."

"I suppose that's true."

"We do all understand that you are one of them, Mr. Green-wing," the Chancellor murmured. I bowed slightly. She smiled at me, then turned attentively to Myrta the Hand. "In this matter we are your pupils, and await the master's instructions."

"My daughter loved her time at Morrowlea. I will be forever grateful that you permitted her that opportunity."

"She wrote an excellent entrance essay."

"She spent long enough on it. Now: I had not previously been given *all* the pertinent details, and so did not know we were to expect a Restoration ceremony. I had thought it was an ordinary ritual intended to disrupt the bindings the Winterturn ceremonies strengthen." She glanced at me. "That one does involve sacrifice, though usually of animals: the bull, the boar, and the stag at this time of year."

"They are used for a semblancing spell." Or by people who wanted to make it look as if someone had used the semblancing spell ...

She shrugged. "I am not a student of the old cult except inso-far as I wish always to fight them. I lost my mother to the Stone Speakers of Loe."

I stared at her. "But you didn't think my father was the traitor?"

"He isn't."

"But everyone thought he was."

"Who would listen to an outlaw?" she replied bitterly. "Enough. Suffice to say that I condemn those who worship the Dark Kings. The plan was to wait until the sacrifice was well-begun and then to disrupt it and arrest the participants."

"Very good. And now?"

"And now that we know that their goal is not the ordinary

disruption, but the full restoration, we must prevent them from making the first cut."

"Surely if we disrupt it—"

But the Chancellor was shaking her head. "Did you not obtain sufficient magical theory in History of Magic? Mr. Greenwing, the spell has already begun; you are already fully implicated in it. As soon as blood is spilled, the gate will open."

Chapter Thirty-Five
Cut Across

A GREY JAY screamed.

It sounded exactly the same as all the rest to me, but Myrta the Hand cursed and set an even faster pace. I felt it hard, and had to concentrate to keep up. Running did not seem to translate to walking at high speed.

"It is my life's work," she said through clenched teeth.

I made what I hoped was an encouraging grunt. I didn't have the breath for anything else.

"I would do *anything* to prevent this from happening. I gave up *everything* to pursue the traitor."

"Traitor?" I asked, or rather gasped.

"The traitor of Loe. Be silent! We're nearly there."

Myrta the Hand was obsessed with the traitor of Loe?

Perhaps *obsessed* was too strong a word. I looked at the portion of her profile I could see from my angle behind and slightly to her side. Her voice was intense, her eyes had a fixed intensity to them. She had lost her mother at Loe.

If I had been an adult when the letters came about my father?

I would have gone to Eil if I'd had to walk there.

She hadn't recognized Ben or Jack, but it had been night ... and I hadn't recognized him, either.

It had never occurred to me to wonder what everyone else whose families were lost at Loe had thought of the news. What did *they* make of the play? Were they as angry as they were scandalized? The Sixth Division of the Seventh Army had contained many Alinorel soldiers. They all had friends, families, wives, husbands, parents, children ...

Myrta stopped at a grouping of shrubby evergreens (junipers? Hal would know) that looked identical to the hundred others we had passed, but which presumably contained an identifying characteristic to her. She gestured the Chancellor and me to draw as close as possible. I wished I didn't smell so badly; the stench rising off my clothing made me want to gag. I had to listen carefully. There was a deep subterranean rumble, tangible through my boots now that we were standing still, just about audible so that the lower dips in Myrta's voice dissolved into the background noise.

"We are very close now," she said in a voice that seemed to fall silent even as it reached me. "We are coming up to the Gate of the Strid, where the Magarran river exits Crimson Lake through the Falls. The Falls will be nearly dry now: the turn will begin to return at noon precisely."

"What causes it?" I asked.

She gave me a reproving glance I felt to the soles of my feet. "We can speak of natural mysteries and magical phenomena later, Mr. Greenwing. Suffice it now to say that we come with some of my people to the Horn. Those coming from the town will be on the far side, the Ivory Tower."

I could not refrain from a small snort of appreciation for the name.

Myrta the Hand ignored me. "Between the two is the upper-most of the three stone bridges. The lower two will be visible be-cause the water is down. I don't know upon which the cult priests will be doing their sacrifice. If it is the uppermost bridge, either side will be able to approach. It occurs to me now that given that it is the Restoration that they are seeking, they might choose the middle bridge as the most appropriately symbolic."

Another jay screamed an alarm.

"They're coming," Myrta said. "Everyone else is in position—it will take too long for anyone else—we must be the ones to go down to the middle bridge. Come. It is nearly noon."

We followed her off the narrow track onto an even narrower and fainter trail that soon petered out at a hole in the rock. This was the burrow of some creature; it was far too small for us. Myrta the Hand seemed to take it for a sign, for she turned, walked a certain distance, turned again, and thus zigzagged us between two out-croppings that I would have sworn, ten feet away, held no possible space between them.

The air was cold, and it had that breathless not-quite-damp feel of incipient snow. The wind swirled around the rocks, chilly even in the heat of our exertions. I followed Myrta the Hand with anxious care. The limestone outcroppings were rough and sharp-grained; I scratched myself simply brushing past. And all the time the stones were vibrating with that deep rumble that rose up into my veins like the sound of the earth's own anxiety.

A deep *boom* echoed through the stones.

I did not need Myrta the Hand to say "They're starting," to know what that meant. I had heard the gongs and the drums, that night at the Ellery Stone, when the cultists had transformed from fools to villains.

"Down the ladder—back to the drop—lead with your right foot. Count—it's forty steps down. Don't step past forty."

I did not even question as she stepped aside for me to go first. I turned so my back was to the drop, saw in the curving bulge of a stone pavement the indentations someone had carved there long ago, and put my right foot in the first. Left in the next. Right. Left. After five steps I needed my hands to keep my balance. Right. Left. Ten steps. Right. Left. Twenty.

Boom

That time I felt the shock coming through the stone.

Above me little flakes of loose rock and plant-matter were pattering down. The Chancellor or Myrta the Hand, presumably, coming down after me. I did not look up. I did not want my eyes blinded with rock-dust at this stage of the proceedings from my own stupidity.

Right. Left—

Boom

Thirty steps.

There was that wail starting up, the high atonal ululation I remembered from the Ellery Stone. It cut across the vibrations, sending up weird harmonies in the stone, as if the whole gorge was a bell or the sound-board of an instrument and it was resounding to the singer's voice.

Aiiieee—aiieeee—aiieee-a-a-a

Boom

Thirty-seven steps. I had to grip tightly with my fingers, clench my toes, as I reached blindly down to the next foothold. If I had started with the left foot, what would have happened? Would I have stepped down confidently to find that there was nothing below me but the Magarran Strid?

Boom

Thirty-eight—thirty-nine—and very carefully, very slowly, very cautiously—

Boom

Forty.

I opened my eyes and turned even more carefully, even more slowly, even more cautiously around before even trying to put down my other foot. I was glad I had.

I stood on a ledge perhaps two feet deep. It was the bottom of a kind of natural chimney that led up the cliff face; as trees and shrubs in the top reaches had obscured the initial drop, so down here the—

Boom

—The arrangement of rocks and fissures obscured the descent. I could not, looking up, even see the Chancellor above me, just rocks white and grey and black from their own shadows.

Boom

The shock that time rattled my chest-bones. I took a breath. Two feet ahead of me the ledge ended as if a knife had sliced it off. To my left there was a bulge of rock and then nothing; to my right an indentation at about hand-height that suggested one was to go that way, around the obscuring outcrop.

Boom

Aiiee—aiieee—ai—ai—aiieee—a—a

Left hand or right? Right seemed to fit better. I turned so my front was to the stone, my right hand in the indentation, my left foot sliding out along what was barely more than a lip of stone. I did not look down to see how far down it was until one reached the water. In normal times it was presumably up here, for there was a line of red scum just breaking over the lip, as if the water had risen to that height and no further.

Boom

It was hard to imagine anything being worse than a seventy-foot drop onto knife-sharp limestone pinnacles already handily stained red, but I thought the idea of the smoothly rushing deadly currents of the Strid a bare inch below your foot might do it.

The narrow ledge lasted only five or six yards before doubling back into the cliff-face in a way that made me very glad I had led with the foot I had.

At waist height there was a tunnel slanting slightly up and to the right.

Boom

Aieee—aiieee—ai—ai—ai

It amazed me that I could still hear that ululation through the vibrations and the booms and the sound of my own slow movements along the stone and the thundering loudness of the circulation of my blood.

I had to kneel to fit in the tunnel. It was very dark.

I stopped there for—I don't know.

***

Boom

Aiieee—aiiieee—ai—aiieee—aiaa—aiaa—ai

Boom

Boom

Boom

***

And had my father been afraid, running up the cliff into the face of the enemy?

Had he been afraid, standing there with the great Sun-in-Glory banner of Astandalas flying over his head?

Had he been afraid, going into the mountain fastness of the Stone Seekers, not knowing if any of the people he sought were alive?

Had he been afraid, standing at the top of the Gate of Morning with his sword and his book of haikus and the knowledge that the way home was going to be shut behind him?

Had he been afraid, turning his oar to foul the movement of the pirate galley?

Had he been afraid, coming home from the reputed dead for the second time?

Was he afraid now?

***

Boom

***

I was not my father. I would never win the Heart of Glory from the hands of the Emperor. I would never win a name for myself as a soldier of Astandalas. I would never be him.

But by the Lady, by the Emperor, by the bees my mother had so loved: I could, and I would, and I did, act to make him proud.

Even if I did stupid things like running off without thinking after my uncle.

I wanted to sit at his feet and learn all that he could teach me by his living presence.

***

Boom

***

I crawled into the darkness.

***

Boom

And then, silence.

***

The other end of the tunnel was hidden from full view by a series of stone pillars.

I came out low, on my hands and knees, and was for a moment dazzled by stripes of white and black. I crouched there, trying to breathe quietly as I caught my breath, trying to listen, trying to ignore the deep vibrations thrumming through the stone into my hands and knees and body until my teeth were shaking from it.

Boom

The wind had died down.

Aiieee—aiieee—aiieee—ai—ai—aiaaa

I crawled forward until I came to the stone pillars. They marched out from the right-hand side of the tunnel mouth, a double row of them like teeth that grow from the top of a cave and the bottom. I blinked as my vision started to clear.

The tunnel came out in what was a slightly larger cave whose mouth was obscured by the pillars or stalactites (stalagmites? I could never remember). They were all stained red, which suggested I had somehow descended *below* the level of the river by climbing *upwards*, which made my head hurt until I remembered that we were at the place where the river launched itself down a series of falls from Crimson Lake in what was presumably an upper valley to the Magarran Strid in its gorge in the lower. The tunnel must have taken me up into a cave formed by the action of the water going through one of the stages of the cataract.

The pillars obscured my view; they also protected me from being seen. I crawled forward on my belly, reasoning that this outfit was already ruined and that the action might help me avoid detection.

If there were anyone on the bridge.

Boom

I slithered forward in the cold red scurf left from the drying foam. Once I neared the pillars I discovered they were not nearly so uniform as they had appeared, nor so orderly. There was a definite way forward between them, zigzagging as if on purpose. I kept scratching myself on various protruding rocks broken rather than worn by the movement of the water as I worked to get close enough to see the bridge and the gorge and the gate.

And then all of a sudden, there they were.

On the far side of the bridge, too high or too low to do anything, clutches of figures I recognized as Mr. Dart, Master Dart, Ben, Hal, Sir Hamish, the Chief Constable, Inspector Quent, and the two lawyers, Mr. Morres and Mr. Tey. They were all looking down, for a moment I thought at me, but then I realized that between them and me was the bridge.

It was not what I'd expected. I suppose I'd thought of a proper bridge, or maybe the old humpbacked bridge over the Rag into town. Not a smooth water-worn arc of white stone stained with reddish scurf like all the rest.

What the red water and the white stone can do ...

Not the higher bridge, brilliantly white, that stood catching the noon sun another seventy-five or hundred yards upstream, another fifty feet above us, arching between the Horn and the Ivory Tower, the two outcroppings marking the egress of the waters from Crimson Lake down the Strid. High up on the very top of the Horn was something moving, but whatever or whoever it was was only a black spot against the sky from here.

Not the lower bridge, another twenty yards downstream and ten feet down, which was black.

On the middle bridge the Black Priest stood. His face-mask of polished silver caught the sunlight as he lifted his head back. He obviously could see the watchers, and equally obviously did not care, for he raised his hands and in his right he held the same wicked bone-white knife the priests had used to kill the cow at the Ellery Stone.

Boom

He did not have a cow this time.

Aiieee—aiieee—aiaaa

On the far bank from me stood my aunt Flora, her eyes wide enough I could see the ecstasy this side of the bridge. She was the one singing, her voice rising and falling, her eyes transfixed, her face mindless.

On the near side of the bridge, only a few yards from me, Hagwood the factor stood staring at the Black Priest and his victim.

Boom

I could not see the source of the booming.

On the bridge my uncle Vorel knelt with as much passive acceptance as the cow at the Ellery Stone had shown. I could not tell if he was bespelled or drugged or simply shocked.

Lady Flora wailed out her inner convictions.

Hagwood shook with horror at his alliances.

The Black Priest lifted his hands and his head until the sun blazed forth from the mirror-mask as if he were the Sun-on-Earth himself.

Sir Vorel, trembling visibly, lifted his chin and raised his eyes and I realized with a wrench of pity and wonder that he was not drugged, not bespelled, not even shocked into insensitivity. He was fully aware, and he lifted his chin to meet his fate.

Where was Red Myrta with her famous archery skills? I thought acridly, and with the thought (sounding so like my grandmother!) I snapped into the world of mortal danger just as the Black Priest cried in a voice like the boom of the drum: "It is time!"

My aunt wailed.

My father started to climb down the cliff.

Hagwood screamed, and screamed, and screamed.

The Black Priest laughed. He reached for my uncle's hair with his left hand, jerked hard to tilt his head back until all my uncle's many chins were visible, and began to lower the knife with easy assurance.

I moved fastest.

Chapter Thirty-Six
The Emperor Card

I LAUNCHED MYSELF at a dead run out along the bridge. The Black Priest did not take notice of me at first: he was laughing as he moved the knife left so he could begin the cut across the jugular. I was on him before he began the righthand movement.

If it had truly been Dominus Gleason I don't think it would have taken very long.

It was not, however, Dominus Gleason.

My three half-seconds of surprise—that anyone was there—that *I* was there—that I was not yet the restored avatar of the Dark Kings—quickly lost all meaning. I gripped his wrist with my left hand and his other hand with my right and then I stood there squeezing with my stupid sausage fingers as my reflection in the polished silver mask started to do strange things.

He was muttering, chanting really, in a voice whose pitch moved eerily between pitches and timbres. I caught words and half-phrases of Old Shaian and wished I hadn't, for the picture they painted was one of madness coiling deeper and deeper into my mind with every syllable.

That is just one way of connecting the signs together, I told myself firmly.

Where was Red Myrta with her arrows?

Where was the Chancellor and Myrta the Hand?

—Where, I wondered suddenly just before I stepped backwards onto him, was my uncle?

He cried out in alarm whose shrillness bespoke far more than the pain of a trodden foot.

I could not spare the attention to look away from the Black Priest. I did not like the look of the Jemis in the mirrored mask. That Jemis was grinning with unholy exaltation, his face illuminated like a painting of a saint or a devil, his eyes insane.

Boom went the drum.

We had nearly deafened ourselves, Hal and I, sitting in the campanile that day we'd broken curfew. We'd fled onto the roofs because we could not bear the vibrations of the sound, the dizzying, deafening, maddening sound like blows to the head and chest. We had lain on the roof-tiles recovering for ages, the sun burnishing me scarlet before Hal looked to see what was going on. Even Hal had admitted to tenderness from the sun, though his skin didn't show the burn as obviously as mine.

On the bridge was like being *inside* the bell as it was rung.

My hand slipped around the straining wrist, and suddenly the bone knife was pointed straight at my eye.

Even in the state of mortal danger, or perhaps especially in that state, I knew an impasse when it saw it. I did not let go; but I did not move, either.

"You have come too early," said the Black Priest in a low, whispery, almost multiple sort of voice.

He had spoken to me like that once before, I recalled, the time when drunk on persiflage and an unfinished game of Poacher with

the Tarvenol duellist I had dithered at the Lady's Cross at midnight
and been invited to the Talgarths' by the Black Priest of the old
cult.

That time he had taken me to the back door and told me to
put a phial of something into the dessert.

Later in the evening I had been sent by the wizard who turned
out to be the White Priest to the back door of the house, and there
I had let the Black Priest over the threshold. He had kissed me—*as
a gift*, he had called it—and made me lose my memory.

Standing there so close to him, as close as I had been on that
dazzled and disturbing evening, I recalled what else he had done
between the kiss and the next moment I remembered.

***

So you are the chosen one, he had said, walking towards me so I
retreated backwards down the hall away from him. *You are the one
whose magic is calling so loudly. I am glad, for so many reasons I am glad
you are the one.*

Why me? I had asked. I was bound by the fascination cast by
his presence, by what the wizard upstairs had been doing, by what
I had been given to drink and to eat and to do.

*The gods choose us for their own reasons. They have chosen you. Re-
joice: you are the way they will return to the world and reclaim their own.
When the time comes you will learn what your rewards are.*

No, I had said, muddled but knowing that this was not anything
I wanted party to. *No, I don't want to. I will not—you cannot make me!*

*We speak for the shadows. The object has no choice in what he casts.
The shadow has choice in what it graces.*

I tell you, no! I will not be party to this!

You have no choice. You are chosen. It is your fate to be bear the glory of the restoration. It is your fate that you, son of one who slaughtered so many of our children, should be the one who will be vessel when the gate is opened. His shade will writhe with torment to see what his beloved son has become.

***

The last move in the game of Poacher before the tales were told—or implied—was to turn over the Emperor Card.

On the Emperor Card—if the players had counted the cards at play properly, if they were able to see from what was kept and what discarded the shape of a story that was not totally dissimilar from the one their opponent actually intended—on the turn of the Emperor Card games were won or foundered or transformed into legend.

The Black Priest had not been the one to make a semblance of my father's body. He had neither killed him nor faked his death.

But he thought he had.

Time to see what hand the other player actually had—

I took a deep breath and with all my strength I pushed the knife away from my face and I screamed with all my might, "*PAPA!*"

***

Several things happened.

Halfway down the cliff my father cried, "Jemis!" with a voice that opened up every single memory of him I had.

On the top of the facing cliff Myrta the Hand cried, "Mad Jack Greenwing!" in a voice in which shock and exultation and triumph mingled like a burst of fireworks.

At my feet my uncle screamed like a little girl, high-pitched and endless.

And the Black Priest for just the barest moment wavered.

I was waiting. I brought my arms together and twisted them until the Black Priest's arms bent around each other and the knife started to bend at an increasingly untenable angle and although he was fighting me again, writhing in my grip and trying to use his feet to unbalance me, I was braced and ready and full of the assurance that I was not going to die today in the sight of my living father, I was going to win and prove myself worthy of being his son—

And then my uncle scrambled to his feet and tried to run behind us on a stone bridge barely four feet wide and covered with algal scum.

He slipped.

I could not help myself. It so instinctive in the face of the helpless terror on his face to want to reach out—

The Black Priest used my inattention to do what I had just done to him. The twisting was as effective as Dominus Lukel had said it would be, I thought distantly as it was my turn to have my elbows twist against their proper direction. My uncle was not quite over the edge of the bridge. He was holding on to the Black Priest's leg, which did not distract or discombobulate him nearly enough.

I supposed I could understand why Red Myrta was not shooting arrows at us now. Even she would be hard-pressed to hit only the Black Priest. I presumed she didn't want to hit me in the sight of so many witnesses of good character and standing, etc. in the community.

Boom went the drum again.

I was looking into the eye-holes of the mask when the sound hit us. The pupils were dilated already with fury and frustration, but I could see a ring of white.

What did he know I didn't?

What *was* making that booming noise, anyway?

My muscles were not going to be able to hold on much longer, I thought distantly. Neither was my uncle. With each sway and twist the knife came closer and close to my face. I wondered what happened if the chosen vessel was also the chosen sacrifice? Did the Dark Kings re-animate the corpse?

Would that be better or worse than being present in your body when they possessed you?

Boom went the drum.

I shuddered with the resonance of the sound. It sounded like the river had when it dropped below me, as I so slowly crossed the tree trunk over the Strid.

—The river.

I wished I had made Myrta the Hand or Red Myrta or someone spend thirty seconds explaining to me what exactly caused the Turning of the Waters, and when it stopped happening.

I dared not look down. I dared not look anywhere but at the white knife so close to my eye I could see it only as a blur of sunlit edge.

There were plenty of times recently I should have spent thirty seconds finishing a line of questioning instead of rushing off to the next thing.

My uncle cried, "Jack!"

Both the Black Priest and I looked not at my uncle but at where my father had just jumped down the final bit of cliff to land on the stone bridge. The Black Priest's expression was invisible behind the mask. My reflected expression still looked insane, but in a more gleeful way. I wondered with the distance that came with the world of mortal danger whether this was what I *did* look like just that moment.

I held on to the Black Priest's wrists and pushed the knife away from me and waited the interminable three seconds while my father ran down the length of the bridge. I was watching, my mind as clear and certain as it had been facing the dragon or running into the Forest. Unfortunately what I was most clear and certain of was that my muscles were overtaxed and were not going to hold very much longer at all.

But it was my task to keep the Black Priest from completing the sacrifice, and I would not fail that.

My father dropped to his knees, grabbed Vorel by the arm, and hauled his brother away from the drop and back towards the safety of the river bank. Others were there now, I saw out of my peripheral vision as I waited to see what would happen next. Several someones were running down the top of the cliff towards the next accessible point, where my father was even now pushing Vorel to go on his own, a flat spot where the line of red scum swirled into a kind of bay, lower than the level of the bridge by a couple of feet.

The Black Priest shoved me with all his strength. I staggered back, lost sight of those on the bank, and as my head snapped back I saw bright spots in the air—

Boom went the drum.

A horn sang out.

It was a hunting horn, the kind fox-hunters used to sound out the hunt. It sang out sweet and loud and penetrating:

Too-ra Too-ra Too-ra

It echoed off the cliffs until its sound seemed to shake the bridge with its power.

Too-ra Too-ra Too-ra-ra-ra

I knew that call. Roald Ragnor had gone on about the county fox-hunting calls for a full half-hour a week ago. He had been drunk, and witty, and I had drunk enough to encourage him to imitate the horn-calls in his own not-very-good singing voice.

Too-ra Too-ra Too-ra-ra-ra

That was the warning-call for a flooding river.

It was my turn to use all my strength to swing the Black Priest around. I could not force his arms back, could barely hold him away from my face, but I could turn us both until I could see up-river, up the gorge, up the Gate of the Strid.

All I could see was white.

The Turning of the Waters—

First the red foam of algal bloom as Crimson Lake came down.

Then the water dropped through a sinkhole or *something* that was opened once every seven years, when the cult priests wanted to do their rituals on the Bridges into Shadows.

And then the waters turned white, white as the Lady of Winter whose season started tomorrow. White for winter, for innocence, and for hope.

White for wool, or mountain clouds, or the wool pulled over your eyes.

White for purity, for divinity, and for death.

White for the full flood of the Magarran river thundering down like a lightning bolt into its Strid.

White for the knife the Black Priest was even now using my distraction to thrust straight at my face.

***

I dropped into a place as far beyond the world of terror as the dream of my mother.

I dropped down into a crouch, knowing that the water had plunged down into the depths of its gorge and was even now leaping up to fill its cataracts to the fullness of their flood.

The Black Priest had to twist his body slightly so that he could correct the trajectory of the knife to my new position.

Knowing exactly what it would mean, understanding for the first time why my father could have stood there at the Gate of Morning knowing there would be no relief, glad that I had had this week of knowing him—

As the knife came down against the pressure of my hands I kicked back against the stone and flipped the Black Priest over my head and myself over my heels off the bridge.

***

The Black Priest hit the water and tore immediately from my grip into the grip of the river.

***

Like so many Astandalans before me—for I was a child of the Empire, whatever the new order might be—I had entirely forgotten the possibility of wild magic.

***

I hit the water and skidded across the surface like a stone across a millpond to fetch up at the feet of Mr. Dart.

***

My father reached down and grabbed my hand to pull me up the three feet to what was now the top of the bank rather than the top of the gorge.

I stood there, catching my breath and my realization that I had not just died in the Strid.

I stared at Mr. Dart, whose eyes were as white as the water.

Far away on the top of the peak the horn-player was now sounding out the triumphant notes of the end of a successful hunt.

"It's the Hunter in Green," Hal said, pointing up. I realized that it was, and that he was shielding Mr. Dart, and that no one else knew who had performed that act of magic.

I took a deep breath, and then another. Mr. Dart put his out-thrust hand back into his pocket, blinking until his eyes were once again blue. My father said: "And just *what* do you think you were doing, young man?"

He was still holding my hand. I smiled weakly at him. "I was hoping we might be able to have some lessons on tactics, Ja—Papa."

"You're alive," said my uncle, staring at both of us. "You were alive the whole time. You're alive."

My father reached up with his free hand to ruffle my hair. "Yes." And he smiled at me. "Yes.

Chapter Thirty-Seven
The Last Will and Testament of Benneret Buchance

MY UNCLE HAD been made Acting Chief Magistrate when Justice Talgarth had been encouraged to take a hiatus while the legal situation with his wife (who had permitted her sister to grow wireweed on their premises) was resolved.

No one was very clear on all of Sir Vorel's crimes, but as he had somewhat piteously asked the Chief Constable to arrest him as soon as he had recovered his ability to speak after crying on my father's feet for a while, it was apparent he was in no fit state to oversee the Winterturn Assizes.

Mr. Etaris, the Chief Constable, made these announcements from the stairs of the town hall at the stroke of ten o'clock on the first morning of the Winterturn Assizes. There was a very good crowd to hear him, bigger even than was usual for the first day of the Assizes. A great many rumours had flowed out of the Forest along with us.

Dressed in a mostly-completed winter-weight suit (I had begged the tailor almost in tears the night before to make sure I had something fit to wear for the morning; he had finished everything except the waistcoat and a few parts of the coat lining), I stood next to Hal and Mr. Dart. Mrs. Buchance and her daughters stood on my other side, with most of the Embroidery Circle close by to give support, and two men in Charese clothing who must have been my stepfather's business partners, here for the Fiellanese portion of his estate; Ben, the Chancellor, and my father stood with Master Dart and Sir Hamish on the other side. It was cold, with the odd snowflake drifting down. I wished the gloves had been ready at the haberdashers'.

For a wild moment I feared that we would not be able to finish the probate of my stepfather's will after all. Then the Chief Constable turned to gesture at Mr. Tey, who stood close by the bottom of the stairs. Mr. Tey floated up the five stairs to stand next to Mr. Etaris, his every movement languid and delicate. Mr. Morres stumped up more normally beside him.

"I am Mr. Tey of the Kingsford Chancery," he said, and gestured delicately at Mr. Morres. "This is my colleague, Mr. Morres."

Mr. Morres nodded. I could see that everyone appreciated his less rarefied approach (and more distantly audible voice) immediately. "We were sent to oversee several cases at the Assizes here, most notably those concerning the inheritance of the Marquisate of Noirell, whose heir had been listed as missing since the Fall, and certain items to do with the new whiskey tax, as well as to conduct some investigations whose results will come with time. We were therefore granted considerable authority by the King. We have consulted the law books and our mandate and are pleased to announce that we may appoint an interim Magistrate for this session. We have therefore chosen Master Torquin Dart, commonly known as the Squire of Dartington."

Master Dart made a harrumphing noise that did nothing to

disguise how pleased he was and strode up the steps to stand beside the lawyers. He spoke with them briefly, nodded, and turned to the crowd. "We will follow the order of cases set by the town council. The first item is the reading of the Last Will and Testament of Benneret Buchance, a merchant of Chare who lived and died in this barony. Clerk of the Court, will you please hand me the document?"

A bony woman in the dark green and white robes of the Assizes presented him with it. Master Dart held it up to demonstrate to the audience that the seals were intact. Then he said, "It is the law in Fiellan that a Will may be read only in the presence of all parties named within it. I shall read those listed on the envelope and request that those so named gather together at the bottom of the steps so that we may go into the court together. Do you all agree and abide?"

There was a rumble of agreement through the crowd. Not very many people had left the square yet, even though the drama should (please the Lady) be through now that Master Dart had been appointed. Surely everyone knew by now that I'd come back to town?

"Mrs. Elinor Buchance. Misses Lauren, Sela, Zangora, and Lamissa Buchance. Mrs. Elinor Inglesides. Mr. Jakory Inglesides. Mr. Harry Zuraine. Mr. Artorin Palaion. Major Jakory Greenwing. Mr. Jemis Greenwing."

He lowered the envelope again. The snow was coming down harder, but that didn't obscure the puzzled expressions. The murmurs and whispers started when my father (still with his eyepatch, still dressed like a barely-solvent gentleman) walked with his head high and a small smile on his face away from Sir Hamish and joined us at the stairs. He clasped me on the shoulder, which I knew was partly for the benefit of the crowd and partly for his own comfort, but which I took for my own, too. I had no idea why my stepfather should have mentioned my father in his will.

***

Master Dart had read out the names in the order in which they were listed in the will.

We sat in the small room given over to such meetings. It had some historical paintings of indifferent artistry on the walls, un-comfortable wooden chairs, and a large desk with a throne-like seat behind it where the Squire sat. The Clerk of the Court sat at a smaller desk to one side to record matters, and we had Mr. Morres present as an outside witness, and another lawyer who turned out to be Mr. Buchance's there for corroboration of any details.

Master Dart harrumphed. "We shall not drag out this process; you have all waited long enough." I squirmed a little, but not much because all my muscles were horribly sore, and because although I terribly regretted not writing and thereby missing the news and the summons, I no longer felt quite so guilty.

"Mr. Safford, will you please give as an account of the writing and witnessing of this will?"

Mr. Safford was an elderly man who looked as if he'd been dried out on a slow fire. I contemplated him, and Mr. Tey and Mr. Morres, and even Master Dart's pleasure at being named Chief Magistrate.

I had absolutely no desire to sit in any of their places.

If I could not be a soldier of the Empire, what then? Perhaps I could work in the bookstore ... we had all the necessary material to prove my father's innocence, which meant he would take over the management of the Arguty estate.

He had lost his factor, for Harry Hagwood had been swept away by the flood.

Mr. Safford cleared his throat. I jumped and looked guiltily at him. He sucked on his teeth for a moment, as if to be sure he held all of our attentions, and then spoke. His voice was a great contrast to his appearance, being as fruity as a Winterturn pudding. "As was his custom, on the birth of each of his children Benneret Buchance revised his will. Upon the birth of his last daughter, Lamissa, which coincided with the commencement of the last year of his step son's minority, he requested me to do a full rewrite of the will. Mr. Buchance wished to ensure that everything would be as he wished it should there be any sad misfortune, as indeed there was. The will's revision took several iterations before Mr. Buchance was happy with it, as he was required to complete several transactions in Chare before all of his points could be assured. The final version was witnessed by myself and by Mr. Farquhart of my offices in May of this year."

After he had come to see me at Morrowlea on his way back from one of those business trips to Chare. He had asked me what I planned to do with myself after I graduated. I had spoken vaguely of sensible plans, although my mind was fragmenting with the later stages of wireweed addiction and the devotion to Lark that would soon turn to betrayal. Mr. Buchance had told me he would see I would never starve: a turn of phrase that immediately pricked me, echoing as it did what my uncle had said to my mother and me when he had kicked us out of Arguty Manor.

I had been proud, I supposed, and foolish, and perhaps truthful to my inner heart when I had told him I expected nothing from him but that he would treat his daughters by my mother equally with those by the second Mrs. Buchance. He had pressed me until I told him that I kept my father's name and kept his inheritance—

I had left him, smarting and angry at myself for hurting him, for I knew how badly he had wanted a son to carry on his name and business and family. And as I had climbed up the hill towards the towers of Morrowlea I had met Lark, who had tilted her head back so she could look at me from under the wide brim of her hat, and she had said, "Oh, let us be rebels, Jemis my love. Tell me about your family."

And I had.

And she had taken that confession, that confidence, and written it as the arguments in her philippic for why Jakory Greenwing should not be admitted into the House of Fame … and if I were correct in my surmise, she had also used it to hire Jakory Lindsary as the basis of *Three Years Gone*.

"Mr. Greenwing?" said Master Dart. "Are you attending?"

I flushed and bowed in my seat. "Yes, sir. My apologies."

He nodded magisterially. "Then we may begin. Here is the Last Will and Testament of Benneret Buchance, born in Hillcrest, Chare, in the thirteenth year of the reign of the Emperor Eritanyr, who died this eighth year after the Interim on the twelfth of July."

> *To my wife Elinor, the rents from my properties in Chare* [an appendix is provided]; *the full ownership of the house on Woolsack Lane and all of its contents except those specifically named below; the third portion of the income from my businesses in Chare* [these were also to be found in the Appendix, said Master Dart].

That was a splendid widow's inheritance, especially since I was

WHISKEYJACK

fairly sure she would also get (as a matter of course) all those moneys not otherwise apportioned out. I did not know the details of either the properties in Chare nor what the third portion of income from his businesses there, but all throughout the kingdom of Rondé (and, I was sure, far beyond its borders) people used the containers devised and produced by Benneret Buchance to store all the foodstuffs that in the past had been preserved with magic.

> To my daughters Lauren, Sela, Zangora, and Lamissa: to each a portion of one hundred and fifty thousand bees, to be allotted to them half upon their majority at 21 and half upon their marriage or their attaining the age of 27.

That made them exceedingly wealthy heiresses. I was pleased that my soon-to-be-confirmed status as Viscount St-Noire might be of some assistance in launching them into society, though I felt that my best efforts in those lines would probably come from cultivating the interest of Hal's Aunt Honoria.

> To my brother- and sister-in-law, Jakory and Elinor Inglesides, the outright title to those properties at no. 8 the Square and in Ragglebridge, and a gift of one hundred and fifty thousand bees to be divided up evenly among their children.

How kind of him to think that Mrs. Buchance might not want to see her children's cousins so far removed from her station. The boys would be able to start businesses or travel or go to universities they might otherwise be unable to afford; and if Mr. Inglesides himself rented rather than owned his bakery, that was all to the good.

> To Harry Zuraine and Mr. Artorin Palaion, the remaining two portions of the income from my businesses in Chare. To Harry Zuraine also the library of books in my study at Woolsack Lane. To Artorin Palaion the library of books held in my offices in Chare.

The two men stirred and smiled when this was read out. They had clearly expected the incomes; equally clearly the libraries meant something to them.

To Major Jakory Greenwing (deceased).

Master Dart paused here to look at Mr. Safford and the others present. "Having learned earlier this week of Major Greenwing's, ah, status, to wit that he is alive and that it is provable he was framed as the traitor of Loe, I consulted with Mr. Morres and Mr. Tey with regards to this Will as well as the many other matters that will need to be sorted as a result of his unexpected happy return. While the law naturally makes a great deal more of those parties named in a will who predecease the one who named them, there is precedent in Fiellanese law for a party named as deceased within the will who turned out subsequently to be alive. In that case the money intended to go for a memorial was granted to the living person as a legacy."

Mr. Safford nodded. "Indeed, the infamous case of Margery Cox. A very clear and apt parallel to this case."

"Thank you, Mr. Safford." Master Dart turned back to the will. I realized I was growing nervous again.

> *To Major Jakory Greenwing, in memory of the wife beloved to both of us and to the honour of the son whom we both love dearly: fifty thousand bees, to be used as Jemis Green-wing directs for the restoration of his good name and the subsequent exhumation and re-internment of his remains.*

"Oh," said my father softly, looking much struck. We were sitting next to each other, so I could reach over the touch his hand. He smiled at me.

> *And finally, to my stepson Jemis Greenwing, who expects nothing and requests nothing of me but my fairness to his sis-*

ters; who is in all ways a son to be proud of; who will believe
my gift to his father's memory sufficient: knowing that a son
who has never faltered in loving and honouring his father's
name will never fail to honour this gift from his stepfather
and use it to the best of his ability, which is considerable:
with no requirements or conditions, I leave the remainder of
my fortune.

I opened my mouth.

Mrs. Buchance was smiling at me.

Mr. Zuraine and Mr. Palaion were also smiling at me.

Mr. Safford said, "Mr. Buchance did ask me to make one condition, should he pass on before he had spoken with you about
your future." I stared at him. He smiled. "He asked me to ask you
to reflect on the power of compounding interest before you make
any plans to give it all away."

My father was smiling at me.

I closed my mouth. There was no one to bow to, so I settled for
saying, "Thank you."

At least it solved the problem of how to get the villagers of St-
Noire through the winter.

Note

Whiskeyjack *is the third book of* Greenwing & Dart. *Book Four,* Blackcurrant Fool, *finds Mr. Greenwing and Mr. Dart going on an unanticipated journey to Orio City, where they encounter much more than they are sent to fetch..*

Please visit the author's website, www.victoriagoddard.ca, for the opportunity to join her newsletter, to be informed about new releases and to receive a free short story, "Stone Speaks to Stone," the true tale of what happend to Major Jakory Greenwing at Loe.

Made in the USA
Las Vegas, NV
28 February 2024

86432514R00236